MISSING MAX

KAREN YOUNG

MISSING MAX

HOWARD BOOKS
A Division of Simon & Schuster, Inc.
NEW YORK NASHVILLE LONDON TORONTO SYDNEY

Published by Howard Books, a division of Simon & Schuster, Inc.
1230 Avenue of the Americas, New York, NY 10020

In association with the literary agency of Books & Such

ISBN 978-1-61664-590-8

Manufactured in the United States of America

Edited by Dave Lambert and Traci DePree
Cover design by John Hamilton Design
Interior design by Davina Mock-Maniscalco

MISSING MAX

1

THEY SAY SOME PEOPLE have a premonition about calamity before it strikes. But Jane Madison felt only irritation when her cell phone rang as she waited in the Mardi Gras crowd to order shrimp po'boys. Checking caller ID, she decided to ignore the call when she saw it was Melanie. Her stepdaughter probably wanted to change her order, but after standing in line for more than twenty minutes, Jane was finally up, so changing was not an option.

The man ahead of her received his order of fried shrimp, calamari, and beer. Loaded down, he turned suddenly and almost crashed into her. Not for the first time that day, Jane wished she were elsewhere. Ordinarily, she avoided Mardi Gras Day in New Orleans, but Melanie was at the age to be enthralled by the uninhibited and often near-depraved behavior all too common at the event. So Jane had reluctantly agreed to take her, even though it meant having to also bring Max. The other possibility for Melanie's calling was that Max was awake. If he were, Christine would know what to do. Having her best friend along made the day a bit more tolerable for Jane.

Teething had made Max cranky and restless lately, but so far he'd been surprisingly docile just watching the goings-on around him from his stroller.

Her cell phone rang again. Apparently Melanie wasn't giving up. Now loaded with two large bags and three soft drinks, Jane looked around for a place to set everything down, but there was no open spot, just hordes of people, literally a crush of humanity. Grumbling, she turned back to the vendor's cart and with a murmured apology transferred the load to his counter and fumbled to click her phone free of her purse. Sometimes Melanie could try the patience of a saint. "What is it, Melanie?"

"Mom, Max is gone!" the girl cried. "Come quick! He was here a minute ago, and now he's disappeared!"

Jane shifted to allow an impatient customer access to the vendor's condiments. "What do you mean, he's gone?"

"Just that! Didn't you hear me? He's disappeared." Melanie's voice caught on a sob. "Hurry! We've looked everywhere, but there are so many people!"

"How could he be gone?" She was used to Melanie's overreacting. Even the girl's friends called her a drama queen. "Let me talk to Christine."

"She's not here," Melanie insisted. "A lady fainted and Christine went into the hotel lobby to help and Julie and Anne-Marie were here and we were talking and Max was in his stroller under the balcony just where you left him and then he was gone!" She drew a shaky breath. "Mom, I'm so scared."

"Christine didn't take him with her?"

"No, no! Listen to me!" Melanie's voice went up another notch. "I'm serious, Mom. He's gone. Someone took him and his stroller and everything!"

Jane felt the first real stirrings of alarm. "Don't leave," she ordered. "Stay where you are, Mellie. And don't hang up. I'm on my way." Food forgotten, Jane hurriedly headed back the way she'd come. People took one look at her face and shifted out of her path.

"I can't just stand here and wait, Mom!" Melanie said in a shaky voice in Jane's ear. "We're going to Jackson Square."

"Jackson—Why?"

"Don't you remember? We saw some policemen there when we were trying to find a place to—never mind, Mom, I'm going there. It's only a block away. I have to hurry!"

Jane barely managed to avoid crashing into a man outfitted in Native American garb, complete with a full feather headdress. With a muttered apology, she skirted around him, keeping the phone pressed to her ear. "I'm a block away, Melanie. Don't go any farther until I get there."

"There's a cop on a horse! I'm going over."

"Okay, but don't hang up," Jane ordered.

Melanie gulped and burst into wild sobs. "Mom, I don't know how it happened! We were all just watching the floats and—"

"Just calm down, Mellie. You can tell me when I get there." Surely there was a logical explanation. Babies didn't just vanish, although in a teeming crowd, it would surely be easier to kidnap— She stopped herself. She would not go there. She would not think the unthinkable. "Can you see Christine?"

"Not really. I told you, she went into the lobby. I mean, I saw the EMTs trying to get through. The lady who fainted is inside and so is Christine."

Christine was the practice manager for a team of internists. Although she'd had no formal training as a nurse, she would certainly know what to do if someone fainted. "I can see the EMT unit now, Mellie. I'm going to stop and talk to Christine just to be sure she didn't take the stroller."

"We saw her run over to the lady, Mom! She didn't take Max."

"I'll just double-check."

The sidewalk was choked with people, but Jane finally reached the hotel where the ambulance was now loading the woman inside. Spotting Christine, she tried forcing her way through the crowd, but she was quickly blocked by an EMT.

"Ma'am, you'll have to stay back and let us do our job."

"I understand, but I have to talk to—"

"I'm sorry, but you can't talk to anyone just now."

Jane craned her neck to look around him and managed to catch Christine's eye.

Christine's gaze went wide with surprise. "Jane. What is it? What's wrong?"

"Do you have Max?" Jane called over the EMT's shoulder.

Christine looked confused. "Max? No. What—"

"He's gone." Frantically, Jane surveyed the sidewalk fronting the hotel where she'd left them. It was still choked with people cheering madly as the parade floats lumbered past. There was no sign of Max or his stroller.

"Where are you headed now?" Christine asked. "I need to get my things inside the hotel and I'll come over."

"Melanie is at Jackson Square. Hurry, Christine."

"I will."

Turning, Jane headed in a rush toward Jackson Square, a full block away. In the distance, the three tall spires of St. Louis Cathedral reached high into a sky that was so clear and blue, it almost hurt to look at it. She put a hand to her heart. *Please, God, don't let this be happening.*

As she pushed through the reveling crowd, she told herself Melanie had to be overreacting. Still, she had a sick feeling in her stomach. The possibility that Max really had disappeared was simply too frightening to be real.

Finally, on reaching the square, she drew a desperate

breath, searching for Melanie. How would she find her in this crowd? She pressed the phone to her ear. "Melanie, where are you? Talk to me."

"I'm on the steps of the cathedral, Mom. Look, over here with the cops. You can see the horse. And I'm waving."

With a rush of relief, she spotted Melanie standing with three uniformed policemen. Jane quickly headed toward them.

One cop held the reins of a horse, which stood patiently, unfazed by the chaotic goings-on. Melanie's friends hovered near her, looking frightened, their eyes scanning the crowd. As Jane approached, she saw a female officer speaking to one of the cops—issuing orders? With a nod, he quickly mounted, cut through the crowd, and disappeared in the direction of the river. Jane did not want to think of that dire possibility.

Melanie was crying, gesturing with her hands as she talked while her eyes anxiously searched the area. Jane's hope that this was all a mistake faded. Down the block on Bourbon Street, floats lumbered past, but in the parklike square, teeming with hundreds of people, how would they be able to find a baby, even in a stroller?

Like Melanie, her frantic gaze swept up and down the square. But there were so many people, so much confusion. Shops were closed, sidewalks jammed. Streets leading off the square were blocked off to accommodate the crowds. Balconies groaned with the weight of those lucky enough to have access. There was an occasional stroller, Jane noted, but none was a familiar blue with yellow-and-blue-plaid trim. With her heart beating frantically in her chest, she approached Melanie and the cops, two men and one female officer.

"I'm here," she said, as Melanie launched herself into Jane's arms. Looking over the girl's head, she asked, "What can you tell me about my baby?"

The policewoman spoke. "Are you Mrs. Madison?"

"Yes, yes."

"Mom, I've told them we shouldn't waste time talking! We need to be looking for Max!"

Jane caught Melanie's arms and angled back enough to see her face. "Mellie, be calm for a moment. Please. Let me talk to these people."

"I'm Officer Cox, Mrs. Madison," the woman said, extending her hand. Jane shook it, nodding mutely. "We've talked to Melanie, trying to get details of exactly what happened. She says she and her friends have thoroughly searched the immediate area where the stroller was parked. Meanwhile, NOPD officers have fanned out looking. But maybe there's a logical explanation. She tells us that there was another adult—"

"Christine O'Brian," Jane said, nodding. "I just spoke to her. She's over there." She waved her hand vaguely. "Some kind of medical emergency. She did not take Max with her."

"And there was no one else with you today? No one who might have felt it okay to take the baby?"

"Without asking me?" Jane stared at her. "No, of course not."

Cox pulled out a small memo pad. "And how old is the baby?" she asked, pen poised.

"Six months. He has b-blue eyes and blond hair." Jane swallowed, struggling to keep calm. "He's wearing a red shirt and denim overalls. White sneakers. He's in a stroller. Navy blue and blue-and-yellow-plaid trim."

"Could he have crawled out of it?"

"He couldn't have climbed out on his own. He—" She turned to Melanie. "Max wasn't out of his stroller, was he?"

Melanie's face crumpled. "No, he was asleep. Just the way he was when you left him with me, Mom." She pressed the fingers of both hands against her lips. "I'm so scared, Mom!"

"We'll find him, Mellie." Jane squeezed the girl's shoulders gently before turning back to the police officers. "How could a baby in a stroller just disappear?" But even as she asked the question, she knew the answer. The stroller didn't just disappear. Somebody had been watching, and when the teenager and her friends became distracted by the fainting woman and the parade and the sheer frenzy of Mardi Gras, that someone had seized the moment to take her baby.

That was the moment when Jane's concern escalated into terror.

"As I mentioned, I've alerted all units in the area, Mrs. Madison," Officer Cox said, touching the radio attached to her belt. "I'm sending out a B.O.L.O."

"B.O.L.O?"

"It means be on the lookout." She spoke briskly into her radio and received a squawked response that was unintelligible to Jane.

As they stood, isolated by the trauma of a missing child, people milled about enjoying Mardi Gras. Some were in costume, others not. Some were drunk, but most were simply reveling in the abandoned spirit of carnival. Jane's gaze strayed beyond Jackson Square where the river formed the east boundary of the French Quarter. Kidnapping a child on a day meant for celebration was obscene. Had she looked into the face of the person who'd taken Max while mingling with the crowd that day?

"Approximately how long has it been since you actually saw the baby, Mrs. Madison?"

Jane struggled to focus. "Twenty—maybe thirty minutes, no longer. I left to get food." She looked at Melanie. "How long after I left did Christine leave, Mellie?"

"I don't know. Pretty soon, I guess. You weren't even out of sight."

"Meaning it could be thirty minutes, give or take," Officer Cox said. Without stating the obvious, both knew a person could travel pretty far in that much time. Even in this crowd.

"We've got to find him!" Jane felt panic rising in her chest.

She stopped, drawing a breath to try to collect herself. With her hand on her heart, she spoke again. "I'm sorry. This is just . . . so—it can't be happening!"

"Please. Come with me." Cox caught Jane's arm and gently guided her toward the cathedral with Melanie following behind. "Let's get out of the crowd."

As they headed to the steps of the cathedral, she added in a reassuring voice, "I know you're worried, but there are hundreds of uniformed policemen on duty today. They'll call me if they spot Max. Meanwhile, let's try to reconstruct what happened. There could be a logical explanation."

"Like what!" Jane cried.

"Someone could have wheeled it away by mistake. Many of these strollers look alike." The possibility was so ludicrous that Jane didn't bother contradicting her. No parent on the planet accidentally claimed a stroller with a strange baby in it.

Jane's cell phone rang. She clicked to talk . . . hoping, hoping. Maybe, just maybe—"Hello!"

"It's Christine. I'm trying to find you. Where are you?"

"Near the steps of the cathedral. One of the officers is on horseback. You should be able to see him. But Christine, we can't find Max."

"Are you serious? He's disappeared?"

"Yes. Oh, Christine . . ." Her voice broke. "I can't believe this."

"I'm on my way, Jane. I'll find you. Meanwhile, I'll be praying."

Turning from Jane, Cox spoke to both officers standing by. "Head over to the hotel where Max was last seen. Someone there might have noticed something." The officers nodded and headed out. "I'm here, Jane." Christine, breathless from running, slipped an arm around Jane's waist and gave her a reassuring hug. "Thank goodness I was able to find you."

"This—" Jane turned to Officer Cox. "This is Christine.

She was with Max and Melanie when I left to . . ." she trailed off, swallowing hard.

"Surely someone saw—" Christine broke off.

"We're working on that now," Cox said. She refocused on Jane. "Are you certain Max was in his stroller when you left?"

"Yes, of course. I checked to see that he was sleeping. He's teething. I knew if he woke up, he'd be grumpy. He would want . . . me." Her voice caught. No time to break down now. "So, yes, he was asleep in his stroller when I left," she said emphatically.

"Mom, let's call Dad," Melanie said. As always, when Melanie was distressed, she wanted her daddy. Christine slipped a comforting arm around the girl's waist. Jane gave Christine a grateful look. With every passing minute, Jane, too, felt the need for Kyle's support.

"Max was definitely asleep in his stroller when I left," Christine said.

With the policewoman leading, they all hurried up the steps to the cathedral. The steps were shallow and worn from the footsteps of the faithful and wide enough to accommodate a crowd. A single look at the officer's expression, and people parted like the Red Sea. An attendant standing at the doors moved aside to let them enter.

The sudden hush inside felt almost eerie. Jane glanced toward the altar with its display of religious symbols and quickly turned to focus on Officer Cox.

For some time, Christine, who was active in her church, had been urging Jane to explore the lack of faith in her life, but she'd resisted. It wasn't that she objected on any philosophical grounds; it was just that she'd never found it particularly . . . relevant. Her life was full and . . . well, busy. On Sundays, rather than getting dressed and going to church, she liked to sit around, read the paper, have a leisurely brunch . . . resting up for the demands of the coming week.

She felt suddenly fearful that she might pay a price for her attitude.

"Try to recollect anything unusual you might have noticed, Melanie." Cox spoke in a calm voice. Jane guessed her tone was intended to steady Melanie and focus her thoughts. "Was there anyone who appeared out of place or was suspicious looking?"

"I-I didn't see anything or anybody like that." She turned to Anne-Marie. "Did you see anything?"

Her friend shrugged. "What was there to see? We were talking, we were all watching the parade and then—"

"And then Max just . . . disappeared!" Melanie said, her voice climbing in panic. "We have to do something!"

"Tell you what." Cox touched Melanie's shoulder. "Let's sit down over here to talk. All of you." With a tip of her chin, she indicated that Melanie's friends as well as Jane and Christine should follow. But Melanie shifted free of the cop's touch.

"We shouldn't be talking at all!" she cried. "We should be looking! We should block off stuff! We should go inside bars and any place that's open! We should stop people and ask if they've seen Max. Whoever took him will get away if we don't do something right now!"

"We are doing something, Melanie," the policewoman said calmly. "Please. Sit." She waited while the group reluctantly perched on the edge of a pew.

"The incident has been reported. Right now officers are on the lookout for Max, but we can't 'block off stuff.' It's not possible in this crowd." Her tone turned brisk. "Now. Let's go over the past half hour once again to be sure we haven't overlooked something. You first, Mrs. Madison."

Jane drew a deep breath. Inside she felt as agitated as Melanie, and she wondered how long she could keep from falling apart. "We stopped at the sidewalk in front of the hotel, beneath the balcony because it wasn't quite as jammed with people, to watch the parade. I left Max with Christine and Mellie to get some food. There were two friends with her." She looked at Christine. "Right, Chris?"

"Yes. And the stroller was right there when I left to help inside the hotel."

"You noticed nothing unusual?"

Christine paused to think. "No. But I was there only another minute or two after Jane went for food. I told Melanie to watch Max and left."

Cox turned to Melanie. "Tell me exactly what happened from the time Mrs. O'Brian left."

"It was—" Melanie began with a guilty look at her stepmother. "Some guys we knew were on a float that was passing by, and the parade stopped, right there. You know how it is, everything's moving and then it's not. It was only for a minute, Mom, honest." Her lips trembled as she met Jane's eyes. "They said when the parade was over that they knew someone on Bourbon Street who had rented rooms with a balcony and they were going to watch the rest of the parades from up there. They invited us too. So then it started up again and they left and we turned around and Max was gone!"

"This is the first I've heard about boys on a float," Jane said sternly. "Did you forget you were responsible for your baby brother?"

"No, Mom." Melanie dashed at tears in her eyes. "I swear to you, it was only a few minutes."

"But long enough for someone to steal Max." Jane knew her words were hurtful, but her concern was for her baby now, not Melanie.

"Mom, please call Dad! Please. We need him. He'll know what to do."

Until a few minutes ago, Jane had been hesitant about calling Kyle in case the whole thing turned out to be a false alarm.

But now, with her stomach in a knot and her mouth dry with fear, she knew it wasn't a false alarm. She sent Officer Cox a questioning look.

"It might be a good idea to call your husband, Mrs. Madison."

JANE REACHED KYLE AT his office on Poydras, but it was thirty minutes before he managed to get to the cathedral. They gathered on the front steps outside, where the crowd seemed to have lessened just a bit.

On the phone, she'd been unable to tell him much except that Max had disappeared. He'd wanted details, but there were none. Now his fierce gaze swept past Officer Cox's serious face and Melanie's tear-drenched cheeks to lock onto Jane.

"Has he been found?"

"No."

He looked stunned. "There has to be a mistake."

"We've looked—" Jane paused, knowing her voice wavered. "They've fanned out to search, but the crowds are monstrous. They haven't turned up anything. It's as if he disappeared into thin air."

"That's impossible. He must still be here somewhere. Someone is bound to've seen him. You gave them a description of his stroller?" He glanced at the police officer.

"Of course, Kyle." Jane rubbed her temple where a sharp pain throbbed.

Officer Cox moved to them, putting out her hand. "Mr. Madison, I'm Sharon Cox, the investigating officer." With a brief nod, he shook her hand.

"Now that you're here, I'd like to suggest we go to the police substation. It's a better place to talk. Once we're there, I'll explain—"

"I don't think we should leave," he said in a firm tone. "And what's to explain? We should be combing the area, knocking on doors, questioning people, looking into garages and courtyards." Glancing outside, he raked a hand over his face. "This is a nightmare."

"Everything you mention is being done, Mr. Madison. N.O.P.D. is on the scene—has been from the start—but we're hampered by the crowd. What we need now is to piece together exactly what happened."

"How can you be certain Max is nowhere nearby?"

"I can't say that with certainty," Sharon said. "But we've found no trace of him. No one has seen anything suspicious." Like Kyle's, her glance strayed beyond the narthex to the reveling crowd outside. "At least they've seen nothing that might be construed as suspicious beyond ordinary Mardi Gras madness."

"It's all my fault, Dad!" Melanie cried suddenly.

Jane knew Mellie needed reassurance from Kyle. She needed to hear him say he understood her fear, that he wasn't angry with her. She needed a hug from her daddy. But from the grim expression on his face it didn't look as if she was going to get any such thing. "Max was with Melanie and her friends, Kyle," Jane explained, trying to keep the tremor from her voice.

"With Melanie?" He frowned darkly. "Why was he with Melanie? Where were you?"

"I went to get us something to eat from a vendor . . . Julie and Anne-Marie were with them—"

"You left our son in the care of a bunch of teenagers to get junk food?"

Melanie made a distressed sound. "Dad, just listen. Please."

"Hush, Melanie." Kyle waved the teenager quiet, keeping his gaze laser sharp on Jane. "I'm waiting to hear what happened," he told her.

"You can't say anything worse to me than I've been saying to myself, Kyle. The kids were hungry. I went to get food.

Christine was with them. It never occurred to me that anything like this could happen."

"Christine?" He turned to glance at Jane's friend then back at Jane.

"There was a medical emergency," Jane said. "Christine lent assistance. She—" Jane stopped, not wanting to cast blame on Christine or Melanie.

Kyle's steely gaze turned to his daughter. "So how could Max disappear if you were watching him?"

Melanie was crying again. "We—we got talking and suddenly the parade stopped and this float was right by us. There were some guys we knew from school on it. They were laughing and goofing off and everything. They threw us tons of beads and stuff. It was just for a few minutes, Dad," she said, pleading for understanding. "I know I shouldn't have taken my eyes off Max! But I thought he was safe on the sidewalk right beside me!"

"Clearly he wasn't beside you," Kyle said.

"But he was only a few feet away, honestly." She put both hands to her cheeks. "I mean, I don't know how long it was, minutes really, but when we looked, he was gone!"

Jane slipped an arm around the girl's shoulders, trying to console her, while inside she was sick with terror.

Kyle stood with his hands on his hips. "Can you estimate how much time passed before you noticed your baby brother was gone?"

When Melanie seemed unable to talk, Cox spoke up quietly. "We've covered all that, Mr. Madison. The parade stalled for about five minutes, so I don't see how it could have been much longer than that."

"But more than long enough for someone to take the stroller and melt into the crowd, then head for only God knows where," Kyle said in a flat tone.

"Possibly," the officer conceded.

"I'm sorry! I'm sorry!" Melanie cried. "I didn't mean this to happen. I'm so sorry."

Jane drew the girl closer. "We know, Mellie. And we'll find him. You'll see. We will." She looked up into Kyle's eyes, her chin tilted. "We *will*!"

They all turned to look as the cop who'd been mounted on horseback appeared, dismounting and moving reverently toward them. His glance skimmed the Madisons before moving to Sharon Cox. "N.O.P.D. has found the stroller."

Jane pressed her fist to her heart. "Oh, thank God!"

The cop gave her a sympathetic look. "I'm sorry, ma'am. The stroller was abandoned . . . up on the Riverwalk." In one hand he held a tiny sneaker. "This is all we found. There was no sign of the baby."

2

SIX MONTHS LATER

WITH THE STRIKING OF the clock at half past midnight, Jane Madison put aside the bestseller she hadn't been able to get interested in, threw off the afghan, and rose from the couch. She removed her reading glasses on her way to the window and stared out at the street. It was dark and quiet.

Melanie, where are you?

Actually, it was only half an hour past her stepdaughter's curfew, but Jane couldn't remember an evening lately when Melanie had made it home even close to that deadline. And so far tonight there'd been no phone call, no text message, nothing to explain why she was late. They'd agreed on a twelve o'clock curfew on weekdays for the sixteen-year-old. In Jane's estimation, it was more than reasonable. The late hour allowed for less sleep than Jane considered necessary, but compromise was crucial with Melanie nowadays. Not that compromise seemed to be working. Melanie still accused Jane of being overprotective, among other things. Lately, the girl had a laundry list of ways Jane didn't measure up as a parent.

Jane again studied the blank face of her cell phone. No text, nothing. Wasn't her reaction understandable? Once a parent loses a child as she had lost Max, wasn't it natural to be apprehensive? Or was it just she? Kyle seemed less paranoid, which could be one of the reasons for Melanie's defiance. Tomorrow, whether Kyle thought it was convenient or not, Jane determined to make him sit down and talk with her about Melanie. Of course, it would mean catching him at a moment when he was willing to talk . . . and that was tricky lately.

She glanced again at the time. Twelve forty-five. It wasn't only Melanie who was late. Kyle should have been home a couple of hours ago, too, and she'd heard nothing from him either. He was in Houston taking a deposition in an important case. Or so he claimed. To him every case was all-important. Now that he'd made partner, he had thrown himself into his career with even more zeal than when he'd been striving for the promotion. And he spent more and more time in the New Orleans office than at home in Mandeville.

She studied the quiet street. Why was it that lately neither her husband nor her stepdaughter bothered to tell her when they were going to be late? That was going on her list of complaints, too, she told herself. How long did it take? Thirty seconds? A minute to send a text message? She was on Melanie's speed dial, for heaven sake! Kyle's too, for that matter.

With a sigh, she turned away from the window and headed for the kitchen. As she stood at the refrigerator, filling a glass with water, her eyes fell on the photo of Max in a spot at eye level. Pain, instant and sharp, stabbed her to the heart. Max, one month before he was taken, his sweet face wreathed in a smile. As always, the spot of strained spinach on his chin tugged at her heart. Oh, he was so beautiful, more precious than life to her.

She turned away to fight despair welling up in her chest. Why was he taken from her? It had been so difficult to even have a baby. She'd suffered through miscarriage after miscarriage for twelve long years, never able to carry a baby to term. Then miraculously there was Max.

Why? Why? Why? It was a question she'd asked of God over and over, trying to understand. She was a good person. She tried to live a moral life. Granted, she wasn't active in a church, but she wasn't evil either. Even Christine, when Jane had pressed her, had trouble searching for some greater purpose in Max's disappearance.

"I don't know why bad things happen to good people," Christine had told her in the early weeks after Max was gone. "That's an age-old question that may not have an answer. At least, no satisfying answer when you're on the wrong side of tragedy."

"So I'm just supposed to accept it?" had been Jane's bitter reply. "Suck it up and keep on keeping on?" But the bottom line was that it was impossible to pick up the pieces of her life after Max, not with a hole the size of the moon in her heart.

Drawing a breath, Jane brushed at tears welling up. She didn't want to dwell tonight on the whys and what-ifs to a God who was supposed to be loving and kind, when her baby had been kidnapped. She'd had plenty of time to do that in the past six months. No, tonight she needed to focus on Melanie and the girl's distressing behavior. But after looking at Max's photo, a whisper of fear had sneaked in to remind her of what could happen to Melanie. Where was she? Darn it, the girl knew how Jane worried when she was late.

Setting the glass aside, she tried once more to reach Kyle, but again got only his voice mail. Maybe he was in flight. At least she hoped he was en route home and not ignoring her attempts to call.

She reached for her address book and paged through it,

looking for Anne-Marie Melancon's number. It was difficult to know who Melanie's friends were or where she chose to hang out now. Everything was a big secret.

Finally she found the number. With a glance at the clock, Jane hesitated only a few seconds before dialing. She regretted the necessity of waking the Melancons at this hour, but hopefully they'd understand. If the situation were reversed, Jane would understand.

Ten minutes later, she was even more worried. After calling the Melancons and getting nowhere, she'd tried three other numbers suggested by a sleepy Anne-Marie, but nobody had seen Melanie, and nobody had any suggestions about how to find her. Jane was once again pacing. Tomorrow was a school day. Where in the world was Melanie?

And where was Kyle?

Unable to bear the four walls closing in on her, Jane went outside to the patio. The night was filled with nocturnal sounds. Situated a block from the north shore of Lake Pontchartrain, the property backed up to a stretch of uninhabited land that teemed with wildlife. For a minute, she stood listening, then shivered a bit at the haunting cries of mourning doves.

To shake off that mood, she moved across the lawn, silvery green in the moonlight, and stood looking at the trees, silent sentinels in the night. Spanish moss dripped from the limbs of cypress not twenty yards from her patio. In rainy seasons, the woods became swampy and inaccessible. She often thought it was nature's way of reclaiming what was never meant to be inhabited by humans in the first place. But now, tonight, the trees were dark and still, and the night was inky black. Sinister.

Sudden movement near a camellia bush startled her. In a moment, she relaxed as a raccoon waddled off, no doubt after raiding Melanie's bird feeder. Jane moved to the edge of the patio and inspected the contraption. Sure enough, it was pretty much empty.

Seeing it, Jane was taken back to the birthday party four years earlier when Melanie received the bird feeder as a joke. Jane, as chaperone, had a sleepless night. Six twelve-year-old girls did not settle down until nearly daybreak. How they'd managed to stay awake so late mystified Jane, who longed for her bed around two a.m. But it was fun. Jane felt a nostalgic pain. A prepubescent Mellie had still wanted Jane as mother and friend. They did so much together then, enjoyed each other, talked, touched, *loved*. They could not have been any closer if they'd been biological mom and child.

And then Max was gone.

At first, the chasm that was to develop between Jane and Melanie was barely noticeable. Everybody in the family was so shocked and grieved that it was a while before Jane realized the extent of Mellie's feelings of guilt. They'd finally put her in counseling. But instead of improving, somehow Mellie's emotional state deteriorated. She began focusing her pain on Jane. She lashed out at the least thing. Where they'd once shopped together, gossiped together, gone to movies, and spent weekends with Jane teaching her to drive, Melanie no longer seemed able to tolerate the sight of Jane.

The psychologist said not to worry, that she'd come around in time. But Jane wasn't so sure. When Melanie came home from school, she went directly to her room. Not only did she not speak to Jane, she didn't even look at Jane. And nothing Jane did or said seemed to break through that wall.

With her arms wrapped around herself, she headed back to the house. The doorbell was ringing when she slid the patio door open. Heart in her throat, she rushed inside. Was this that moment all parents feared? Were the police coming to tell her there'd been a horrible accident? She fumbled with the dead bolt, finally got it, then stared in surprise at Christine O'Brian.

"I'm sorry," Christine said, impulsively catching Jane's arm when she gave a start. "I scared you and I didn't mean to. But I saw your lights on and Daniel isn't home and I wondered if by some chance he could be over here."

"Come in, Chris." Still a little shaky, Jane closed the door. "Melanie's not in yet either, and it's way past her curfew. Could they be together, do you think?"

Christine rubbed wearily at her temples. "I have no idea. Daniel's so secretive lately. And moody, you wouldn't believe. He's almost a stranger." She gave Jane a bewildered look. "What's happening with our kids, Jane? They never used to be so . . . so difficult."

"When you get an answer to that, be sure and tell me," Jane said. "It's late, but since neither one of us can sleep, you want a cup of tea?"

"May as well, but no caffeine for me at this hour." Christine followed her to the kitchen and waited while Jane filled a kettle at the sink and set it on the stove. "Kyle's sleeping?" Not waiting for an answer, she added dryly, "I guess he's like Ben. When anything approaching trouble crops up, he lets me do the worrying and he sleeps through it."

Trying not to sound as bereft as she felt, Jane said, "Kyle's not here."

"Out of town again on business, huh?"

"In Houston. But he was due back hours ago."

Christine glanced at the wall clock. "Must be a really late flight. He'll be exhausted."

Jane took two mugs from the cabinet and selected herbal tea from a canister. "I guess, but I'm exhausted too. The way Melanie is behaving lately is driving me crazy. I can't reach her anymore, and I need Kyle to step up to the plate. He's the only one she'll listen to now."

"No surprise there. Mellie's always been a daddy's girl."

"Which leaves me out in the cold nowadays." When the kettle whistled, Jane lifted it and filled both mugs. She set Christine's in front of her and leaned against the counter, cupping her hands around the warmth. After a moment or two, she said, "Melanie's not the only one I can't reach anymore, Chris. Kyle has become so withdrawn, I sometimes think he takes those out-of-town trips just to escape. Or maybe to get away from me and all that I remind him of."

"I can't believe he wants to get away from you. He loves you." Christine was thoughtful as she stirred her tea. "If he's like Ben—and a lot of men—actually saying what he feels is difficult. Men don't vent like women do."

"I suppose. But having Kyle turn into a ghost while Mellie morphs into a stranger makes our home a shadow of what it used to be. I don't see how we can keep on like this. I feel like a person poised on the edge of an abyss and any minute something is going to push us all over into it."

"Your family has suffered horribly, Jane," Christine said gently. "Not that I'm an expert—far from it—but six months is really not all that much time to adjust to something like that, is it?"

"But wouldn't we cope better together than apart?" Jane knew she sounded bitter, but she had plenty reason, didn't she?

"All three of you are different people with different personalities," Christine said, seeming to pick her way through a minefield. "It makes sense that you'd cope in different ways."

Gathering her thoughts, Jane studied the floor. "Melanie's a teenager. She feels responsible for Max's disappearance so it makes sense that she might have trouble coming to terms with that. I accept that she doesn't choose me as confidant . . . or comforter. But Kyle . . . I really need him to share with me what he's thinking and feeling. We need to be together to make it through this, Christine. And we're not. "

Christine gave a helpless shrug. "I don't know what to say, Jane. But you know that I care about you, and that I'm praying for you."

Jane shifted uncomfortably as she watched her get to her

feet. Her friend's prayers hadn't done much so far. She smiled sadly and said, "It's enough to know I can count on you just to listen, Christine. I'm grateful for that."

"I've got to get back in case Daniel calls." With a glance at the clock, Christine took her mug to the sink. "Thanks for the tea. If you hear anything, give me a ring, will you?"

"Of course."

THE HOUSE SEEMED MORE empty and lonely than ever after Christine left. But it was only a few minutes later that her cell phone rang. With a glad cry, she lunged toward the table where she'd left it. Good news or bad?

"Hello?" she said, breathless from hurrying. No one answered, but she could hear background noise. Voices like that of a blaring TV set.

"Hello? Hello! Mellie, is that you?"

But no one answered.

"Kyle?"

Still no answer. Jane pressed the receiver to her ear and struggled to identify the sounds on the other end of the line. It really did sound like a TV program turned up to maximum volume.

But just then headlights swept across the front of the house. She clicked the phone off and hurried to the window, willing the car to stop out front. When it did, she closed her eyes in blessed relief. Had it been Kyle, he would have tripped the garage door, so it had to be Melanie. Worry and fear were instantly replaced with righteous fury.

She recognized Daniel O'Brian's Mustang, dropping Melanie off. Christine would be relieved, but why they'd both ignored curfews was baffling. Both had always been such good kids, but that didn't make Jane any less furious. Daniel and Melanie had played together since childhood and still attended the same high school, although he was a year and a half older. Jane wished she knew Melanie's other friends as well as she knew Daniel.

She had the words of a stern lecture at hand. Yet she resisted yanking the door open to confront them both on the spot. Instead she took a deep breath and waited. Kyle complained lately that Jane undermined her own authority by being on Melanie's case constantly. Okay, she'd give them a minute or two to say good night, and then Melanie was going to get an earful.

By the time they reached the front porch, Jane heard Daniel's voice. She couldn't hear what was said, but she could tell he was angry. And because that was unusual, curiosity overcame anger. Maybe, just maybe, she'd get a clue as to what in the world was going on with Melanie lately.

She heard Daniel clearly.

"Nobody's ever going to believe how this happened, Mel. I don't even know how it happened. You said everything was okay!"

What on earth? Jane frowned, straining to hear Melanie's reply, but it was too soft. In contrast, Daniel didn't seem to care who might hear him.

"Everybody's gonna freak when they find out!" he said. "This is major trouble."

Again, Melanie's reply was mumbled. Jane guessed she didn't want to be overheard. Truly intrigued now, Jane heard no more conversation, only the jangle of Melanie's keys. Daniel must have left. Not waiting for Mellie, Jane turned the lock and pulled the door open just in time to see Daniel taking off in his Mustang with a screech of tires.

"What is going on, Melanie?"

Melanie rolled her eyes. "Hello, Jane."

Jane. It still gave her a pang when Melanie called her that.

When had it happened that she stopped being Mom? With Max's disappearance, of course. "What were you and Daniel arguing about?"

"Since you were listening, you tell me." The girl's face was set, her tone hostile. She would not look at Jane.

"Are you in some kind of trouble, Mellie?"

"I'm tired." Shouldering around her stepmother, Melanie took the first step on the stairs. "I'm going to bed."

"No! You stop right there!" Jane caught her by one arm. "You aren't going anywhere until you explain a few things. Have you looked at the time? You're two hours past your curfew. We're going in the den, and I want an explanation."

"Oh, give me a break!" Melanie broke away, but she turned from the stairs and stormed off toward the den. Jane followed, determined not to let her get away with open disrespect.

"Sit, Melanie."

Huffing with disgust, Melanie flopped onto the couch. "Okay, let's get this over with."

"Fine with me," Jane said. "Let's hear your explanation."

"I'm sorry," Melanie said without a trace of sincerity. "I forgot my watch and lost track of the time."

Jane simply stared at her.

"It's true!" Melanie crossed her arms over her chest and tilted her chin. "I didn't realize it was so late."

"I might believe that if you were half an hour late," Jane said, struggling to hang on to her patience. "But even with no watch, you had to know it was past your curfew, Mellie."

"I said I was sorry."

"What were you two *doing*?" Jane tried to keep the exasperation from her tone, albeit unsuccessfully. "Christine was frantic, just like me. Where did you go? Was there anyone besides Daniel with you?"

"A thousand questions as usual. Can't all this wait until

morning, Jane? I'm really tired." With her arms still wrapped around herself, Melanie leaned over and rested her head on her knees.

"I'm tired too." Jane gazed down at the girl's dark hair, thinking she *did* look exhausted. She longed to offer comfort, to touch her and not be rejected. But it had been a long, long time since Mellie had welcomed Jane's touch.

Melanie stood up. "Good, we're done, right?"

Baffled, Jane struggled wondering how to handle the situation. She wished Kyle were here. She tried calming her tone and keeping her irritation in check. "No, we are not done. You didn't bother to ask permission to go anywhere, Melanie. Put yourself in my place. With no note, no voice mail, no text, I was really worried. Did you set out to simply ignore the house rules or did something come up, something I'd understand? I'm willing to listen to any reasonable explanation."

"If you're so willing, you can wait until tomorrow, can't you?"

"No! And sit back down. You're not blowing me off this time. I'm getting to the bottom of this now. Tonight."

Melanie sat, shoving her fingers along the nape of her neck and fluffing her hair out. "So, have at it."

Jane was almost defeated by such open impudence. But she was the adult here, wasn't she? "Melanie, I'll ask one more time. Where were you and what were you and Daniel doing all this time?"

"Talking!" Melanie cried. "In his car. Okay? Now are you finished?" She started to rise.

"Finished? Am I finished? Did you hear a word I said? No, I am not finished. And you're not getting up from that couch until I say you can. Now, where were you? And simply saying in Daniel's car is not good enough."

"Out." A shrug of her shoulders. "Around."

"Show some respect, I mean it! Don't be snarky with me like I'm one of your girlfriends. I'm your mother."

"My mother is dead," Melanie said coldly. "Breast cancer. Remember?"

Jane sighed. "Oh, Mellie, you know what I mean. Why are you making this so hard?"

"Daniel picked me up after school. We went for pizza."

"And it took ten hours?"

Melanie flipped her hair again. "We were pretty hungry."

Jane propped her hands on her hips and glared. "You're supposed to call me if you're going to be late. We discussed this. You agreed to the rules."

"Rules. Rules. You're obsessed with rules, Jane," she said angrily. "There are too many rules around here! I can't keep them all straight."

"Well, here's another one, Miss Smart Pants. You're grounded. I want you home within thirty minutes after school for the next two weeks. And no computer, no text messaging, no talking on the phone."

"Whatever." Rolling her eyes, she radiated disgust.

"And no driving privileges."

"I know, I know. I'm grounded, crucified, dead, and buried."

Confounded, Jane stared at her. "What is the *matter* with you tonight?"

"I'm a screwup, in case you haven't noticed. I can't do anything right. I know you hate me. You may as well say it to my face."

"Don't be ridiculous. You know that's not true. But if you continue in that rebellious tone, I'll see what else I can think of to change your attitude!"

With an insolent shrug, Melanie turned her face away.

"Look at me when I speak to you!" Jane cried in frustration.

"I'm trying to understand what's wrong, but you behave as if I'm the enemy. I'm not. I only want what's best for you, but you make it so difficult, Mellie. You are not an adult yet, and you can't just do what you want when you want! Now, I'll ask you once again. Where were you, and what were you doing tonight?"

"What do you *care*?" Melanie shrieked, suddenly springing up from her seat. "Most of the time you don't even know I exist, so stop pretending that you're so concerned, okay?"

"What are you talking about? What do you mean I hardly know you exist?"

"You know what I'm talking about, Jane." Tears suddenly welled in her eyes. "You're bugging me about rules and curfew and stupid stuff like that, but it's all for show. It ticks you off that I'm out late, but that's because you know parents are supposed to do that."

"So it's wrong that I'm doing what a parent is supposed to do?"

Melanie looked at her. "Can I please just go to bed?"

"What's going on here?" Startled at the sound of her husband's voice, Jane wheeled about to find Kyle standing in the doorway frowning at them.

"Kyle." Jane drew in a deep breath. "I didn't hear you come in."

"I can believe that." With his briefcase in one hand and his jacket in the other, he scowled at Jane as he dropped both on the nearest chair. "With all the shouting, you couldn't hear thunder."

"Daddy!" Melanie rushed over to Kyle, burying her face in his shirt. His arms went around his daughter as he looked over her head at Jane. "It's two o'clock in the morning. Why isn't Mellie in bed? For that matter, why aren't you both in bed?"

"She just got home, Kyle. Daniel dropped her off a few minutes ago . . . two hours past her curfew. I was trying to find out why. And not getting very far," she added on an acid note.

He sighed, pulled back, and caught the girl's face in his hands. "Go to bed, Mellie," he said gently. "Tomorrow's a school day." He dropped a kiss on her forehead.

"Okay, Daddy." She gave him a contrite look, then left the room without another glance at Jane.

Jane clutched the sides of her head, gritting her teeth. "We've got to do something, Kyle. She's completely out of control. It's maddening. I'm at my wit's end."

"And I'm bushed. We'll talk about it tomorrow." He turned and headed toward the stairs. "Right now, I'm going to bed."

"That's it? That's all you have to say?"

Pausing at the foot of the stairs, he glanced at his watch. "At two oh five a.m.? Yeah, that's all I have to say. Whatever we need to talk about, it'll keep until morning."

Jane watched him climb the stairs. Shaking her head, she went about securing the house and turning off lights. But inside she was seething. Darn it, he wasn't going to get away with sticking his head in a hole. They had a real problem. Maybe a part of Melanie's rebellion was an attempt to reach her father. He'd been so remote lately that she'd have to practically faint at his feet to get him to notice her. Maybe Jane would remind him of that.

He was undressing when she walked into their bedroom. She watched as he stripped off his shirt and tossed it into the laundry hamper. "Why didn't you call and let me know you were going to be late, Kyle? I expected you hours ago."

"My flight was delayed. We actually took off but returned to the airport because some character looked suspicious. He was booted, but the airplane had to be inspected from stem to stern. They issued an order for us not to use our cell phones."

"And once you landed in New Orleans, you didn't call me because . . ."

"Because I thought you'd be sleeping."

"For heaven's sake, Kyle. You—"

"I'm sorry." He scrubbed a hand over his face looking exhausted. "I should have called anyway. So do me a favor and drop it for tonight, will you?"

"I suppose I have to."

"We'll talk tomorrow, Jane." Stripped down to his underwear now, he got into bed and turned off the lamp.

"Did the deposition go wrong?"

"Hmmm."

Whatever that meant. As Jane watched, he settled on his side, his back to her. She had little choice but to turn and get ready for bed herself. She'd always envied Kyle his ability to fall asleep quickly. Even if he was troubled, it never seemed to keep him awake, whereas Jane was at the mercy of her emotions. If she was upset or angry or frustrated or worried, sleep was impossible.

She was all of that tonight.

In the bathroom, she brushed her teeth with a vengeance, creamed the makeup from her face, slathered on a moisturizer, then changed into a gown and finally got into bed beside him. She lay for a minute thinking that there had been a time when he would have been eager to make love after being gone for even a single day. Now, she realized with a frown, she couldn't remember the last time they'd made love. Couldn't he see how that hurt her? Did he care?

She stared up at the revolving ceiling fan. They used to be so happy, but Max's disappearance had stolen the joy from their lives. For the second time that night, she pushed thoughts of her kidnapped baby from her mind.

What in the world to do about Melanie? In spite of counseling and Jane and Kyle's careful handling, she did not seem to be getting better. According to her therapist, Melanie was unable to rid herself of her guilt for Max's disappearance.

If only Max could be found . . .

* * *

Morning routine was always hectic, but because she'd gone to bed after two, Melanie was off to a late start. She had to rush to get to school on time, meaning Jane had no opportunity to talk to her about the night before. What did surprise Jane was that Kyle didn't leave for his office right away but lingered, pouring himself a rare second cup of coffee.

He stood at the sink in a crisp white shirt and smoky blue tie, trim pants, and shined shoes. Jane still felt a little catch in her heart at the sight of her handsome husband. Dark hair, clear gray eyes, and an athletic build made him stand out. Upon meeting him for the first time, while it was nice that they shared a common career, what really touched her heart was learning he was raising a three-year-old daughter since losing his wife to breast cancer. Before Kyle, Jane's few relationships had been short term and without passion. It still surprised her how quickly she'd fallen in love with Kyle.

But they waited to get married until Melanie was five years old. And being so young when her mother died, the girl didn't remember much about Laura, so she'd been eager to have a "real mommy." For Jane's part, loving Kyle made her eager to fill that role. So Melanie's rejection baffled her as much as it hurt.

Gazing into her coffee, Jane wondered how to broach the subject to Kyle. "You're getting a late start today," she said, offering a smile.

"Yeah." He turned and emptied what coffee was left in his mug and reached for a paper towel. "Did you get a chance to talk to Melanie before she left for school?"

"No. She overslept, of course. I had to practically drag her out of bed, and when she finally got up, she had to rush like mad to catch carpool." Studying him now, Jane paused with her hands cupping a warm mug. He seemed to have something on his mind. Maybe last night's fiasco had finally gotten to him.

He tossed the paper towel. "Let me guess. You picked up right where you left off last night."

"No, Kyle." Exasperated, she added, "We didn't talk at all. She barely managed to grab a muffin and a bottle of juice. Not much of a breakfast, but better than nothing."

When he didn't comment, Jane set her coffee aside and stood up. "We need to talk about last night, Kyle. I'm worried about her."

"She doesn't have a car," he said. "Who had the wheels?"

"I told you—Daniel. And when they got to the door, he was giving her the devil over something. Whatever it is, he seemed to think if we found out, we'd be upset. 'Freaked' was the word he used. I got nowhere asking Mellie what he meant. You know how stubborn she can be." She heaved a sigh. "What in the world are we going to do, Kyle?"

"She's sixteen, for Pete's sake."

"And sixteen is a difficult age, I get that. But it's no excuse." Jane gazed unseeing out the window, utterly mystified. "She's so resentful of me, though I can't think of anything I've done to make her feel that way."

"Can't you?"

Caught up in her own thoughts, she missed the wry note in his voice and went on. "She absolutely adores you, Kyle. Maybe you can say something to bring her to her senses."

"I'll talk to her."

Skeptical, she asked, "And when would that be? You've been gone for three days. And you missed her this morning." She held up a hand when he seemed ready to argue. "You'll go back to your office and bury yourself in this or that case, Kyle. Don't deny it. And you'll forget about the trouble at home." She set her coffee cup on the table with a thump. "You can't. Not this time. You have to deal with this. Now."

"And what will you do, Jane?"

"What?"

"I don't see you spending much time nurturing Melanie. When you aren't at your job, you're with a bunch of strangers at Child Search."

"Those people are suffering, Kyle. They've lost children. For some, more than one. I know what that's like. If I can help a grieving parent, I think it's time well spent."

"Maybe your time would be better spent if you focused on your family. Melanie is grieving over the loss of a child too. Her baby brother. Maybe acting out is the only way she can get your attention. Have you thought of that?"

She stared at him, genuinely speechless. Hadn't he heard a word she'd said?

When she stayed mute, Kyle continued, "It's not only Melanie who hasn't been able to get your attention, Jane. It's me too."

She was shaking her head. "I can't believe this."

He sighed. "I understand your obsession. It's—"

"My obsession?"

"Yes, your obsession. To find Max. But you still have a family—which you seem to have forgotten. With all the time you give to your quest and Child Search, Melanie and I get the leftovers . . . distracted leftovers, I might add."

"That is not true!"

"Jane. When was the last time you fixed dinner instead of picking something up at the deli or grabbing takeout from somewhere? When was the last time you went to a movie with Melanie? When was the last time you noticed either one of us?"

"I notice you all the time! I have a lot on my plate, same as you, Kyle. When was the last time you puttered around the kitchen? Or vacuumed, for that matter? Or are cooking and cleaning exclusively my jobs?"

"This is not about who cooks and cleans and you know it."

Jane sputtered and propped her hands on her hips. "Besides, how would you know since you're constantly working or out of town?"

"I'm out of town because I have several cases that require it, Jane. I don't hop a plane just because I like flying. I made partner because of the time and effort I devote to my career." He grabbed his jacket off the back of a chair. "Which is more than you can say at the moment. I'm surprised you haven't been reprimanded for neglecting yours."

"Why are you talking to me like this?" she cried. "You know how hard it's been to keep my head above water since Max was taken. I'm doing the best I can."

"And maybe Mellie is doing the best she can too."

"I don't see you spending a lot of time with her," Jane shot back. "Why is it up to me?"

"Then maybe both of us are guilty." He sighed and raked a hand through his hair.

The gesture made her heart ache. How long had he been bottling up so much resentment? Lord, she felt like an idiot.

"This isn't getting us anywhere, Kyle," she said quietly, ready to call a truce. "I need to finish dressing, and you should probably go before we both say something we'll regret."

He paused, wearily rubbing his forehead. When he looked up, he had a bleak expression on his face. "Has it dawned on you, Jane, that we're living half a life here?"

She frowned. "What do you mean, half a life?"

"You in your world, Mellie, and me in another. Or maybe we're in separate universes since you don't seem to have a clue."

She was momentarily struck that he said the same thing she was thinking. What did that mean?—that he didn't want to live with her? It was a chilling thought. "Have you thought it might be because I *feel* like half a person since Max was taken?" she demanded angrily. "And unlike you burying yourself in cases and Melanie going age-sixteen-crazy, I'm at least doing something about it."

"Like what, Jane?"

"I'm doing everything I can to try to find him!"

"Of course you are," he shot at her as if he'd suddenly had as much as he could take. "Since it's your fault that he's gone."

She was stunned. "I've explained a million times that—"

"I don't care how many times you explain, Jane. You know that the streets are literally crawling with predators at Mardi Gras. You should never have left Max with a teenager."

"I left Max with Christine!"

"You should never have left him at all!"

Jane flinched at the ferocity of his attack. She'd spent hundreds of hours blaming herself for Max's disappearance, but it hurt even more to know that Kyle blamed her too. She felt shocked and blindsided.

"Maybe you should ask yourself if there's blood on your own hands," she said, her volume rising.

He glared at her. "Meaning what?"

"Our son could have been kidnapped by one of the sleazy types you deal with, Kyle. But have you spent a minute looking into that possibility? Wondering if Max's disappearance could possibly be laid at your door?"

Instead of defending himself, he turned his back on her and shrugged into his suit coat, obviously bent on leaving. Or escaping, she thought. No surprise there.

"What's the deal?" she asked. "Did I hit a nerve?"

But taking a cheap shot gave her no satisfaction. At the beginning of the investigation into Max's kidnapping, they'd all dissected every facet of their lives, personal and professional. The N.O.P.D. team had turned both their offices inside out looking for a connection. Nothing was found.

She sighed, giving over. "Okay, Kyle, enough. We started this talking about Melanie and what to do. But we've wound up screaming at each other. What's the point when we have way more important issues on our plates?"

With his back still to her, Kyle paused, then turned slowly. "Actually, the way we're screaming at each other probably means that we both need time for some serious thinking."

She stared at him in confusion. "About Melanie?"

"No. About us." He rubbed the back of his neck, looking miserable. "I don't know about you, but I need some space, maybe try and work through some things."

"Things?" she asked, bewildered.

"Haven't you wondered lately whether our relationship is what it ought to be? I mean, we've lost Max and—"

"We haven't lost Max! Don't say that!" Her voice quivered with fright. Giving up on her baby was not an option. "We're going to find him."

"Okay, okay. I'm sorry. But what we're going through can put a strain on any relationship. That's what I'm trying to say. Or maybe it's just me. Whatever. I think we need to back off from each other for a while as we try to work through this."

"This isn't a relationship, Kyle. It's a marriage."

"It's not much of a marriage at the moment," he said. "You can't deny that."

Her heart was beating hard. She couldn't deny that their marriage was shaky. The research about families facing tragedy supported that theory. But she couldn't believe Kyle had come to such a drastic place without her having a clue.

"Are you telling me you want a divorce?" she asked, afraid to hear what he'd say.

He took a long time weighing his thoughts. "To tell the truth, I'm not sure what I want. I just know that continuing the way we are isn't working. It seems logical to take some time to try and figure out what I want."

"And how are you going to do that, Kyle? Are you leaving? We can work through this, but only if we're together."

"We're not together now, Jane. It's like I said, sometimes I feel as if there's an ocean between us."

"Well, I don't!" she cried.

He studied her for a long moment. "Let me ask you something."

She braced herself. After the bombshell he'd just dropped, she didn't know what to expect . . . just that it wouldn't be good.

"Do you think you're the only one in this family who is suffering because Max is gone?"

"What kind of question is that? Every one of us was devastated when Max was taken."

"Then why do you act as if only your heart was broken? Why do you hold your pain and suffering up to us as if ours doesn't match yours? You immerse yourself in your grief and in finding other folks' kids while you shut me and Mellie out. That's what I mean by obsession. I can't cope with it anymore."

"You are leaving!" she said, aghast at the thought.

"I don't know! But I had a wife. Mellie had a mother. Neither one of us has that anymore."

His words were so devastating that she couldn't speak for a moment. "So what are you going to do, Kyle? What am I supposed to make of all you've said? "

"I don't know the answer to anything right now, Jane. I just need . . ." He shook his head, his gaze falling before hers. "I don't know. I just need some space."

"Well, I hope when you figure it out you'll let me know." She heard the nastiness in her tone, but it was understandable, wasn't it? He could hardly expect hearts and flowers after what he'd just told her.

He looked relieved as his cell phone rang. "I need to take this," he said, after glancing at the screen. He headed to the door. "I'll try to wrap up my day before it gets too late tonight."

A storm of emotion raged inside Jane as she watched him leave. Even if she could have thought of something to say to stop him, his heart was closed and locked. First Max, then Mellie, now Kyle. She was losing everyone!

KYLE DROVE ACROSS THE Causeway Bridge berating himself for the way he'd talked to Jane. He'd meant to explain himself so she'd understand how unhappy he was. But if he'd been in a courtroom in front of any judge on the planet, he would have been sternly admonished for the way he handled himself. The way he hit her cold had surprised him as much as her. But once he started, it was as if a volcano inside him had been heating up to pitch point. His anger and frustration had erupted like molten lava. And now he felt worse. It was no wonder Jane had looked shell shocked.

He studied the still, gray surface of Lake Pontchartrain. His life was like that body of water—gray, without joy, empty. And no matter how she might deny it, Jane was the reason. She had left Max unprotected, and now he was gone. Her obsession for finding him didn't absolve her of her part in his disappearance. Until now, he hadn't known how angry he was with her about that. Or how much he blamed her for robbing him of his son.

His son. Max. As always, when he allowed himself to think of his baby boy, he wanted to scream and curse and damn the fates that had taken him. The torment of not knowing whether Max was dead or alive was with him every waking minute. Jane might hang on doggedly to the belief that they'd find him one day, but he'd passed that point about a month into the search. Statistics didn't lie. If a kidnapped child wasn't found within twenty-four to forty-eight hours after the abduction, he wouldn't be found alive.

He squeezed his eyes shut. He started at the blare of a car horn too close beside him and swerved back into his own lane. It wasn't the first time he'd let distraction bring him dangerously close to an accident on the bridge. And it wasn't the first time he'd wondered about his carelessness in doing so. Was it carelessness? Or was it something else? A fatal crash on the Causeway would be a sure cure to his pain.

The coward's way out.

He knew that voice. He'd heard it most of his life since, at seventeen, his father had committed suicide. After that, he'd been full of rage. For years he'd been unable to even think of his old man without choking on his anger. It got better after his first marriage, but only with Melanie's birth was he finally able to love unconditionally. And then, like his father, his wife was taken. If he hadn't met Jane after Laura died, he wasn't sure he would ever have felt his world could be right again. But now, thanks to Jane, his peace of mind was again destroyed. It was so damned unfair that Max was taken. Hadn't he lost enough in his life? First, his father, then Laura. And now Max. How much was a man supposed to take?

3

Jane was still shaken when she arrived at her office. She'd driven with a death grip on the steering wheel, her mind reeling in the aftermath of Kyle's bombshell. They'd disagreed before—what married couple didn't? She wasn't sure what hurt more, that he blamed her for Max's kidnapping or that he was so unhappy that he was considering leaving.

Oh, dear God, maybe he's having an affair. Her stomach knotted at the thought, but she pushed it away. No, Kyle wouldn't do that. Yes, he was angry, frustrated, unhappy, and at sea in his mind, but his moral compass wasn't out of kilter, she told herself.

But was he truly so disillusioned that he couldn't decide which way to turn? As an attorney, she was known for her insight into dealing with families in crisis. How could she be blind to her own husband's needs?

She stopped at the break room, Kyle's words still resounding in her head, and poured a cup of coffee. As she sipped, her gaze went to her reflection in a glass window. Heavens, she looked like death. She would have to gather herself before anyone saw her. Plus, she had tons to do after allowing a backlog of work to accumulate. Since Max's disappearance, she'd been unable to concentrate properly on her case load. Kyle was right about one thing. She was neglecting her career in her zeal to find Max. That was something she could change, and she resolved to start that day.

With coffee in one hand and her briefcase in the other, she hurried past Michelle Guidry's desk, murmuring a greeting to her overworked paralegal without meeting her eyes. Michelle had been issuing urgent reminders lately in a valiant attempt to get Jane's attention to pending cases. But it was so hard to keep up . . .

At the door of her office, she surveyed the files covering every available surface and fought an urge to simply turn and leave. And go where? To her house and be faced with its emptiness? To her bedroom to wonder and worry about whether Kyle would be there tonight to share it. Worst of all, to be faced with the sight of Max's empty crib? She had no good options.

Get a grip!

She moved to her chair and settled her briefcase, then lifted the cup to her lips with shaky hands. Coffee sloshed onto her blouse. Her white blouse. With a groan, she searched for a tissue but found the box empty. What else could go wrong? Eyes closed, she dropped her head in her hands.

"Jane."

Startled, she looked up. Henri Robichaux, the senior partner of the firm, stood in the doorway, the door she should have closed before sitting down and wallowing in self-pity being open. "Oh, Henri, hello. I didn't hear—"

"You look upset," he said, pulling the door closed. "Something wrong?"

She managed a weak smile. "No, no." She waved a hand at

the stacks of material on her desk. "I was just about to tackle the Guilliot file."

Robichaux lifted one skeptical eyebrow. "That's partly the reason I'm here, Jane. René Guilliot called me at my home this morning. He—"

"Oh, I'm sorry, Henri. René and I have played phone tag for a week now, but he shouldn't have called you at home." While Henri watched, Jane scanned the glut of files and luckily spotted Guilliot. On top, thanks to Michelle. She opened it, only to find a bright orange Post-it, the color coding meaning *urgent*. Michelle had made a list of things to do on the case, some of which Jane should have done days ago. "There's no need for you to get involved, Henri. I'll take care of it."

"It isn't only about the Guilliot case that I wanted to see you, Jane. There are other issues."

"Issues?" She lifted her gaze to his.

"Hmm." He remained standing at the door. "We do need to talk."

Sensing trouble, she sank into her chair. "I know I haven't reached my billable hours quota yet, but—" She reached to open the file drawer on the side of her desk, but Henri stopped her.

"That won't be necessary." He glanced at his watch. "Five minutes. In my office. Please."

It was an order. And coming from the senior partner who'd been Jane's mentor, not a good sign. She spent four of the next five minutes in the restroom trying to remove the coffee stain from the center of her blouse, but it was still faintly visible when she finally entered Henri's office. He motioned her to a chair, and with bitter coffee roiling in the back of her throat, she sat.

He got to his feet and moved around to the front of his desk. As he settled on its edge, he was shaking his head. "This is difficult for me, Jane. I had such great hopes for you when you first joined the firm. You were bright, focused, and ambitious, all the qualities we admire and require here. I understand you've had to cope with a terrible personal tragedy, but unfortunately work goes on."

He paused as if seeking words, letting his gaze rove beyond Jane to the view of a sprawling live oak outside. "You may think I'm being harsh and unsympathetic. I hope not. But I'm simply in a position here where the partners have run out of patience. They've demanded action from me regarding your work." He paused. "And accountability from you."

"They're critical of my work?" In spite of the fact that she'd missed a few deadlines, Jane was stunned. She had graduated law school in the top five percent of her class. Instead of accepting a position in one of the large law firms in New Orleans, she'd chosen the small firm, Robichaux and Hendricks, located here in Mandeville, a bedroom community north of Lake Pontchartrain from New Orleans. Since joining the firm, she had taken some of the most difficult cases, wrapping them up successfully. She had a gift for resolving difficult situations that arose when divorce was an issue.

"The partners are not critical of your work, Jane," he said in a gentle tone. "They're critical of your failure to handle hardly any work lately."

"I know I've missed a few deadlines, but—"

"A few? Jane, you've filed continuances in more than a few cases. Just in the last month, you've rescheduled more appointments than you've taken. Michelle admitted you spend more time on matters relating to the Child Search organization than you do on your cases. It's a worthy cause, and I understand your commitment to its mission, but when you're on our clock, your responsibility to the firm should come first. We do occasionally accept pro bono work, but we can't sacrifice a majority of any associate's time on pro bono. If you feel so compelled to work for Child Search, you should resign from this firm and go to work there."

She stared, genuinely shocked. "Are you asking for my resignation, Henri?"

"Not now. Or, not yet, I should say." Robichaux held a pen, idly clicking it. "But I'll be honest. I'm at odds with the partners about you, Jane. They do want your resignation. What I want is for you to buckle down, clear the backlog of work you've allowed to accumulate, and do the job you were hired to do. And if you can't do that . . . or don't choose to do that, then I *will* have to ask for your resignation."

Shaken, she said, "I don't think I can clear the backlog in a few days." It galled her to have to acknowledge that there was a backlog, but in the face of his ultimatum, she had no choice. "It'll take some time, but I can do it. I will do it."

"How much time?" He offered her a smile.

"Can I get back to you? I'll need to sit down with Michelle and go over each case."

"It's Friday. Take the weekend. Give me an answer Monday. I can hold them off that long, Jane, but no longer." He slipped the pen inside his jacket and looked directly at her. "About Michelle. I don't want you thinking she was a willing participant in answering our questions. As your assistant, she was extremely reluctant to talk."

"Yes." She hated that Michelle had been put on the spot for her sake. She was hardworking and loyal to a fault. "I'm lucky to have Michelle. We're a team. We'll get right on this."

"Well, you both have a big job in front of you. If you need additional help, I can—"

"No. No, we'll handle it." She was on her feet now, desperate to escape. "Was there anything else?"

When he paused, she guessed there was more, but to her relief, he simply shook his head and waved her out.

WHEN JANE RETURNED TO her office, Michelle was waiting. "I'm sorry, Jane," she said, her eyes anxious. "They've been all over me for the last couple of days. I tried to cover, but—"

Jane put up a hand. "Michelle. I'm the one who should be apologizing for landing you in such an uncomfortable position. I'm sorry. You warned me, but I didn't listen. We both know why." She rubbed a dull ache between her eyes. "What I've got to do now is work up a plan to get back on track. I'll need—" She stopped when the phone rang. "If that's René Guilliot, tell him I'll meet with him this afternoon when I've had a chance to review the file. I don't think we've missed a court deadline on his case . . . yet."

Michelle read the caller I.D. "It's Christine O'Brian. She's on your calendar for lunch today."

"I can't do lunch today!" Jane waved a hand at the stacks of files. "Look at this."

"And while you're gone," Michelle continued, ignoring Jane's protest, "I'll clear your desk of all files except the most pressing. I've already made a list. We can spend the afternoon working up a plan. As for Guilliot complaining about you to Henri Robichaux, he's worried that his wife will take him to the cleaners after the divorce . . . as he deserves. If she gets half his money, it'll be poetic justice. He's been unfaithful for years. Besides, he's got more money than God."

"He's our client, Michelle," Jane reminded her. "Whether we like or approve of him or not, we're honor bound to represent him professionally."

"Don't remind me." She made a face while still covering the phone's mouthpiece. "And before you cancel lunch with Christine, may I say that you look as if you could use an hour with your best friend." She smiled kindly.

Jane felt a wave of emotion. After she swallowed the lump in her throat, she said, "Well, it was my lucky day when you came to work for me, Michelle. You've been covering my backside for a while now, haven't you?"

"Of course not!"

"Of course, yes. And that's no doubt the reason Henri didn't fire me outright today. So thank you. I'll see that you get a raise if I have to take it out of my own paycheck!"

Michelle laughed and glanced at her watch. "I won't hold you to that, but I will remind you that we only have a couple of hours before lunch, time enough to review Guilliot's file and return his call. And if you have to hold your nose while you do it, I won't tell."

By lunchtime, Jane was badly in need of a sympathetic ear. Christine surely filled the bill. Jane watched her friend threading a path through the restaurant, smiling and greeting half a dozen diners, including the frazzled waitress who bussed tables. Christine's warmth was only one of many traits that drew Jane to her. Besides being happily married to Dr. Ben O'Brian, one of the finest pediatricians in town, and with three teenagers, she managed the medical practice of a team of internists and was active in her church and civic affairs. All of which she seemed to handle effortlessly while maintaining a positive outlook. Whatever her secret, Jane wished she had some of it.

She rose as Christine approached the table. After a hug, Christine held on to Jane's hands and studied her with a critical eye. "What's wrong?"

"Hello to you too." Jane's smile was weak. She pulled her hands free and sat down. "Iced tea is coming for both of us. That okay?"

"You know it is."

After they ordered, Christine fixed her gaze on Jane's face. "Is it Melanie? I gave Daniel such a scolding last night when he finally got home! No wheels for two weeks, which includes the big game this weekend." She frowned thoughtfully as she shook out her napkin. "Frankly, I expected more of a reaction from him than I got. I think he has something big on his mind, but you know kids. It could be as trivial as a bad haircut or as momentous as wrecking the car."

"I got the same reaction from Melanie, only worse. It ended with my learning nothing and both of us shouting at each other. She's grounded too." Jane sighed. "I'm worried, Christine. There's something going on, but she won't talk to me anymore."

Christine squeezed lemon into her iced tea, taking her time as if working up to saying something difficult. Finally she said, "There aren't many things I can think of to make Daniel act so . . . so out of character. Your mind runs away from you at times like this, Jane." She looked up anxiously. "I've ruled out drugs. I'd know. I see enough of that at my job. Maybe . . . and this is just wild speculation, but I tell myself maybe he's gotten himself into trouble with a girl."

"No." Jane instantly dismissed that. "Not Daniel. And as difficult as Melanie is, I don't believe she's sexually active."

"I guess I'm more suspicious than you," Christine said with a wry smile. She reached for a sugar packet. "We've certainly preached abstinence to Daniel from the time he understood where babies come from, but reality is what it is."

"You don't think Melanie and Daniel are having sex, do you?" Jane asked, dismayed now that the idea had been planted.

"No. To tell the truth, I think there's something wrong, but call me naive. I trust Daniel not to stray that far from all Ben and I've tried to teach him." She took a sip of tea and smiled ruefully. "Hopefully, our effort has not been in vain . . . but you never know."

"Daniel persuaded Melanie to go to your church's youth group for a while," Jane said, thoughtfully. "I'm assuming there would have been a strong emphasis on being responsible about sex." She sighed. "But that was before Max was taken. She quit going."

"I know," Christine said, adding sadly, "which was just when she needed it most. But I still have hope she'll start back in time."

Jane knew Christine hoped she and Kyle would show some interest in attending her church, too, but Jane couldn't sit through a church service listening to meaningless words about a loving and caring God when she didn't see any personal evidence of it.

Christine reached for her glass before saying, "I only brought up the subject of sex because it's something Daniel might feel he couldn't discuss with me or Ben, but if you're so certain . . ."

"I'm not certain about anything, but I just can't see it. I know they've been friends since they were in kindergarten, but that's not the same as boyfriend and girlfriend." She frowned, shaking her head. "No, Chris, I know Melanie's a pain right now, but I don't think she'd act out in that way. And Daniel is so responsible. I just don't think that's the problem."

"We can hope." Christine smiled ruefully. "Daniel's moodiness is probably no better or worse than any other teenager's. But it's different with your family. Your situation is complicated by real trauma, Jane."

Jane pressed her trembling lips, unable to speak for a minute. Christine reached over and covered her hand. "You just have to hang in there, hon. Be there for Melanie. Be patient. She'll come around. I know it."

Jane wasn't so sure. No amount of patience and understanding on Jane's part seemed to matter so far.

Christine sat back with a shrewd look. "You haven't answered me yet about why you looked as if you'd lost your best friend." She smiled gently, adding, "And I know that hasn't happened."

"Do I look that bad?"

"You could never look bad. Worried, maybe. A little . . . freaked out, as Daniel would say. But with those model looks, no amount of teenage torture can make you unattractive, Jane. So . . . is it something you can share?"

Jane had a brief reprieve as the waitress appeared with their orders. She looked at her salad but couldn't bring herself to taste it. She drew a shaky breath, laid her fork down carefully, and looked at Christine. "What was Ben's reaction to your lecturing Daniel last night?" she asked.

"His reaction?" The question seemed to puzzle Christine. "He added a few well-chosen words of his own. All our kids jump when Ben speaks." She paused. "Why?"

"It didn't go anything like that at my house last night. Kyle happened to arrive in the middle of the shouting match. And it wasn't Melanie he blamed, even though he knew she'd been ignoring curfew and the house rules lately."

"He blamed you?"

"He said I was so busy taking care of strangers at Child Search that I'd forgotten my first obligation was at home . . . as wife to him and mother to Melanie. He said it was likely that Melanie was behaving badly because I was neglecting her."

"Ouch."

Tears sprang into Jane's eyes, and she paused to hold them in check. "He said I was obsessed with looking for Max. Can you imagine? It was so unfair, Christine. It really hurt."

"Oh, Jane . . ."

Jane frowned, toying with her utensils. "He said some awful things . . . we both did."

Christine's face softened with sympathy. "We all have moments like that, Jane. Anyone who's been married more than ten minutes knows there're times when we just lose it. We say things then that we're sorry for later."

"I said that to Kyle . . . or tried to." Jane stared glumly at her plate. "But once he got started, it was as if all the anger he'd bottled up just spewed out like hot acid."

With her fork suspended in midair, Christine frowned. "Any mother would bristle at being accused of neglect."

"It wasn't only Kyle. Last night Melanie threw it in my face that I wasn't her real mother. Maybe they're both ready to dump me."

Christine lowered her fork and eyed Jane sternly. "No way, Jane. Mellie popped that off in the heat of battle. Whatever's going on inside that brain of hers, it isn't thoughts of your not being her 'real' mother." She used her fingers to make air quote. "First of all, she was too young to even remember her birth mom."

"Yes, but she had a birth mom, and I'm not it," Jane said.

Christine studied her for a long moment. "Has Kyle given you some idea that that's what's going on here?"

"No, not really. But we're a blended family." She made a face. "I hate that term. Anyway, I've never felt like a stepmother to Melanie, whatever that means, but it's the only thing I can think of to explain how hostile she acts around me now."

"Besides being sixteen and spoiled rotten?"

Jane managed a wry smile. "There is that."

"However," Christine tucked her fork into her salad, "it doesn't explain why Kyle is acting like a spoiled brat too."

Jane watched wistfully as a couple across the room greeted each other with a kiss. "Apparently there's more going on with Kyle than I dreamed," she said. "Since he was on a roll, he decided to tell me how unhappy he is."

"You're unhappy too," Christine said, unimpressed. "Your child has been kidnapped."

"But I don't need to deal with it by seeking space away from him to think things through."

"Away from him? In what way?"

"He didn't say." Jane set her fork down. "He's not sure what he's going to do, just that he needs space."

"Oh, please."

"To do what, I asked, but he was vague." Jane sighed. "I'm not sure what he's thinking, Chris. But he was clear on one thing. He blames me for leaving Max and giving a predator a chance to take him."

Christine's mouth dropped.

"Yeah." Jane flicked at a bread crumb on the tablecloth. "He says it's my fault and he's just not sure he's able to deal with it anymore."

"Your fault? Come on . . ."

"That's what he said."

"So what's his plan?"

"He's questioning whether or not our *relationship* is worth saving," Jane said bitterly.

"As in a divorce?"

"If he's so unhappy, wouldn't that be the logical way out?"

"Oh, I can't believe that, Jane. Not now. Not when your lives have been turned upside down. Not when Melanie is in an emotional tailspin. She needs a mom and a dad. All of you need the stability of marriage."

After Kyle's words last night, Jane doubted the stability of her marriage. "Chris, do you think my search for Max has become an obsession?"

Christine touched her lips with a napkin. "I don't know. Seems to me any mother whose child was kidnapped would go all out to find him. I certainly would. If that's obsession, then a lot of mothers in your shoes are obsessed, I would think. I can't see how it's a bad thing."

"Me either. But I can't give up, Chris." Tears sprang to her eyes.

Christine's tone was sympathetic. "I can't believe Kyle would want you to give up."

"Maybe not, but he may be too tired to deal with my obsession."

Christine leaned forward to make her point. "Jane, he's as

torn up over Max as you. Each of us deals with emotional pain our own way. Thinking it's your fault absolves him, although in fairness to him he probably isn't consciously thinking that. Our minds can play tricks on us."

For a minute, Jane studied the rose in a bud vase on the table. "I do spend a lot of time at Child Search. Maybe he's right to be resentful."

"If blaming you is Kyle's way to absolve himself, then your time at Child Search is probably your coping mechanism," Christine said thoughtfully. "I am definitely no psychologist but I don't think there's anything wrong with a healthy coping mechanism. It's sure a lot better than turning to tranquillizers or alcohol."

Jane felt like bursting into tears. She was lucky to have a friend like Christine. It was comforting to hear her practical and down to earth advice when her own world was so chaotic.

"With Child Search and your job," Christine went on, "plus your efforts to keep Max's case alive at the N.O.P.D., you can't have much time or energy left over. Keeping to that schedule would be crushing to anybody. When is the last time you and Kyle were together, just the two of you? For dinner out, or just for an evening doing nothing special, maybe watching TV or reading, but just doing it together?"

"It's been a long time." Jane realized she'd thought much the same thing last night when it dawned on her that she couldn't recall when she and Kyle had last made love. "I don't remember the last time for any of the above," she admitted in a quiet voice.

"Then maybe he just needs a little attention. And the only way he knows to get it is to shock you. Telling you he's rethinking your relationship surely got your attention, didn't it?"

"Uh-huh." The pain of those words still ached inside her.

Christine looked at her, smiling gently. "He loves you, Jane. I've been your best friend for how many years? Ten? Twelve?

Anyone could see he was besotted from the first time he ever looked into your gorgeous blue eyes. Your relationship used to be wonderful. He wants that again."

"But, Christine, he's given up on ever finding Max. It's asking the impossible of me."

"Yes, I can see that." There was sympathy in Christine's voice.

Jane set her water glass down. "If it were you and this were happening, what would you do?"

"After praying?" Christine lifted her hands as if to say, what else?

"Which doesn't work for me . . . as you know," Jane said in a wry voice. "Your God let me down when He took my child."

Christine reached for Jane's hand and squeezed. "It hurts me so much when you say that, Jane. God doesn't promise that bad things won't happen to good people, but faith is His comfort when it does."

Still, Christine's God had taken her baby. So her faith didn't work for Jane. Maybe for some people—for many people apparently—but not for her.

She cleared her throat, dabbed at tears in the corners of her eyes, sat up straight, and picked up her fork. "Short of heavenly intervention, do you have any other advice for me?"

"No, not really," Christine said. "But I'll still pray—because God isn't out to hurt you. I know that for certain." And with that, she picked up her fork to finish lunch.

JANE FELT A LITTLE better after that. Back at her office, she forced herself to concentrate on the most urgent of her cases. It was a mammoth task. The backlog was worse than she realized. But things could always get worse, she discovered when she found a minute to check her voice mail. A message to call Detective Sam Pitre of the N.O.P.D., as always, stirred a host of emotion—hope that he would tell her they'd found Max, or fear of the worst, the dread possibility that she couldn't bring herself to even think.

She sat for a few moments, taking deep breaths to prepare herself. In the six months that Max had been missing, she'd had many conversations with Detective Pitre. At first, she called every few days, hoping for some break in the case, some little something to help her keep on keeping on. But there was never anything, not the slightest thread of a clue. He had been patient with her, understanding her fear that if she didn't keep reminding them of Max's kidnapping, they'd let the case grow cold.

In fact, it was Sam who suggested she get involved in Child Search. It had been an eye-opener. She never realized how many children disappeared without a trace every day, never to be heard from again. She was determined that would not be the case with Max.

Sam answered on the first ring. "Jane, I always feel bad making these calls," he began. She could hear his intake of breath. "It's about Max."

Jane closed her eyes. With a heavy feeling in her chest, she asked, "What do you mean?"

"N.O.P.D. was called by H.H.S. after they moved on a complaint of child abuse. The kids—about eight of them—were all crammed into an apartment in Algiers. They immediately removed all eight. N.O.P.D. arrested two people, a man and a woman. Turned out, at least three of the kids were unrelated to them. I'm guessing most of them won't be, but we don't know yet. Anyway, since they were so young and the couple isn't talking, we haven't been able to figure out how the children came to be in the care of these two lowlifes."

Jane felt a rush of relief and excitement—one of these babies could be Max!

"Um, that's the reason I'm calling, Jane. One of the youngest looks to be around a year, maybe a little more, just about—"

"Just about Max's age?" Hope soared in Jane. "You think—"

"I just don't know. He's the right age, he has blue eyes and blond hair, and he looks like Max, but—"

"But what? What!"

"I hate to put you through this again and possibly another false alarm. But I think someone should come down and check out whether this little kid might be Max."

"Someone? I'll come down. Tell me where." Jane was already on her feet. With the phone cradled between chin and shoulder, she yanked her blazer from the coat rack. "I can be there in forty-five minutes."

"Wait, Jane. He's . . . This baby is in bad shape. You should know that and be prepared for pretty grim stuff. Like I said, I don't know if it's Max, but the kind of shape he's in, who knows?"

Bracing herself, Jane asked, "How bad?"

"How to begin? First off, he's dehydrated and malnourished. I don't know when he last had a bath. But the worst thing . . ." He hesitated, taking in a deep breath. "The worst thing . . . after we got him to the hospital, they found a fracture in his left arm. The doc's unsure how long ago it happened and how it happened remains a mystery at this point. But it's in a cast now."

"That's monstrous!" Jane cried. "Who *are* these people?"

"Two drug-addicted transients. We think they're connected to a ring of thugs trafficking in child porn."

Jane couldn't bear to hear any more. "Which hospital?"

"Children's."

"I'll be there as soon as I can," she told him. "I assume you've called Kyle?"

"I tried, but couldn't reach him. I left a voice mail, but he never returned it. I felt you'd want to know . . . just in case it—"

"Just in case it could be Max. Yes, I would. I do. Thanks, Sam. I'm on my way."

It was a trip she'd rather not make alone. She'd been down this road three times with high hope, and each time she'd been disappointed. Once—and the worst—she viewed the dead body of a baby boy. But she always had Kyle at her side, providing emotional support. How would she endure the disappointment alone if, as before, the baby was not Max?

On the other hand, if it was Max and he was alive . . .

No, best not to let herself go there. Not yet.

On the way out of the building, she pressed the speed dial for Kyle's cell, thinking that in spite of the way they argued that morning, this was something they needed to face together. But she got his voice mail and left a message. She hoped he'd get word and be at the hospital by the time she got there. Did he say he'd be at the firm's downtown offices today? She'd been so stunned when he left that she couldn't remember. Or maybe he didn't say anything about his day. She suddenly realized that they'd gotten out of the habit of sharing their daily schedules.

Thankfully Kyle called as she approached the New Orleans city limits.

"I just spoke to Pitre," he told her. "I've been in court. I'm leaving now. How far away are you?"

"About fifteen minutes from the hospital," she said, exiting the interstate. She knew it would take him at least that long to reach Children's. "I'll meet you there."

"Why don't you let me do this, Jane? There's no point in putting both of us through it again. Chances are—"

"I want to be there, Kyle," she said. "If it is Max, I want to touch him and hold him."

"Did Pitre tell you this kid is in pretty bad shape?"

"It doesn't change anything." She turned onto Tulane Avenue. "I'm going," she repeated.

"I only wanted—" She heard him sigh. "Okay. I was just trying to save you the pain of going through it again."

"I can't just sit back and wait for you to call me when there is the remotest chance that this time it could be Max, Kyle. I have to see for myself."

"Then I'll meet you in the lobby." He ended the call.

Jane dropped the phone into her purse and sat at a traffic light, thinking. Kyle obviously didn't understand. Yes, it was painful. And her hopes might be dashed yet again. But she'd spent six months in a living hell waiting for the moment Max was found and brought home. How could Kyle not get it?

As she turned into the hospital's parking garage, she recalled Christine's question. She and Kyle had rarely been together lately, just the two of them. Could it be that she had been the first to distance herself emotionally from Kyle and Melanie? In her zeal to find Max, was she jeopardizing everything she held dear?

SHE FOUND SAM PITRE waiting for her at the elevators. "Good to see you, Jane."

"Thanks for calling." She glanced toward the entrance doors. "Kyle should be here any minute."

"I know. He returned my call only a couple of minutes after I spoke to you."

"Just as a matter of record, Sam, in the future, I want to be notified first of any and all matters relating to Max's disappearance. That includes instances like today, no matter how difficult. And no matter what Kyle may tell you."

His eyes narrowed. "What makes you think I wouldn't do that anyway, Jane?"

"You did wait to call me."

Sam was obviously puzzled, but she was saved further questions when his gaze shifted beyond her right shoulder. "Here's Kyle now."

Jane turned and watched her husband approach. Until this morning when he'd revealed his feelings, she would have rushed headlong into his arms. And then together they would have followed Sam to the area where the baby waited. But now, after one look at his stern expression, she realized that would not be the way they handled this situation today. With just a fleeting glance at Jane, he spoke to Sam.

"Detective." He extended his hand.

"Like I said on the phone," Sam began, "this is a hard one."

"Yeah." Kyle looked at Jane. "No trouble getting here?"

"No trouble," she said. She felt a chill all the way to her bones. It was like talking to a stranger. Was it her? Or Kyle? Or both of them gingerly making their way through an emotional minefield?

"The baby is sleeping," Sam said. "I checked with the nurse a few minutes ago. We can go right up."

Kyle pulled in a deep breath. "Let's do it."

4

PEDIATRICS WAS ON THE second floor. Jane's stomach was in a knot, and her heart raced as she stepped from the elevator. Moving on sheer grit, she walked between Kyle and Sam down a hall painted sunshine yellow and decorated in bright, cheery art. Even the flooring had a whimsical pattern. Every effort had been made to make a child's hospital stay a positive experience. But it was still a hospital.

Somewhere a baby cried, a sound that never failed to twist Jane's heart. She passed rooms with beds occupied by infants she could see through tall rails. Parents hovered, touching, crooning, coping. Some faces were stamped with fatigue. There was nothing so exhausting as caring for a sick child. Jane yearned to be able to do it again.

This could be it, she told herself. Her long search for Max could soon be over. The nightmare that began on Mardi Gras

Day could end now. Today. She was almost light-headed with hope and fear as they approached the nurse's station.

A tall, red-haired nurse looked up, and Sam flashed his police I.D. "We're here to see the baby who was admitted this morning by H.H.S.," he said. "I called an hour ago."

"Oh, yes." She turned to Jane. "He's still sleeping, poor little guy. It was necessary to anesthetize him to set his arm, so he'll be really groggy for a while, but you can go on in." She picked up a chart. "Just so you'll know what to expect, he has an IV to hydrate him, and we've added antibiotics to treat an ear infection. But his physical injuries can be overcome with time and good care. What he may have been subjected to emotionally . . ." She gave a helpless shrug. "Who knows."

With the chart in her hand, she left the station and walked directly across to the room where the baby slept. Once inside, Jane saw there were four cribs, all occupied by children of various toddler ages. Two were girls. The third was a little boy who was standing in his crib, gazing solemnly at them with wide brown eyes.

The nurse moved to the crib farthest from the door. "He's here."

But Jane's eyes had already locked on to the sleeping baby boy. She was almost sick with anticipation as she approached the crib. Beside her, Kyle seemed remote. It was Sam who gave her shoulders an encouraging squeeze, falling away as she took the two steps that brought her close enough to look at the child's little face.

Her heart quickened. Blond hair, the shape of his head, a sweet hand tucked close to his lips just as Max did. That little thumb at the ready. Could it be? Max would be six months older than when she'd last seen him. This baby boy seemed to be about that age. But she was able to see only a portion of his face in profile. She reached for the blanket and gently pulled it away. Leaning down with her face even with his, she studied the tiny nose, soft mouth, impossibly long lashes that lay feathery blond on his cheek.

Jane made a soft, anguished sound. "No, no-o-o-o," she whispered as a wave of bitter despair washed through her. "It's not Max."

Clutching the steel bars, she rested her forehead against the cold metal. She always told herself she was prepared for disappointment, that the chances of finding Max like this were a thousand to one, but she was never truly prepared for the reality of looking at a little boy so like Max and finding it was not her baby.

Gathering herself, she let her gaze wander over the child who, after all, was somebody's baby. He lay flat on his back with his tiny hand curled near his face. The other arm was in a cast. A part of her was guiltily relieved that Max had not suffered the abuse that showed on the face and body of this child. But at least this boy was alive, rescued. She would not allow her thoughts to go further. Instead, she reached through the bars and gently touched his blond head. His hair was as soft and silky as down on a baby chick.

Beside her, the nurse quietly lowered the railing. "He has no other injuries other than his arm. I was told the arrested couple claimed he had fallen out of his high chair, but we don't know if that's true. All the kids in that apartment had various signs of abuse, so we can't believe much of anything they say."

"We can go now, Jane," Kyle said in a low voice.

She glanced at him. His face was a blank mask, his mouth set. Whatever emotion he felt was expressed only in a stern frown. Before, in viewing other children in their quest to find Max, she had seen tears on his cheeks. Then they had held each other and wept. But today . . . nothing. Tenderly, she tucked the blanket around the boy and stepped back. "I'd like pictures of the other children who were removed from those people," she said to Sam once they were out in the hall. "It could be that they match some of the kids registered as lost or stolen at Child Search."

"That won't be a problem," Sam said. "I'll send them to you in an email."

Beside her, Kyle was still remotely silent.

"Do you have any leads on the identity of the other kids?" she asked when they stopped at the elevator. Somewhere there were frantic parents. Today, her own anguish had not been eased, but someone's somewhere would be.

"Not yet," Sam said. "And most of them are too young to be able to tell us anything useful. But I'll let you know." He gave her a sympathetic smile. "And I'm sorry we haven't gotten a lead on Max yet. But Jane . . ." He waited while both she and Kyle stepped into the elevator. "I promise you, I haven't given up. I never will."

The elevator doors slid closed, and Jane was left alone with Kyle. With his eyes looking straight ahead, he finally spoke. "Are you headed back to your office, or are you going to Child Search?"

"Why do you ask?"

"I know you, Jane." He turned his head then to look at her. "You're fired up after seeing that baby, even though it's Marilee's job as administrator to follow up with those kids and try to get them reunited with their parents. But you'll charge in with the best of intentions—I'm not arguing that—and throw yourself into the search with all the zeal of a missionary."

"Instead of going back to my office, which is what you think I should be doing?"

"Frankly, yes, since Marilee is fully capable of handling *her job*."

She shook her head wearily as the elevator stopped and opened. "Well, you're wrong on one count. I'm not going to Child Search. I wish I could, but I'm buried at work and can't. So I'll have to leave it to capable Marilee."

She walked beside him across the hospital foyer to the exit, and when they were outside, she stopped. “How do you do it, Kyle? How do you look at that little boy and not care?”

“Unlike you, I don’t always telegraph everything I feel, Jane.” Turning away from her, he dug in his pockets for his keys. “Where are you parked? The garage isn’t safe for a woman alone. I’ll walk you to your car.”

After coming in from bright sunshine, the shadowy garage did seem a little spooky. The third level where Jane had parked was now almost empty. Or maybe it was simply her mood, she told herself. Beside her, Kyle was silent, texting on his iPhone. Maybe an urgent matter needed his attention, or maybe he didn’t want to talk to her. Jane wasn’t certain. But she was glad not to be alone in the garage.

Once they were on the third floor, Kyle stood at the elevator, keeping her in sight while she walked to her car. Still several yards away, she unlocked it with her remote. And it was as she passed a car parked several slots from hers that she noticed someone was simply sitting in it, unmoving. Her first thought was that they might need medical attention, but then the person moved slightly, pulling a baseball cap low over his face. Or her face, she couldn’t tell between the dimness in the garage and the car’s tinted windows. But something about the way he—or she—just sat there was odd. It was weird, but you saw all kinds at a hospital, she told herself. Still, with Kyle watching, she wasn’t overly concerned. She climbed into her car, backed out, and drove down the ramp, glancing in the rearview mirror at Kyle, who was still texting. He never looked up.

Jane used the drive back across Lake Pontchartrain and the voice of Sarah McLachlan on a CD to seek some sense of calm. Aside from the crushing disappointment of yet another failed lead, she would never understand how anybody could hurt an innocent child. But better not to dwell on that.

Sometimes the twenty-five-mile long bridge seemed endless, but today she found herself going through a mental checklist of action to recommend to Marilee at Child Search. First thing on the list: Sam's email. She'd follow up with him if he didn't send those kids' pictures right away. She wished she didn't have to return to her office and instead could go straight to Child Search, but duty called.

Traffic was lighter than usual, so she took a handheld recorder from the console to make a few notes. Unlike Melanie, she wasn't quick at texting and especially not while driving. Besides, recording her thoughts meant she could add details not possible when texting.

But just as she began to talk, she realized a car had come up behind her and was staying pretty close. Too close. Tailgating was dangerous anywhere, but on the Causeway it could be lethal. She frowned, wondering at the recklessness of some drivers. The bridge was virtually clear of traffic, and there were two northbound lanes with ample opportunity to get around her. There were no shoulders and nowhere to go in a collision except over the railing and into the water.

She shivered at the thought and slowed down to let him pass.

But after a few moments, she realized the driver wasn't going to come around. And if she should need to use her brakes, he would be unable to avoid slamming into the rear of her car. Now she was really getting nervous. With her hands tight on the wheel, she gave a quick glance in the rearview mirror.

She blinked, looked again. She recognized that car! It was the same one that was parked in the garage with the strange person sitting in it. Jane settled back, shaking her head. She'd had too much coffee. She was so jittery that she was seeing things.

Suddenly, she was jolted from behind. Panicked, she wrenched the wheel and managed to keep the car in the lane. What had happened? But with a quick glance up at the mirror, she knew. Incredibly, whoever was driving that car had intentionally rammed into her. Now her heart was thumping madly, and it wasn't from coffee nerves.

Someone was trying to push her into the lake!

She had a death grip on the steering wheel, hoping to be able to control the car if she was rammed again. But suddenly the driver behind her accelerated and with a loud roar shot past. Within seconds, the car was so far ahead on the bridge that she couldn't tell anything about it except that it was a dark maroon color and an older model sedan.

"It all happened so fast that I didn't have time to get his license." Jane, still shaken, accepted a cup of tea from Michelle. "It was all I could do to keep my car between the lines so I wouldn't go sailing over the guardrail into the lake."

"I think you should call the police," Michelle said. "You could have been killed."

Jane was thoughtful, looking into her teacup. "I did. But since I couldn't come up with a solid description of the car or driver, they told me there was not much they could do. I'm just thankful he didn't hit me hard enough to cause a serious accident. I think he just wanted to scare me." She gave a short laugh. "He definitely did that."

She set her cup down. "Here's the funny thing, Michelle. I'm vague on make and model, but I recognized the car. It was parked in the garage when I left the hospital. But why would he be following me? And why would he do something like that?"

"You think it was a man?"

Jane shrugged. "I don't know. All I saw was a blurry face

with sunglasses and a ball cap with the bill pulled so low that it was impossible to tell what sex the person was."

"I can't imagine a woman trying something like that."

Jane choked a little when tea went down the wrong pipe. "I can't imagine anyone trying something like that!"

Michelle plopped a stack of files onto Jane's desk. "Well, thank goodness, you survived it. So now, can you settle down enough to concentrate on these files?"

"I have to," she said on a sigh. "I have to get my act together."

IT WAS FULLY DARK before Jane felt she'd made enough progress on the files that she could leave. She glanced at her watch. Seven o'clock. She dialed Melanie's cell to check that she was honoring her grounded status. After five rings, she finally answered in a sullen voice.

"Hi," Jane said, injecting a bright tone. "Were you sleeping?"

"No."

"You sound a little groggy."

Big sigh. "It's boring sitting around here . . ." She paused, then added in an accusing voice, "since I'm totally alone."

"I know. Sorry to be so late. I had to clear a few things off my desk, and it took longer than I anticipated," Jane said. "I was thinking about dinner. How about—"

"No you weren't. You were thinking about me being grounded, and you want to make sure I'm here. Well, relax. I'm here . . . bored, bored, bored."

Jane gritted her teeth. "Don't you have an English paper to write?"

"Yes, but Daniel has the research, and since I'm locked up here, I'm out of luck."

"Then call him and get it," Jane said evenly.

"It's got maps and stuff. And some of it's on his computer. I need to print out stuff. I need to go over there, Jane."

"Oh, Mellie." Jane sighed with exasperation. "Why do you have to make everything so complicated? You can go over and get the research, which should take you no longer than an hour. And before you go, how about taking that pack of chicken tenders out of the freezer for me? Oh, and chop a few vegetables, celery, carrots, onion. You know. I'll do a quick stir fry when I get home."

"I can't do all that and be back in an hour."

"It'll take about fifteen minutes, Melanie. Do it."

Jane flinched as Melanie hung up on her. So much for her hope that they might have a civil meal together, albeit late. They might eat together, but they'd both probably wind up with indigestion. Kyle, of course, wouldn't show up at all. She checked her voice mail just in case, but there was nothing.

Heading for her car, she felt depressed. It had been a horrible day, and she had no desire to go home to an empty house. Now that she knew Kyle was struggling with questions about the future of their marriage, there was bound to be tension. And Melanie would pick up on it. Or maybe she already had.

But now, with a free hour before she needed to go home, Jane decided to stop at Child Search. Getting there was a pleasant drive, even in the dark. The road ran along the shore of Lake Pontchartrain, lined with huge live oaks draped with Spanish moss. Their aged beauty had survived countless storms and always gave Jane a sense of peace. The same was true of Child Search, despite the fact that the old Victorian house that Marilee had managed to snag for the organization was in dire need of repairs. At least it had adequate space and the roof didn't leak. Yet.

The reception desk was manned by a volunteer who was talking on the phone. She greeted Jane with a smile and motioned toward Marilee Stokes's office. Child Search tried to keep its doors open until ten o'clock in the evening, but that was possible only if volunteers were on hand. The telephones were manned 24/7—it was a lifeline for distraught parents.

Jane tapped on the open door of Marilee's office and felt a rush of emotion when the administrator looked up from her computer and smiled a welcome. Here was the one person who truly understood her anguish.

"Jane." Marilee rose and walked around her battered desk, a reject from the public library, to give Jane a hug. "I got your email. I'm sorry it wasn't Max."

Tears sprang to Jane's eyes and she dashed them away. "It's hard not to hope, you know?"

Marilee touched her forearm in a gesture of comfort.

"So, what about the other kids?" Jane said.

"They're entered into our database, but so far, no nibbles." She closed the door and drew up a chair for Jane. "The kids are possibly hundreds of miles from their homes, but at least they're safe and in the system now."

Instead of returning to her chair behind the desk, Marilee leaned against it, crossing her ankles in front of her. "I can see by your face that you've had a long day. Shouldn't you have gone home instead of stopping here?"

To an empty house? To brood over Kyle's rejection? To look at Melanie's angry face? Jane attempted a nonchalant shrug, not willing to unload the details of her troubles on Marilee. "Kyle is working late, and Melanie is grounded again and in a very bad mood, but hopefully starting dinner." She managed a bright smile. "So I'm free for an hour or so."

Marilee nodded. "Well, I have hope we'll know something about those children within a day or so."

"Other than that," Jane said, "what kind of day have you had? Give me some good news, please. I've handled more than my share of dark stuff today."

"I actually have some good news," Marilee said. "But it's

personal. My daughter Ellen and her husband are moving here from Houston next month. He's being transferred by his company, and she's been hired by the university in their English department."

Jane smiled, envying the loving relationship Marilee had with Ellen. There had been a time when she and Mellie were that close, and she hoped they would be again. But she feared it would be a long road to travel getting there.

They were busy discussing possible places for Ellen to live when a tap sounded on the door. The volunteer at the front desk stuck her head inside. "A woman is out front, Marilee. Her ex-husband has taken their six-year-old daughter and disappeared. Can you break away and talk to her? I've given her a cup of coffee and tried to calm her, but she's beside herself."

"Of course." Marilee got up.

"She's waiting in the first interview room," the volunteer added.

Neither Jane nor Marilee hesitated. Both left the office and headed down the hall to the interview room. The distraught woman halted in her pacing, looking up as they entered. Jane's heart turned over at the stricken look on her face. Her eyes were frantic, her hair in disarray as she raked through it with trembling fingers. "You have to help me!" she cried, rushing to them. "He has Remy and I don't know where they are."

"We will help," Marilee said in a soft voice, slipping an arm around the woman's waist. "Try to calm down a little so we can get some information from you."

She guided the woman to a large sofa and sat down beside her. Jane took a seat opposite them. "I'm Marilee Stokes, and this is Jane Madison. And you are—"

"Shelly Delchamps." She drew in a breath, trying to calm herself. "My ex-husband is Bernard Delchamps. Bernie. Everybody calls him Bernie." Her voice took on a bitter note. "It sounds nice, doesn't it? Sort of boyish, but he's a monster. He . . . I . . . I am so afraid that he will hurt Remy."

"Physically?" Marilee asked.

Shelly pressed her fingers to her lips, looking at both of them with abject fear in her eyes. "He hates me for leaving him. To punish me, he'll kill her."

JANE DROVE HOME FEELING sad and outraged by Shelly Delchamps's story. The woman was so desperate to find Remy that she willingly revealed the sordid details of her marriage. Bernie's verbal abuse began almost before their honeymoon ended. His foul temper made it impossible for him to keep a job, for which he blamed Shelly. After an accident in which he was badly burned, he turned brutally violent. At first, it was only Shelly who got the brunt of his rage, but when he turned on Remy, she found the courage to leave him.

For Marilee and Jane, it was an all-too-familiar scenario but one that never failed to touch Jane's heart. The how and why varied, but to Jane, the bottom line was simply that a mother was dealing with the loss of her child. It helped Jane cope with her own pain to focus on another parent facing what she lived with daily.

It was almost nine thirty when she opened the door to a silent house. It dawned on her that if Kyle's unhappiness made him decide to end their marriage, this would be what she would face when she came home: stark silence. Every day, every night. To the end of time.

She dropped her purse and keys on the foyer table and headed upstairs, hoping, hoping that Melanie was home. With the bedroom door closed, who knew? It was almost never open now.

Jane tapped lightly. "Melanie?"

"What?"

Jane sighed at the rude tone yet was glad she was there. "I'm going down to fix something to eat. You want to keep me company?"

"No. I'm not hungry."

Jane tried the door and found it locked. "You need to eat something, Mellie."

Melanie opened the door and met Jane's eyes with a stony look. "Really? Like what, raw chicken? Oh, or maybe now that you've finally managed to tear yourself away from that place, you'll finally get around to cooking for your family?"

Jane rubbed her temples wearily. "I'm sorry, Mellie. I know it's late, but I got caught up in a case at Child Search. A woman—"

"I am so not interested in anything happening over there, Jane. You said you'd be here in an hour. I was here, you weren't. As for dinner, forget it. I ate pbj. Good thing I didn't wait for that stir fry you were gonna make." With that, she closed the door in Jane's face.

Jane stood without moving for a few seconds. *I guess I deserve that.*

With a sigh, she turned and headed down the hall to change out of her suit. Once in her bedroom, she hoped to find some sign that Kyle had come home. But there was nothing. The room was as neat as when she'd left that morning. He wasn't traveling, so what was he doing? She remembered once hearing a friend say that after the clock struck the midnight hour, nothing good happened. Jane stepped out of her skirt. It wasn't midnight—not yet.

Where was he? What was he doing?

She realized suddenly how tired she was. Since Melanie wasn't hungry, there was no point in cooking only for herself. After the rotten day she'd had, her appetite was gone anyway. Kyle surely would have picked up something on his own.

But where was he?

It was two a.m. when he finally came home. She lay watching while he quietly undressed in the dark. Once in the bed, he turned on his side away from her. Jane considered asking where he'd been and why he hadn't called. She knew he'd probably have a perfectly reasonable explanation. At least, she hoped he'd have a reasonable explanation. She stared up at the ceiling fan. Maybe it was something unreasonable. She froze for a moment, wondering again if there might be another woman. But no, she pushed that thought away. Kyle wouldn't. Still, out of common courtesy, he should explain why he was so late coming home. She shouldn't have to ask. She shouldn't have to force him to talk to her. She considered telling him about the incident on the bridge, but if he wouldn't share his day, she wouldn't share hers.

KYLE TRIED NOT TO wake Jane the next morning. Moving quietly, he took what he needed to wear from the closet and went to the guest bathroom to shower and shave. He had to be in court early, and he still had some preparation to do. It should have been done the night before, but by the time he was able to get back to his office last night, he was exhausted and wanted to go home. It had been one hellish night.

"What's going on, Kyle?"

With half his face shaved, he met his wife's gaze in the mirror. "I'm shaving. And then I'll be getting dressed to go to the office, Jane."

"Why did you sneak out of our bedroom?"

"I wasn't sneaking. I was trying to be quiet so I wouldn't wake you. I know you had a restless night."

"And with good reason, thanks to you."

He rinsed foam from his razor and put it on the edge of the sink. "Can we have this conversation tonight, Jane? I have to be in court at ten. I need to review about two hundred pages of text, so I don't have time to talk."

"How long would it take to tell me where you were last night until two a.m.?" she demanded.

"It was business."

"What kind of business?"

"I'm a lawyer, Jane. I occasionally have clients who prefer meeting away from my office. You know that."

"So you were with a client?"

Kyle dropped his head down, shaking it wearily. Jane could be as stubborn as a mule when she set her mind to something. It was a good trait in a lawyer, but this morning it was a pain.

"Was your client a man or a woman?" she asked.

He looked at her frowning. "What difference would that make?"

"A lot if it was a woman. Was it?"

He said nothing for a long moment. Was this what they'd come to? he wondered. She thought he was cheating? "Do you really believe I would do that, Jane?"

"I don't know!" she cried. "You're acting so strange. You're staying out to all hours. You won't say why and with whom. What am I supposed to think?"

"I don't know what you're supposed to think, but I know you're supposed to trust me. This is what I was talking about yesterday." Disgusted, he tossed a washcloth in the sink. "I was with Sam Pitre," he told her. "I said it was a client because I didn't want to go into it this morning."

She looked confused. "You were with Sam Pitre until two o'clock in the morning? Why?"

"Because I wanted to talk to those two creeps about where they got those kids. I wanted to know if it was possible that they might have a lead to Max. I called Sam because I knew he could fix access for me."

Jane's eyes went wide with surprise. "What happened?"

"He didn't want to, but I pulled some strings, and he had to let me in the jail. Believe me, I would've had a lot more fun doing whatever it is you suspect of me."

Jane clasped her hands and pressed them to her heart. "Did you find out anything?"

"No. I had a photo of Max in my wallet, but if they recognized him, they covered it well."

"You talked to both of them?"

"Yeah. But separately. They're housed in different areas of the jail." Kyle reached for a towel and rubbed it over his face. "I could have skipped it altogether for what I got out of them. They both seemed borderline paranoid to be questioned. They're small potatoes, I think, but they're tied in with a big organization. I got the idea they're worried that if they talk, they won't survive even in prison."

He brushed past her at the bathroom door, scooping up his clothes as he went. "I guess I can go back to the bedroom now," he said.

"I'm sorry, Kyle." She turned with him. "I overreacted."

He looked at her. "I wasn't trying to keep secrets from you, Jane. I had to find out for myself, without giving you more stress."

"I can take any amount of stress if it's related to finding Max!"

"I didn't want to put you through anything else. And if nothing came of it, you'd never need to know."

"Here we go again, Kyle. When will you get it that I want to be totally involved in whatever is happening to find my son?"

"Your son?" He gave her a hard look. "He's my son, too, Jane. And when will you get it that I'm not just sitting around waiting for the investigation to turn up something useful? I'm pushing, I'm calling, I'm digging. Not a day goes by that I don't do something. And it's pretty frustrating."

She was caught off guard. Was this another instance when she'd been blind to what Kyle was doing? Thinking? Had he been active all along, but not sharing it with her?

She gave a resigned sigh. "It would be good if you'd tell me what you're doing, Kyle."

"And it would be good if you'd trust me, Jane." He tossed the towel in the hamper and glanced at the clock on the wall. "I need to get going."

She needed to get going too. She dressed quickly for work, but the scene had left Jane more bewildered than angry. It was good to know that at least Kyle was not sitting on the sidelines and leaving Max's case entirely to the police, but it was frustrating that he didn't feel he needed to keep her in the loop.

Once at her office, she determined to behave professionally. She needed to prove to Henri and the partners that she was serious about catching up on the cases assigned to her. It wasn't easy to put out of her mind the possibility that some lead might come from the despicable characters that had abused those poor children, but she would just have to trust Sam Pitre to do his job. And Kyle to follow up . . . for the time being.

So, by the end of the day, she felt good about the amount of progress she'd made. She was also more than ready to wrap it up and go home. Tonight, she thought, she would make a good dinner for her family. She might rail against the conventional wisdom that, as wife and mother, she was chief cook and bottle washer at home without much help from her husband or teenage daughter, but until things were on a more even keel there, that was the way it was.

The autumn sun was low in the west as she walked to her car. However, something about the way the car looked struck her as a bit off. With the glare of the sun in her eyes, she had to get closer to figure out what was making it list sideways like that. And then she gave a sound of sheer disgust. She had a flat tire!

She spent a few minutes checking her spare and another scant ten seconds wondering if she'd be able to fix it herself. Those TV shows demonstrating the art of fixing a flat tire were for entertainment, she realized, not real life. And Kyle, of course, would be across the lake, at least an hour away. The dealership where she'd bought the car was closed at this hour. She was fast running out of options when one of the office cleaning crew appeared.

"You need some help, Mrs. Madison?"

"Do I ever!" She wanted to hug him. "Can you fix this, Arthur?"

"No problem."

As she watched, he made short work of the job, checking the condition of her spare first, then setting about removing the damaged tire.

"I bought my car only a few months ago," she told him. "How could I have a flat?"

"Stuff happens, Mrs. Madison." Now that he had the tire off, he searched for the damage. "Looks like you've got a nice, clean puncture here on the side, see?"

Jane removed her sunglasses to get a better look. "Did I run over a nail or something?"

"Not with the damage being on the side, no." He studied it, frowning. "Hmm, that's funny."

"What?"

"Actually, it's such a clean cut that it looks like it might've been done with a knife." He stood up, squinting from the sun in his face. "You got any enemies? Anybody mad at you?"

She looked at him, astonished. "No, of course not."

"Well, I could be wrong, but I'm thinking somebody slashed this tire."

Could it be? Jane felt a cold chill climbing up her spine. A near-disastrous encounter on the bridge and now this? Suppose the two incidents weren't random acts? Suppose they were connected? Suppose someone was deliberately setting out to . . . to . . . what? Harass her? Scare her? If so, they were doing a pretty good job. Or was she becoming a bit paranoid? Or maybe that was the intent—to shake her confidence, to steal her sense of security.

But why? She bent her head, resting it against the wheel. Didn't she have enough to cope with?

Sighing wearily, she picked up her cell phone and dialed 911 and was told to stay put and wait for a police unit. She'd prefer calling Sam Pitre, but this was local and out of his jurisdiction. Besides, a tire-slashing was, at most, a minor misdemeanor. Sam had bigger fish to fry in New Orleans.

But as she sat alone in the deserted parking lot waiting, she had a sudden, creepy feeling that she was being watched. She looked around for Arthur's pickup, but it was gone. She was alone. She glanced quickly at the rearview mirror but saw nothing. Then, toward the rear of the building in a thick growth of wax myrtle, she caught a flash of color as if something—someone?—moved. Or did she? Was she letting a couple of scary experiences freak her out? True or not, she decided not to wait around for the police. When 911 answered her second call, she told them she'd wait in the parking lot of the nearest supermarket.

Why was all this happening to her?

5

ONCE AGAIN SHE WAS late getting home. Same as last night, she trudged up the stairs and knocked on Melanie's door. "It's me, Mellie."

"Oh, goody." Melanie opened the door and simply looked at her.

"I had a flat tire."

"So?"

"I left you a voice mail," Jane said. "And I'm in no mood to hear any back talk. I'm tired. I picked up Chinese takeout. Do you want to share it with me?"

"No, I made myself a smoothie. Last night pbj, tonight a smoothie. So, you're off the hook. As for Dad . . ." She shrugged. "Whatever."

"He's home?"

"Who knows?"

Jane resisted getting pulled into more pointless back and

forth. This time, before Melanie could slam the door in her face, she turned on her heel and headed to her bedroom.

As last night, the room was quiet and empty. She tried to reach Kyle at his office, but his assistant told her he was in conference with a client. She'd tell him about the flat tire when he got home. Right now, she was interested in digging in to that Chinese takeout. She'd had only a yogurt and a handful of almonds for lunch. As soon as she changed into something comfortable, she'd eat whether Kyle was home or not.

Her mouth fell open in shock when she opened the closet. There was nothing but empty space where Kyle's clothes should have been. Everything was gone—his shirts, his pants, his suits, his ties, his shoes.

Stunned, she stood staring, not knowing what to think. He must have come home at midday to do this. With her heart racing, she rushed into the hall, making for the guest room. She opened the closet and found his things. For a minute, she wasn't sure whether she felt relief or fury. He hadn't moved into a hotel, so he wasn't leaving her. Yet. But there was something so . . . so cowardly about doing this on the sly.

Slowly, she returned to their bedroom—or what used to be their bedroom. Did Melanie know? Was she in her room vicariously enjoying what she knew would shock Jane? No, as badly as their relationship had deteriorated, Mellie could not be that mean-spirited. On the other hand, she wouldn't have believed Kyle could be so cruel.

Jane gazed blankly around the room. If she'd had any doubts about the depth of her husband's unhappiness, this settled it.

But what to do about it? How to proceed now? She loved Kyle. She loved Melanie. With Max gone, they were all she had. She didn't want to lose either of them. But was it too late? Was the damage so deep and so wide that it could not be repaired?

With her hands shaking and a sick feeling in her stomach, she changed into jeans and a T-shirt and left the bedroom. At Melanie's door, she hesitated. Maybe she should make more of an effort to persuade her to come downstairs. Maybe she should try harder to find a way to heal what was wrong between them.

She knocked softly. "Mellie, I know you've had a smoothie, but how about coming down and keeping me company while I eat?"

No response, only dead silence.

"You know you love Triple Dragon," Jane said in a coaxing voice. "C'mon. Let's enjoy it together."

Still no response.

"Tell you what, I'm going to heat it up, and it'll be ready in a few minutes. What d'you say?"

Melanie didn't say anything, but Jane refused to think she'd be able to resist Asian food. It was a big favorite in their family.

Five minutes later, she had it ready. Stepping to the bottom of the stairs, she called out, "Mellie, come and get it! Chinese needs to be eaten piping hot."

Jane tried to appear nonchalant when Melanie appeared. And she noted with relief that the girl's expression wasn't quite so surly. "Let's set a place for your dad just in case he can make it tonight," she said.

"Fat chance," Melanie muttered.

Jane ignored that. "We'll need the trivet to set this on," she said, removing a dish from the microwave. "Oops, I forgot the chopsticks. Will you get them? I'm gonna learn to use them if it kills me, so I need the practice. Next time we go out to eat sushi, I'll be as good as you and your dad."

Melanie didn't comment, but she did root around in the drawer for chopsticks. When she had them in her hand, she dropped them on Jane's plate with a clatter, but took more care in placing napkin, utensils, and chopsticks at Kyle's place at the table. No, Jane thought, she didn't seem to know about her dad's moving to the guest room.

Jane set the steaming dish on a trivet and surveyed the table for a second. "Okay, I think we're ready."

Melanie had poured herself a tall glass of milk, surprising Jane since she usually preferred tea or water. But she didn't comment. Whatever she wanted to drink was okay with Jane, so long as she was willing to sit at the dinner table and at least pretend they were a normal mother and daughter. Well, stepdaughter. Melanie had made that crystal clear lately.

Dishing up a generous portion of Triple Dragon, Jane set it in front of her. "There. Doesn't that smell delicious!"

Melanie took one look at the steaming entree, went still and pale, and suddenly leaped up and dashed out of the kitchen. Stunned, Jane wasn't sure what was wrong. She left the table and found Melanie in the powder room bent over the toilet throwing up.

"Mellie, what on earth!"

"Leave me alo-o-o-ne!" It was a wail, and she was again overcome with violent heaves. It was mostly strawberry smoothie, Jane noted, thinking the drink must have been the cause of her upset stomach.

"You must have a touch of food poisoning," she said when Melanie seemed done. "Where did you buy that smoothie?"

"Mango Tango."

"Well, don't ever go there again." Jane opened a box of wet wipes and handed it over. Melanie took one and buried her face in it.

"Don't mention Triple Dragon to me ever again," she muttered.

"I won't," Jane said, "but I don't think you should avoid Triple Dragon forever when it was a smoothie that made you sick. Or maybe you have a virus. Is something going around at school?"

"Maybe . . ."

Jane sighed. "You'll probably want to lie down awhile. I'll bring you some ginger ale. That's good for an unsettled tummy."

"Nah, I think I'll go back to the kitchen and make myself another pbj."

Jane stared at her in surprise. "What?"

"I know it's gross, but now it's over, and I'm hungry."

"Are you sure?"

It was a surreal mood at the table when they were seated again. At least it seemed surreal to Jane. Melanie, wolfing down her favorite—peanut butter and jelly sandwich—acted as if nothing unusual had happened.

Jane took her cue from that. Although her appetite was gone, she sat down and pretended right along with Melanie. "So, did anything interesting happen at school today?"

Melanie looked at her. "Does it ever?"

"You used to think so."

"Well, I got over it."

"How about your friends?"

"What about them?"

Jane gave up.

After a stressful day at work, a flat tire, and finding her husband had moved out of their bedroom, she was ready to crawl into bed and pull the covers over her head. A part of her was glad Kyle wasn't here. That meant they could put off explaining to Melanie why he had moved into the guest room. She'd be interested to hear his reasoning herself.

SHE MET KYLE THE next morning at the coffee pot. She had not wanted to talk to him when he came home the night before. She hadn't trusted herself not to throw something at him, so she'd closed their—*her*—bedroom door. He'd tapped softly around eleven, but she ignored it. And had spent another long, sleepless night.

"We need to talk, Jane."

She leaned against the counter, cradling her coffee in both hands. "No kidding."

"I didn't mean for you to walk in cold last night and find I'd moved my things. I was going to be here when you got home, but a client called as I was leaving my office. He was in jail on a DUI. I went over and didn't get away until nearly eleven."

"They must be getting to know you pretty well at the jail," Jane said, looking out the window.

He didn't reply to that. "I wanted to explain when I got home, but I guess you weren't in any mood to listen."

"I was in a pretty rotten mood on finding my husband had moved out of our bedroom without bothering to tell me. So, yes, you might say that."

"It was probably just as well. We were both tired, and the discussion would probably not have been productive."

She turned to look directly at him. "You sound like a lawyer, Kyle. Don't talk to me like that. I'm your wife, not a client."

"I tried to tell you the other day that I needed some time to myself to think things through. That's what I'm doing. That's *all* I'm doing. "

"And you can't think in our bedroom?"

His gaze shifted to the window. "I don't know. I guess not. I just feel I need—"

"Space," she said. "It's that space thing again. So, okay, you have it, Kyle." She turned to leave.

"Wait."

She stopped. "What?"

"I shouldn't have said I blamed you for what happened to Max. I apologize for that. I'm just looking to blame someone."

"Then blame the person who took him."

"Yeah." He stared down at his coffee.

She paused, eyeing him narrowly. "So, is that it? We're done here?" He looked as if he wanted to say more, but when he didn't, she walked to the door carrying her coffee. "Oh, I almost forgot. I had a flat tire yesterday, and I'll need a new one. Could we swap cars? Do you have time to take mine to the Lexus dealer today?"

"Yeah. Where were you when it went flat?"

"At my office. Arthur Collins was still in the building cleaning. He came out and fixed it for me. He said somebody punctured it with a knife or something."

Kyle looked stunned. "Did you file a police report?"

"I did, and they were underwhelmed. Said it was probably a vandal. I asked Arthur if he'd noticed anybody in the parking lot who didn't belong, and, of course, he hadn't."

"You should have called me."

"You mean you would have chosen me over a drunken client?"

He gave her a straight look. "C'mon, Jane."

"I'm going upstairs to take a shower," she said. "I'd rather not be around when Mellie comes down and wants to know why you're sleeping in the guest room. I'll leave it to you to handle that."

NEXT MORNING, JANE WAS seated at her dressing table, drying her hair, when Melanie burst into the room. "What is going on, Jane?"

Jane turned the dryer off and set it down. She pushed her hair back from her face. "You can see what's going on. I'm getting dressed as I do every day." She met Melanie's eyes in the mirror. "How are you feeling this morning? No more nausea?"

Shifting her gaze beyond Jane, Melanie suddenly noticed the empty side of the walk-in closet. "Why are Dad's clothes gone? Where is he?" Her voice went up an octave.

"Did you check the porch? It's Saturday. He's probably out there reading the paper."

"That's not what I mean and you know it! Dad slept in the guest room. Why? What have you done?"

"She hasn't done anything, Melanie."

Jane stood up as Kyle appeared.

"I've decided to sleep in the guest room for a while," he said.

"Why?" Melanie demanded. "Are you getting a divorce?"

"You don't need to be worried about this, sweetheart," he said. "It doesn't concern you."

Melanie stared at him in astonishment. "It doesn't concern me? I don't need to be worried when my father decides he doesn't want to sleep in the same room with his wife? Are you kidding me?"

"This is between Jane and me, Melanie. It's not something you need to get involved in."

"It has everything to do with me!" she cried. "You're doing this because of Max. And don't try to tell me anything different. It's my fault he's gone, and because he's gone, Jane doesn't think about anything except finding him and she's been such a horrible wife to you that you've decided to get a divorce!"

"Jane is not a horrible wife to me." Kyle raked a hand through his hair, looking frustrated. "Try to calm down."

"Okay." She pressed her hands to her hips. "I'm calm. So, are you getting a divorce?"

"Nobody said anything about a divorce," he said with exaggerated patience.

"If you aren't, then what? Why would you start sleeping in the guest room?"

Kyle gave Jane an imploring look. For a second or two, she thought about letting him stew in the juice he'd stirred up, but the impulse died with a glance at Melanie's stricken face. "Your dad and I are going through a bad patch, Melanie," she said gently. “You know things have not been exactly happy around here, so it sometimes happens that people—couples—need to step back and take a little time to think things through. That’s how couples work things out. We are not getting a divorce.”

“I don’t believe you,” Melanie said.

Which was no surprise since Jane didn’t believe it either. “Then I guess you’ll have to just stick around and wait to see what happens.”

Melanie’s eyes clung to Jane’s for a long moment before turning to Kyle. “I got it right, didn’t I, Dad? Jane spends so much time at that place that she doesn’t care about us anymore. She made you move out of the bedroom, didn’t she?”

Wearily Kyle rubbed his face. “You have it all wrong, Mellie. We’ve all been under great stress since . . . ah, these last few months and—”

“Since Max was taken, that’s what you were going to say, isn’t it? So go ahead and say it.”

Kyle sighed, then tried another approach. “You know from your counseling that these issues are difficult for families to resolve, Mellie. We’re no different from other families who go through something like this.”

“You can’t even say the words, can you, Dad? Max was kidnapped. Somebody snatched him right out in broad daylight when I was supposed to be watching him. It was my fault. And now you’re taking the first step to getting a divorce by moving into the guest room.” Her lips trembled as her eyes filled with tears. “And that’s my fault too.”

Kyle took a step toward her, but she put out a hand to stop him. “No, don’t you even try to lie to me. I don’t want to hear anymore.” Her voice rose as she began backing out of the room. “I hate this place! I hate you! I hate both of you!” Bursting into sobs, she turned and ran.

“Melanie! Come back here!” Kyle took a step, but Jane caught his arm.

"Let her go, Kyle."

Shoulders drooping, eyes troubled, he stood looking at the door. "I messed that up royally, didn't I?"

"I don't know what would have been the right way to tell her. I'll call her therapist and try to get an appointment early next week. Maybe she can help sort it all out."

"I didn't want to upset her so," he said.

"Really?" Jane wondered exactly what reaction he'd expected. Melanie had suffered extreme emotional trauma when Max disappeared. She saw her father's action in moving out of their bedroom as more upheaval in her life. "We're not a family anymore, Kyle, and Melanie knows it."

MELANIE LEFT THE HOUSE by way of the back porch. As she picked her way across the lawn, she texted Daniel, hoping he would pick it up though it was pretty early and he liked to sleep late on Saturdays. But she really needed to talk to him. She stood at a hedge of azaleas separating the two properties. Overhead, in a magnolia tree, some kind of bird was singing his heart out. How could the world be so ordinary with birds singing and the sky so blue when inside she felt so miserable?

She was wiping tears when her cell phone vibrated. Drawing a shaky breath, she tried bringing the text from Daniel into focus.

"Mt u n bk."

She waited with her eyes on the O'Brian's patio. And then Daniel stepped out of the house.

"What's wrong?" he said the minute he got close enough to see her.

"Everything." She felt a pang seeing the look on his face. Daniel was not as sympathetic as he used to be. Her fault, she accepted that. But what was done was done.

"What does that mean—everything?" Daniel asked.

"I think my dad and Jane are getting a divorce."

He rolled his eyes. "C'mon, Mel. That's crazy. Your dad isn't going to divorce Jane, especially now. It would be . . . well, mean. Really awful."

"You mean because Max is gone?"

"Well, yeah. It would be . . ." He shrugged, searching for the right word. "Mean."

"Well, what about this? His stuff is moved out of their closet and he's sleeping in the guest room. And I don't think my dad is mean. I think he has every right to leave because Jane doesn't think about anything except those stupid people at Child Search. If she paid more attention to my dad, this wouldn't be happening."

Daniel sighed. "Is this why you got me out here, to trash Jane some more? You need to get over that, Mel. Jane's always been a great mom, and she's sad. Who wouldn't be? She's lost her little boy same as you've lost your little brother. Can't you cut her some slack?"

"Not when she's destroying our family!"

"She is not destroying your family. She's just trying to get through this, same as you."

Melanie closed her eyes, heaving a sigh. "I guess you think the answer to getting through is to start going back to church, is that it, Daniel? 'Cause I know that's your answer to everything."

"Well, it couldn't hurt. Specially with big problems. Like having somebody take your little kid."

"Well, what difference has it made so far? You prayed for my little brother to be found. Didn't you? Didn't you?"

"The whole town prayed for Max to be found, Mel."

"Then why didn't we find him?" She looked at him with tears bright in her eyes. "Answer me that, Daniel."

6

Tension at the Madison house during the next few days was so thick it was as if a dense fog had settled in and saturated everything. It seemed to Jane they were all weighed down with uncertainty and stress and feelings too complex to be spoken. Every morning she faced Melanie's angry face and Kyle's blank features. Meanwhile at work, she was clearing the most pressing cases and making headway in the long list. Henri told her that the partners were still disgruntled, but with the level of work she was turning out, they were willing to cut her some slack.

She wished it were as easy to remedy the problems in her personal life.

She stopped Kyle in the hall Wednesday morning. "Can you hold up leaving for a few minutes?" she asked in a low tone so that Melanie wouldn't hear. "I need to talk to you."

"Okay." He followed her downstairs. "What's up?" he asked when they reached the kitchen.

"I'm worried about Melanie."

Kyle gave an impatient sigh. "Is this about her attitude again?"

Jane forged ahead, "Every day she gets home from school and goes straight to her room and sleeps. You must have noticed this weekend that when she wasn't eating, she was sleeping."

"Teenagers need more rest than adults," Kyle said with a shrug. "You don't think she's just being typical?"

"It could be that, but I'm wondering if it's clinical depression. I'm going to mention it to her therapist if we can get her to go. She's made excuses and cancelled the last two appointments I made for her."

"I'll talk to her," he said, jangling his keys in his pocket. Jane could see he wanted to get away.

"Good. That's what I hoped you'd say. We can't be too careful, Kyle. We don't want more tragedy."

With his hand on the door, he stopped, frowning. "You think she's suicidal?"

"I don't know. I can't reach her anymore. That's why I'm telling you."

"Okay." He opened the door to the garage. "I'll handle it when I get home tonight."

In spite of Kyle's apparent willingness to "handle" the problem, Jane was still troubled. There was something going on with Melanie, but with things so tense between them, she couldn't do much about it. She had her hands full just getting her up in the mornings and out the door to school.

Now, reaching the top of the stairs, she realized there was no sound of life in the girl's bedroom. She must have shut off her alarm again and gone back to sleep. Or forgotten to set it after studying late the night before for an exam, an exam she couldn't afford to miss.

Jane tapped on the door. "Melanie, wake up. I'm leaving in thirty minutes, and I'm not waiting for you again this morning."

There was still no sound. "Melanie, did you forget you've got an exam? Get up." Still nothing. Annoyed at first, she had a chilling thought. And quickly opened the door. Melanie lay still, on her side and facing away from Jane. Holding her breath, Jane walked to the bed and gingerly touched the girl's shoulder, sighing in relief at the warmth of her skin. She would scold herself later for overreacting.

"Melanie, c'mon, wake up."

Melanie stirred and made an irritated sound. A second or two passed as she came awake but didn't move.

"You are going to be late, Mel. You've got an exam, remember?"

Startling Jane, Melanie turned over abruptly and threw back the covers, clamped one hand over her mouth and made a wild dash for the bathroom. She barely made it to the toilet where she was violently ill.

"Oh, no, you've got another virus!" Jane exclaimed as the girl retched and retched. When she seemed done, Jane thrust a few wet wipes into her hand and ran cold water over a washcloth. Melanie leaned against the wall, weak and pale as a ghost. Jane gave her the cloth and watched as she pressed it to her face. "What rotten timing," she said sympathetically. "Getting a virus on the day of your toughest exam."

Melanie said nothing, simply stood with her eyes closed and her hands on her tummy looking wretched. Seeing she was shaky and unsteady on her feet, Jane slipped an arm around her waist. "Here, let me help you back to bed."

Melanie shook her off, took a few deep breaths, and dropped the cloth in the sink. "I think I'm okay now," she said, but her eyes were closed and she still seemed to need support to stand. "I'm taking a quick shower. Don't leave without me. I want to go to school."

Jane studied her face with a worried frown. "Oh, I don't know, Mellie. Usually with stomach flu, you'll feel okay a few minutes after upchucking and then the nausea returns. You don't want to be at school if that happens. These things usually last about twenty-four hours." She dropped the cloth in a hamper. "I'm sure your teachers will understand. Actually, they'll have to. These things are contagious. You can take a make-up exam."

She then gathered up the tissues to toss. The trash can was full, almost overflowing. Melanie tended to wait forever before dumping trash. It was a bone of contention between them . . . among many. Jane pulled it out and was on the point of compacting the overflow to make room for the soiled tissues when she realized what was in the trash. Frowning, she stared at the labeling on the discarded box. She gave Melanie a quick, puzzled look before bending down and picking it up.

"What is this, Melanie?"

Melanie sat down abruptly on the lid of the toilet. "You can see what it is, Jane."

"It's a pregnancy kit." Jane gazed at it in disbelief. "Why? What—"

"Why and what? Do I have to draw you a picture?"

"Oh, my God," Jane whispered. "Are you pregnant, Melanie?"

"That's what all this puking is about, Jane."

For a second, Jane was too shocked to think. This couldn't be. But, oh, it was. She felt a sudden rush of sheer, unadulterated fury. Like a red tidal wave, it slammed into her brain. "Don't you dare start with the sass, Melanie. I want a straight answer from you, and I want it now. Are you pregnant?"

Melanie gave an elaborate sigh. "Yes, I am pregnant."

"I don't believe it," Jane said. "You can't. You wouldn't—"

"I can. I would." Melanie jumped up. "I did! So now you've got a real reason to hate me, right?"

Jane was floored. Still holding the pregnancy test kit, she realized that all the signs she'd noticed and hadn't been able to make sense of suddenly made sense. Awful, horrible sense. Her sixteen-year-old stepdaughter was pregnant. She was aghast, stunned into incoherence.

"You—how—who?" She finally got it out. "How far along are you?"

She shrugged. "I don't know. I haven't seen a doctor." Melanie took the box from Jane's hands and flung it across the room. "And now you know."

"What on God's earth were you thinking!"

"I'm sixteen," she said. "We don't think, remember?"

Jane said, "You don't even have a boyfriend. Who is the father?"

"You don't need to know that," Melanie said. She reached into the cabinet and took out a bath towel. "And I don't want to answer any more questions now. What I do want is to get ready for school." She looked at Jane. "Am I going to get a little privacy to do it?"

Jane's mind reeled with the implications of this fresh disaster in her family. "Is it Daniel?" she asked.

"Did you hear me? I'm not telling, so you may as well stop with the questions."

Jane stared at her stepdaughter as if looking at the face of an alien. Who was this person now glaring at her? What had happened to the sweet young girl she used to be?

"Jane—" Wagging her fingers, Melanie motioned to the door, but Jane felt stuck to the floor, appalled and sick to her stomach. As for Melanie, her color was back. She looked rosy and healthy. Amazingly, there was no sign that she'd been violently ill five minutes before.

As if seeing that Jane was disinclined to leave, Melanie shrugged and began bustling about in the bathroom, taking out a fresh washcloth and towel, turning on the shower, selecting shampoo and finally, peeling off her pj's and tossing them in the hamper. Jane's dazed gaze fell to the girl's teenage tummy looking for evidence of pregnancy. Was she a bit more rounded than usual? No, not really. This child could not be pregnant, she told herself frantically. This had to be a bad dream.

"You can't leave, Melanie," she managed to say. "We have to talk about this."

Melanie pulled back the shower curtain. "You want me to miss my exam?"

"No, but . . ."

"Then we can't talk. I guess you can stand there and watch me take a shower."

Jane finally left.

THE DRIVE TO SCHOOL normally took about fifteen minutes, and in that time, Melanie sat stubbornly silent beside Jane while the shocking news that she was going to have a baby was like an elephant in the back seat. Nothing Jane said—no threat or cajoling or exasperated demand—seemed to faze her. Melanie refused to talk.

Jane had pounced once they pulled out of the driveway. "How long have you been sexually active, Melanie?"

Her reply was an insolent shrug.

"You knew about birth control. Why weren't you using it?"

Another shrug. More silence.

"For heaven's sake, just tell me who the father is!"

Face turned away, mouth set stubbornly.

"Well, at least tell me this. How far along are you?"

Stony silence.

Jane felt like reaching over and grabbing her by the throat and shaking words out of her. "Does anyone else know?" she demanded through clenched teeth.

Silence.

Finally, in front of the school, Jane stopped the car and made one last attempt. "Is that why you were arguing with Daniel at the door last Friday night? Was it about this?"

Melanie opened the door and got out. With Jane watching impotently, she wove her way through a gaggle of students and up the steps to the entrance. And without a backward look, she went inside.

The impatient honk of a car horn behind Jane prodded her back into morning traffic. But her hands were shaking on the wheel. Besides feeling wildly frustrated, she was furious. How could Melanie be so irresponsible? Was it a one-time thing? Had she gotten carried away on a date? But she didn't date, at least, only rarely and on special occasions. A thought struck. Was it rape? That possibility made it imperative that Melanie open up and talk.

Jane thought back, trying to recall a moment when she'd noticed Melanie seeming unduly anxious. Or upset. But there was nothing. Melanie had had a lot of problems, but they'd all seemed connected to Max's disappearance. Never, ever had Jane suspected that she was sexually active. On the contrary, she and Kyle had often felt relieved that her troubled behavior didn't seem to take her in that direction.

What naive fools they were.

Jane felt sick recalling Christine's suspicions. What if Daniel were the father? What an awful situation for both families. Jane braked abruptly, almost plowing through a red light. What a horrible mess.

Instead of driving on to her office, she turned in at a supermarket parking lot. She was too upset to talk to her husband and drive. Hands still unsteady, she found her cell phone and called him.

"Kyle, it's Jane. I need to talk to you. Can you break away and meet me?"

"Now?"

"Yes, now. It's important."

"Are you serious?"

She ignored the impatience in his voice. "I wouldn't call otherwise."

"Then no," he said flatly. "I've got a packed schedule. I promised I'd talk to Melanie tonight and I will."

"I need to talk to you before that, Kyle."

"Talking isn't going to be helpful in our situation just now, Jane."

"This isn't about our situation," she said. "It's about Melanie. And not what you think. It won't take long. If you can't break away now, then meet me for lunch. You do take time for lunch, don't you?"

He ignored her sarcasm. "Melanie's at school, isn't she? We can talk when I get home tonight."

"Yes, she's at school. I just dropped her off, but—"

"Then, can't it wait, Jane?" He was clearly annoyed, but Jane suddenly had enough. Their world was turned upside down, and Kyle clung to his job as if it were a life raft. Then he had the nerve to lecture her about her work at Child Search.

"I am going to be at Charlie's Grille at noon, Kyle," she said, spacing her words evenly. "I wouldn't bother you if it wasn't a matter of dire importance. So do whatever you have to do to make time for your daughter. Trust me; you're going to drop your teeth when I tell you." Without waiting to give him a chance to argue, she ended the call.

FROM THE PAINED EXPRESSION on his face, Kyle was still obviously annoyed when he spotted Jane at Charlie's Grille. She had ordered a sandwich for him and a cup of soup for herself. She had absolutely no appetite. Kyle might lose his appetite, too, once he heard what she had to tell him.

He took a seat and looked pointedly at his watch. "I have a meeting at one o'clock."

"I'll be brief." She watched him peek between the slices of bread to check what kind of sandwich she'd ordered. Seeing it was a Reuben, he gave her a half-smile and thanked her. Now that she'd had a few hours to think, she felt sympathy for him, knowing how he'd feel once he heard why she'd forced a meeting. She wished she didn't have to give him this news—she knew the pain it would bring him.

After taking a bite, he brought a napkin up to his lips. "What was so all-fired important that it couldn't wait until tonight?"

"Brace yourself, Kyle," she said. "Melanie is pregnant."

As she guessed, he almost dropped his sandwich. "What?"

"I think you heard."

"No, you aren't serious."

"I wish." She pushed her soup away. "When she told me, I was as stunned as you look now."

"She told you this? When?"

"This morning after I witnessed a bout of morning sickness. I thought she had picked up a virus." Jane's mouth twisted with irony. "Silly me."

Kyle was shaking his head in denial. "It can't be. She's still a child. She wouldn't—"

"She would. She did. She admitted it. She even seemed . . . defiant about it."

Kyle shoved his sandwich away, then looked at her soup. "Are you done?"

"Yes."

He stood up. "Then let's go."

With a sigh, she slipped out of the booth, taking her purse, and walked with him out of the restaurant after he paid for their uneaten lunch.

"Now," he told her once they reached her car. "Give me the details."

Even though she knew Kyle's personality, she wondered at his ability to focus on facts rather than emotion in the face of this incredible situation. He was ready to confront the reality head on. She, on the other hand, had been struggling just to get beyond the shock.

"I don't have any details," she said. She described Melanie's attitude on the way to school. "I thought you should know before you got home tonight. Maybe you can get her to open up. She made it plain this morning that she's not about to tell me anything."

"I can't believe this."

"But now at least we know why she's been sleeping so much. And eating everything she can get her hands on." Jane's mouth twisted with irony. "I feel like such an idiot for not figuring it out before now."

"Who's the father?" he asked.

"I told you, she's not talking. So I don't have a clue."

He looked beyond her, clearly troubled, but whatever his thoughts, he kept them to himself. After a minute, he gave a deep sigh and reached into his pocket for his keys. "No point in our discussing it here when we don't know anything," he said. "I was already planning to be home early tonight."

"I'm glad to hear it." She turned to go.

"Wait," he said. "I meant to tell you that I followed up on your police report about the flat tire. You may be visited by a detective asking questions."

"Why? I told them everything I know . . . which was not much."

"They're coming anyway. It's what cops are supposed to do. I didn't like it that they seemed to dismiss it, especially after that bridge incident."

"Then you think they could be connected?"

"I don't know, but I consider both criminal acts. They promised to alert the security people at your office to be on the lookout for suspicious persons hanging around. Anyone doing this stuff and getting away with it is sometimes tempted to try again."

"Okay." That incident had upset her, but in the face of Melanie's pregnancy, it was suddenly a very minor blip in the cosmos. She opened her car door, but he stopped her again. "What?"

"Don't start anything with Melanie before I get home. Wait for me."

She nodded and with a vague wave of her hand got in her car. This was one situation where she would gladly defer to Kyle. Dealing with the pregnancy of a sixteen-year-old was beyond a stepmother's pay grade.

That day seemed interminable to Jane. She'd found it difficult to concentrate on the inane details of her cases when her mind was whirling with Melanie's bombshell. So it had taken some fierce mental discipline, but she knew Henri and the partners were watching eagle-eyed. She was more than relieved when it was time to go.

She wasn't surprised to find the house empty. With her secret out, Melanie probably wished to avoid questions as long as she could. But she'd have to come home eventually. And she'd be hungry. Jane smiled humorlessly at the irony of that. Food was irresistible when a woman was pregnant.

She was removing a shrimp-and-pasta casserole from the oven when Melanie finally appeared. One look at the girl's face and she was glad she'd promised Kyle to wait with the questions until he got home. With Melanie's chin set at a mutinous angle and her eyes sparking, it would have been a futile effort on Jane's part anyway.

"How was the exam?" Jane asked on her way to the table.

Melanie tore off a big chunk from a loaf of French bread. "I aced it."

"Honors English, right?"

"Yeah. We had to write an essay."

Jane set the casserole on a trivet. "What did you write about?"

"Wicked stepmothers."

Jane gave her a startled look.

Melanie laughed, helping herself to a banana. "I'm kidding, Jane. I wrote about my life with two lawyers as parents. Rather, as one parent and one stepparent. And don't look so stressed. I didn't tell the truth."

Why was the girl determined to rile her? Trying to have a normal conversation with Melanie was like negotiating a minefield. Thankfully they were interrupted by sounds from the garage. For the first time in weeks, Kyle was home before dark.

"Will you set the table, please?" she asked Melanie, who gave her an exaggerated look of astonishment.

"What?" the girl said. "We're eating before the interrogation?"

Jane, struggling for patience, turned away without comment. Maybe, just maybe, she would react to Kyle with less disrespect. He came into the kitchen a few minutes later.

"Hey, kitten." He gave Melanie a hug and looked over at Jane. "Something smells great."

"I've made a shrimp casserole," Jane said, thinking he didn't appear to share her apprehension. Apparently, he was going to pretend all was well until he was ready to mention the elephant in the room. "We can eat as soon as Melanie sets the table."

"I'll just wash up," Kyle said. "Won't be a minute."

"This should be interesting," Melanie muttered around a mouthful of banana.

"I was thinking the same thing," Jane said, handing plates to her.

* * *

Looking back, Jane marveled that they managed to make it through dinner while ignoring the subject all were obsessing over. But they did. Conversation centered on school, Melanie's exams, a couple of Kyle's cases and Jane's as well. At one point, Melanie asked about the abused children that had been discovered a few days earlier.

"They haven't identified the little boy," Jane told her. "But somebody will recognize him once his profile circulates through the system."

"What will they do to those people?" Melanie asked.

It was Kyle who answered. "Child endangerment is a serious crime. And if they're found guilty of kidnapping, all the more. They'll go to prison. Hopefully for a long time, but it's hard to tell."

Melanie looked at Jane. "Didn't you say that those people were actually the real parents of a couple of those kids?"

"Yes. At least, the couple claimed they were their natural children."

Without being told, Melanie stood up to collect their plates. It was her job, but Jane usually had to remind her. "It's hard to understand why some people have babies and don't seem to appreciate them," she said, opening the dishwasher.

"It is puzzling," Jane said quietly.

"And then to some parents," Melanie said, "kids are their whole life."

"Fortunately, most people value their children," Kyle said.

"Yeah, but for those who don't, haven't you ever wondered why God lets just anybody have babies?"

Jane knew without a doubt that, tonight of all nights, neither she nor Kyle wanted to get into a philosophical discussion on that subject.

"That's why," Melanie continued, as she busily wiped the surface of the counter, "I don't really believe in God."

Jane gave Kyle a meaningful look. It was time to get to the

subject that was uppermost in their minds. Taking the cue, Kyle stood up.

"Now there's a subject that's too deep to go into tonight, I think." He dropped his napkin on the table. "But there is something that we need to talk about, Melanie. Come back here to the table and sit down."

"Well, finally!" Melanie tossed a sponge into the sink. "I was beginning to wonder if Jane had decided to keep my little secret just between us girls."

Kyle frowned. "So what Jane tells me is true? You are pregnant?"

"I guess so."

His brows rose. "You guess so?" He flicked a glance at Jane. "I thought there was no doubt."

"I only have Melanie's word that she's pregnant," Jane said. "But she told me she hasn't seen a doctor."

He frowned again. "Then how can you know, Mellie? You're sixteen years old. Pregnancy is . . . Pregnancy means . . ." He gave an exasperated sigh. "This is ridiculous. I thought it was settled. I was told—" He turned to Jane. "You led me to think she definitely is pregnant."

Kyle shifted his gaze to his daughter. "Well, Melanie, what about it? Is it really true, or are you simply trying to shock us?"

"I'm really pregnant," she said in the same tone she might have used to tell them she was really getting a headache. "That test kit is the third one, so I'm pretty sure. It's three months since I had a period. According to what I found on the internet, that makes me about eleven or twelve weeks, I'm not sure which."

Both Jane and Kyle stared at her. If it were her intent to shock them, Jane thought, she had succeeded. "You're possibly twelve weeks pregnant, and you haven't thought it necessary to see a doctor?" Jane asked.

Melanie shrugged nonchalantly. "I didn't think I needed

one so soon." She put both hands on her tummy as if to prove to them that she wasn't showing yet. "You saw me naked this morning, Jane. You couldn't tell, could you?"

Jane simply shook her head, speechless.

"So stop and think," Melanie went on. "I'm sixteen. It would be kind of complicated to go to a doctor. Besides, I'd have to have insurance, wouldn't I?"

Kyle gave Jane an amazed look. "This is incredible."

"Yes," Jane said faintly. Gathering herself, she said to Melanie, "Tomorrow I'll call my gynecologist. It's clear that you don't realize what you've gotten yourself into. Pregnancy is a complex medical condition, if not the most complex."

"But it's the only way to get a baby," Melanie said.

"You're too young to have a baby," Jane said firmly. "You have the rest of your life to do that. First you need to grow up; you need to find the right person to share your life with. People don't have babies first and then finish all the rest of that at a later date! That's crazy."

"Jane." Melanie leaned forward in her chair and looked directly at her. "Listen to what I'm telling you. I know I have lots of time to find a good guy, get married, and have children." She glanced at her father before switching her gaze back to Jane. "That's not why I've done this."

"What are you talking about?" Jane demanded.

"Yes," Kyle chimed in. "What are you saying?"

"I was responsible for Max's being taken," Melanie said. "This baby is not for me . . . it's for you."

7

Kyle stared at her with a stunned look on his face. "What do you mean?"

Melanie inhaled and looked first at her dad, then Jane. "I got pregnant to replace Max," Melanie said. "You and Jane can have the baby."

Jane managed to recover before Kyle. "That is the most preposterous thing I've ever heard, Melanie! Are you out of your mind?"

"No." Melanie made an impatient sound as if Jane and Kyle were purposely being thickheaded. "And before you freak out, Jane, just think about it. Didn't you have a hard time getting pregnant with Max? And didn't you finally have to go to one of those fertility clinics? And didn't you have to try three or four times before in vitro worked?"

Jane was shaking her head. "What does that have to do with anything?"

"Everything," Melanie said. "It has everything to do with

my getting pregnant. You'll be forty years old on your next birthday. Your chances of having another baby are not good."

Jane could only stare at her.

"So," Melanie continued, "I knew there was only one way we could have a baby in this family. It would have to come from me." She glanced at Kyle. "You'd have a baby, a blood relative, not some adopted kid." She flashed them a bright look. "This way, you'll know what you're getting."

Jane, speechless, sent a look of amazement to Kyle, who seemed at a loss for words as well. Melanie, however, wasn't finished. She turned her attention fully to Jane.

"Except I didn't know you and Dad would decide to get a divorce. It's too late to do anything about my being pregnant." She gave a helpless shrug. "I couldn't just change my mind about something like that." She rubbed her belly. "The baby's in there. According to a book I'm reading, he's already the size of a peanut."

Jane was appalled. Clearly Melanie didn't grasp the consequences of what she had done. "Who is the father, Melanie?" Jane asked. At least they deserved to know that much.

"Yeah," Kyle said, finally finding his voice. "Who was foolish enough to go along with you on this?"

Melanie looked down at her hands. "I'm not going to tell you his name. For one thing, it isn't his fault. I don't want him to feel any responsibility for the baby. It wouldn't be fair."

"Are you saying you didn't tell him you were using him to get pregnant on purpose?" Jane asked in a shocked voice.

"It sounds bad when you say it like that," Melanie said in a defensive tone.

"But you didn't tell him what you were up to?"

For the first time, Melanie looked uncertain. "I did it for . . . um . . . honorable reasons."

"But you weren't honorable enough to tell someone who obviously cared about you that you planned to get pregnant?"

"It wasn't like that!" she cried.

Kyle was staring at his daughter as if she'd turned into a stranger. "I can't believe you would do something like this, Melanie."

Tears sprang into her eyes. "But I did it for you, Daddy." Her lips trembled. "I mean, I did it for you both—Jane too. I didn't know you were going to get a divorce."

"That is absolutely irrelevant, Melanie!" Kyle said, raising his voice. "Can't you see what you've done? It's selfish and thoughtless. Do you have any remorse about that?"

Melanie shrugged without saying anything.

"Have you thought who the victim is in all this, Melanie?" Jane asked quietly.

"The father is not going to be responsible for the baby," Melanie said. "I really mean that."

"I'm not talking about the father," Jane said. "The victim in this . . . this scheme is the baby. An innocent child."

"Jane is right, Melanie," Kyle said.

"But the baby will have a good life," Melanie insisted. "He will have you and Jane as parents. At least, he would have until she"—she threw a hard look at Jane—"messed everything up."

"This is not about me and your dad," Jane said. She stood up. "I think we're done tonight . . . unless you'd like to reveal the name of the baby's father, Melanie." She waited, looking at Melanie, who lifted her chin stubbornly, but remained mute. "As I said, I'll make an appointment for you to see a doctor as soon as possible. Pregnant women have special needs, you'll soon realize. And you should begin taking prenatal vitamins."

Melanie's stubborn expression was still in place. "In primitive societies, women have babies without all the fuss and bother that we have. They just squat somewhere and have him, then go about their everyday work. It's no big deal."

Kyle rose from his chair. "Go to bed, Melanie. We're done here for tonight."

Melanie looked as if she might continue to argue, but Kyle pointed to the stairs. “I said go, Melanie. And I mean it.”

When she left and they heard the sound of her door closing upstairs, Kyle sat down. “What an unholy mess.”

“Yes.”

“How could she have come up with such a crazy scheme?”

“I don’t know.”

“How could she think Max could be replaced like . . . like a puppy?” He dropped his head into his hands and spoke in a muffled tone, “What are we going to do, Jane?”

“Are you and I ‘we’ now, Kyle?”

“Of course, we are.”

“So move back into our bedroom.”

He sighed. “Can we stay on topic, please?”

Jane drew a deep breath, rose, and began clearing the rest of the dishes from the table. “I’m taking her to a doctor as soon as I can get an appointment. After that . . .” She shrugged. “I don’t know. We’ll need to think this through carefully. Consider all options.”

He looked up. “Do we have any options?”

“Yes, of course. If we decide to do nothing, she’ll have the baby, but then what? Adoption might be the best thing.”

“Maybe we shouldn’t allow her to have the baby at all,” Kyle said.

“Are you suggesting abortion?” Revulsion made Jane shake her head vehemently. It had been so difficult for her to conceive that the very thought of abortion was abhorrent. “No, Kyle. We have to persuade her to give him to a deserving family.”

“Okay, but”—Kyle was on his feet, pacing—“she’s sixteen years old, Jane! How would she be able to make such a serious decision?”

“But abortion is a far more serious decision, Kyle,” Jane said. “There will be consequences in years to come regardless of which choice she makes. In addition to the guilt of abortion, she could harbor deep resentment if she feels forced to do that against her will. Even if she made an adoption plan, she could end up feeling as if she's been robbed of her child."

Kyle stopped his pacing and looked at her. "So, what? We just let her keep it? She's still got two more years of school. She's too young to be a mother to a puppy, let alone a child. That leaves us—you and me—parenting him. Isn't that the same thing as going along with her crazy scheme to replace Max?"

"No baby can replace Max."

"No, of course not." He paused for a beat or two, then managed a crooked smile. "The baby is my grandchild. I'm human enough to want to know him, Jane."

"Lucky you." She didn't mean it to sound snarky, but it did.

Kyle drew in a frustrated breath. "But are we able . . . or willing to parent another child? She sure isn't capable. And she won't be for another couple of years."

"That's assuming we're still married two years from now."

Seeing he didn't have an answer to that, Jane let it go.

"I think Daniel is the father," she said quietly. "I just can't imagine Melanie being intimate with anybody else. It has to be Daniel."

"I can't imagine Melanie being intimate with anybody!" Kyle said.

"Well, there's only one way to be impregnated, Kyle," she said dryly.

He was silent for a minute, thinking. "If you're right, I wonder what Christine's reaction will be."

"And Ben," Jane added. She tossed a towel on the counter in frustration. "What was Melanie *thinking*?"

"She told us what she was thinking." Kyle's gaze was fixed on the darkness outside the kitchen window. "She was thinking to replace Max," he said softly. "God help us."

* * *

THAT NIGHT, LYING ALONE in her king-size bed, Jane couldn't sleep. Sometimes when she was troubled, she talked things out with Christine. Staring at the ceiling, she imagined telling Christine. She would be shocked, yes, but she had a warm and loving heart—Jane knew she would sympathize with Melanie's reasoning. What Jane wouldn't give for some practical wisdom now, but on this, she'd have to muddle through on her own. It was just that . . . sometimes she felt so empty, so hopeless. What was that old song? Is this all there is?

Her gaze turned to the window where the O'Brians' house appeared dark and peaceful. Kids all tucked in, Ben and Christine together, everything all right and tight. A couple bound by love and family and faith.

She threw an arm over her face as if she could block the despair that came at her from all sides. She was a good person, she obeyed rules, she gave to charity, she tried to "do unto others," so why were bad things, one after the other, happening to her? What was the message she was supposed to get here? Was that how a loving God worked? Or had her rejection of God brought disaster down on her?

Was Melanie right? Was there no God?

LYING ALONE IN THE guest room, Kyle was sleepless. He felt as if the dark pit he'd fallen into six months ago was yawning wider and sucking his whole family down with him. He could see that Jane had already been pulled into it, and now Melanie was at risk. She might be just a kid, but she knew the point at which all the color had gone out of their lives. Her scheme to fix everything was crazy, but he understood the reason she'd done it.

Where was his son? Who had taken him?

His client base contained a host of characters who could've had a part in his disappearance, and Jane's cases, too, were fraught with negativity. Divorcing couples could be ticking time bombs. But he'd spent countless hours going through his files, scrutinizing every possible individual he'd ever represented, every questionable case, looking for the one that might be "the one." And he'd found nothing.

After a while, he'd felt nothing. He'd simply shut down emotionally. And even though his life was unraveling, he didn't know how to change that.

Turning his head, he gazed at the closed door. A part of him longed for the solace he'd once found in Jane's arms. He'd once been so in love with her, so captivated by her intelligence and personality, her humor and her loving heart. They'd been so in tune with each other, so compatible in their wants and needs. But he wasn't the person he once was. And neither was Jane. They were both broken, both fundamentally changed. So Melanie's pregnancy was simply one more blow to the crumbling foundation on which he'd built his life.

JANE WENT TO HER office Thursday morning determined to do what Kyle was so good at, compartmentalizing the issues that were a source of turmoil in her life. First, she made an appointment for Melanie to see an obstetrician. Melanie had informed her on the way to school that morning that she wasn't going to let Jane take charge of her pregnancy, not with everything that was going on with her dad. She intended to handle the whole thing by herself. Jane was so fed up with the girl that she was almost glad to wash her hands of the situation. She wouldn't, of course.

The next issue was Child Search. She would have to pull back on the number of hours she volunteered there. Marilee would understand. Her priority had to be her personal life—Kyle and Melanie. Maybe it should have been all along. She just wished they appeared to need her as much as those at Child Search needed her.

Midmorning, Michelle stuck her head in the door. "Your ten o'clock appointment is here, Jane."

"The Chastains?"

"Uh-huh. And they're in rare form."

Bess and Dennis Chastain were divorcing after thirty-two years. Dennis had fallen in love with one of his employees, a woman who was only three years older than his daughter. The business was worth several million dollars, and Dennis was determined that Bess wouldn't get a big chunk of it.

With a resigned sigh, Jane rose, gathered up the Chastain file, and moved from behind her desk. "Are they in the conference room?"

"Yes. You may need a flak jacket," Michelle said with a smile. "They had a nasty argument in reception before I could usher them to the conference room."

"Is Jay here yet?" Jay Rawlins was Dennis Chastain's attorney.

"Yes, but he couldn't control Dennis in reception. And Bess was almost as bad. I don't know what'll happen once they're behind closed doors."

An hour later, she was weary of her role as referee. Bess had grabbed the spreadsheet of Dennis's assets that Jay laid on the table. "Do you think I'm an idiot?" she screamed at her husband, waving the paper across the table from him. "I know for a fact that you claimed four million dollars on our income tax just two years ago, and I know that number was lower than the truth." She ripped the spreadsheet in half and threw it at him. "Guess again, you miserable, lying cheat!"

Jay Rawlins cleared his throat uneasily. "Mrs. Chastain, there's no need to use that kind of language. My client—"

"Is a disgusting excuse for a human being!" Bess hissed, nailing Dennis with blood in her eye. "You're not dealing with a twenty-six-year-old bimbo, Dennis. Before you shacked up with your secretary, I'm the woman you slept with for thirty-two years. I know how you think. I know how you are deep down in your despicable soul. So get real."

"Bess," Jane said quietly, "try to calm down."

"Calm down? Calm down?" Bess repeated, chest heaving. "I'll calm down when I see a fair accounting of our assets, not this . . . this insulting piece of garbage." She seared Dennis with another angry look. "You hear that, Dennis?"

"I hear a raving maniac," Dennis said, now on his feet. Leaning across the table, he lowered his voice to a menacing snarl. "And I'll see you dead before I give you another dime."

Bess, unfazed, put her hands on her hips. "You'd like that, wouldn't you? If I drop dead, you'll have it all." She laughed bitterly. "I guess you wished that had happened last year when I got breast cancer, didn't you?"

He glared at her. "You want the truth?"

Jane stood up. "Enough, both of you!" She raised her hands, palms out. "You should hear yourselves. You both need to sit and calm down." She turned to Jay. "It's obvious that these aren't accurate numbers. You need to talk to your client about the law and impress upon him the consequences of fudging the numbers."

Dennis was still on his feet, red-faced and furious. He switched his gaze from Bess to Jane. "I told Jay you'd try and bleed me dry." He used his thumb to thump his chest. "I've spent thirty years in business chewing up and spitting out lawyers like you for breakfast. You keep egging Bess on, and when I'm done with you, you'll know you've been in a real fight."

"Is that a threat, Mr. Chastain?" Jane asked.

"It is what it is!" Dennis shot back. "If you think you'll get away with helping this witch rob me in the name of fairness, think again. There's more than one way to skin a cat, lady, and I know 'em all."

"Dennis, Dennis." Jay caught his client's sleeve and tried to tug him down into his chair. "You're out of line, man. This kind of talk isn't helpful. Let's all settle down and try to work something out."

Jane was shaken but determined not to let this lunatic know it. "This meeting is over," she said and began gathering up papers and stuffing them into a file. "Bess, I'll call you when Jay and I have another proposal for you to consider." And with her heart racing, she turned and walked out.

8

She was still unsettled at the end of the day when she shopped at the grocery store to replenish her nearly empty pantry. Acting on Kyle's accusation that she was neglecting her responsibilities as a homemaker, she needed to have supplies on hand if she planned to make dinner for her family regularly, especially with Melanie eating for two. The girl needed balanced meals, and Jane was determined to see that she got them whether Kyle showed up or not.

The crowd in the store was mostly women who, given their business attire, had come from work, many with children in tow. The younger ones were belted in carts. Jane found it hard to look at any small child without feeling heart-wrenching pain. She wondered what her reaction might be when she was faced with seeing Melanie's baby every day. Would it make the pain less? Or would she feel even more anguish?

She forged a path to the produce section. Melanie would

probably balk at eating veggies, but she needed a superhealthy diet now. Meat was the only item left on her grocery list. She was at the poultry section when Christine appeared beside her.

"You look as if you've had a bad day," Christine said, giving her a hug.

"That's an understatement." Jane dropped a package of chicken breasts into her cart. "You wouldn't believe what vicious things divorcing couples say to each other." She made a face as she studied the cost of jumbo shrimp. "Or to the opposing party's lawyer."

"That would be you?" Christine moved her cart to let a customer pass. "What happened?"

Jane told her about the meeting with the Chastains, not mentioning names or private details. "It was a threat, Christine. There was blood in that man's eyes. And I'm telling you, if he appeared here in the store, I would run for the nearest exit. I think he was actually ready to do me physical harm."

Christine followed her to another aisle. "Who knew a specialty in family law could be dangerous?"

"Unfortunately, it's one of the most dangerous," Jane said. Pausing, she reached for a bottle of olive oil. "It's sad when love turns to hate. Two people who were once happy being married suddenly want to kill each other." She put the bottle into her cart and added with irony, "along with their lawyers."

Christine frowned. "Didn't you have a similar incident in your office with a crazy client a couple of years ago?"

"Hmm," Jane said. "How could I forget?"

Jane's client had reacted violently upon learning she would not get custody of her little boy. She'd lunged across the desk and physically attacked Jane. She was later diagnosed as mentally ill and hospitalized.

"Today's skirmish was not that bad," Jane said, "but scary anyway. And neither has mental illness as an excuse for their behavior." She moved her cart to let another customer pass.

"They were so angry with each other that they couldn't seem to control themselves." She shuddered, remembering.

"It almost drives you to consider another line of work," Christine said dryly.

"That's what Kyle says."

Christine's eyebrows rose. "What, two lawyers in one family is one too many?" she asked.

Christine was teasing, but Jane was serious. "No, he just thinks divorce law puts me in jeopardy when I could be in a safe legal specialty like real estate law or"—she wrinkled her nose—"bankruptcy, both of which would be boring, boring, boring."

Christine put two cans of tomatoes into her cart. "Sounds like Kyle is coming from that age-old husband thing—looking out for the little woman. When Ben starts making noises like that, I ignore him . . . without actually letting him know it, of course."

"When I need to consult Kyle on decisions about my career," Jane said grimly, "I'll ask. Until then, I think I can handle it."

Jane reached for a box of whole-wheat pasta, but she saw Christine's frown and regretted the implications of her statement. Though lately she knew it was true—when had she stopped caring what Kyle thought?

"Actually, it's rare that people go off like those two this morning," she said to Christine. "I used to think I could bring something useful to the table when a couple was thinking about divorce, but now I don't know, Chris. If I can't keep my own marriage together, how can I offer anything constructive to other troubled couples?"

Christine patted her arm. "You're too hard on yourself, Jane."

Maybe, Jane thought, but saying it didn't make it so . . . or change how she felt about her ability to help others. "I was thinking last night, Chris. Why is this happening to me? I mean, if there is a God, why is He heaping so much trouble on me? Is there some message I'm supposed to get out of having my baby kidnapped? Am I supposed to somehow . . ." She searched for words, "find a lesson in all this? Doesn't seem like a very loving God to me."

"I wish I had a nice pat answer," Christine said, obviously dismayed, "but I don't. I do have a suggestion for some short-term relief. How about the four of us, you and Kyle, Ben and I, having a nice dinner out tonight? We could go to that new seafood restaurant, check out the gumbo and stuffed crabs. I hear it's pretty good."

Jane would love it, but she needed to see that Melanie had a nutritious meal, and if she didn't prepare it, the girl would settle for a bowl of cereal. Or pbj, which she appeared to be craving lately. Besides, she couldn't make any commitments for her and Kyle now. They weren't a couple anymore. They were . . . what? Two people living in a house, but separate.

She was on the point of politely refusing when, at the end of the aisle, she caught a glimpse of a woman pushing a cart with a small child in it. As her gaze narrowed on the child, she did a double take. He looked so much like Max . . .

She put out a hand blindly to Christine. "Christine! Turn around. Look!"

"What?" Startled, Christine turned but saw nothing.

"I think I just saw Max!" Jane cried.

"What? Where?"

"The end of the aisle!" Jane bolted away from her cart to find the woman. "Get the manager!" she shouted. "Tell him keep everyone inside. There's a woman with a kidnapped child in the store."

She dashed past surprised shoppers in the aisle. At the end, she turned and ran headlong into a stock boy who was stacking cans of something on an end cap. He gave a yelp as the display collapsed sending cans rolling willy-nilly to the floor. Losing precious seconds and desperately afraid she'd lose the woman, Jane danced and dodged, trying to stay on her feet.

She had to stop her!

When she finally reached the next aisle, she saw several people with carts, but none with a child.

Christine came up beside her, out of breath. "I told a clerk to get the manager and block the exits," she said, huffing and puffing. "Which direction did she go?"

Jane shook her head, frantic and frustrated. "Down this aisle, but she can't have gone far. Quick, go to the front of the store and I'll head this way."

"Right." Christine hurried off, saying over her shoulder, "I'm calling the police too."

Jane was almost running, glancing right and left, desperately searching for the woman and the baby—her baby! Rounding the corner of the last aisle, she stopped short. An abandoned cart blocked traffic. She looked around for its owner, but could see no one. In the cart were a few items, but what gave Jane a pang was a box of animal crackers. The kind that had a little string handle. It was opened. She quickly scrutinized the shoppers in the aisle, thinking to find whoever belonged to the cart, but had no luck. And there was no woman with a baby who looked like Max. But somehow, Jane knew—she knew!—this was the cart. And Max had been in it.

She stood with her heart racing and her gaze frantic, searching, searching. There were women with children—several of them—but not the one woman she was looking for. That woman seemed to have disappeared into thin air. Jane almost cried out loud in despair. Where was she? A woman with a small child couldn't just disappear. She put shaky hands to her mouth and drew a breath to try to calm herself.

I am not giving up! She's here. I know she's here.

She made her way hurriedly to the front of the store and quickly spotted Christine at the customer service window.

"This is the child's mother," Christine said, as Jane approached. "Jane, this is Mr. Morton." Jane nodded at the squat man.

"I have people watching the exits from the time your friend told us what happened. No one with a baby has gone out."

"They must have gotten out!" Jane wanted to scream with frustration.

"There's the service entrance in the rear," Mr. Morton said, "but no customers are allowed back there, only authorized personnel. She'd be spotted."

Christine made a strangled sound. "We're talking a kidnapper here, Mr. Morton! What's to keep her from dashing through whether she's spotted or not?" She looked at Jane in dismay. "If she went out that way, she's gone."

"I could check," Mr. Morton said, but obviously skeptical.

"Thank you," Jane said. "And hurry. Please."

As he scurried away, obviously glad to leave an awkward situation, Jane turned to Christine. "I'm going outside to check the parking lot. She had to have a car. Meet me out there after he checks the back of the store, okay?"

"Yes, of course."

Jane hurried out the main exit and quickly made her way toward a sea of cars and people in the parking lot. She was not likely to find the woman waiting around, but there was nowhere else to go, nothing else to do. The area was crowded with rush-hour shoppers, but none of the people she saw resembled the woman she was looking for. And with dusk falling, it was almost impossible to see inside cars.

As she stood feeling crushing despair, Christine appeared beside her. "Morton said nobody saw anything in the back. Same thing out here?"

"Yeah." Jane's gaze was fixed on the busy parking lot. "Even if she drove right past me in a car, I don't know if I would recognize her. It all happened so fast."

"This is incredible, Jane."

Jane nodded, her arms crossed and close to her body. "I didn't imagine what happened, did I?"

"Only you would know that," Christine said. "So tell me exactly what you saw."

"I looked up as a woman passed at the end of the aisle. There was a baby boy in her cart. When I saw his face, I knew it was Max."

"Like I said, incredible . . ."

Jane frowned. "But now that I've had a few minutes to calm down, I guess I can't be absolutely certain. I mean . . . babies change a lot from six months to twelve months, don't they?"

"Sometimes, but not always. You were after that woman in a flash."

"It was instinct. And I just had one quick glance. Barely three seconds." She gave Christine a pleading look. "But I'd know my own child, wouldn't I?"

"You would." Christine handed Jane her purse. "What details did you notice? Was he wearing a jacket? A cap?"

"He was all bundled up, but no cap." She slipped her purse strap on one shoulder, thinking. "She was wearing a baseball cap. The woman. I remember that."

"Can you describe her?"

Jane thought back for a minute. "I don't think I registered much about her. My eyes were on Max. I was so stunned that all I could think about was getting to him."

"And they were all the way to the end of the aisle?"

"Yes. You couldn't have seen them. Your back was turned."

Christine touched her arm. "That's a pretty good distance, Jane," she said gently.

"Meaning I'm probably mistaken," Jane said. She'd been galvanized by an incredible surge of adrenaline, but now it was gone, and she felt drained and a little shaky. "You think this is just wishful thinking on my part?"

"I think that if I were you and I saw a baby boy and thought for a second it was Max, I would have torn that place apart to find him."

"He looked so much like Max," Jane said with a note of wonder in her voice.

"It's odd that we never glimpsed her again in the store." Christine was also scanning the parking lot. "How could she just disappear?"

"I don't know." Jane's eyes were cloudy with thought. "I'm trying to remember. I think the collar of her jacket was upturned, so with the baseball cap, I couldn't see much of her face." She met Christine's eyes. "Her hair was in a pony tail that stuck out of the cap."

"You remember the color of her hair?"

"Blond," Jane said instantly. "Bleached blond."

"Seems you saw more than you realized," Christine said. "And you don't think she looked even vaguely familiar?"

Jane was shaking her head. "No, I really don't." She stood for a minute with her gaze fixed at a point in the distance, so caught up in thought that she didn't realize a police car had pulled into the parking lot until it stopped at the store entrance.

"Well, they're finally here," Christine said

Two uniformed policemen got out of the patrol car, one a huge man, the other much shorter and overweight. The tall one started for the store entrance, while his partner stayed behind at the vehicle.

"Hello! We're over here," Christine called, waving. "I made the 911 call."

"I'm Officer Burnett," he said. "You called about an abduction?"

Jane spoke up. "My baby was kidnapped in New Orleans at Mardi Gras six months ago. I thought I saw him in the store with a woman. "

"Where are they now?"

Christine made an impatient sound. "We don't know. We lost her."

With barely a glance at Christine, Burnett focused on Jane. "Do you think you can describe her?"

"Only in the vaguest terms," Jane said. "Her hair was blond, and she wore a baseball cap. I think her jacket was a dark color. The baby—" She hesitated as her voice went a little unsteady. "The baby was wearing a red jacket. It happened so fast. One second she was there at the end of the aisle, and the next she'd disappeared. We searched all over the store."

"Did anyone else see her?" he asked.

Jane sighed. "No, only me."

"Uh-huh." Burnett wrote in a small notebook. "You want to come to the station and file a police report?"

"I don't know how it would help," she said doubtfully. "A blond woman with a child is hardly unusual."

"It's your call, of course. But if you think of anything else, give us a call." Burnett tucked his notebook into a back pocket and turned to go back to the car. His partner was already behind the wheel. He paused at the car, looking back at Jane. "I take it the case is active at N.O.P.D.?"

"Yes."

"Who's handling it?"

"Detective Sam Pitre," she told him.

He nodded. "I know him. Good man. I'd mention it to him." He touched the bill of his cap. "Good night, ladies."

Jane stood with Christine for a moment after they drove off. "They think I'm a hysterical female," she said.

"Who cares what they think?" Christine said. "As long as they respond the next time we call 911."

Jane fell in step with her to go back into the store. "Maybe it was my imagination, Chris. But if it really was Max, how likely is it that someone would chance being seen with him in a grocery store less than a mile from where I live?"

"I'd say fairly," Christine said. "Someone who's heartless enough to kidnap a child in broad daylight would surely do something like that."

Jane stopped. "You know what, Chris. I think I will file a police report. It couldn't hurt. I'll check out here and go straight to the police department."

"I think that's smart. As for checking out, that's if our groceries haven't been returned to stock," Christine said, as they made their way back to where they'd abandoned their carts.

"Please. I don't have enough energy to do my shopping all over again," Jane said.

"At least you won't have to cook when finally you get home," Christine said. "That is, if you and Kyle will join us for seafood tonight."

Jane had forgotten all about the invitation.

"I'll have to let you know," she said. That was how she would have to handle everything now—as an individual. Not as half of a married couple.

JANE'S CELL PHONE RANG as she was loading groceries into her car. Thinking it could be Melanie, she dug deep in her purse to find it. She flipped the phone open and looked at the screen. With a frown, she saw that the caller's name and number were not displayed. Instead, what she saw was the word Unknown. Not Melanie after all, but there was something about a ringing phone that she couldn't ignore. There was always a chance it could relate to Max.

"Hello?"

She heard nothing at first and assumed it was a wrong number. Then, on the point of disconnecting, she heard the sound of a child crying. She couldn't disconnect then, not so soon after the sighting of a look-alike Max in the store. She stood listening, frowning. It wasn't the cry of a newborn, which was a distinct sound no mother could ever mistake. It was more like the cry of a small child.

"Hello? *Hello!*" Jane waited, hearing background noise. It sounded like a noisy party. She heard loud music and people talking. And laughing. A bar? But why would anybody have a crying child in a bar?

"Hello?" she repeated, feeling a growing sense of unease. "Who is this?"

"Oops," someone said in a playful voice. Man or woman? Jane couldn't tell. "Sorry about that . . . Jane." The line went dead.

Jane?

Jane stood very still with her gaze focused over the parking lot on nothing in particular. First, a little boy with an uncanny resemblance to Max spotted in the store. And now a call from someone she couldn't dismiss as a wrong number with a crying child in the background. Someone who knew her and knew what had happened to her baby. When she added the incident on the bridge and the tire slashing, it was suddenly frighteningly obvious that she was the target of some sick person's evil intentions.

But who? Why?

Moving numbly, she climbed in behind the wheel with her cell phone still in her hand. She tried to tell herself that she could be letting her imagination run away with her. That she would go crazy if she let herself get caught up in wild speculation.

But what if it wasn't speculation? What if she'd just seen Max and the person who had him had just called to be sure she knew that? *That* was a terrifying thought.

Forget filing a report with the local police. Her fingers shaking, she dialed Sam Pitre's number.

9

KYLE SHOWED UP THAT night as she and Melanie were sitting down to dinner. It was the second night in a row. Jane suspected he was making an effort because of Melanie and not because he wanted to save their marriage. But he appeared haggard as if he hadn't been sleeping well alone in the guest room. She certainly wasn't. But at least he wasn't sleeping somewhere else. She hoped. She guessed they were both finding it difficult making their way through the minefield that was their life now.

She decided to delay mentioning the incident at the market and her call to Sam until after dinner. And since they avoided any contentious subject—including Melanie's pregnancy—dinner was almost pleasant. Anyone looking on might think them an ordinary family.

"I may as well tell you this now, Jane," Melanie announced abruptly over dessert. "I'm not keeping that appointment you made for me with your doctor."

And with that, the almost pleasant atmosphere evaporated. Jane folded her napkin and put it beside her plate. "You don't have any choice, Melanie. You have to be monitored by an obstetrician throughout your pregnancy. If you don't think about yourself, think of your baby."

"Right," Kyle said. "All kinds of things can happen, Mellie, so you're seeing a doctor."

She stood up and carried her plate to the sink. "I didn't mean I wasn't going to see any doctor," she said. "I meant I wasn't going to Jane's doctor. I don't want you butting in, Jane, which you would do if I went to Dr. Roberts. That is who you chose, isn't it?"

"So how are you going to pay?" Jane asked. "You'll need our insurance card."

Melanie looked at Kyle, ignoring Jane. "See, Dad, what I want doesn't count, right? I have to do what I'm told even if I hate it?"

Having a baby at sixteen was bad enough, but if choosing her own doctor would make her less hostile, then so be it. "Do you have someone in mind?" Jane conceded.

"Yes, I have. I went to see her today. I don't have to tell you her name."

Kyle stood up. "Okay, Melanie. That's enough. You have to tell us the name of your doctor. You're under age. You aren't going through a pregnancy without us knowing your doctor and, furthermore, checking her credentials."

"They told me you might say that," Melanie said, "but it doesn't make any difference. I have a legal right to keep everything confidential. I don't have to tell you her name or anything else."

"Is this a free clinic?" Jane asked, watching as she scraped leftover salad from her plate. "I hope not. You need quality care, Mellie. You can't be sure what you might get in a free clinic."

"I'll tell you this much," Melanie said as she rinsed her plate at the sink. "I met this doctor at Christine's church. That should make you feel better."

"It doesn't," Kyle said sternly. "I want to know her name, and I want to know it now!"

"No, Dad."

Jane was shocked. Even for Melanie, this was over the top. "What if there are complications?" Jane asked. "What if something happens and you need to see your doctor and we don't know who to call?"

"You can call 911," Melanie said blithely. She put her plate in the dishwasher, closed it with a bang. "I'm going to bed now," she said over her shoulder. "I'm sleepy."

Kyle appeared bewildered as he watched Melanie climb the stairs. "You think she's okay?"

"She's young and healthy," Jane said. "And as for her doctor's name, we'll get that when we get the report from our insurance." She paused, giving Kyle a look of bafflement. "Sometimes lately I feel as if I've been picked up and dropped into someone else's life."

"Me too."

While Jane tidied up the kitchen, Kyle went to the espresso machine. Once it had been a shared pleasure after dinner. But it had been a long time since they'd done that. These days, Kyle usually retreated to his office and closed the door.

"I had a strange experience at the grocery store," she said, watching him go through the familiar ritual.

"Strange?" He flipped the switch to start brewing.

"You'll think I'm crazy."

"Try me."

"I thought I saw Max today."

He turned, giving her a sharp look.

"I'm not sure," she said hurriedly and told him what happened, including the phone call. "I just wish Christine had seen them too."

"If it was the person who took Max, that would be pretty risky to show up where you often shop," Kyle said, looking thoughtful.

"I told you you'd think I was crazy."

"I didn't say that. And I didn't mean that. The phone call happened right after the encounter in the store?"

"Yes. I've been getting a lot of wrong-number calls lately." She took two small cups down from the cabinet. "But this one freaked me out. I heard a child crying, and the caller said my name. So coming right on the heels of that encounter in the store . . ." She trailed off, leaving the rest of her thought unspoken.

"What do you mean, you get a lot of wrong-number calls? Here? Or on your cell?"

"On my cell," she said. "And before you ask, no name and number are ever displayed. I've assumed they were probably salespeople making blind calls, but now . . . after the call tonight, I'm wondering . . ." She watched him fill two espresso cups, just like old times. "I'm not sure what I'm wondering."

"And the caller didn't say anything except your name?"

"No. Well, she did apologize, but in a snarky voice. It sounded as if a party was going on or maybe it was from a bar."

Kyle was frowning as he passed a tiny cup to her. "You should mention it to Sam. He might be able to trace the number. Or numbers."

"I did call him. I almost talked myself out of it, but when I got thinking . . ."

"What did he say?"

"That he'd check my phone records and maybe we could trace the calls. That he'd follow up with those two officers who came to the grocery store. He told me I should have reported the tire slashing to him as well as to our local police." She gave a rueful shrug. "He was a little put out with me that I hadn't connected these incidents and called him before. And to tell the truth, I felt sort of dim in being so tardy in putting it together too."

"So what's he going to do?"

"He'll get back to me, he said."

"Okay, good. But that'll take a while." He paused, clearly troubled. "I'm with Sam. You're getting phone calls, your tire was slashed, and now it appears someone wants you to think you've seen Max. There could be a reasonable explanation for the phone calls, but not the other stuff. If anything else happens, I want you to tell me then, don't wait."

"Actually, there was something else, but I dismissed it as a malicious prank by somebody getting kicks out of terrorizing a lone woman. It was when I was on the Causeway. Someone was tailgating me, and just before speeding off, he purposely bumped into me from the rear."

Kyle stared at her. "When were you going to get around to telling me that?"

She shrugged. "We weren't exactly talking much, if you recall." She held the tiny cup, thinking back. "What struck me as odd was that it looked like a car I'd noticed earlier in the hospital garage."

"I'm not liking any of this," Kyle said, with a restless move. "It sounds as if you're being stalked, Jane."

She was stunned. It was so incredible that her first thought was to deny it but . . . could he be right? With all the incidents put together, it did seem ominous. "What can we do?"

"I don't know. Yet." He set his cup on the counter. "Stalking is a sneaky, cowardly act meant to terrorize. I'm calling Pitre. But in the future be ultracareful. Don't stay late at your office. In fact, try not to be out after dark at all. And I'll try to get home early too."

Jane waited as he talked to Sam. She could hear only Kyle's end of the conversation, but it was obvious that Sam was on top of it. That he was in touch with the local police. It felt good to hear genuine concern for her in Kyle's voice. As she sipped the espresso he'd made for them, she felt a tiny lessening of her earlier fear. This was the way it should be, the two of them joined in harmony to cope with the extraordinary circumstances complicating their lives.

When he rang off, she said, "Should we tell Melanie?"

"Yeah, I think so," Kyle said. "But let me do it. I don't want to tell her too much."

Jane turned on the dishwasher, grateful that at last there seemed to be a truce between them. For the first time in weeks, she and Kyle were talking without anger or spite tainting their words. It was a welcome respite.

But not enough, she learned later, to bring him back into their bedroom. When she went upstairs, he didn't follow.

For the next few days, Jane stuck close to home. She learned through Henri that the partners were pleased with her efforts to catch up, and, barring a catastrophe, she felt they probably wouldn't ask for her resignation anytime soon. It was the end of the month and she was at her computer entering billable hours when Henri appeared at her desk.

"Jane, we have a problem."

"What is it?"

"Nate Strickland scheduled a deposition in the Leon Waters matter this afternoon at two." He paused. "You're familiar with that case?"

"Yes." More than familiar. When she'd fallen behind, the Waters case had been taken from her and passed to Nate Strickland, who was fresh out of law school. As well as the nephew of one of the partners. Jane had felt embarrassed and humiliated at the slight. Nate had spent the first few days boning up on the case and the next month interrupting Jane with questions on what to do next.

"Nate just got a call from his wife," Henri said. "She's in labor and the baby is four weeks early."

"Oh, dear." She sat up. "So, what do you need from me?"

"The witness is flying in from Little Rock. Nate agreed to take the deposition at the Airport Marriott for the convenience of the witness, who is catching an eight o'clock return flight. I'd like you to take the deposition." He glanced at the stack of files on her desk. "Can you make it?"

For about three seconds, Jane considered refusing. She could tell Henri about the bridge incident a few days ago and that Kyle thought she should avoid the possibility of another encounter. But she was still in the process of proving to Henri and the partners that she took her job seriously. She had to do it.

"I'll be glad to do it, Henri. Where is the file?"

"It's on Nate's desk." Rubbing his hands together, he smiled. "I knew I could count on you, Jane."

WITHIN MINUTES, SHE WAS easing onto the Causeway with some apprehension, but this time nothing was out of the ordinary. Traffic moved along with no glitches, no one following, no one bumping her. She met the witness at the Marriott, took the deposition, and was back in her car by noon, which was when she decided she had time to see Sam Pitre and still make it back across the lake well before the rush hour.

The N.O.P.D. First District was at the edge of the French Quarter on North Rampart Street in what was once the Old Bank of Louisiana Building. Today, as always when she entered, she was struck by a sense of history. The building had been built in 1826 by a firm of famous architects. And, briefly, after the Civil War, it had been the state capitol. Inside now, twenty-first-century technology enforced strict security, but it was impossible not to feel ghosts of the city's illustrious past.

Sam smiled with real pleasure at the sight of her. "Jane.

This must be ESP. I was just thinking about you. In fact, I was going to call."

Jane felt her heart skip a beat. "Tell me."

"It's about those kids we rescued a few weeks ago." He came around his desk and closed his office door. "I know you were concerned about their welfare." He touched her arm to guide her to a chair. "Here, sit down. That can wait." When she was seated, he propped a hip on his desk in front of her. "What brings you to the French Quarter today?"

"A deposition. This one I got through without bloodshed."

"Family law." He smiled, shaking his head. "It sounds benign, but I bet you could tell some stories."

She gave him a humorous version of the scene in her office with the Chastains. "Michelle tells me the next time I schedule one of those meetings, I need to put on a flak jacket."

Sam's smile faded a bit. "She's joking, but I've been at crime scenes where disgruntled clients have left a lawyer crippled or, once as I recall, dead."

"Speaking as a cop," she said dryly.

"I am a cop. You be careful."

"I will, Sam," she said. "Now, please tell me they've indicted that horrible couple."

"Close, but not quite. They pleaded guilty to several counts of child endangerment."

"They knew they wouldn't get much sympathy from a jury," Jane said.

"A jury would throw the book at them," Sam said. "This way, they're sentenced at the judge's discretion, which won't be light, I promise you."

"What about the children?"

"You saw the report, didn't you?"

"No. I haven't seen any report."

He frowned. "I sent it to Marilee at Child Search. She didn't tell you?"

"I haven't been in for a while, Sam. I'm cutting back on my time there." She gave a wry smile. "I'm told I need to spend more time with my family and my day job."

"You're told? C'mon. I have trouble believing you'd let anyone tell you something like that."

She laughed shortly. "I didn't like hearing it, but I tell myself that constructive criticism is helpful."

"Are we talking about your job or your personal life?"

"Both." He studied her, narrow-eyed. "Did I sense something a little off between you and Kyle at the hospital?"

Jane realized she had waded into deep waters. She studied her hands. "We're no different from other couples who have lost a child, Sam. It's been a very rocky road. I don't think anyone can truly understand if you haven't been there."

"I have been there," he said.

She looked up in surprise. "What?"

"My ex moved a thousand miles away and took my son with her. I know that's not the same as what you've been through, but it's tough."

"I didn't know."

"I never mentioned it. But sometimes I miss him so much that when I'm alone in my apartment—especially in the middle of the night—I swear I can hear his voice."

"The same thing happens to me . . . a lot," she said. "It's hard."

"Yeah." He managed a crooked smile. "But at least I can see Tray as often as I can afford to fly to Sacramento."

"Tray?" She smiled gently.

"Samuel James Pitre, the third."

Her gaze went to a framed photo of a grinning toddler on the credenza behind his desk. "How do you bear it, Sam?"

"I fill the days and nights with work."

"And I volunteer at Child Search."

He was studying her face. "You've done a lot of good, Jane."

She got up out of her chair and moved to the window, looking down on Rampart Street at tourists riding in a horse-drawn carriage. When she first married Kyle, they took Melanie on a carriage tour of the French Quarter. She was terrified by the horse. It was Jane she clung to until the ride ended. She shook her head, sad that those days were long gone.

She turned back to find Sam watching her, looking troubled. "I need to get back across the lake, Sam. But first . . . I know Kyle told you about my seeing Max and the phone calls." She waved her hand. "And all the other stuff."

"Yeah," he said. "The local police have been busy. They've interviewed the manager and the clerks at the supermarket. And they've talked to your office cleaning people about the slashed tire. Nobody saw anything."

"Kyle thinks I'm being stalked."

"Considering the string of incidents, it's a logical conclusion."

"But it's been several days now and nothing's happened." She gave a nervous laugh. "I was on the lookout for that car when I drove the Causeway today, but he never showed up."

"He?" His eyes narrowed. "You think it was a man?"

"I don't know. I couldn't tell."

"How about when you heard your name in the last phone call? Was it a man or a woman?"

"Again, I couldn't tell. There was so much background noise." She paused as Sam settled back in his chair.

"I know you need to be in the city sometimes to do your job, Jane, but considering the stuff that's happening, I'd like to see you staying close to home. Don't go on the Causeway if you can help it."

Jane felt heartened and, at the same time, anxious over his attitude. He was clearly concerned about her. She picked up her purse, ready to go. "You think it's that serious?"

"I think you can't be too careful." He walked with her to the door. "Someone took your child, and if it really was Max you saw at the store, it puts the case in a whole new light."

"But it's bad news mixed with good news, isn't it?" she asked, looking up at him. "I mean if it really was Max, then we know he's alive."

"It's a definite possibility."

In spite of Sam's sober warning, Jane wasn't thinking much about being safe as she got back on the Causeway heading home. She was too caught up in the possibility that there was a break in the case. And trying not to invest too much emotion in hoping. She was afraid of it now. She was afraid of more crushing disappointment. For with disappointment came pain. With Kyle so distant and Melanie so hostile, she didn't think she could survive much more pain.

KYLE WAS SEATED ALONE at a restaurant downtown. He often found it beneficial to conduct business at lunch, but today his client had cancelled at the last minute. He wasn't much interested in eating, but he would have to order something. It had been a long time since he'd enjoyed food. Since Max's disappearance, his appetite had mostly disappeared too.

He was studying the menu without enthusiasm when suddenly the chair across from him was jerked out and a man sat down.

"Enjoying your lunch, counselor?"

Nothing friendly about that smile, Kyle thought. He carefully closed the menu and laid it aside. "Joseph Kaski, right?"

"You recognized me, eh? That's surprising. I don't have the wardrobe I used to have."

That was an understatement. Beneath a cheap hooded jacket hanging on his emaciated frame, Kaski wore a T-shirt emblazoned with a New Orleans Saints logo. Not one article of this clothing looked as if it had been washed lately. Including Kaski.

"It's been a while."

"Six months."

Kyle didn't offer to rise and shake hands with a man he'd last seen in court, weeping like a baby. That had been after the judge found him guilty of bilking his business partner, Kyle's client, out of two and a half million dollars. "Has it been that long?"

"Seems like a lifetime to me," Kaski said. To anyone listening, the conversation might have sounded ordinary. But there was nothing ordinary about the nervous tic on Kaski's face or the fanatical light in his eyes. Alarmed, Kyle knew from past experience that Kaski was a loose cannon. Anything might happen. Hopefully, the maître d' was watching.

"How've you been, Mr. Kaski?"

"How would you be if you'd lost your home, your business, and your reputation, and on top of that your wife divorced you and your two sons were too embarrassed to be seen with you?"

"I'd feel bad," Kyle said, finally catching the eye of the maître d', who watched them with a condescending smirk. If he could see the look on Kaski's face right now, instead of smirking, he would be buzzing for the bouncer. This was not the kind of place that employed a bouncer, but today might be the day they needed one. Kyle hoped he wouldn't have to assume the role.

He settled back in his chair, thinking to present a calmness he didn't feel. "I'm sorry you're having personal problems, Mr. Kaski."

"You're sorry."

"Yes, I am. Now if you'll excuse me." He looked intentionally back at his menu.

Kaski leaned forward with a menacing look and spoke in a low tone. "You were the slimy character who cost me everything, mister! Don't sit there and tell me you don't know a reason I might have a bone to pick with you."

"You had legal representation, Mr. Kaski. Top-of-the-line legal representation, as I recall. You should be talking to your lawyer, not me."

"You think I didn't try? You think I didn't haunt his office after the deal went down?" Kaski's mouth twisted in a sneer. "After the two of you sold me down the river."

Kyle knew better than to try to reason with a man in denial. Kaski had been in a no-win situation although he'd proclaimed his innocence to the end. The fact that his lawyer had kept him out of jail was evidence of good—even superior—legal representation.

Kyle folded his napkin and made a point of looking at his watch and again catching the eye of the maître d'. "I have an appointment in a few minutes, sir, so I'll ask, why are you telling me this?"

"Two reasons. One is that I want to hear you admit that you had a hand in ruining my life."

"I'm a lawyer, Kaski. I did my job, representing your adversary. If you have a complaint, it should be made to the lawyer who represented you."

Kaski gave a short laugh as he dug from his jacket pocket a section of folded newspaper. "It's a little late for that now. Take a look at the number two reason."

He shoved the paper over to Kyle. "This was in today's *Picayune* . . . on page eight."

Kyle hadn't yet read the newspaper. He glanced at the page and saw nothing relevant. "Mr. Kaski, I need to—"

"Look again, down toward the bottom, on the left." He jabbed his finger at the page.

Kyle sighed, but scanned the headline, and read out loud. "Missing man found dead in Atchafalaya Basin." He frowned, looking up at Kaski. "I don't see—"

"Read on."

Kyle paused, feeling a premonition of bad news from the look on Kaski's face. He read the first few words of the article and stopped short when he read the name of the dead man. "Thomas Parker," he murmured. Then, looking up at Kaski, "your lawyer."

Kaski smiled evilly. "He's nobody's lawyer now."

"You don't seem shocked," Kyle said.

Kaski laughed. "What goes around comes around, as they say." He picked up the paper. "They think he drowned. Parker was big into bass fishing. Traveled to bass tournaments all over. He told me that once. That would have been before he double-crossed me." He pretended to scan the article casually. "You wouldn't think a seasoned sportsman would fall out of his boat and drown like that, would you?"

Kyle felt sick watching Kaski savor details of his lawyer's death, smiling with a Charles Manson gleam in his eyes.

"How long ago did this happen?" Kyle asked.

"Who knows?" Kaski gave an exaggerated shrug. "If a body's been in water for a few days, it's hard to tell when he fell in."

"Fell in."

"Yeah." Kaski picked up a shaker of salt and studied it. "They found him in brackish water. There's salt in brackish water. Not as much as is in the Gulf, but enough so that the forensics people would have trouble trying to pin down a time of death."

"You seem to know a lot about it," Kyle said.

Another shrug. "Nah, I'm just killing time in front of the TV now, you know? It's amazing what you pick up watching that stuff."

Was the man admitting he killed Parker? Kyle longed to get up and call Sam Pitre. But he knew Kaski wasn't done.

Kaski replaced the salt and looked directly at Kyle. "Here's a funny thing about Parker. Well, I guess funny isn't quite accurate, but anyway, seemed he couldn't get any luck but bad. I should take some comfort in that, I guess, but for my part, it's hard to rake up much sympathy . . . considering."

Kyle guessed from the look on Kaski's face that he was gearing up to deliver his knock-out punch. "You'd know how it is," Kaski went on, "you having had some bad luck too?"

Kyle frowned, eyeing him warily. "I don't follow."

"Parker lost his son six or seven months ago. You heard about that?"

"No," Kyle said carefully, getting a heavy feeling in his chest. "I didn't. And I don't know where you're going with this, Kaski, but if it's about Max, you better spit it out. Now."

Kaski drew out a long sigh as if pondering the mysteries of a cruel fate. "Who said anything about Max? We're talking about Parker. About his teenage son. The one who hung himself. Happened in their barn. Kid had two sisters who were big into horses."

Stunned, Kyle had his cell phone out thinking to call Sam Pitre. Kaski would be long gone by the time Sam got to the restaurant, but it was worth a try. "You killed Parker's son?"

"I'm not saying I did . . . or I didn't." Kaski stood up abruptly but leaned over and pointed out an item on the menu. "Seeing as how you haven't ordered yet, I recommend the pompano en papillote. Comes baked in paper. They're famous for it . . . but you'd know that, wouldn't you? Me, I can't afford it anymore, but it used to be my favorite."

"Did you take Max? Do you know anything about my son?" But Kaski was already making his way toward the door.

"Mr. Madison, is there a problem here?" The maître d' gave a distasteful look at Kaski as he brushed past.

Kyle rose, determined not to let him get away, but as he got close to the front of the restaurant, Kaski suddenly, with a mighty heave, overturned a table and shoved it at Kyle. While Kyle swerved to avoid it, Kaski hefted a chair and tossed it at

Kyle's head. He ducked, but not quick enough. A leg of the chair caught him on the temple.

Pain exploded in his head. For a second or two, he saw stars. Then, shaking his head to clear it, he realized the maître d' was grasping his arm, leading him to a chair. The restaurant was abuzz with curiosity. Realizing it, the maître d' stepped in front of Kyle.

"I do apologize for that, sir," he said, thrusting a dinner napkin into Kyle's hand. "But he seemed to know you. He called you by name, which is why I didn't stop him at the door."

"It's okay." With the napkin pressed to his temple, Kyle looked out the window, trying to find Kaski. But he'd disappeared, melting into the lunchtime crowd that swarmed the sidewalks on Canal Street.

"Mr. Madison?"

Kyle looked blankly at the maître d'. "What?"

"Shall I call an ambulance?"

"No, I'm okay," Kyle said, in spite of the throbbing pain in his head.

The maître d' looked toward the window where Kaski was long gone. "It's apparent that that fellow was experiencing some . . . ah, stress."

Kyle took a twenty-dollar bill from his wallet. Murmuring that he had an appointment, he left.

10

KYLE WENT DIRECTLY TO his office. He couldn't remember the last time he'd been this angry. His assistant rose as if to ask him a question, then when he met her gaze, she sat back down and clicked on her computer. To prevent being asked about the bandage on his temple or a lot more unwelcome questions, he personally cancelled all his afternoon appointments and opened the case file of the client who'd brought charges against Joseph Kaski.

It had been one of many cases he'd looked at after Max was taken, but nothing in it had suggested that Kaski—or anyone connected to Kaski—was linked to the kidnapping. And reading it now revealed nothing new. Even after the bizarre confrontation in the restaurant, he found it difficult to believe Kaski would have been so deranged that he would kidnap an innocent baby. On the other hand, the man's obvious glee over Thomas Parker's death was alarming. It was plain he'd wanted to plant in

Kyle's mind the suspicion that Parker's demise and his son's suicide were not accidents.

But was he so deranged that he murdered Parker and his son? And if so, could he have taken Max?

Kyle buried his face in his hands at the thought of his tiny son meeting such a fate. He wouldn't believe it. Jane's incredible sighting at the grocery store had given him hope that Max would be found alive and well. But he couldn't ignore the possibility that such a connection might exist. Closing the file, he left his office, got in his car, and drove to Sam Pitre's office.

"Parker's body was found in Terrebonne Parish," Sam said after Kyle was done telling him about his encounter with Kaski. "That takes it out of Orleans Parish jurisdiction. But I can pull up the initial report and get some information." He began typing with two fingers.

"Even if the autopsy reveals drowning as the cause of death," Kyle said, "that doesn't clear Kaski, does it? According to the newspaper, Parker was found near his boat in a remote area of the Atchafalaya. I don't see how an experienced fisherman could fall out of his boat and drown in a swamp."

"Could've had a heart attack," Sam said, still clicking keys.

"Which would show on his autopsy."

"Here it is." Sam paused, reading. "Cause of death was drowning, Kyle. The medical examiner found water in his lungs."

"An autopsy would have revealed a heart attack," Kyle said.

"It would." Sam pushed away from his computer. "But it didn't."

"That doesn't prove Kaski didn't push him out of his boat," Kyle said.

"No, but considering where he was found, the number of days he was in the water, and there not being any sign of trauma on the body, he—"

"How do you know that?" Kyle demanded.

"The M.E. would not have certified the death an accident if he had found any visible trauma. In his opinion, it was not a homicide."

"So if he did murder his lawyer, he gets away with it?"

"It's possible." Sam was shaking his head.

Kyle touched his bandaged temple and winced. "It could be that he hunted me down just to jerk my chain, Sam, but I don't think so. He looked like a man capable of murder."

"He'll find he's opened a can of worms messing around in this case," Sam said grimly. "So to start with, why don't you tell me the details of the case that connects you to Kaski."

Kyle briefed him, giving out as many details as he was legally able to. When Kyle was done, Sam put his pen down and rocked back in his chair, stacking his hands behind his head. "What was your client's name?"

"Jefferson Adams. And if Kaski did have anything to do with Parker's death—and his boy's—it beats me why he wouldn't have chosen to take out his frustration and anger on Adams instead. As co-owner, Adams got everything. He's sitting in Kaski's office as we speak, reaping the benefits of the settlement."

"Maybe Adams will be next . . . if Kaski is the diabolical killer he's trying to make us believe he is. Or, like you say, maybe he's just trying to jerk you around."

"Which doesn't change the fact that Parker is dead and so is his teenage son." Kyle focused on a magnolia tree visible through the window. "And my son is missing." His gaze shifted back to Sam. "That's too much coincidence, Detective."

"It is," Sam agreed. "But I don't see how we tie it into Jane's seeing Max at the store. With a woman."

"About Jane," Kyle said. "I don't think we should mention Kaski to her. At least not until we know for certain that it's simply the ravings of a disturbed man."

"Whatever you say," Sam said.

Kyle wasn't sure how to interpret the detective's expression, but he had a clue from Sam's next words.

"Everything okay with you two?"

Kyle frowned. "Why would you think otherwise?"

Sam shrugged. "I picked up some chilly vibes when the two of you came here a couple of weeks ago."

"Everything's fine," Kyle lied.

Obviously skeptical, Sam waited a long moment, studying Kyle's face. But he let it go. "By the way, I was able to get a subpoena today and access the records of Jane's incoming cell-phone calls. Several calls originated from the same throwaway phone. There's no way to trace the caller's name, but I was able to trace the cell towers and pinpoint the general location."

"And?"

"Some here in Mandeville, some in Baton Rouge."

"Really?" Kyle thought a minute. "In reviewing the Kaski case today, I turned up information that Kaski had a fishing camp somewhere on the river above Baton Rouge."

"I'll check it out," Sam said. "If he's on hard times, as he told you, he might be using a throwaway phone."

"But why call Jane and not me?" Kyle asked.

Sam lifted his shoulders, shrugging. "Jane would be the most vulnerable. But that's pure speculation. Let me look at this clown a little closer. I'll keep you posted."

When Kyle left a few minutes later, he felt pretty certain that if Kaski was involved in Max's disappearance, Pitre would soon know. But it bothered him that the detective had picked up on the tension between him and Jane. As messed up in his head as he was about his marriage and his future with Jane, it wasn't anybody else's business. Especially Sam Pitre's.

Jane made a conscious effort to settle down over the next few days and focus on the things that were within her control rather than stewing over things she couldn't control. She would have thrown herself into her work at Child Search, but between her caseload and making more time at home, little was left over for Child Search. The good news was that she was truly on top of things at her job. She'd had a string of successes. Today she'd finally managed to effect a compromise between a long-time client and the woman's stubborn ex-husband after they'd fought for eighteen months. It felt good.

When Jane pulled into her garage that evening after a quick stop at the supermarket, Christine slipped in before she could click the remote to close it. It was just as well, she thought. She couldn't avoid her friend forever.

"Hello, stranger."

"Christine. Hi."

"So . . . where've you been hiding?"

"Work, work, work." Jane reached in the car and grabbed a couple of sacks from the supermarket. She handed one to Christine and moved to the door. "After refereeing a contentious case between two hardheaded exes, I then battled half of Mandeville, or so it seemed, to pick up something for dinner tonight at Winn-Dixie. What's going on with you?"

"Nothing as interesting." Christine dropped a sack on the counter in the kitchen and leaned against it, clearly intending to stay and chat. "But I've been concerned. You've missed the last three sessions at Curves. You skipped book club. I've left three voice mails."

"I'm sorry, Chris." Jane put a gallon of milk in the refrigerator. "Is everything okay?"

"As okay as ever." As Jane took a kettle from the stovetop and filled it with water, she desperately wished she could tell Christine just how un-okay everything really was. Instead, she said, "I'll make us some tea."

"Is it Kyle?"

When Jane hesitated, Christine made a pained sound. "I'm

sorry. You don't have to answer that. It's none of my business." She paused a beat or two, then went on, "It's just that I'm so worried about you, Jane."

Jane turned to look at her, trying to come up with words when she couldn't truly explain. "Kyle hasn't moved out . . . yet. And I do need your friendship, Christine. Don't ever doubt that."

"Well, is it Melanie?"

Jane gave her a quick look. "Melanie? She's fine. Why would you think she isn't?"

"Because I haven't seen her either. Usually, she's in and out of the house with Daniel constantly, but lately she's as elusive as you are."

"Did Daniel say anything?"

"About what? About Melanie not being around?" Christine watched Jane rummage around in a cabinet selecting tea. "No. I would grow old waiting if I expected a teenage boy to tell me what was going on."

"Teenage girls aren't much more communicative; at least Melanie isn't." Jane held up a box. "Is Earl Grey okay?"

Frowning, Christine took the tea bag. "Is this about Kyle? Is Melanie choosing sides with him?"

Jane sat down, relieved that the conversation now focused on problems that were safe to discuss. "She's definitely siding with Kyle, but wouldn't you expect that? I'm the stepmother as she's only too happy to remind me. And often."

Christine made a face. "Teenagers can be such tyrants, can't they? It's all about me, me, me."

"Just wait," Jane said. "You've got two girls coming up after Daniel."

"Lovely," Christine said dryly.

Jane was thoughtful as she opened a tea bag. "Or maybe not, Christine. Your girls may stay as sweet and even-tempered as they are now." She sighed. "Mellie used to be sweet and even-tempered."

Christine dropped a tea bag into her cup. "You mustn't let her steal your joy."

"Joy? You've got to be kidding." Jane rose as the kettle whistled. "There is no such thing in this house. Mellie is so angry with me."

"I guess, from Melanie's point of view, it doesn't help that Kyle is sleeping in the guest room," Christine said after a few moments.

"I have to do something to win her back, Chris. I just don't know how. She hates me."

"She doesn't hate you. She feels responsible for Max's being taken. You've done everything humanly possible to ease Melanie's guilt, Jane. She'll get beyond this. I'm praying for her. And you."

But will you pray for either of us when you find out what she's done, Christine?

Jane brought the kettle over to the table and filled both their cups, returned it to the stove, and sat down. "When I think of my life as it was six months ago, it seems like a dream, Chris. I was so happy. We were *all* so happy. I can't imagine ever feeling real joy again."

"You will . . . and you'll win Melanie back. I know it."

"She's making me the villain in all this—it's so unfair!" Jane cried in a frustrated voice. "Why do I have to be the lone person holding the key to Melanie's problems?"

Christine stirred sugar into her cup. "Who said life was supposed to be fair?"

"How about just sometimes? I'd settle for that."

"Oh, come on." Christine smiled over her cup. "She'll come around . . . at least by the time she's twenty."

Jane laughed, feeling a rush of affection for her friend. How she wished she could pour out her heart fully and hear Christine's down-to-earth advice. But until she knew who the father of Melanie's baby was, she couldn't say anything.

Christine gazed thoughtfully into her cup. "We need to figure out a way for you to regain Melanie's trust. You can't expect her to find fault with Kyle. She's always been a daddy's girl. That'll never change. But she needs to realize that she needs a mommy too. That would be you."

Melanie did indeed need a mommy right now . . . in the worst way. Christine had that right. Jane just had to find a way to work that miracle.

KYLE APPEARED THAT NIGHT as Jane was adding final touches to dinner. He seemed to be making it a regular thing to show up now. She knew the reason was his concern for Melanie, and not her. Yet she was glad for it. She'd baked a chicken with wild rice and veggies, simple and nutritious. They might not notice her efforts in the kitchen, but Jane was actually beginning to enjoy cooking. It was only as she turned from the stove and took a good look at him that she saw his bandaged temple.

"What happened?" she exclaimed.

"It's just a scratch," Kyle said. "I should have ducked, but didn't."

"Someone hit you?" Melanie asked, wide-eyed.

"It's nothing. A disagreement over a case that happened a long time ago."

Jane gave him a long, studied look. "And you tell me that family law is dangerous."

"I stand corrected," he said dryly. "What's for dinner?"

"I've been thinking," Jane said a few minutes later when they were eating. "Labor Day weekend is coming up. Melanie, why don't we take off and go to the beach?"

"No, thanks," Melanie said without missing a beat.

Kyle looked at Jane. "Do you mean Gulf Shores?"

"Yes, it only takes a couple of hours to drive there. I could call and check if the condo we rented a couple of years ago is available." She had been pregnant with Max then. The memories would be painful, but maybe they would be healing too.

Melanie stood abruptly and took her plate to the sink. "You two can go. I'm staying here."

"I can't make it," Kyle said, "but there's no reason why you can't go with Jane. It'll be good for you to have some quality time together."

Jane shot Kyle an exasperated look. Suggesting quality time with Jane was a surefire way to turn Melanie off. "I was thinking you might invite Anne-Marie," she said. "Remember what a great time you had together the last time we were there?"

Melanie put her plate in the dishwasher and gave the door a firm slam. "I need to go upstairs and work on an essay for Honors English." She took only a step when Kyle spoke.

"Melanie!"

She stopped and without turning dropped her head back and, heaving a huge sigh, looked up at the ceiling. "What is it?"

"What is it?" Kyle muttered a curse under his breath. "For starters, it's rude to flat-out refuse Jane's idea to go to the beach for no reason. I'd think you'd welcome a change. Why wouldn't you want to go?"

Melanie turned and gave him an insolent look. "Why wouldn't you?"

Yes, why wouldn't you? Jane watched Kyle struggle to keep his temper. It was unusual for Melanie to show him disrespect. Jane, of course, was always fair game.

Jane knew he didn't want to spend a weekend in a condo and be forced to share a bedroom with her. And to tell the truth, Jane didn't like the idea any better. When he decided to sleep with her again—if ever—she wanted it to be his idea and for the right reason.

Kyle gave a tired sigh. "You know why I'm not going, Melanie. But that doesn't mean you and Jane shouldn't go. You could spend time walking the beach, watching the sun rise and set.

Bring your camera along and take some shots. It's been a long time since I've seen you pick up your camera. You used to love doing that too."

Melanie looked at Jane. "Is this an order? Do I have to go?"

Jane felt her throat go tight. Tears were very close, but she couldn't let Melanie see how easily she could hurt her. Or Kyle. Neither should be given that satisfaction.

"No, you don't have to go, Mellie," she said quietly and rose to clear the table. "We'll do it another time."

TO JANE'S SURPRISE, BOTH Kyle and Melanie stayed at home for most of the weekend. On Saturday, Kyle took care of a few chores around the house, leaving only to go to Home Depot or the car wash. Melanie worked at the computer on an English assignment . . . alone in her room, of course. Jane puttered in the yard. The activities of the family were reminiscent of how it used to be. But instead of being comforted, Jane couldn't shake a feeling that disaster lurked around the corner.

Sunday morning, after fixing breakfast for Kyle and Melanie, she went out to the patio with the newspaper. As she sipped her coffee, she inhaled the sweet scent of magnolia from the huge tree that shaded the patio. With the paper forgotten on her lap, she was watching two blue jays squabbling over turf when she heard sounds from next door.

Christine stood on her patio. Jane guessed she must have attended early church, as she didn't usually see the O'Brians on Sunday until well past lunchtime Now, spotting Jane, she waved and began making her way across the lawn.

She frowned when she got close enough to look at Jane's face. "Well, that makes two of us who didn't sleep well," she said.

Jane set her mug down. "Is it that obvious?"

"To someone who knows you pretty well, yes." Christine

removed her sunglasses to reveal red, puffy eyes. "These bags are the result of a splitting headache. I spent most of the night walking the floor worrying about my teenage son."

"Daniel?"

"He's the only teenage son I've got." With her sunglasses perched on top of her head, she eyed the mug in Jane's hand. "Got any more of that?"

"Inside. Help yourself." While Christine went inside for coffee, Jane opened the newspaper. She was reading the advice column when Christine came back. "Maybe Dear Abby could advise me on getting back in Melanie's good graces," she said. "I suggested a trip to the beach, but she wasn't interested."

"Take me," Christine said. "I'd love a weekend to do nothing but listen to the surf. Oh, I forgot. I've got three kids who'd want to tag along. Well, two of them would." She took a sip of coffee. "As for Dear Abby, after she advises you, maybe she could suggest a way for me to figure out what's bugging Daniel."

Jane held her breath. "What makes you think something's bugging him?"

Christine rested her mug on one knee and looked out over the lawn thoughtfully. "He's never been moody, but lately he's like a bear with a thorn in its paw."

"He was out late last night?"

"Yeah. Till three a.m." She was frowning now as she gazed out over the lawn. "It's so unlike him to behave like that. What could he be doing at that hour?"

"He won't say anything?"

"Nothing. He's grounded, of course." She made a face. "Now I'll have to take him to school, which means I have to leave for work a full half hour early." She shook her head, her gaze in the distance. "Which reminds me," she said, setting her coffee on the small table between them. "Why has Melanie stopped riding to school with him?"

"You think she would tell me?" Jane sighed. "Who knows? She asked if she could ride in with me a couple of weeks ago, but she wouldn't tell me why."

About the time I found out she was pregnant.

"I guess they outgrew each other," Christine said quietly with a note of regret in her voice. Hearing it, Jane wanted with all her heart to tell Christine what she suspected about Melanie and Daniel.

"Was Melanie out last night?" Christine asked.

"No, she had an Honors English assignment and, as far as I know, she worked most of the weekend on it."

"Well, at least that's a productive way to spend her time." Christine slipped her sunglasses on again and turned to Jane. "I can't believe she would pass up a weekend at Gulf Shores."

"It was *my* idea," Jane said. To her dismay, she felt tears suddenly welling in her eyes. She turned, trying to control them, but it was no use. They spilled over and streamed down her cheeks.

Christine sprang up. "Oh, dear, Jane." She thrust a napkin into her hand. "I'm so sorry you're having such a problem. I know that girl is going to wake up someday soon and realize what a great mom you are . . . have always been."

Jane mopped at her tears as Christine patted her back.

"I can't believe I'm blubbering over this," she said in choked voice. "I hope what you say is true, Chris."

Both turned suddenly when the patio door slid open and Kyle stepped out. Jane's first impulse was to hide her face to keep him from seeing that she'd been crying. But with one look at him, she forgot. Something was wrong. She felt a flutter of alarm.

"What is it, Kyle? What's wrong?"

"I've just been listening to the news on the local channel," he told them. "George Crandall has been arrested."

"That's Dr. Faye Crandall's husband, isn't it?" This from Christine. Faye Crandall was one of the physicians in her practice.

"That's the one," Kyle said. "According to the TV reporter, he's been running a racket from his law office."

"Oh my." Jane set her coffee on the table. "What kind of racket?"

"Don't tell me. Let me guess," Christine said. "It has to do with adopting babies."

"You know about it?" he asked, frowning.

"No more than is public knowledge. He's the guy to see if you want to adopt a baby and don't want to wait. If you have the cash, George Crandall is your man."

"That's not illegal," Jane said. "It's not something I'd ever consider, but I know someone who seriously considered going to him when she couldn't conceive. The way she explained it to me is that George Crandall matches birth mothers with adoptive couples, skipping the hassles you have to cope with in a traditional adoption process. The adoptive parents pay all the obstetric expenses plus a hefty fee to Crandall. When the baby's born, it's handed over, problem solved."

She looked questioningly at Kyle. "So why has Crandall been arrested?"

Kyle sat down. "I only know what I heard on TV. It's well known that George Crandall is the go-to person to short circuit the system to adopt a baby. The problem is that Crandall has more customers than babies. So to meet the demands, it's alleged that he's been buying babies."

"But how do you buy a baby?" Jane asked.

"They don't stock them at Wal-Mart," Christine said.

"According to the TV report," Kyle said, "he pays minor teenage girls to get pregnant, and after paying all her expenses, he gets the baby."

"That's horrible!" Jane said.

"It's also pretty risky," Christine said, "even if you get beyond how reprehensible it is."

"Turns out," Kyle said, "he was still unable to harvest enough babies, so the police think he began getting infants from other sources, no questions asked about where they came from."

Jane stared at him with wide eyes. "Oh, Kyle, do you think—?"

"I'm not thinking anything yet. But I've just spoken to Sam Pitre. I told him I want to know the age of every male child Crandall has sold in the last seven months. And I want details as to how he got those particular babies."

Jane unconsciously clasped her hands to her heart. "Do you think it's possible that Max—"

"I don't know, Jane," he said. "Let's not jump to conclusions yet. Sam had the same thought as I had when Crandall was arrested. So he's already on top of it."

Jane's eyes filled with tears again. *Please, please, let this be the day we find Max.*

It was Christine, not Kyle, who rose and, with an exclamation of sympathy, put her arms around Jane.

11

JANE FORCED HERSELF TO complete her to-do list the next day before leaving her office and driving across the lake to see Sam Pitre. Her urgency to know about George Crandall overcame her nervousness about driving the Causeway. Maybe, just maybe, she would find out that Max was one of the "sold" babies. And they would find him. And her life would be complete again.

Sam appeared unsurprised to see her. "Jane. I can guess why you're here."

"George Crandall," she said simply.

"Yeah." He closed the door and waved her to a chair.

Jane perched on the edge of it and gave him a pleading look. "Please tell me you have details on all the babies."

"Some of them, but not all, Jane." He rubbed the back of his neck, looking tired. "If you'd called, I would have saved you a trip. We've subpoenaed Crandall's records, and I've spent the last twenty-four hours poring over them. Whether we have them all or not, we aren't sure."

He saw the look on her face and added hurriedly, "Don't worry. I'll eventually see everything, but it's not the same as if the case were here in Orleans Parish."

"I don't know if I can stand this!" Unable to sit still, Jane rose and began to pace. "Max could very well be one of those children. He could have been placed with parents who live in . . . in . . . Alaska! In the Middle East, for heaven's sake! Time is passing." She stopped, giving him a look of anguish. "Don't they understand how we parents"—she tapped her heart—"feel when there is even a glimmer of a possibility that our child—my baby—might be one of the stolen ones? And if he is, I might be able to touch him again. I might be able to hold him again . . ." Her voice failed. "K-kiss him again."

He moved from behind his desk to go to her. "We understand that, Jane," he said quietly. "Believe me. The detectives in Metairie are doing their job by the book. If the case were on my desk, I'd be doing the same thing, acting the same way."

She nodded mutely, but she couldn't stop tears filling her eyes. Turning away from him, she took a deep breath. "I'm sorry, Sam. You're right. I'm just so—" She couldn't finish and couldn't hold back a sob.

Sam touched her hair lightly. "Ah, Jane, I wish I could do something."

She made an inarticulate sound and turned her eyes up to his. He looked at her face, wet with tears, and took her in his arms. She broke down then, weeping in pure anguish, needing the comfort and sympathy he offered. She so much needed the reality of touch, of warmth and strength and caring, all the physicality that had been missing in her life for weeks now. She was starved for it. She wanted it. Craved it.

For a few moments out of time, she basked in sweet words

murmured in her ear. He wasn't just the detective who'd seen her through the horror of Max's kidnapping. He was a trusted friend. And as he held her close, their bodies flush, she was suddenly aware of the scent of him, of his strength, his masculinity. She gasped, horrified at what was happening. And filled with shame, she pushed free.

"I'm sorry!" she exclaimed, turning away in panic. "I didn't mean for that to happen. I don't know what I was *thinking*!"

Whatever he replied, she missed in a frantic scramble to find her purse and scoop up her car keys that had fallen to the floor. To escape. Without looking at him, she rushed to the door. "I have to go! I'm sorry. I shouldn't—"

"Jane, wait!" Sam was at her side. He caught her arm. "Don't run away. And don't apologize. There was nothing wrong in what just happened. In fact, nothing did happen."

She stood without looking at him for a long moment, her back to him, her shoulders tense with absolute certainty that something had happened. For a dangerous moment, she had come close to crossing a moral boundary, and she was shocked.

She turned, raised her eyes to his. "You're wrong, Sam. Something did happen. And I do apologize. It was my fault. I have to go."

"No, Jane. Hear me out first, please. And then you can go."

Sam's hand fell away, but something in his troubled gaze held her in place. His eyes clung to hers as he searched for words. "I know there's trouble between you and Kyle."

She wanted to object, but before she could, he rushed on, "No, wait, let me finish. I'm not about to judge two people whose child has been kidnapped. But when you stood looking at that little kid in the hospital, why didn't Kyle have his arms around you? Whatever you needed at that moment, Jane, you didn't get it from Kyle."

Jane put her hands to her cheeks and made a sound, a short,

humorless excuse for a laugh. "I can't believe I'm listening to this. It is so inappropriate."

"Maybe so. But if you were my wife, Jane, there would be no circumstance—even the kidnapping of our child—that would alienate me from you. If you were mine, I would walk through the fires of hell before that happened."

Jane looked at her watch. "It's nearing the rush hour, detective," she said in a cool voice. "I need to leave. Please let me know if you find anything."

Sam looked at her for one long moment, simply looked. But in the end, he said no more, just sighed and told her to take care driving home.

She escaped as if the devil himself nipped at her heels.

THE TWENTY-FIVE-MILE DRIVE ACROSS the Causeway bridge seemed endless to Jane. She was so caught up in shock and shame that even if her stalker had appeared, she might not have noticed. How had she allowed herself to fall into the arms of a man who wasn't Kyle? She was mortified that she might have given Sam Pitre reason to misjudge her.

She fumbled for a tissue to wipe her eyes. With traffic whizzing past, she needed to see where she was going. What else could possibly go wrong in her life? she wondered, as the tears streamed in spite of her efforts to mop them up. And why was she weeping again? she thought in disgust. She never used to be such a wimp, such a screwup, such a pitiful excuse for a wife and mother and all-around person! For a minute she was steeped in despair. Oh, she needed *something*! Or someone. The road she'd traveled lately seemed endless, stretching out in front of her, dark and long and perilous.

When her cell phone rang, she was tempted to just let it ring. There was no one she wanted to talk to, or at least no one that she'd be able to talk to honestly, no one on whom she could unload the miserable circumstances of the day and be offered the understanding and consolation she needed. Not even Christine. Especially Christine.

She sighed. It could be Melanie. She dug it out and flipped it open without checking caller ID.

"Hello."

No response. She was in no mood to put up with another crank call. "Hello!" she barked.

Still nothing.

"Who is this!" she demanded angrily. "Why are you calling me? Who are you? What do you want?"

Silence.

Regardless, someone was on the line, someone who was getting a kick out of bugging her like this. Instead of frightening her, today it made her mad. Forgetting traffic and safety and courtesy, she lit into the caller full bore. "Listen, whoever you are! I want you to know that I've reported you to the police. You may think you're hiding, but these phone calls can be traced. Furthermore, this kind of harassment has serious consequences, and I will not hesitate to push for maximum punishment when you're exposed. I'm a lawyer, and I know how to do it."

The caller laughed. Laughed! And hung up.

Jane felt a rush of white-hot rage. For a minute, she was so furious, she could barely breathe. Telephone harassment was so craven, so gutless. What kind of sicko would keep doing this? If somebody wanted to tell her something, he ought to be man enough to say it to her face!

She was so distracted that it was a minute before she recognized the sound of a police siren coming up behind her, blue lights flashing. Instinctively, she glanced at her speedometer, blinked at her speed, and then realized she was the patrol car's target. She wasn't just a few miles over the legal limit, but a lot.

She slowed and, with the cop crowding on her tail, drove

meekly another quarter of a mile to a space on the bridge designed for breakdowns and speeding idiots.

A perfect end to a miserable day.

By the time she got home, she was no longer crying. Or railing at the anonymous caller. Or cursing her stupidity in getting a speeding ticket. But if she hoped she'd be able to slip inside and erase signs of her rotten day, she was wrong. Any other time, who knew when Melanie would deign to show up after school? But today—of course today!—when Jane snuck into the kitchen from the garage, there she was.

"Wow, what happened to you?" Melanie asked. "That is not the way to apply eye makeup, Jane, unless you're going for the raccoon look."

"Very funny," Jane snapped. She stopped at the sink and ripped off a paper towel. "You're home at a decent hour for a change. What's up?"

"Surprise. I live here."

Jane moistened the towel and dabbed at the blotched mascara but said nothing. She refused to be drawn into yet another silly confrontation. After the day she'd put in, she couldn't trust herself not to unravel. All she wanted was to get upstairs and close up in her bedroom—the room she had all to herself now, thanks to Kyle's abandonment—and pull the covers over her head.

"So, I can see you haven't had a good day," Melanie said, munching a cracker loaded with peanut butter. "And since nobody at your office makes you cry, I guess you've been holding hands with that bunch at Child Search again. I mean, what's fun about listening to people tell their creepy stories? Don't you ever get tired of that?"

Jane turned to look at her. "Don't you ever get tired of being a brat?"

Melanie was caught off-guard for a beat or two. But she recovered quickly and retorted with matching sarcasm. "Why would I? I'm so appreciated here."

"You'd be more appreciated if you made just a slight effort to be civil."

"Why should I be civil? I'm nobody to you. And I know you hate me."

Jane threw the used towel at the sink in disgust. "Why do you keep saying that, Melanie? It's ridiculous. I have no reason to hate you."

"You blame me that Max is gone."

Jane's control slipped. How much abuse was she supposed to take from this insufferable child? "If you're so convinced that I blame you, maybe I have good reason!" she said hotly. "You were supposed to watch him and you didn't. And now he's gone!"

"So you do think it's my fault!" Melanie cried.

"Yes, it's your fault! You know it's your fault!"

"I knew it! I knew you were thinking that. You've been thinking it all along and lying about it. I wish I'd never seen you. I wish Daddy had never met you. I wish Max had never been born!"

"And I wish I didn't have to put up with a spoiled brat!" Jane said. "You're rude; you're thoughtless. You're so self-centered that you expect everybody to put up with whatever you dish out. Well, I'm sick of it! You hear me?"

"The whole neighborhood hears you!" Melanie screamed.

"So what! I don't care!' Jane took two steps forward and shook a finger in Melanie's face. "And don't let me hear you say that about Max ever again! How dare you, you little twit! He's gone, and then you have the nerve to think you can get pregnant and replace him? Nobody can replace him, Melanie. Nobody. Ever!"

Melanie sniffed and made for the door. "I don't have to listen to this."

Jane caught her sleeve as she went by. "Yes, you do." She gave her a little shake before turning her loose. "For once you'll listen until I'm done. I have treated you with kid gloves for six months, and to what end? The more I try, the worse you behave. What is your problem, Melanie? Doesn't everybody love you enough? Don't you have enough privileges? Don't we all walk on eggshells around here for you?"

She paused to take a breath, totally unmoved as Melanie's face changed and she burst into tears. "And stop acting like you're the one we should feel sorry for," Jane said with disgust. "My baby is gone to God knows where, and you're here whining and making life even more miserable for everyone in this house. Well, here's a bulletin for you, Miss Smart Pants, I'm not putting up with it anymore!"

"I'm telling Daddy everything you said. And just wait. You'll see whose side he's on."

"Like that's a big secret?" Jane gave a harsh laugh. "You know what, little girl? You can have your daddy. If you think he's so wonderful, take him. I don't want him!"

"I knew it!" Melanie cried, dashing tears from her eyes. "You finally admit it. You never loved him. You never loved me. It's no wonder God took Max away from you. He knew you didn't deserve him."

Enraged at the sheer cruelty of it, Jane lifted her hand in a burning desire to hurt, to maim, to vent the unbearable pain. But when Melanie cringed and scrambled backward out of the line of fire, Jane suddenly came to her senses. For a split second, she was appalled at herself. And then, covering her face with both hands, she was engulfed in shame.

"I need a minute," she said in a shaky voice. Trembling, she sat down heavily in a chair, wishing the floor would open up and swallow her. She'd loved and cared for this girl, had treasured her as a precious gift. She'd probably despise her forever now. But she was the adult here, she told herself, and Melanie was the kid. Pregnant or not, the girl was an immature brat. But she was Jane's brat.

So, for the second time that day, and a little sick to her stomach, Jane drew a fortifying breath preparing to apologize. Forcing herself, she looked at the girl's surly face. "You probably won't believe this—or forgive it—but I'm sorry about that, Melanie. I got carried away. My excuse is that I've had a horrible day."

Feeling old and exhausted, she got to her feet, whether to try to give Melanie a hug or to escape she wasn't sure. But Melanie put out a hand to keep her at a distance.

"Don't you even—" she hissed, her face twisted into a spiteful mask.

Jane waved a hand weakly. "Don't worry, I won't."

"Good." Melanie gave a rude, humorless laugh. "And after all you just said, don't think you can have my baby now, even if you beg me. Not in a million years. I would give it to a stranger before I'd let you have it. I hate you!" She turned and ran out of the room.

JANE WASN'T SURE HOW it came about that she decided to go to Christine later. She simply realized that she was in a bottomless pit of despair. She had alienated Melanie, she'd betrayed her marriage vows by falling into Sam Pitre's arms, she'd been harassed by that spiteful caller, and she'd gotten a speeding ticket! All in the span of one afternoon. So, when she saw Christine arriving home from her job, she headed over without giving herself a chance to think twice.

Christine took one look at her and without a word pointed Jane to the den and went upstairs to check on her kids. Jane went where she'd been told and, in spite of the dire state of her emotions, felt welcomed as she settled into the familiar family room. She sank down onto the big, cushy sofa and put her hands up to her aching temples. She was so upset that she didn't even hear Christine return.

"Is it Max?" Christine asked. "Is he one of Crandall's babies?"

"No," Jane said. "Or rather, we don't know yet. Could I have some ibuprofen?"

"It's in the kitchen. I'll get it." She was gone no longer than a minute. When she got back, she had the painkiller in one hand and a bottle of water in the other.

Jane heaved a tired sigh as she popped the cap off the ibuprofen. "This ranks right up there with one of the worst days I've ever had in my life, Chris."

"What happened?"

Jane was shaking her head dismally. "Where to start?"

"Let me guess. Melanie."

"I just ruined any chance I ever had to mend my relationship with her." Jane repeated the argument, leaving out Melanie's threat to give her baby away. "I blamed her for Max being kidnapped."

"Oh, dear."

"I don't really." Jane paused, thinking, then shook three tablets into her palm. "Actually, I'm not sure that's true. Maybe I do blame her, as ugly as that sounds. But if it's true, I've done a good job denying it to myself . . . until today."

"She's hormonal, Jane. Sixteen-year-olds are ruled by their hormones."

And even more so when they're pregnant.

"I know this is no excuse, but it was bad timing on Mellie's part to sass me when I was already feeling so miserable. I just wanted to go upstairs and try to put this awful day behind me."

"All because you exchanged a few heated words with a rebellious teenager? That's an extreme reaction."

Jane drew a deep breath. "It's not only that. I got a speeding ticket."

Christine's mouth twitched with the effort to hide a smile. "Now that's really bad behavior."

"I was going eighty-seven miles an hour, Chris."

"Ouch. That'll be some ticket to pay. But, hey, now might be a good time for you to put in a call to that sexy cop you and Kyle know so well. Maybe he'll take pity on you." When Jane blinked, she added, "Just teasing, hon."

Jane gazed moodily at the three tablets in her palm. "Yeah, and it might work, too, as that sexy cop just made a move on me today."

Christine stared, mouth open. "You are kidding me."

"I wish. I really wish." She looked up into her friend's eyes. "Detective Pitre knows there's trouble in my marriage, Chris. And as nutty as it sounds . . . and as shocked as I was over it, he seems to think he can step into my neglectful husband's shoes."

Christine was still staring. "You *are* serious!"

"He apparently was, if you can believe that."

"Of course, I can believe it. You're a beautiful woman. He's taken a personal interest in your case. And the man is not married." Christine took the cap off the water bottle and handed it to Jane.

Jane swallowed the tablets with a swig of water and set the bottle on the floor beside her. "It worries me that he thought I might be . . . available."

"Have you been giving out signals that you'd be unfaithful to Kyle?" Christine asked.

"No, of course not. At least, not that I was aware of. But he guessed our problems . . ."

"I don't think he's seeing anything that others don't." Christine sat on the sofa beside Jane and reached over, patting her knee. "Anybody who's been around you and Kyle can see that things are different. There was always a special something that set the two of you apart. Now that something is missing. Well, maybe not missing, but sort of lost in the awful trauma you're living."

"What's missing is Max."

"Yes." Christine looked sadly sympathetic. "It's so hard, Jane. I know that."

Jane drew a shaky breath. She knew Christine would pray about it, and for once she didn't dismiss that. Considering her state of mind today, it was oddly comforting.

"So . . ." Eyes teasing, Christine began ticking things off on her fingers. "Sam hit on you, you got a speeding ticket, Melanie behaved badly, and you did too. Is that all that happened today?"

In spite of herself, Jane laughed. "Except for another call from my anonymous friend, yes, that's all."

"You got another one?"

"Yes. And I gave him a piece of my mind, to which he simply laughed."

Christine's expression turned serious. "It was a man?"

"To tell the truth, I'm not sure. The laugh was low and sarcastic, but it could have been a woman, I guess."

"And nothing was said, no words?"

"Not this time, no. But he stayed on the line while I ranted and raved and threatened to have him arrested. I got so hot and bothered that I forgot to pay attention to my driving, and that was when I got the ticket. Once I find him, I'm gonna sue for the cost of that ticket!"

Christine didn't find her humor funny. "I am not liking this at all, Jane. Has it struck you that someone might be stalking you?"

"Kyle and Sam Pitre think so." She paused. "For sure someone's irritating me, harassing me, bugging the dickens out of me . . . It's creepy, wondering what he might do next."

"This is so frustrating," Christine said. "A person would

have to be truly sick to keep doing that. And potentially dangerous. You be careful, Jane."

THE ODD SENSE OF peace she felt when she left Christine didn't last long. She let herself in through the garage and found Kyle standing in the kitchen studying the speeding ticket she'd left on the table.

"What's this?" He held it up, frowning.

"You can see what it is." She scooped up her suit jacket from the back of a chair intending to go upstairs. "It was dumb. I was an idiot. Let's leave it at that."

Scanning it, he looked at her with an incredulous expression on his face. "You were going eighty-seven miles an hour?"

She stopped, took a long breath. "You can save the lecture. I got that from the cop when he wrote the ticket." She could see that he wasn't going to quit. "You want details? I got another crank phone call, Kyle, and on the heels of that, I was stopped for speeding. But my horrendous day wasn't over, no, not even close. I walked in the door of my home and in seconds found myself screaming at Melanie." Jane stood with her hands propped on her hips. "Does that explain why I'm headed upstairs to lick my wounds?"

Kyle tossed the ticket back on the table. "Did you get the ticket on your way to Sam Pitre's office or on your way home?" he asked.

"Excuse me?"

"You were in his office today. Was that before or after you got the ticket?"

She felt color rising in her cheeks. Kyle couldn't know what happened, could he? But nothing had happened, she reminded herself. She had stopped Sam before anything happened. Still, it was with an effort that she managed to meet his gaze head-on.

"What exactly are you trying to say? Is there some reason I shouldn't have gone to Sam's office?"

"None. But I was just a little surprised when the sergeant who has the office next to Pitre mentioned you'd been there a few minutes before me."

She felt a rush of dismay at what Kyle might have seen—and misinterpreted—had he walked into Sam's office while she was there. "I wanted to hear about George Crandall straight from Sam," she said. "That's why I went."

"Okay . . ." Kyle said as if waiting for her to go on. When she didn't, he said, "I got some strange vibrations from Pitre that didn't have anything to do with George Crandall."

Jane's heart was beating fast. She felt guilt and shame and a host of other complicated emotions. And she was sure every one was written all over her face. "What kind of strange vibrations?"

"I," he paused as if he didn't want to say it, "I think he's got a crush on you." When she opened her mouth to deny it, he held up a hand to stop her. "I know that's an old-fashioned word, but it's what came to mind when I talked to him today."

"It's ridiculous."

He was watching her closely. "Only if you have no interest in returning his feelings."

She suddenly felt the same rush of anger that had made her scream at Melanie earlier. How grossly unfair that he was acting as if he cared whether she had a crush—stupid word!—on another man when he hadn't touched her in weeks! When he hadn't slept in their bedroom in ages. When he'd told her flat-out that he wasn't sure their *relationship* was worth saving! And now he wanted to know if she was interested in the attentions of another man? Well, let him wonder.

"What's your point, Kyle? I'm tired. I want to go upstairs."

"What about dinner?"

She glanced around the kitchen, realizing she hadn't given a thought to dinner. "I won't be cooking tonight. Maybe you and

Melanie can order pizza. I don't think she'll want me to join you after what happened." Seeing his frown, she said, "She'll give you all the details, trust me."

"What did you do?"

She gave a short laugh. "I'll just say this. When she paints me as a horrible witchy stepmother, she'll be telling the truth."

12

Kyle stood for a long minute after Jane left. He wanted to stop her so they could talk, but he was afraid she would throw his words back in his face. He needed to make her understand why he had gotten so far off track. Being married to Jane had made him a happy man . . . until Max was taken. The realization that he loved her, needed her, had been growing in him, but it had taken about ten minutes in Sam Pitre's office to bring it into sharp focus.

Kyle felt like an idiot for thinking Sam wouldn't notice their marital trouble. For six months, Pitre had been at the forefront of their anguished search for Max. It was no wonder he would be the one she would turn to.

"Your wife is one in a million," Sam said. "She's been brave and strong in a no-win situation. But it's telling on her. I've seen what happens when parents go through this. I'd hate to see it happen to you." When he saw Kyle's face, he'd shrugged. "I'm just sayin', man."

Because it hit home, Kyle was defensive. "What do you mean? That you know my wife better than I do? Has she been crying on your shoulder?"

Sam gave him a disgusted look. "Have you given her reason to?" Without waiting for an answer, he said, "Give me a break, Kyle. I can't believe you'd even ask a question like that. She's loyal to a fault, and you're a lucky man. You want my advice, you'll go home *tonight* and tell her that."

Kyle left feeling as if he'd been kicked in the chest. It was hard to admit it, but Sam was right. He'd been thinking of himself when he moved out, not Jane. And just at a time when he should have been her rock.

Now, standing in their kitchen, he faced some scary truths. He had done major damage to his marriage, and he had to figure out a way to repair it. While he'd been walking around in a fog of self-pity, Jane seemed to have adjusted to the situation. She'd adjusted to sleeping alone. How long would it be before she chose to be alone, period?

Tired and worried, he slowly climbed the stairs. Pausing at the top, he looked longingly at the master-bedroom door. The firmly closed master-bedroom door. His desire to try to set things straight would have to wait. As a lawyer, he knew that timing was crucial when he needed to persuade an adversary to accept a bitter-tasting compromise. And he had no doubt whatever that Jane was bitter over his abandonment. God knew she had cause to be.

What had he been thinking to assume Jane couldn't understand what ailed him when she was suffering the same pain? So why had he thought it would hurt less if he closed himself off from his wife? They both feared their little boy was lost to them forever. What would really hurt, he realized, was if he no longer had her.

He stopped at Melanie's door. He was sure to get an earful as to why Jane was the worst stepmother ever and how wonderful it was going to be when she didn't live in the house anymore. Added to his shortcomings as a husband, Kyle was seeing his failings as a father. It was one more black mark that he hoped Jane would not throw back in his face.

"Melanie." He tapped lightly on her door.

No response.

"Melanie, I want to talk to you. Open the door."

"I'm already in bed, Dad."

"Why? It's early. Are you sick?"

Big sigh. "No, I'm not sick. I'm reading."

Grouchy, he thought. Not a good sign. "This won't take long, Mellie. Open up."

He heard a few rustling noises and then the sound of a book—or something—dropped to the floor. A moment later she opened the door, but just a crack, not enough that he could see her face.

"I guess Jane has been trashing me again," she said.

"You guessed wrong," Kyle said. He conjured up a smile. "You don't object to a few minutes with your daddy, do you?"

She heaved another heavy sigh and opened the door fully. "What is it?"

For a second, Kyle was struck by the way she looked. Her dark hair—so like his own—curled softly around her pretty face, a face so like her dead mother's. It was free of any makeup, which was rare. She was about thirteen when he caved on the rule forbidding makeup, after which she painted and primped herself lavishly. But tonight, no paint, no powder. She'd obviously been crying. Her eyes were puffy. Her nose was red and shining. But even so, there was a glow to her skin, a dewy softness that was at once both beautiful and dismaying to him. Was it the pregnancy? His baby girl was having a baby! He still had trouble believing it.

"You don't look like a happy camper, Mel. You want to talk about it?"

She teared up instantly. Her lips trembled, and she pressed her fingers to her mouth until she found her voice. "Did she tell you what she said to me?"

He moved to her, put an arm around her shoulders, and walked her over to the bed. Pulling back the comforter, he motioned her in under the covers, much as he'd done when she was a little girl, and sat on the edge of her bed. "Now, tell me what she said."

"She told me it was my fault Max was kidnapped. That I should have been watching him and I didn't and that I'm a bad person."

"She said all that?"

"Well, maybe not the part about being a bad person, but that's what she meant." She wiped at her eyes with shaky hands. "I knew she felt that way, and now she proved it. I'll be glad when you get a divorce from her, Dad. She's a horrible person."

"How long have you felt that Jane was a horrible person?" Kyle asked. "Seems like only a few months ago you loved her a lot and thought of her as a pretty good mom."

"That was before Max was kidnapped, Dad. She changed after that."

"And you didn't?"

"No!"

"You're sure about that?"

"Maybe I had a little trouble getting used to not having Max around, but now I'm just glad you've seen the light too. You were right to move out of that bedroom. I was kind of upset at first when it happened, but now I see it was right. The best thing that could happen now is to divorce her. That is the plan, isn't it?"

Kyle stared down at his hands, feeling the full weight of his folly. Who could blame a kid for putting the most obvious interpretation on what he'd done? "I'm not getting a divorce,

Melanie. And I made a mistake by moving out of our bedroom. It hurt Jane, and I don't know if she'll be able to forgive me."

"What are you talking about, Dad!" she exclaimed. "Didn't you hear what I just said? She told me flat-out that I was to blame for Max being kidnapped! That's so mean. It's cruel. I'll never forgive her for it. And I won't forgive you if you start trying to make up with her."

"She's had some stress today, Melanie. Sounds as if things sort of escalated when the two of you argued, and she lost her temper. She probably regrets some of the things she said. I bet she'll apologize tomorrow."

"She's already apologized," Melanie said in a petulant tone, "but you can't make mean things disappear just by saying you're sorry. I meant it when I said I won't forgive her."

"That's up to you, of course. But seems like I've heard you say some pretty mean things to Jane lately. If you apologize, do you want her to throw your apology back in your face, too, hmm?"

She set her mouth in a stubborn line. "It doesn't matter, because I'm never apologizing."

Kyle studied her face, thinking he probably hadn't made much headway in resolving the thorny problem. But then again, he hadn't set a very good example for his daughter in dealing with thorny problems. He leaned over and kissed her cheek, then stood up. "I'll leave it for now, Mellie, but I'll be making some changes, and I expect you to do the same."

She gave him a suspicious look. "Changes like what?"

"Watching your mouth, to start with. You've gotten away with some pretty unattractive behavior lately, and I've been remiss as your dad in not stepping in to put a stop to it. I can't undo what Jane said to you tonight, and I can't force you to forgive her, but you will not be rude and disrespectful, and that's an order."

"You're on her side now!" Melanie cried. "I can't believe what you're saying, Dad!"

"We're a family, Mellie," he said quietly. "There's no taking sides. We're all in this together. Whether we find Max or not, we still have one another . . . you, me, and Jane."

Disgusted, Melanie flopped over, her back to him, and pulled the covers up to her chin. "I'm going to sleep now. Close the door when you leave."

JANE SLEPT FITFULLY THAT night and finally, after looking at the clock too many times, decided to get up. It was five a.m. In the bathroom, she stood looking at herself in the mirror and thinking she'd aged twenty years since Max was taken. Sam Pitre must be pretty hard up to even consider coming on to her. Moving to her closet, she found a running suit and sneakers. She didn't usually run; she preferred Curves. But maybe a little jogging would clear the cobwebs. Or not. Couldn't hurt.

She slipped out of the house quietly. The sun was barely up, the lawn and landscaping glistened with dew. Birds in the trees were awake and singing. The whole world was set for the beginning of a new day. Jane stood for a minute and vowed to make it a good one. She needed to put behind her the stress of yesterday, and the mistakes. She needed to apologize to Melanie, and hopefully they could get beyond that horrible scene. And with that upbeat mind-set, she started jogging.

She was barely out of sight of her house when she realized she wasn't alone. Glancing behind her, she saw the runner was a woman, but she wasn't gaining, so Jane wasn't unduly concerned. A neighbor keeping in shape, she decided. There was probably no reason to panic. She was bound to meet up with other runners.

And she did. Several times. Which made her comfortable

taking the trail that branched off and wound through a wooded area that eventually opened up to the lakefront. Ahead, she could see glimpses of it. She felt invigorated and virtuous at doing something that felt so good for a change. When she got there, she told herself, she would sit for a while. She loved just looking at the lake and hearing the sound of the wind and water.

And because she was daydreaming, she was caught off guard by what happened next. As she reached a tall cypress tree and rounded it in a tight curve, she was suddenly struck violently from behind. She cried out and went tumbling headlong—and painfully—to the ground. Stunned, she took a moment to gather herself. Her cheek throbbed, and the heels of both hands were scraped and stinging.

"Hey, lady, you okay?"

Jane looked up into the face of a young man. He was in a tank top and shorts, his skin glistening with sweat. "I think so." She took his hand and let him haul her up onto her feet.

"Looks like you took a bad tumble."

"Did you see who did it?" she asked.

"Huh?" He was shaking his head. "I didn't see anybody. You saying somebody did this on purpose?"

Jane studied the thick growth beyond the cypress tree. "He came out from behind that tree. He must have taken off through there."

"I'm walking you to the lake," he told her. "You need to call the cops. You got a cell phone with you?"

"I do. And thanks for your help. I appreciate it."

Two Mandeville policemen dropped her off at her house half an hour later. She found Kyle standing at the coffee pot in T-shirt and pj bottoms, fresh from his morning shower. Seeing the look on his face—pensive, troubled, deeply thoughtful—as he watched the pot, she paused in the doorway. He was about to look even more troubled.

"G'morning," she said.

He gave a start when he saw her face. "What happened? Where've you been?"

"I went for a jog. It seemed a good idea at the time. But I was mugged."

Stunned, he put out a hand, cupping her cheek. "You're hurt. Your cheek is bruised." He sucked in a quick, worried breath. "What else, Jane?"

"If you're asking was I raped, no. Just . . . assaulted. Whoever it was shoved me from behind and I hit the ground hard. That's the reason for the bruises."

He took her hands, turned them over. "Your hands need cleaning with antiseptic."

"They're okay. They look worse than they are."

"You had your cell phone, didn't you? Did you try calling me?"

"I called the Mandeville cops instead. I gave them a statement, vague as it was. They brought me home."

"You should have called me, too, Jane," he said quietly.

"Maybe."

"It was your stalker."

She nodded, reaching for a cup. "Probably. But don't bother to ask. I don't know any more than I told you. Male or female, I couldn't tell. It happened so fast. Just a blur coming up behind me as I went around the curve at that big tree." She looked down at her scraped hands. "Then *boom*!"

"Whoever it was, he must have been watching the house," Kyle said.

"Well, duh . . ."

"We need to call Sam Pitre. This is escalating into real danger."

"I already called him."

He appeared to be at a loss for words as he watched her pour a cup of coffee. "We need to talk, Jane."

"I know. I'll apologize to Melanie," she told him. "The things I said were inexcusable. She may not even listen, let alone forgive me, but I'm giving it my best shot, so you don't need to nag me."

He rubbed the back of his neck and met her eyes in a wry look. "After what just happened, you expect me to start nagging you?"

"I don't expect anything anymore, Kyle." She took cream from the refrigerator and poured it into her coffee. "Frankly nowadays, I never know what's coming next, so . . . as I said, no expectations."

With a tilt of his chin, he indicated the table. "Let's sit. No nagging, I promise. Okay?"

"Okay . . ." Jane put the cream back in the refrigerator and took a seat. "Shoot."

"Did you have a bad night? Was that why you went for a run this morning?"

"Not surprising, is it, considering?" Propped on her elbows, she spoke over the rim of her cup.

"Were you worried about Melanie?"

"Along with about ten other things, yes."

"I was awake too. If I'd known you were jogging, I would've joined you." He added with a wry note, "Now more than ever, I really wish I had gone with you."

"Nothing would have happened then. My stalker is a sneaky coward. I'm only harassed when I'm alone."

Kyle gazed down into his cup for a long minute before looking up at her. "I've been thinking, Jane. We can't continue like this. You and I in separate bedrooms, Melanie playing one of us against the other, people gossiping about us, speculating all kinds of things. I want it to end."

Jane suddenly felt sick in the pit of her stomach. Considering, the day's positive beginning had truly been a cruel joke. On her. With great effort, she kept the apprehension she felt out of her voice. "So, is this where you finally get around to telling me you want a divorce?"

"No!" He gave an emphatic shake of his head. "I'm saying just the opposite, Jane, but obviously making a mess of it. I want to put the trouble that got us into this situation behind us. I want us to be a family again."

It was the last thing she expected to hear, so it took a minute for her to take it in. She was relieved that he didn't want a divorce after all, but she was curious to know what was behind his sudden change. "What exactly is the trouble that got us into this situation, as you see it?"

Instead of giving a ready answer for that, he seemed to search for words. "Max's disappearance," he said hesitantly. "And the way we reacted, I guess. All of us, me, you, Melanie. It made for a perfect storm in our family."

"I believe you called my reaction 'obsession.' "

He gave her a distressed look. "I was wrong to criticize your efforts to find Max. I was looking to fix blame, and I refused to look too closely at myself. I was the one who was supposed to take Melanie to the parades that day, and I cancelled. I put my work ahead of my promise to my daughter. So you stepped in. And because you went, you had to take Max. If I'd kept my promise to Melanie, we would have Max with us today."

Jane noted that Melanie was still "my daughter," not theirs. But whatever motivated him to make such an admission, it was good to hear him acknowledge that what happened was a perfect storm of circumstances. "My family is falling apart," Kyle was saying in a troubled voice. "I can't let that happen." He leaned forward in his eagerness to make his case. "Melanie is in crisis, Jane. She's sixteen, she's pregnant, she's confused, and she's angry. For her sake, we need to be united. It would be the worst thing for her if our family shattered. If we're together again, it'll give her the security she needs to get through this."

As Kyle leaned forward, Jane moved back in her chair. So this was basically about Melanie. Kyle wasn't thinking of mending their broken *relationship* because he loved Jane and wanted a real marriage. No, he wanted to present a happy face for his pregnant daughter. And, amazingly, he thought it would be okay with Jane to go along with such a farce. How obtuse could a man be? She felt like throwing her coffee at him.

"Melanie's pregnancy could destroy her future," he went on. "You and I can prevent that. I plan to be a better father, a better husband. I'm ashamed that it took me so long to see what's important in my life. It's you, it's Melanie. It's our family. That's what I'm trying to say. That's what I'm trying to fix."

He reached over and covered one of her hands with his. "Jane. It was stupid of me to move out of our bedroom. It's my fault that Mellie did what she did, that she's been treating you so mean. She's scared at the thought of the breakup of her home. With Max gone, her home represents what little security and love she has left."

"So, besides playing at being a mom to Melanie, what do you want from me, Kyle?"

He seemed thrown by her blunt question. "I want us to be together again. I want to take my things from the guest room and move them back into our bedroom where I belong."

"And you think that'll fix everything? Forget Melanie for a minute. We'll be sharing a bed, sleeping together again, and everything you found so dissatisfying about our marriage and so unsatisfactory about me—all that is okay now? You're over it."

"No, no, that's not it at all." He was shaking his head, ready to argue, but she wasn't done.

"What about my *obsession* for finding Max? Is that quirk in my personality less aggravating now? Have I convinced you that I'll be an acceptable wife?" She put up a hand. "No, don't bother trying to talk me around to your way of thinking, Kyle. It's not happening."

"You're misunderstanding all this, Jane. It's nothing like that. I was wrong. I'm asking you to give me another chance."

Jane stood up. "I'm trying to figure what brought about your change of heart. It's too abrupt for me to believe it. I haven't seen any evidence that you were rethinking whatever you felt when you walked out." She narrowed her eyes looking at him. "So why is our relationship suddenly worth saving? For Melanie's sake? To present the illusion of stability to your daughter? All the reasons you were unhappy had to do with me, but now it's all about Melanie?"

"Listen, Jane—"

"No." She stopped him again. "Look, I'm ready and willing to help Melanie get through this dark time, but I'm not willing to welcome you to our bedroom for her sake. So don't go to the bother of packing up."

There was no time to say more, as Melanie's steps sounded on the stairs. Jane quickly moved to the stove to begin making breakfast. Melanie might be ticked off at Jane, but she wouldn't pass up a meal. Thank pregnancy for that.

"I'll have scrambled eggs ready in a minute," Jane said as Melanie came into the kitchen. "Will you make some toast, please?"

Melanie didn't reply, but she didn't refuse either. She popped two pieces of bread in the toaster and took butter from the refrigerator.

Kyle, still sitting at the table, rose. "Mellie, how about making a couple of extra pieces?" He moved to the cabinet. "I'll set the table."

Jane wasn't sure who was more surprised—her or Melanie. Kyle never ate breakfast except rarely on a weekend. In the act of breaking eggs in a bowl, she added two more without comment. "These will be ready in a minute. There's fresh orange juice in the refrigerator and strawberries. You need fresh fruit, Mellie."

Until that moment, Melanie hadn't looked directly at Jane. Now, seeing the bruise, she gasped. "What happened to your face?"

"I went jogging this morning. I fell."

Kyle spoke before Melanie could comment. "I'll get glasses and napkins."

For the next few minutes, they worked in silent, albeit somewhat edgy, harmony. And once they were seated at the table, Jane decided to take advantage of the odd lull in hostilities to offer her apology to Melanie.

She spread a napkin on her lap and took the plunge. "There's no excuse for what I said to you last night, Mellie. I am so sorry. I lost my temper. I really did have a horrendous day, and things seemed to pile up on me, one after another, but I shouldn't have taken it out on you. To tell the truth, I was as shocked to hear myself as you must have been. I hope you'll be able to forgive me."

"Wow, nice speech," Melanie said, after popping a strawberry in her mouth. "Do they teach you that stuff in law school?"

Jane sighed. She hadn't really expected much in the way of forgiveness from Melanie, but her attitude did get so tiresome.

"Melanie Ann Madison," Kyle said suddenly. "Have you forgotten the talk we had last night?"

"Dad!" Melanie threw half a strawberry at her plate. "Have you forgotten that she blamed me for Max being kidnapped?"

"And she apologized. Very sincerely, I thought. Now it's your turn to accept her apology."

Melanie's face set stubbornly, her eyes shooting daggers. Jane guessed the girl would rather walk on hot coals than accept her apology. She also wondered what good a forced apology would be. Maybe more harm than good.

"It's okay, Mellie," she said. "I crossed a line in what I said, and you're right to be angry and hurt. I don't blame you for what happened to Max. The person to blame is the one who took him."

But Kyle was having none of that. "Wait a minute. Who fixes breakfast for you every morning, Melanie?" he said. "Who drives you to school every day? Who is it that bites her tongue when you're rude and disrespectful, which is often? And you throw a sincere apology back in her face?" He was fiercely disapproving. "Seems to me that Jane has been one very long-suffering parent to you, and yet you continue to behave like an ungrateful brat. I think we've all had enough of that . . . whether you're pregnant or not."

Melanie's face crumpled and her eyes filled with tears. "So I'm just gonna have to pretend everything's okay around here while you suck up to her trying to get her to let you back in the bedroom?"

Wham!

Kyle banged his palm on the table, shocking Jane and Melanie. "Did you hear what I said, Melanie? As of this minute, if you have something to say, it had better be respectful."

Melanie scraped her chair back abruptly and rushed toward the door.

"Hold it!" Kyle barked. "Didn't you forget something?"

She wheeled about and stalked back to the table. Without a word, she collected her plate, glass, and silver and put them in the dishwasher. She turned then, looking only at her father. "Am I done now?"

He held her gaze without replying long enough so that her face went pink. When he still didn't speak, she huffed and finally looked over at Jane. "I don't know about forgiving you but . . . apology accepted," she said in a curt tone.

"Thank you, Mellie. I think."

"Now?" she said insolently to Kyle.

He shook his head and gave a resigned sigh. "Go. You've got about fifteen minutes before Jane has to leave. Don't make her wait for you."

IN THE SILENCE AFTER she left, Kyle sat with a defeated look on his face. "Will she ever come around?"

Jane rose to collect both their plates. "Emotions are on a roller coaster during pregnancy. A lot of what's driving Melanie is hormonal. We have to hope that after the baby is born she'll be less . . . volatile."

Kyle watched Jane load the dishwasher. "She seems determined to throw everything we want to do for her right back in our faces."

Jane stood at the sink, washing the skillet she'd scrambled the eggs in. "Think of it from her point of view," she said. "She believes she's done a pretty generous thing by volunteering to give us a baby. And we turn around and decide we're not sure we want to be a family anymore. She could be thinking she made this amazing gesture for nothing."

"Well, if that's all it takes to sweeten her up," Kyle said in a no-nonsense tone, "we'll soon have peace and harmony in this house again . . . because we are going to be a family again. I know you're not ready to accept that, but I can wait until you're ready. I'm a patient man."

"Here." She shoved the washed skillet into his hands. "Make yourself useful again. Dry."

13

Melanie was fed up. What she'd done by getting pregnant was an act of pure love. And it was pretty unselfish. But everybody was treating her as if she'd done something awful. How about instead of criticizing her, they'd try looking at it from her side? She was the one facing nine months of misery. It was her breasts that were tender and hurting; she was the one who'd thrown up at school every day for a week until her doctor gave her some pills. Now she was so sleepy in the afternoons, she couldn't concentrate. She'd actually gone to sleep one day in geometry class, and when the teacher woke her up, everybody had laughed like crazy. On top of all that, her dad was being cruel and Jane was mean to her. The way she figured it, she'd made a big mistake. Everybody thought so. Okay. She could take care of it. Today.

Lunchtime at school used to be fun, but now she preferred to eat alone. After she was done, she called Daniel. They had barely spoken lately, but she was in a bind, and he used to be her best friend. She thought she'd be able to talk him into what she needed. Considering.

"Did you drive to school today?" she asked when she finally reached him.

"No, I'm grounded," he told her. "You know that. What do you need?"

"A ride to the mall. After school. Today. It has to be today."

Daniel made a sound that told her he thought she was a pain. That really hurt.

"You want to go shopping and it has to be today?"

"Something like that," she said. "But if you can't help, forget it. I'll figure something out."

He gave a big sigh. "Okay, Mel. Michael Benton has a car. He offered to let me ride to school with him until my grounding is over, but Mom nixed it. I'm riding the bus now. I'll ask him if he'll drop you at the mall. But why is it so important that you can't wait for the weekend when Jane could take you? Are you still fighting with her?"

He was always trying to get her to make up with Jane. But he didn't know the real Jane. He hadn't heard what she said last night. He didn't have to live with someone who blamed him for her baby being kidnapped and ruining her life.

"I need a ride to the mall, Daniel," she told him patiently, "not a lecture on getting along with my stepmother."

He hesitated as if he'd like to say more, but in the end, all he said was, "Michael will probably do it. Where do you want him to pick you up?"

"In the parking lot. I'll be waiting beside Michael's car. At three thirty, Daniel. Don't forget."

"I won't forget." He paused again. "Are you feeling okay? You're not . . . sick or anything?"

"I'm fine." She hung up before he could say anything else. Because she'd been so quick to get away, she realized she hadn't even thanked him. She felt a little bad about that, but she was on a mission that was way bigger than forgetting to say thank you.

MICHAEL BENTON WAS A few minutes late getting to his car. And because Melanie owed him for the favor of taking her to the mall, she didn't say anything. But she was on pins and needles by the time he appeared. What she was facing was pretty awful and she didn't need more stress. Also, it didn't make her feel any better that Daniel was with him. He always saw right through her, no matter what the deal.

"Sorry we're late," Daniel said as he opened a rear door of Michael's Mustang for her. "Michael had to check with the coach about something. It took longer than we thought."

Michael slid in behind the wheel, flicking a glance at her over his shoulder. "Hey, Mel, how you doin'?"

"I'm great. Thanks for the ride, Michael."

"Hey, no problem." He started the Mustang with a roar and gunned it toward the exit. "How 'bout that quiz we had in geometry? I thought it was a killer."

"I think I made a pretty good grade," she said, pressing her palm to her tummy. Lately, she didn't like riding in the back seat. It made her nauseous.

"Way to go," Michael said, grinning at her from the rearview mirror. "If I slept through class, I'd be lucky to make a passing grade."

Daniel turned to look at her, scowling. "You were sleeping in class?"

"Just once," she said dismissively and turned her face to the side.

"The whole class about cracked up when Blakely had to wake her up," Michael said, chuckling. "But, heck, Mel gets geometry even with her eyes closed." He snickered at his own joke, apparently not noticing that Daniel and Melanie weren't laughing.

Melanie was relieved when they reached the mall. "You can let me out at the main entrance, Michael," she said. "And thanks for the ride."

Daniel looked at her with suspicion. "Is Jane picking you up?"

"No, my dad is." She hadn't called him yet, but she would when she was ready. Getting home was the least of her worries right now. She opened the door to get out. "See you tomorrow."

"Wait a minute." Daniel got out and looked at her over the top of the Mustang. "Are you sure you're okay, Mel?"

She shrugged. "Yes, why?"

"I don't know. You just look . . . funny."

"It'll pass." At least, she hoped it would. She didn't know what condition she'd be in when it was time to go home. She turned, waving a hand without looking back, and hurried to the mall entrance.

But she was inside only long enough to watch and be sure Michael pulled into traffic and kept going before she went back out the door where she'd entered. It was sort of a long walk to her destination, but it was not so far that she couldn't make it on foot. It was on the same side of the road as the mall, she'd checked. The traffic was horrific this time of day and she wouldn't want to try and cross.

Still, it took fifteen minutes to get to the clinic. She'd researched it on the internet at school today and had called to make an appointment. She'd been thinking about it anyway. It was the best thing to do to fix everything. Hardly anyone would know. She hadn't told anybody but Jane, her dad, Daniel and the people in the doctor's office.

She just wished she felt better about it. She put her hand on her abdomen. Her conscience bothered her when she thought of the tiny embryo floating inside. That was how she preferred thinking of him, a tiny embryo. When she thought of him as a baby, she saw Max's little face. And when that happened, she got a little queasy about her decision.

Like now.

No, she told herself. She'd already made the decision. It hadn't been definite before, but after Jane said all those things, now it was.

By the time she got to the clinic, she was more than a little nervous. All sorts of thoughts were jumping around inside her head as she stood outside the door. She was suddenly aware that what she was about to do was truly awesome. Once it was done, there would be no turning back. Maybe she should have mentioned it to somebody, gotten some advice. Like who? She was cut off from the people she used to turn to. It took a few minutes, but she finally got hold of herself. Then, with a good, deep breath, she opened the door and went in.

It looked like any other doctor's office inside. There were several people in the waiting room, two around her age—maybe a year or so older—a couple of women who looked to be in their twenties, and sitting in a corner away from everyone else was a woman who looked as old as Jane. Why would she be doing something like this? Melanie wondered, thinking she looked too old to make a stupid mistake.

With her hand pressed to her abdomen, she walked to the little glass door where a receptionist was doing something with paperwork. Or maybe she was a nurse. Melanie couldn't tell. The woman looked up, smiled, and reached to slide the glass open. "May I help you?"

"I called this morning," Melanie said. "I have an appointment for three forty-five. I'm sorry I'm late. The person who gave me a ride—" She stopped. "Anyway, I'm supposed to see a doctor."

"Is this your first visit?"

"Yes."

"Then you'll need to fill this out." She pushed a clipboard with a form attached to it through the opening.

Melanie sat down across the waiting room away from the others. She glanced at the form, but didn't write anything. Instead, she studied the people who were waiting. The two twenty-somethings were chatting with each other. They'd both seen the same movie and were talking about it, how it was hilarious. They'd see it over again, it was that good. If they were here for the same reason she was, they didn't act like it was a big deal.

But across the room from her, a younger girl didn't look so unconcerned. She seemed nervous and fidgety. She kept looking at her watch and the door. Maybe she was waiting for someone.

The girl next to her was dressed all in black. Even her nails were painted black. Her hair stood up in spikes that were tipped in bright green. But the worst was the body piercing. She had a silver stud at the center of her lower lip, plus one on the side of her nose and one near an eyebrow. Wherever else, Melanie didn't want to think. She was looking mostly bored with the whole thing and reading a fashion magazine—which, considering how she was dressed, hadn't made much of an impression, Melanie thought.

Just then a nurse opened the door to the examining rooms and called a name. One of the twenty-somethings stood up. "Nice meeting you," she said to the person who'd chatted with her as they waited.

"Same here," her new best friend said.

Melanie stared down at the form. In spite of the—what was the word?—ordinary stuff going on in the waiting room, she didn't think what she was about to do was ordinary. Not even close. And was it the right thing to do? She wrote the date and was hesitating over filling in her name when the girl watching the door spoke.

"Did you get the sonogram yet?"

Melanie looked up from the form. "Are you talking to me?"

"Yeah." The girl put a hand on her tummy. "I was just in there, and they said would I like to do a sonogram. When I saw it, I told them I needed to take a few minutes to think. I mean, when you see the picture, it's clear as a bell that it's a baby."

"What'd you think was in there," the girl with the spiked hair asked, "a rabbit?"

"Hey," twenty-something said, "show a little respect."

Spiked hair huffed and returned to her magazine.

Ignoring her, the other girl managed a smile . . . sort of. "I guess I really didn't let myself think until I saw it. I was just upset over the idea of having a baby and my boyfriend was supposed to be here with me, but it looks like he's held up in traffic or something."

"Maybe you should wait until he's able to be here with you," twenty-something said. "It's a big step."

"You know, I think you're right." The girl stood up, scooped her purse off the chair. At the door, she said to Melanie, "Be sure and have the sonogram."

Melanie scanned the form, still hesitant about writing her name. A lot of questions needed to be answered. When was her last period? How many pregnancies had she had? How many full-term pregnancies? How many abortions? At that point, Melanie stopped reading and leaned back in the chair. She felt sick. But there was a much more terrible pain somewhere in the vicinity of her heart. What was she doing?

She was staring at the space for her name when the interior door was suddenly opened and a girl about her own age came rushing out. Close behind her was an older woman.

"What is the matter with you, Lisa? I thought we had settled this. You know it's what we have to do. Now come back in here and let's just get it over with!"

The girl stopped and turned to face the woman. "I don't want to, Mom. Don't make me. Please don't make me."

"I already have three kids to take care of, Lisa. I don't need another one."

"You won't have to take care of my baby," the girl said in a pleading voice. "I'll quit school. I'll do everything for him. Please, Mom."

"Excuse me," the receptionist said from her cubicle behind the glass window. "We have a consultation room. You'll have some privacy there to discuss your decision—"

"Now see what you've done!" Ignoring the receptionist, the woman caught the girl by the arm and marched her to the door. "We are going outside to the car and talk. And when we come back in here, I don't want any more whining out of you, Lisa. We're doing this today, as scheduled, and that's final."

When they left, the receptionist said to those in the waiting room, "I'm sorry about that. Let's put it down to stress, shall we?" She glanced at the clipboard on Melanie's lap. "You about done with that, honey?"

"Not yet." Melanie waited until the receptionist had again closed up in her cubicle before looking down at the form. But instead of seeing the lines and questions to be filled out, she saw the terrible look on the face of that girl. And the absence of any compassion on the face of the mother.

Jane would never act like that.

The thought came out of nowhere. If Jane were with her right now and she suddenly felt really awful and changed her mind at the last minute, Jane would be okay with it. Actually, Jane would never be here at all because she would have flat-out told Melanie how wrong it was and she would have seen to it that Melanie never got this far.

She stood up suddenly, losing her grip on the clipboard, which fell on the floor with a clatter. Spiked hair looked up, rolling her eyes. But there was something else in the expressions of twenty-something and the older woman who had not said a word. Sympathy? Understanding?

Melanie bent and picked up the clipboard, took it over to the glass window and left it on the narrow shelf. She didn't say a word to the receptionist.

Once outside, she leaned against the brick wall of the clinic, cradling her abdomen with both hands. Her heart was beating so hard it almost made her dizzy. And tears streamed down her face. She wiped at them with her fingers, but they kept flowing. She had never felt so awful in her whole life. And somehow she had to figure out a way to get home.

She wasn't sure how long she stood there in a miserable fog when she felt a touch on her shoulder.

"Hey."

She jolted with fright and turned . . . and found herself looking at Daniel. She hesitated only a split second before throwing herself into his arms.

He held her close for a minute while she bawled like a baby, then spoke gruffly in her ear. "What have you done, Mel?"

"N-nothing." She pulled back, shaking her head, her eyes still streaming tears. And seeing the look on his face, she repeated, "I mean it, Daniel. I swear. I couldn't do it."

He gave her a narrow-eyed look as if trying to decide if she was telling the truth, then gave a brief nod. "Thank God for that," he said, thrusting a paper napkin in her hand. "Here, dry up. We need to get away from this place."

"How?" she asked, sniffing and mopping tears. "You didn't come with Michael, did you? I don't want him to see me."

"Jane drove me. She's waiting to take you home."

"Jane? You called Jane?" Suddenly her tears dried up.

"Yeah. Who else? I told her I thought you might have

something like this in mind. It upset her about as much as I figured it would." He gave her a little shove toward the parked car. "You can do some stupid things, Mel, but this is about the stupidest."

She shrugged out of his reach. "I don't want to get in any car with Jane."

"Tough. I don't feel like hitchhiking." He scowled at her, as angry as she'd ever seen him.

"You hate me, don't you, Daniel?"

"Nobody hates you," he said with not an ounce of sympathy. Or patience. He took her elbow in a tight grip and stalked toward Jane's car. "You hate yourself, Mel . . . and for no good reason that I can see. But killing your baby isn't the way to make things right."

She almost had to run to keep up with him. "I just wanted things to be the way they were," she said in a stubborn voice.

"We can't always get what we want."

She threw him a sidelong glance. "How come you aren't saying something about God and how what I was about to do is wrong and I'll go to hell and stuff?"

"Because I'm too disgusted right now!" He stopped at the side of Jane's car and reached around Melanie to open it. "Get in."

Melanie did . . . with a huff. She didn't look at Jane, who was probably getting ready to deliver one of her lectures.

Daniel closed the door with a hard slam and climbed in the back seat.

Sure enough, Jane started right in on her. "Oh, Melanie. Why didn't you tell me what you were planning?"

Melanie stayed stubbornly silent. She felt bad enough without having to admit it to Jane.

"She didn't go through with it," Daniel said in a surly voice from the back seat.

Mr. Helpful, Melanie thought darkly.

"I guess she's got some sense after all," Daniel said. "She backed out before it was too late."

"Thank God," Jane said fervently. "And thank you, Daniel, for having the courage to call me."

"I figure it's about time to set the record straight," he said, and Melanie thought he seemed to be calming down. "I've been going round and round in my head with this, and it's just not something that can be fixed. It is what it is, a baby. We both have to face that, Melanie."

"You wouldn't have had to face anything if you hadn't told Jane," Melanie said angrily. "I planned to do this on my own."

"Stop acting like a jerk, Mel," he said. "You think we could go through this whole thing and nobody would ever know who fathered your baby? Get real, Mel. It was bound to come out."

"So you're gonna tell Christine and your dad?"

"Yeah. Tonight. Soon as my dad comes home."

"They're gonna be so mad at me," Melanie said, now more scared than mad. The O'Brians had always been nice to her, but after this they would probably want to kill her. She must have made some kind of distress sound because Jane reached over and touched her arm.

"Daniel is doing the right thing. And whatever happens, your dad and I will be right there."

Melanie felt her lips tremble, but she tried not to start crying again. Jane, glancing over, met her gaze. "You've been under a lot of pressure. But we'll make it through this together, you'll see. As for Christine and Ben, if it would be easier, Daniel, I'll call and invite them over tonight and we'll tell them together," she said. "But I warn you both. It won't be pretty. They'll be shocked and angry. And they'll have a lot of questions."

The knot was back in Melanie's stomach. If she'd known having this baby would stir up so much trouble, she wouldn't have done it.

WHEN THEY GOT HOME, Jane stopped Daniel before he left the garage. "I know it was difficult to call me today, Danny. It was the right decision."

He gave an embarrassed shrug. "I should have said something before, but it was . . . I don't know. I just couldn't figure out what to do."

"In the end you did the right thing. That's what's important."

He glanced at Melanie who stood beside the car trying to look as if her world wasn't crumbling around her. "It hasn't been as hard for me as for Mel." He managed a crooked smile and gave her a thumbs up. "You did the right thing today, too, Mel." And with a wave of his hand, he headed home.

ONCE INSIDE THE HOUSE, Jane called Christine. Fortunately, Chris and Ben had no plans for that evening, so she asked them to come over after they were done with dinner.

"We'd love to," Christine said with happy surprise in her voice. "In fact, don't make dessert. I have a Key lime pie from last night and most of it was left over. I'll bring it."

Jane considered refusing the pie since the evening didn't promise to shape up as a happy occasion where anybody would enjoy a dessert. Not even Key lime pie. But she couldn't tell Christine without explaining. She worried about how the O'Brians would react once they knew they were about to become grandparents.

Melanie hovered nearby as she talked to Christine. But

once she hung up, Melanie scurried upstairs, so Jane didn't have a chance to discuss the nearly disastrous decision the girl had made that day. Not that she would have opened up anyway. Melanie had a difficult evening ahead of her, and piling on wouldn't help. She'd get enough of that when Christine and Ben were finally told the truth.

She reached Kyle on his cell. "What's up?" he asked.

"Why do you think something's up?"

"I can hear it in your voice. Is it Melanie?"

She sighed. "Isn't it always? When do you expect to get home tonight? I've invited the O'Brians over. They'll be here at eight o'clock."

"Are we having a party?"

"Melanie and Daniel have decided it's time they told his parents she's pregnant. I thought it best to do it here."

"I guess this means Daniel is the father?"

"I haven't been told that in so many words, but that's how it appears. Try to get here before they come over, Kyle. Melanie needs to tell you what happened today too."

"It'll take me about an hour to get there. I was planning to be home by six at the latest."

One more evening when he planned to be home in time for dinner with his family. He really has had a change of heart, she thought. Then she reminded herself that it was concern for Melanie that brought about the change, not her.

But the best laid plans often went awry. Ten minutes later, Kyle called to say he'd been involved in a minor traffic accident. Someone had plowed into the rear of his car at a red light.

"Are you okay?"

"I'm fine. But I'll have to stay here until the police report is done. It looks like the driver who caused it is two cars behind me. Which means three vehicles are involved. I don't think I can possibly get away from here for at least an hour. Maybe longer. Then I still have the drive home and it's rush hour. I think I'll be able to make the meeting with the O'Brians. Do you want to fill me in now on the phone, or will it keep? Oh, wait, forget that. The cop is headed this way. I'll try to call you back. If not, I'll see you at home."

Kyle finally arrived a few minutes before the O'Brians, so Jane had no time to tell him anything. She ushered them in, noticing that Daniel was not with them. He must know he needed to be here. She glanced up and saw Melanie at the top of the stairs, her phone in her hand. Texting Daniel, Jane guessed.

"This is a treat," Christine said, giving Jane a one-armed hug while balancing the pie with the other. "I'm supposed to be dieting, but I skipped white carbs at dinner so I could have pie without a guilty conscience."

Kyle reached around Jane to shake Ben's hand. "How are you, Ben? I saw in the paper where your practice has added two more physicians. Business must be booming."

"Folks keep having babies." Ben grinned. "Daniel has his heart set on Vanderbilt. I figure it'll take most of my commission on the deal to pay for his freshman year."

Jane watched the two men drift toward the den. Folks did indeed keep having babies, but he was in for a shock. She hoped Daniel's college plans would not be ruined.

"Do we want to eat this now or wait a few minutes before digging in?" Christine asked, smiling.

"I'll take it to the kitchen. Have a seat in the den." With the pie in hand, Jane went to the kitchen. She was starting a pot of coffee when Melanie and Daniel came in from the garage.

"I thought you were still upstairs," Jane said.

"I told Daniel that we might as well get this over with quick," she said.

Jane paused, but a look at their faces told her that it would be torture if they had to wait while the grown-ups chatted and ate pie. "Okay, if that's what you want, let's do it. Are you going to tell your story, Melanie? Or would you rather I did it?"

Thinking, Melanie chewed on her lip. "I'd rather you did it," she said, "but that would make me seem even more of a loser. I'll tell them how I managed to get pregnant and then try to make them understand that Daniel didn't know anything about it."

"Hey, I'm not a total innocent here," Daniel said. "You wouldn't be in this fix if I hadn't . . . well, you know, if I hadn't been right there with you."

"What is going on here?" Christine demanded at the door.

Melanie's gaze flew to Jane in panic. Daniel groaned and he bent his head.

"Oh, Christine," Jane said, "this is not the way we wanted to tell you."

"Tell me what? It can't be what I heard." She was looking hard at Daniel.

"I'm sorry, Mom," he said.

"Can we all go to the den?" Jane interrupted.

Christine ignored that. "Is Melanie pregnant?" she asked Jane.

It was Melanie who answered, not Jane. "Yes, ma'am. And it's my fault. If you're mad, be mad at me, not Daniel."

"Daniel is the father?" Christine asked with a look of incredulity on her face.

Melanie glanced over at Daniel.

"Yes, Mom, I'm the father."

When Christine seemed struck dumb, Jane repeated, "Let's go to the den, Chris. Ben should hear this."

"No," Christine said, looking at Daniel as if he'd turned into a rank stranger. "It's not possible."

"Yes, Mom."

"What . . . Who . . ." Floundering for words, Christine finally managed, "You're only seventeen, Daniel."

"Please, Chris," Jane said, "I know you're shocked. We all are. Melanie needs to tell you how this happened. But in the den where Ben and Kyle can hear."

Christine sliced the air with an impatient hand. "I know how this happened. There's only one way pregnancy happens. What I don't know is why!" She gave Daniel an anguished look. "I trusted you, Danny. After all our teaching, after all our caution about how this kind of thing can ruin your future and knowing how wrong it is . . . how could you?"

Standing straight, Daniel looked squarely at his mother. "It was a big mistake, Mom." He reached for Melanie's hand. "Me and Melanie, we've both had time to know just how big a mistake it was."

Christine was still in the throes of shock. She gave Jane a bewildered look. "How long have you known about this?"

"About Melanie's pregnancy, only a few weeks, but I didn't know that Daniel was . . . involved until today. I've wanted to talk to you, Chris, you can't know how much, but until Melanie revealed the father, I couldn't say anything."

Christine looked appalled. "Are you saying that Melanie has been sexually active with more than one boy?"

"No!" Melanie said, looking horrified at the thought.

Jane made a motion to try to usher them to the door. "Please, let's get out of the kitchen."

Christine looked shocked and angry, struggling to take it all in. And regardless of anything Melanie said, Jane guessed Chris wouldn't be persuaded this was anything except a major disaster for her family. Such a transgression would have dire consequences. And they had two impressionable younger daughters. Reasons enough, Jane thought, for Chris to be furious. And from the look on her face, she was not going to let Daniel and Melanie off the hook easily.

Jane hesitated as everyone finally filed out of the kitchen. The next hour was bound to be fraught with the kind of emotion that could end friendships and leave scars that might not heal for years to come. Maybe now would be a good time to breathe a prayer, she thought. In any other such circumstances, Christine would be the one to stop and take a moment to pray.

But Jane didn't know how.

14

Christine marched across the den and sat down beside Ben, who took one look at her and frowned. "What's wrong?"

"Everything. We weren't invited over for a pleasant evening," she said grimly. "We were invited to hear that Melanie is pregnant and Daniel is the father."

"What?" Ben gaped in disbelief.

Christine appeared ready to weep. "You heard me, Ben." She gazed in bewilderment at Daniel as if hoping he would say the whole thing was a bad joke. "They're pregnant."

Ben looked at Daniel. "Is this true, Dan?"

"Dad, just hold on. Just give Melanie a chance to—"

"It's not Melanie I want to hear from," Ben said sternly. "It's you. What—"

"Stop!" Melanie stood in the middle of the room, holding up both her hands. "Stop it! Please let me tell you what happened, and then if you want to scream at Daniel, okay. I guess. But I need to say something first."

"No, not yet," Ben said, still focused on Daniel. "First, I need an answer from Dan. You can't just throw something out like this and expect me to sit back and wait to ask questions. Is it true, son?"

"Yes, Dad. But you need to hear the whole thing from Mel."

Before Ben spoke again, Melanie grabbed her chance. "Here's what happened." She took a deep breath. "I knew it was my fault that Max was gone and Jane could never have another baby, because it was so hard to get pregnant with Max in the first place. So after a while, it came to me that I could replace him."

She glanced quickly at Christine and Ben. Both appeared as astonished as Jane and Kyle had been.

"Yeah, I can see you pretty much think the same as Dad and Jane. But to me, it was a good idea."

Ben leveled a stern look at his son. "And you went along with this craziness?"

Daniel refused to reply. Instead, he gestured mutely with one hand to Melanie. "No, he didn't," she said. "I told you, it was all my idea. I didn't tell Daniel what I planned, but we'd been sort of growing together as girlfriend and boyfriend for a while. We've always been careful about not getting too caught up in . . . well, you know, passion? But I knew that I could probably get Daniel to a point where he might sort of . . . ummm, lose control?" She gave the adults a look as if expecting them to understand. No one said anything.

She shrugged. "And it worked," she said.

Christine surged up from the sofa. "I've never heard anything so . . . so—"

"Manipulative?" Ben put in angrily. "Calculating?"

"Yes, sir, all that." Melanie's lips began to tremble. She

swallowed hard. "I don't know why I didn't see that before it was too late. What I did was awful. I know you'll consider it a sin, and I have prayed a lot about it, and I hope God can forgive me." She seemed unaware of the startled look she got from Daniel. "The worst thing was that I didn't realize how Dad and Jane would feel about it. I thought they'd be glad, but they weren't. And Daniel certainly wasn't. If you could have heard him when I finally told him, you'd know he wouldn't ever have gone along with my plan."

"Scheme," Christine said. "But it appears that he did go along with having sex."

Melanie shrugged, unwilling to defend herself. "So today I went to a clinic to solve the problem."

"Oh, no," Christine whispered, with a hand over her heart. "You had an abortion."

"No, I didn't," Melanie said. "I thought a lot about it because it just seemed like a baby was a big problem instead of a good solution." She raised her eyes to Daniel's. "Once, right after Jane found out about it and was so upset, I told Daniel that was what I was going to do, but he freaked out. He told me he would never forgive me if I did that. I think that's how he guessed where I was going today, and he got Jane to hurry over to stop me."

"But I didn't have to," Daniel said.

Melanie looked down at her hands, suddenly tearful again. "But I messed up our friendship, Daniel. You know it did. You wouldn't even look at me, you were so disgusted."

"I wasn't disgusted," Daniel said. "I was wondering what the heck I was going to do with a baby."

"It wasn't supposed to be *our* baby! Doesn't anybody understand that? I was going to give him to Dad and Jane, but then everything went all crazy when it looked like they were getting a divorce."

"We're not getting a divorce," Kyle said adamantly. "We're going through a bad patch, but couples do that, Mellie."

"But do they stop sleeping together? You moved out of the bedroom, Dad."

Jane put up a hand. "Let's not get into our marital problems."

"Daniel said all along it was pretty stupid," Melanie said gloomily. "I guess it really was."

"Not to mention how dishonorable it is and unfair to Daniel," Ben said. "You seduced him, Melanie."

"Hey, Dad," Daniel said, frowning at his father. "I might not have known the plan, but I definitely played my part in getting Melanie pregnant."

"This is too incredible to be true," Christine said. She looked at Jane and Kyle. "Since you've had some time to puzzle this out, have you decided what to do? Melanie is too young to care for a baby. And Daniel"—her voice broke, but in a moment she went on—"Daniel has plans for college. He is not old enough to take on the responsibility of a child."

"I have to, Mom," Daniel said. "I can't just act like the baby doesn't exist."

"I want Dad and Jane to have the baby!" Melanie cried. "That would solve everything."

Kyle shot a quick look at Jane. "We'll have to get back to you on that," she said.

THE O'BRIANS LEFT SOON after. Nobody had to say what a drastic change this meant for both families. It was written on everyone's face. Christine promised to be in touch, but Jane worried that their friendship—like Daniel's future—was threatened.

"I guess the whole world hates me now," Melanie said dolefully.

"Hate is a pretty strong word," Kyle said, surprising Jane by his stern demeanor. "Behavior has consequences, as Jane and I have often said to you, Mellie. The O'Brians have a right to be angry. You're not going to be their favorite girl-next-door after this. From their point of view, this situation jeopardizes their son's future."

Jane watched Melanie tear up again. A lecture coming from Kyle was more effective than anything she might say. She wanted to offer comfort but stayed mum instead. Maybe it was time for a little tough love.

"Ben and Christine were shocked," Kyle went on. "If I were them, I would be too." Melanie was crying openly now. Seeing it, Kyle relented. "I thought you were pretty brave tonight, Mel. It's hard for anybody to admit a mistake. That takes courage, and you did it."

Melanie twisted her hands, tears streaming. "But I still have a baby inside me. That's a big problem."

"It is. But you're not alone. Jane can help you," Kyle said. "Pretty soon you'll need someone who's been there and done that."

Melanie gave Jane a wary look. "Daniel told me the same thing."

"He's standing by you," Kyle said. "That takes courage too."

"No, that's not what I mean," she said as Jane handed her a tissue. "Daniel thinks Jane's the best person I should be looking to for help." She blew her nose and met Jane's eyes. "But I told him I've been so nasty and I've said so many hateful things, no way would you want to have anything to do with helping me. And I wouldn't blame you."

"Of course I'll help you," Jane said briskly, resisting the urge to fold and forgive all. "What are mothers for?" She waited a beat to see if Melanie bristled at that. When she didn't, Jane added, "You need a friend right now. We can start Lamaze classes. I'll be your coach."

"You really mean it?" Melanie's eyes were again bright with tears.

"I really mean it. You can always count on me." Love for this child began to flow again. In a moment, she wouldn't be able to keep from reaching out to the daughter of her heart if not of her body. But, she reminded herself, it would have to come from Melanie . . .

"My friends are never going to speak to me again," Melanie said woefully.

"Maybe a few won't," Jane said, "But if it happens, we'll get through it . . . together.

"Oh, Mom . . ." With a wrenching sob, Melanie threw herself into Jane's arms, wailing in her misery. "I'm sorry . . . I'm so sorry. I've messed everything up. I lost Max and I didn't mean to and I've been so stupid! I just didn't know how to fix everything."

"Hush, baby," Jane whispered, closing her eyes, so thankful for a breakthrough at last. So thankful to be Melanie's mom again. To be able to comfort her, to have her daughter back. "You're not stupid. You made a very unselfish gesture for reasons that seemed right to you. It was a little crazy, I have to say, but you're not the only person to make a mistake. We can learn from our mistakes."

Over their daughter's head, Jane met Kyle's eyes and she saw that they were misty. He swallowed hard, and Jane knew he was struggling to keep a guard on his emotions. And suddenly, something inside her own heart eased and she knew that everything would indeed be all right. In time.

Melanie was emotionally exhausted. She went to bed early, leaving Jane and Kyle alone together. One issue in their personal life—Melanie's pregnancy—now seemed less of a problem. Telling Ben and Christine was a big step forward. Another was Melanie's admitting she needed help and agreeing to accept it from Jane. Some of the weight was lifted from Jane's heart.

"What happened in the accident?" she asked Kyle once they were back in the den. "Was anyone hurt?"

"Only a busted lip for the woman who caused it. She had twins in car seats. She took her eyes off the road when one of them threw his sippy cup. The driver in front of her had stopped, and she plowed right into him. He plowed into me."

"Her children weren't hurt?"

"No, they didn't even seem upset." Kyle's gaze locked with hers. His eyes were dark and troubled. "I don't want to talk about that, Jane. I want to talk about us."

Jane perched on the edge of the sofa. She couldn't tell by the look on his face what he might have in mind. What, she wondered, did she want to hear from Kyle? Was she being unreasonable to feel resentment that he'd abruptly moved out of their bedroom? That he didn't see the hurt he'd caused by doing that? "Okay," she said, "I'm listening."

"I think I lost you last night at 'hello'," he said wryly. "So before I try again, tell me this, Jane, are you thinking of leaving me? Have I been such a bonehead that you don't love me anymore?"

Jane, shaking her head, stared down at her hands for a minute before looking up at him. "Why don't you try to tell me what you intended to say last night?"

"It wasn't all about Melanie," he said in a troubled voice. "I'm worried about her, or rather, I was worried, but I knew that in time her problem would cease to exist. Sooner or later, she'd be off to school or married or somehow caught up in her life. So, here's what I should have said first. It dawned on me that I was looking at a life without you, and it was empty, hollow."

He got up from his chair, walked to the sofa and sat beside her. "I meant it last night when I said it was stupid of me to move out of our bedroom. After Max was gone, something inside me just seemed to wither and die. The joy in my life was gone."

"I know," Jane said softly.

"He was just such a great kid. I loved him so much. I had such plans for him." His voice went gruff with emotion. "But I made a gigantic mistake in somehow linking my sorrow to you when you were grieving too. I'm sorry for going off track that way. Max belonged to both of us, and we belong together, not sleeping apart and going our separate ways."

He managed a somewhat ironic smile. "About the only right thing I said last night was to ask for a second chance."

Jane tipped her head, studying his face for a long minute. "That's it?"

"I'm not a complete bonehead," he said, his smile holding. "So no, that's not it. I love you. I should have said that first, up front."

"Oh, Kyle . . ."

He paused as if waiting for her to . . . what, she wondered. Throw herself in his arms? And when the moment stretched out a little too long and she didn't reply, she saw concern in his dark eyes.

"You don't have to let me back into our bedroom," he said, adding ruefully, "at least not now, tonight, but I can always hope. I'm just laying out how I feel and promising I'll do whatever it takes to repair the damage I've done . . . if I can. If you can forgive me, Jane, we can get beyond this. I don't know what else to say. I just lost it there for a while."

"Max is still gone," she reminded him. "You weren't the only one whose joy was stolen. I found solace in working at Child Search. You didn't ever seem to get that, Kyle."

"I get it now. And it's another mark against me that I was critical about something that obviously helped you. If I'd been able to find help anywhere—at anything—maybe we wouldn't be having this talk now. Instead, all I seemed to see was how empty and dark my life was."

Empty and dark. Jane knew those beasts. Kyle made a restless, anguished move. "Will we ever get beyond this, Jane?"

"I don't know." It was a lie. In her heart, she knew. Never.

Kyle's eyes were full of pain. "Will there ever be a time when it won't hurt so much?"

"Chris tells me I need to put everything in God's hands," she said, not bothering to hide her skepticism. "She claims that everything happens according to His plan, that everything has a purpose. But here's the catch—we mortals may not be able to comprehend it."

"I'm not sure I can ever go along with that," Kyle said after a considering moment.

"Same here." Jane looked beyond him with a thoughtful expression. "If He has a purpose for everything but He doesn't tell us what that purpose is, how can we trust Him?"

He was shaking his head. "You should be asking Chris, not me."

"I came across something as I was reading a couple of nights ago," she said. "It said that just because you believe in God doesn't mean all your problems are solved, all your pain taken away."

"I take that to mean there are no guarantees," Kyle said.

"I don't expect guarantees, but I don't expect my child to be kidnapped either. You know that when Max was first taken, I was so devastated it was hard just to get up in the morning. I couldn't eat, couldn't sleep, I sure couldn't pray. And then after the shock subsided a little—because life must go on, or so they say—I was so angry. I couldn't get past thinking I'm a good person, so why has God done this to me? I really wrestled with that question."

"And now you don't?"

"It's the strangest thing. Maybe it's acceptance, although I'll never accept that Max is gone forever. Nor will I ever cease to search for him. But I'm now thinking life really must go on. Isn't life itself a gift?"

Kyle was studying her intently. "Where do I fit in this new outlook you have?"

"I was never the one who had doubts about our marriage, Kyle," she said quietly. "That was you."

"I don't have doubts anymore. I see our marriage—our family—as the most truly real and meaningful part of my life. So, if you've forgiven God for taking Max, can't you forgive me for going off track?"

"I didn't say I forgave God, though maybe I'm working on it."

"So, could you also work on forgiving me?"

It was rare that Kyle felt uncertain about anything and, until now, seldom with her. In their marriage, she had often felt that he took her love for granted. Had this tragedy changed that? Or did he take for granted that once he ate a little humble pie, all would be as it used to be?

"We were both broken after losing Max," she said. "We both struggled just to keep on keeping on. You went one way and I went another."

"We should have gone one way together," he insisted as his eyes roved hungrily over her face.

"We should have but we didn't. And we didn't have a road map for tragedy. Maybe that's a fringe benefit that comes with faith in God; who knows?" She studied his face for a long moment. "You told me you needed time and space, Kyle. Well, I think now I do too."

"So you're turning the tables?"

"This is not a contest! You hurt me. Behavior has consequences as you just reminded Melanie tonight. I need time to think through the damage that was done and to work on how to get beyond it."

"What if you can't? What if the damage is too much?"

She managed a bittersweet smile. "Maybe you should try praying."

15

JANE TOOK HER COFFEE out to the patio the next morning. It was a cloudy day and still cool enough before heat and humidity set in. Kyle was driving Melanie to school. He told Jane he planned to cancel his morning appointments and spend the time at home. She was okay with that as there was nothing pressing on her calendar, though there was plenty pressing on her mind.

She wasn't sure what was uppermost—the O'Brians and Melanie's pregnancy or Kyle and their marriage. After last night, she supposed she would forgive him . . . eventually. Working together, they could at least try to recapture what they'd once had. Many couples did. They were not unique in that. But Jane knew her world would never be truly right again without Max.

She looked up at a sound from next door. Christine was making her way across the yard to the patio. Jane felt a pang seeing she'd brought her own coffee, meaning she would not be going to Jane's pot to help herself as she usually did. Was it to be this way? Had the unwelcome news that they were to share a grandchild blighted their friendship?

"Morning," Christine said, unsmiling.

"Hi. How are you, Chris?"

"Not so good." She held up a hand when Jane would have spoken. "Save it, please. I need to have my say. I spent the night rehearsing it."

Jane waved a hand in a mute go-ahead, her heart sinking.

"I'm so furious over this whole fiasco that I don't know if I'll ever be able to look at Melanie without wanting to throw something at her, Jane." In her rush to "have her say," Christine's face was flushed and she was breathing hard. "I know, I know. She didn't put a gun to Daniel's head, but what healthy teenage boy wouldn't go for the deal she offered," she said, adding bitterly, "sex with no strings attached."

"Chris!"

"My son didn't stand a chance."

"Your son had free will. He could have refused." Jane set her cup down carefully. "You make it sound cheap and disgusting. These are our children, not street hoodlums. Think what you're saying, Chris."

"It was cheap and disgusting! And don't try to tell me how selfless her motive was. This is a classic case of the end not justifying the means."

"What makes you think I would ever condone what she did? Kyle and I were as flabbergasted as you."

"She has ruined Daniel's life!"

Jane's back stiffened with indignation. Melanie's life was hardly shaping up to be a picnic. And what happened to all Christine's talk for the last six months about faith as a rock to carry you through adversity? Was it good only when preaching to someone else about adversity?

"Melanie's our daughter," she said. "Are we supposed to

throw her out on the street? Do you want us to send her to school with a scarlet letter on her forehead? And as I recall, sex outside of marriage is just as much a sin for the boy as it is for the girl."

Christine's eyes suddenly filled with tears. She sat down heavily. "I'm sorry, Jane. It's just that—" She broke down, weeping. "He's s-so young! He had such a bright future. He had a *scholarship*!" Digging into her pocket, she pulled out a crumpled hank of tissues. "He d-doesn't know anything about being a father," Christine said piteously. "And what am I supposed to say to his sisters? Your brother ignored all our teachings, and now he's going to be a daddy? Oh, it's just too much! I can't believe this is happening."

The same words Jane had said a thousand times when Max was taken. How odd, she thought. While Christine's faith seemed to be foundering, she found herself seeking a source of spiritual comfort. Where was that strength and comfort she'd spent six months preaching to Jane about? But meeting her friend's tear-drenched eyes and seeing how genuinely devastated she was, Jane decided to cut her some slack. "What's done is done, Chris. We both know you can't cancel pregnancy when it's an inconvenience."

"An inconvenience?" Christine took her face out of the wad of tissues. "They're sixteen and seventeen, Jane. They know nothing about—"

"Birthin' babies?" Jane said, fighting a smile. It was a line from the classic movie *Gone with the Wind*, which she'd watched together with Christine more times than they could count.

Christine paused for a long minute and simply sat looking at Jane. She then shook her head and smiled reluctantly. "Well, I said I needed to speak my piece and now I have and I feel like . . ."

"Crap?"

"Not that bad, I guess. Just kinda . . . well, yeah, kinda crappy." She took a good swallow of her coffee. "Can we start over?"

"I'm so sorry this has happened, Chris."

Christine sighed, studying her shoes. "It took a lot of courage for Melanie to face us all last night. I guess I wasn't very Christlike in the way I reacted."

"We do things when we're shocked that we wouldn't do otherwise," Jane said. "You should have seen me when I realized she wasn't coming down with a virus but was having morning sickness."

"Is that how you found out?"

"Yeah. She suddenly jumped up and ran to the bathroom and vomited." Jane gave a rueful shrug.

Shaking her head, Christine looked out over the dewy lawn. "Even for Melanie, hatching a baby for you and Kyle is a little over the top."

"You're telling me."

"No baby can ever replace Max, no matter who he is," Christine said softly.

"No," Jane said.

Christine drew in a breath and, as if turning a corner in her mind, leaned over and set what was left of her coffee on a table. "Okay, we're having a baby. I'm gonna be a grandma. *We're* gonna be grandmas. We didn't anticipate anything like this before we were forty, but it is what it is. Any ideas for what happens next?"

Jane gave a sigh of relief. "None whatsoever . . . except that I've been invited back into Melanie's life. I'm now Mom again and not Jane. We're going to Lamaze classes together."

Christine's face was still blotched from crying, but she smiled. "Aww, that is so incredible."

"And I'm allowed to go with her next time she sees her doctor, who, by the way, is someone in your church." She gave Christine a rueful look. "But I couldn't ask you about her before now because you'd want to know why."

"Anne Severn."

Jane nodded. "Yeah, Dr. Anne Severn. Is she good?"

"She's the best. She must have been biting her tongue when we were in a meeting at the hospital last week."

"I'm not sure she knew the baby was Daniel's." Jane smiled into Chris's eyes. "You know Daniel has shown real honor in this situation."

"I suppose," Christine said, but with a note of doubt. "It's still disappointing. After all our teaching and warning him about getting himself in a sexual situation where he might forget caution, he did just that . . ."

That was true, of course, and Jane couldn't find much to argue in Daniel's defense since he hadn't refused when Melanie deliberately set out to seduce him. How many young males would have refused?

Jane gazed down into her coffee thoughtfully before putting into words what she needed to say. "There's still the issue of the baby's future, Chris."

"I wrestled with that half the night," Christine said, "when I wasn't railing over the situation."

"I don't see marriage as a viable option between these two children," Jane said. "What about you?"

"No. No, indeed not."

"And I don't think Melanie will want to repeat that experience at the abortion clinic."

"Thank God for that."

"There's always adoption."

Christine reached over and touched Jane's arm. "Oh, Jane, we can't let that happen. Can we?"

Jane smiled. "I'm glad you nixed that option. I don't want strangers raising our grandchild."

"Jane. Please don't take this the wrong way. But with Max still missing, would it be too hurtful to have Melanie's baby in your home?"

"Kyle and I talked a long time last night. He wants to come back to our bedroom. He wants me to forget it ever happened."

"I'm sure he does."

Jane's gaze strayed beyond the patio to the yard. "I can't, Chris. Not right now. Oh, I know we'll get beyond this, but we've still got things to work out . . . at least, I have."

"You can't just forgive him?"

"We had other issues before Max was taken, so it wasn't possible to keep on like that."

"I'm no psychologist," Chris said, "but it seems to me when a tragedy of that magnitude strikes, stuff just happens." There was real sympathy in her eyes. "I wish I could have been more helpful."

"You've been a wonderful friend, Chris. I will always be grateful."

"Your heart was broken," Christine said.

"So." Jane straightened. "Now we have this little bundle of joy coming. I've been wondering if after Kyle and I patch up our differences, we just might do what you suggest and what Melanie had in mind. Adopt him."

"Do you know it's a boy?"

"No. And neither does Melanie." She studied her hands for a minute. "What do you think, Chris? Could it be this baby is a gift and we've just been blind to that possibility?"

"A gift from God?" Christine said, smiling at her with open affection.

"Well, speaking of that," Jane said, setting her coffee on a side table. "I think I would like to go to church with you Sunday."

"Oh, I would love that," Christine said.

"Yes, of course you would," Jane said dryly. But her smile

faded as she went on in a reflective tone. "But I still have questions; don't misunderstand. I'm not jumping on the Jesus wagon."

"I'm just so glad that you're at a point where you're not turning from God to seek an answer in places where you won't find it." Christine reached over and squeezed Jane's hand. "And that's my sermon for today."

They were smiling at each other when Kyle opened the glass door behind them. He must have returned from taking Melanie to school and gone straight up to take a shower. His hair was wet and he brought with him the scent of soap and freshness. But a look at his face and Jane's heart dipped. "What is it? What's wrong?"

He had his cell phone in his hand. "Sam Pitre called. He has photos of the children George Crandall placed. He wants us to come down to look at them. There's a possibility one of them is Max."

Jane was on her feet before he finished and so was Christine, who gave Jane a quick hug.

"I'll be ready in five minutes, Kyle." Jane rushed past him and dashed up the stairs.

Please God, let it be Max. Please, please, please . . .

THE TRIP TO SAM'S precinct office in the Quarter took almost an hour. On a good day, the Causeway was a long, boring twenty-five-mile stretch of nothing but gray water. Today it seemed twice that. Jane tried to keep her thoughts reined in, tried to prepare herself for disappointment. It was always better not to hope too hard. But it was so impossible not to. Without it, how would she have been able to survive until now?

Kyle reached over and brought her hand up to his lips and kissed it. "I know what you're thinking."

"If I hope too hard," she said, "I'll just be let down when it turns out he isn't in one of those pictures."

"Me too."

She pressed her cheek against his hand, glad that on this one crucial part of their lives, they were together.

"So let's talk about something else while we're crossing this bridge."

"What, the weather?" She looked out at the vast expanse of water kicking up whitecaps. In fact, the sky was heavy with clouds signaling the approach of a weather cell. Hopefully, a good thing. They needed rain.

"I want to talk about those phone calls you're getting and the assault on the jogging track," Kyle said. "With everything that happened last night, the fact that the stalker seems to be getting more brazen has me worried. We need to find him before you get hurt, Jane."

"Sam says the calls can't be traced any more than they have been. And the police found nothing in the area where I was jogging."

"We can't trace the calls to a specific locale, but we can change your cell phone number." He paused. "On the other hand, if the calls are from the person who kidnapped Max, I'm hesitant to change your number."

"It's sick and depraved behavior. And it's horrible if he's the one who has Max."

When he went quiet again, her thoughts went straight back to where they were going and why. "Do you think it could possibly be Max this time?"

"I don't know, Jane. I'm hoping."

She closed her eyes. *Please, please . . .*

WHEN THEY REACHED SAM'S office, Sam gave Jane one quick intense look, which she met with as much composure as she could manage. She was still embarrassed about her behavior the last time she was in his office. She edged a little closer to Kyle, a move that was not lost on the detective. But she soon lost her self-consciousness. Her entire being was focused on why they were there—to look at the collection of photographs and the possibility of seeing the precious face of her baby.

"Where are they?" she asked abruptly, unable to contain herself.

Without a word, Sam turned his computer so that Jane and Kyle could see what was displayed. Jane's heart was beating wildly as Sam tapped a few keys and a full page of baby faces materialized. With Kyle's hand resting warm and strong at the small of her back, Jane braced herself to look.

"Crandall's been busy," Kyle murmured, as he studied the photos.

It struck Jane, even as her eyes frantically scanned the small faces, that she wasn't alone today as she'd been the last time she and Kyle faced this ordeal. This time they were together, sharing hope and fear.

"I didn't call you until we were pretty certain that we had photos of all the kids he placed," Sam said. "Most you see here were voluntary adoptions. Crandall was known to be generous to mothers who, for one reason or another, chose to give up a baby. He paid all expenses and even threw in a bonus for some."

"But he couldn't keep up with the demand," Kyle said.

"Right." Sam leaned back and waited while Jane moved closer to the laptop, scrutinizing the tiny features of each and every child.

"Some of these are so blurred," she said, squinting at a grainy photo.

"Here, you can enlarge any you want to look at closer." Sam put the curser on the face of a baby, and it filled the screen. "It's still blurred, but you get a better look."

With her heart beating hard and her breath caught in her throat, she studied the little face and felt familiar, crushing disappointment. "No . . . that's not Max."

"Look at this one," Sam said, moving the curser to a toddler. "Except that his hair looks darker, I thought he could be—"

Again, Jane braced herself, hoping . . . hoping . . .

And again, bitter disappointment. "No," she said. "I can see the resemblance, too, but it's not . . . it's not Max." Her voice caught, and she pressed fingers to her lips. Kyle reached for her wordlessly. She turned her face into his chest and struggled to hold back tears. And after a minute, held fast by Kyle, she felt the pain in her heart ease. She wasn't alone.

"I'm sorry," Sam said quietly.

Jane nodded mutely.

Sam closed out the site. "I wish I didn't have to subject you to this, but—" He shook his head. "This little kid looked so much like Max, and he was from Mandeville . . . Crandall said he was given up voluntarily, but the guy's such a liar that I wanted to hear it from you that it wasn't Max."

"You did the right thing, Sam," Kyle said, still holding Jane close.

She pushed back and wiped her eyes with a tissue. She even managed a weak smile. "Kyle's right," she said. "Don't ever hesitate to call us. One of these times might be the key."

She paused, noticing an exchange of looks between Kyle and Sam. "What?" she said, eyeing them with suspicion.

Sam scratched his beard, hesitating. "Well . . ."

Kyle broke in. "Is it about Joseph Kaski?"

"Yeah."

Jane blinked. "Who?"

"What is it?" Kyle asked.

"After your encounter, I took a closer look at the police report filed on Thomas Parker."

"Who is Thomas Parker?" Jane demanded.

Kyle waved a hand meant to tell her to hold on a minute, which only made her more determined to push. She gave him an indignant look. "Tell me, Kyle."

"Parker and I were the attorneys in a fraud case. Parker's client was Joseph Kaski. My client was Kaski's business partner. Parker recently drowned while fishing." Kyle sighed, as if he hated having to tell her the rest. "A few days ago, he found me in a restaurant and started ranting and raving over the outcome of the case, hinting that he was somehow connected to Parker's death . . . and his son's death before that." Kyle touched his temple. "This? It was Kaski. He was tossed out, but not before he beaned me with a chair."

Jane held his gaze for a minute, sensing there was more, but she decided to wait until she heard from Sam. "So what about him now?"

"The M.E. stated the cause of Parker's death as drowning," Sam said. "I wasn't able to find anything to dispute that. If Kaski killed Parker, as he hinted to you, Kyle, he's likely to get away with it. There's just no evidence placing him out in that swamp. But I had a talk with Parker's wife. She's pretty much in a state of shock over losing her husband and her teenage son in the space of a few weeks."

Jane had a tense feeling in her chest. "Teenage son?"

"Yeah," Sam said, "suicide. He was sixteen."

"How awful," Jane murmured in heartfelt sympathy.

"Here's what interests me." Sam tapped a few keys and pulled up what appeared to be crime-scene reports. "Mrs. Parker and both her daughters insist that no way would Braden—that's her son—kill himself. They are convinced he was murdered."

Kyle moved so he could see the screen. "Were these part of the police report?"

"Yeah. And here's what I thought you'd want to see. It's kind of buried under other paperwork. A neighbor claims he saw Braden talking with someone a short while before he died. Mrs. Parker says none of Braden's friends were near the barn that night. The cops shrugged it off as a mother and sisters' natural inclination to deny suicide."

Kyle straightened, looking at Sam. "I take it you aren't going along with the homicide cops?"

"I'm thinking to look a little deeper."

Jane said, "As in maybe the stranger could be Kaski?"

"The way I see it, when he crashed Kyle's lunch to tell him about Parker and his son, he set himself up as a prime suspect. He's either stupid, crazy, or just plain evil."

Jane was shaking her head, trying to process the information. "Why didn't you mention this before, Kyle?" She held up a hand. "Don't bother saying it. You didn't want to worry me." She shifted her gaze to Sam. "So both of you believe this man, Kaski, could have a hand in Max's disappearance?"

Kyle, not Sam, answered. "He sure seemed to have something up his sleeve . . ." He frowned at the memory. "He is one creepy guy."

"You believe he would do these things—kill a father and son—as an act of revenge?"

"I'm going by what he told me at the restaurant. Before he beaned me. It could be nothing. But he knew any mention of Max would make me crazy whether it was a pack of lies or not."

"It's a red flag I don't intend to ignore," Sam said.

"How long ago did their son die?" Jane asked.

"About the same time Max disappeared."

"So if he sought revenge by murdering that boy . . ." Jane pressed a fist to her heart. She found she couldn't say it. She had to hang onto the belief that Max wasn't murdered. That he was alive and well somewhere, being loved and cherished. So that someday they would find him.

Kyle pulled her close with an arm across her shoulders. "This is all speculation, Jane," he said gently. "I didn't mention it because it probably doesn't mean anything."

Jane shook free of his arm. "You two still don't get it, do you?" She sent them both blazing looks. "I don't care if it's just the tiniest scrap of information or suspicion, I want to know." Her voice broke slightly. "I . . . w-want to know!" Her voice rose as she struggled with emotion. "What about that do either of you not understand?"

Kyle said to the detective, "We're thinking of having her number changed, but if it's the kidnapper, should we?"

Sam frowned and turned to Jane. "Did he say anything in that last phone call to give you an idea that he had Max?"

Some of her outrage faded. "No, he just listened while I gave him a piece of my mind."

"Don't do that again," Sam said.

She looked puzzled. "Why not?"

"It just encourages him. In fact, I'd advise you not to answer any calls unless you recognize the number. If this is someone who really wants to reach you, he'll eventually leave a voice mail. It won't be any fun if you don't pick up." Sam stood up the walk them to the door. "And no more jogging."

On the trip back across the Causeway, Jane tried not to dwell on the plight of the children who'd been victimized by George Crandall or her disappointment in yet another failed chance to find Max. She thought of the parents and children out there who might soon be reunited now that Crandall's heinous activities were known. What kind of evil possessed a person to take another's child?

She pulled out her cell phone. "I think I'll call Marilee. I want to be sure she gets a heads-up on the children that weren't in Crandall's clutches legally. Could be that some of them are on our Child Search list."

"Sounds good," Kyle said, his attention on traffic as they approached the Causeway.

Marilee was a bit breathless when she finally picked up. "I'm so glad to hear from you, Jane. Several times lately an individual has called asking specifically for you. We've tried to explain that you're a volunteer and we can't say when you'll be here, but whoever this is has been so insistent—almost rude—that I've been tempted to give instructions to refuse any future calls."

"You haven't given out my phone number, have you?" Jane asked in alarm.

"Absolutely not. You know our privacy policy for our volunteers."

"I know the policy, but someone has been harassing me by calling my cell and then refusing to talk. It could be the same person who's calling Child Search. Is he leaving any messages for me?"

"No, nothing. This is troubling," Marilee said in a worried tone. "I'm going to caution the volunteers to be firm in putting this person off if she calls again."

"She?" Jane repeated sharply. "You know this person is female?"

"Well, I haven't actually taken any of the calls, but that's what I'm told."

The fact that it was a woman took Jane off guard. She was busy adjusting to this new fact when Marilee added in a hesitant voice, "I don't suppose you could find time to come in for a few hours, could you, Jane? We miss you here. Our volunteers are all wonderful people, but you just seem to have a special gift."

"I'm sorry, Marilee. I know it must seem as if my commitment to Child Search has faded, but that's not the case at all. It's just that I have a lot going on. I'll try to schedule some time very soon."

She closed her phone and sat for a minute, thinking. "Someone is calling me at Child Search, Kyle."

"Someone?" He gave her a quick glance. "About what?"

"She won't say. It's a woman. She insists on talking to me personally, and she won't leave her name, so I can't call her back." She watched the whitecaps kicking up on Lake Pontchartrain and felt chilled. "It's creepy, Kyle. I was so disappointed today that none of those babies was Max, but I'm getting this odd feeling that he's near. That it's all about to come together and we'll know."

"Is that a good feeling or a bad one?"

"I wish I knew."

16

After leaving off Kyle at home, Jane spent the afternoon at her office, doing her best to concentrate, but she could not shake a feeling of impending . . . something. She hoped it was a positive something. By the end of the day, she'd accomplished quite a lot in spite of her distraction. Plus, she felt her career was back on track after Henri thanked her in a staff meeting for taking the Leon Waters deposition for the favored Nate Strickland. He'd then added, for the benefit of the partners, a nice compliment acknowledging how she'd closed a particularly difficult case to the advantage of a valued client.

On her way home, she stopped and picked up Chinese takeout. She wasn't sure she had anything on hand that wasn't frozen, and she didn't want to shop. Melanie would be hungry. Now that she and Mel were in a good place, maybe she'd be willing to take on the responsibility of grocery shopping.

Arriving home, she clicked the garage door and pulled alongside Kyle's car.

Melanie was sitting at the computer when she came into the kitchen. "I've got Chinese," Jane announced. "We should eat it now; otherwise, we'll have to reheat it, and it's never as good warmed over."

Melanie stood up before Jane was done speaking. "Great! I'm starved." She took the bag from Jane, but held it at a distance with a cautious look. "Tell me there's no Triple Dragon in here."

"Not after what happened the last time. It's three different entrees, chicken, beef, and shrimp, but I can't remember exactly which ones." Jane was smiling as Melanie unloaded the food. "Where's your dad?"

"A package was left on the front porch," Melanie said, inspecting the first container. "He's getting it."

Kyle came into the kitchen carrying a medium-size box. "This is odd. It's marked private and confidential and addressed to the Madison Family. Did you order something?" he asked Jane.

"Not that I recall." She glanced at the box. "Who's it from?"

"No return address," he said. "And no postmark."

"Why don't we eat first, Kyle? It'll keep."

"Yeah, why don't we?" Melanie said as she opened a cabinet. "Let's do paper plates, okay?"

"Sounds good to me." Jane sat down and opened a container. Shrimp with vegetables. It smelled delicious. She'd skipped lunch after taking the morning to go to Sam's office so she was almost as famished as Melanie.

"Am I the only one who's curious about a package that's marked private and confidential and has no return address?" Kyle asked, eyeing it suspiciously.

Jane scooped out a generous helping of rice. "Open it if you're so curious," she said. "Mellie and I are eating."

Kyle chose from a block of knives and cut through the tape sealing the box. He frowned as he removed shredded paper. Jane happened to glance at him just as he got a good look inside. He drew back sharply from the box as if it contained a snake.

"What is it?" Jane asked.

"Nothing." His face grim, Kyle quickly stuffed the shredded paper back in the box. He picked it up, obviously intending to take it away.

But Jane was up now and stopped him. "I want to see."

"It's somebody's sick idea of a joke," he said in an uneven voice, clearly shaken. "Finish your dinner. I'll take this outside."

Melanie was on her feet too. "I want to see, too, Dad."

"No." Kyle's tone brooked no argument, and Melanie hesitantly stepped back. But Jane saw he was upset by the box's contents. She caught up with him before he reached the door leading to the garage.

"Stop, Kyle. I want to see what's inside."

"You don't need to see this, Jane."

She put her hands on her hips. "Have we had this discussion?"

With a heavy sigh, he set the box on a chair. "Brace yourself."

She grabbed a handful of shredded packing and looked inside the box.

Her breath caught on a gasp.

Melanie pushed past Jane to see for herself. One look, and she sat down, hard. She pressed both hands to her mouth. "Oh, no, is it . . ." Shaking her head, she couldn't finish.

"No, it's not." Jane quickly went to her, caught her face in both hands, and forced her eyes up. "It's not real, Mellie. It's only a doll."

"Are you sure?" Melanie's eyes were wide with horror.

"Yes."

Melanie nodded and swallowed with a sick look. "I'm okay. It was just such a . . . a shock."

"It is that." There was a grim note in Kyle's voice. "Which is why I didn't want either of you to see it."

In spite of a feeling of utter revulsion, Jane moved to get a better look. The doll was very realistic, life-size. The tiny throat had been slashed open and something red had been applied to look like blood. Paint? Nail polish? It was impossible to tell without getting closer, without touching it. And Jane did not want to touch it.

But she was drawn closer in spite of the revulsion boiling in the back of her throat. Because what the doll was dressed in looked horrifyingly familiar. She put out one shaky hand and cleared away more shredded paper so that she could be sure. Yes, a T-shirt with appliqués of dancing penguins. And denim overalls with an upscale label. As she turned it over and saw the handwritten word printed with an indelible sharpie, her heart almost stopped. A cry came from her then, a wail, a deep and wrenching howl emanating from the pit of her soul. She put her hands up to her face and rocked back and forth as waves of anguish washed over her.

"It's Max, oh, dear Lord, it's Max, it's Max."

Kyle crouched down beside her and forced her to look at him. "Jane, it's only a doll. Just as you told Mellie, it's only a doll."

"No, no, no," she cried. "You don't understand. Those clothes, those little overalls, they belong to Max. His name . . ." She stopped as tears gushed from her eyes. "I wrote his name on the back of the label. Whoever sent this—" She gave him an agonized look. "Oh, Kyle . . ."

Kyle stood up abruptly, a bleak expression on his face. "Yeah. Whoever sent it has Max."

She nodded mutely.

Melanie edged closer to the box, as if drawn to something

she knew would be ugly. Like Jane, her movements were hesitant and uncertain. But before she had a chance to lift the flap on the box, Kyle stopped her.

"No, don't touch anything, Melanie." Kyle already had his cell phone out. "I'm calling Detective Pitre. He needs to see this. They can take it to the forensics lab. Maybe there'll be fingerprints. Maybe they'll be able to trace it."

And maybe Max will be found.

Jane, still in a state of shock, watched with soulless eyes as he called Sam. For almost seven desolate months, she had refused to accept that Max was lost to her forever. She'd clung desperately to the fantasy that he had been taken by someone who would love him and take good care of him. Now she was faced with this hideous box, the contents of which told her just the opposite. Whoever had Max was not a loving parent but was using him to torture her.

Two DAYS PASSED BEFORE the forensics were in on the package. Jane insisted on going with Kyle to Sam's office to hear the details.

"There are prints all over the box," Sam said. "Whoever packaged it didn't bother to try to conceal them. They're on the tape, on the doll, even on the address label." He swiped a hand over his face and sighed, looking as disheartened as Jane and Kyle felt. "They're not on file in the AFIS, which means he's probably never been arrested."

"It also means that it wasn't Kaski," Kyle said. "He was arrested, so his prints would be in the system."

"Right," Sam said.

The AFIS, Jane knew, was the Automated Fingerprint ID System. "I guess you can't tell if it's a man or a woman," she said.

Sam shook his head. "Unfortunately, no. I'm sorry."

"Whoever it is," Jane said, "why has he waited this long to let us know he's out there?'

Sam shrugged. "Who knows? Maybe he likes seeing you suffer. Sickos who do this kind of thing get their kicks that way."

She was shaking her head helplessly. "Who hates me so much?"

Kyle slipped an arm around her. "Don't, Jane. We can chew over this until we're blue in the face and never figure it out. What we need to do now is focus on trying to find him." He looked at Sam. "He's bound to have left something, made some mistake."

"What about the box?" Jane asked. "Wouldn't it have some DNA?"

"Yeah." Kyle looked ready to hit something. "But with no suspect, that's useless."

"I'd try the neighbors," Sam said. "Since it didn't come via the post office, UPS, or FedEx, maybe someone noticed when it was dropped off."

Kyle was shaking his head. "We called every neighbor. Nobody noticed anything."

"Then we'll just have to go with what we have." Sam spread his hands in a helpless gesture. "The box and the doll are still being examined by our people in the forensics lab. If there's anything to be found, they'll find it."

"Have you picked up Joseph Kaski?" Kyle asked. "He's eliminated from this incident, but he's still a suspect in my book."

"Kaski has no official residence now, but we'll find him. I personally questioned his wife. She said she had no idea where he was, said he's mentally unstable and that she's broken all ties with him."

"Well, that's just great," Kyle said in disgust. "So how do you plan to find him if he's homeless and crazy?"

"We'll find him, Kyle," Sam repeated evenly. "Meanwhile,

my advice to you both is to go back to Mandeville and let N.O.P.D. handle this."

"I WON'T HOLD MY breath waiting," Kyle said to Jane skeptically as they headed home across the Causeway for the second time that day. It was now almost dark and the weather had steadily deteriorated. The surface of the lake—from what she could tell—was choppier than ever. A storm was definitely brewing.

Just what we need, Jane thought darkly. "I've been thinking, Kyle. You know how you can have a tiny nagging feeling that there's something you know and yet you can't quite put your finger on it?"

"Yeah," he said, concentrating on overtaking a truck.

"Never mind." Jane could see he wasn't really listening. He was caught up in his own thoughts as she'd been ever since looking inside that box and seeing a horrible facsimile of her baby. So she let her thoughts wander, trying to pin down the elusive . . . something that danced on the edge of her memory. Tantalizingly out of reach.

But dwelling on it would drive her crazy, she decided. "I still have the feeling all of this is reaching a crisis point," she said a few minutes later. "I know it in my bones. Whoever took Max is a psychopath, right?"

"I don't know, Jane."

"Well, for the sake of argument, let's suppose he is."

"Okay. What's your point?"

"I don't know if this applies in every case of psychopathic behavior, but at some point the satisfaction or thrill—or whatever emotional sensation he's getting out of this—soon might not be enough. At least, I've read that's fairly common with people like this. As a result, he'll feel compelled to take more risks. And if that happens, he'll make mistakes. Which means, we could have a better chance of finding him."

She turned, looking at Kyle's profile as he drove. "I guess you don't necessarily agree," she said.

He gave her a quick glance before turning back to the road. "I don't agree or disagree. It makes sense, sure, but it's also pure speculation."

"Or wishful thinking?"

"You describe textbook behavior for psychopaths," Kyle said. "But you don't know whoever took Max is a psychopath. After seeing that box with its grisly contents, I'll grant you we aren't dealing with an ordinary, garden variety criminal. He could very well be a psychopath, but he's definitely somebody who's out to hurt us, you or me or both of us. He doesn't seem satisfied just to have taken our son. He wants to keep us in pain. I mean, he gave us better than six months to adjust to the loss of our child, and just in case we've managed to get over it—"

"As if we could ever get over it," Jane murmured.

"It seems he wants to renew the agony," Kyle said. "It tells me he definitely has some personal ax to grind. Maybe he imagines a particular injustice for which we're responsible."

"You could be describing Joseph Kaski."

Kyle nodded. "I'm going to be very interested in what Sam gets from Kaski . . . if he ever finds him. But for all we know, Kaski could be halfway to Canada by now."

"If he's the one, he could have had someone else box up that doll," Jane said. She let her gaze wander back to the surface of the lake. "I've been trying to come up with any of my clients who'd harbor resentment for the way a case turned out, but—"

"That list could be as long as your arm."

She was shaking her head, already having spent hours and hours trying to pinpoint a likely case. But she'd sifted through everyone she thought could be a possibility and still came up with nothing.

"You could have missed something," he told her. "Like I missed the Kaski thing. The problem with trying to figure this stuff out is that we think rationally when we should be thinking in the same twisted way as a kidnapper. If I'd looked at my file on the Kaski thing, I would have passed on it. Actually, I did look and passed on it."

"Hold that thought," she said as her cell phone rang. "It's Child Search."

Marilee answered. "Jane, I've just had a very strange phone call. You remember I mentioned a person who kept calling, insisting on talking to you?"

"Yes." Jane shifted the phone and clicked the button to speaker so that Kyle could hear.

"I issued orders that my volunteers were not to continue trying to reason with this person, but we had a new volunteer today and she took the call. I worried over whether to bother you with this, but it was just so strange that, well, I felt I should mention it."

"What is it, Marilee? Mention what?"

"When the woman learned that we were not going to be a go-between and pass messages to you, the woman became so irate that she began spewing out obscenities and the vilest threats, so much so that our new volunteer motioned me over to listen. I finally took the phone and told her that we were not going to tolerate abuse and that her number would be blocked in the future."

There was a tremor in Marilee's voice, revealing how upset she was. "Jane, she laughed, and it was such an evil cackle that it sent chills up my spine. She told me not to bother blocking her calls as she wouldn't be calling again anyway. But that I should give you a message."

"A message?"

"Yes. She said, 'Tell Jane I have the other shoe.' "

"What?"

But even as Marilee repeated the words, Jane knew. She went as still as death. For a long minute, she didn't even breathe. But her mind raced. Back to the day Max was taken. To the moment when the cop appeared on the steps of St. Louis Cathedral pushing her baby's yellow-and-blue-plaid stroller. To that moment when she'd looked at it and saw that her baby was not in it. No teething ring, no sippy cup, no plastic Baggie with goldfish to snack on. One thing only was in the stroller: a single shoe. Max's tiny sneaker.

"Oh, oh—" Jane felt her heart stop and then start up again, galloping as madly as her thoughts. She turned to Kyle in shock. "A woman has called Child Search asking for me and claiming she has Max's shoe."

"Jane, Jane . . . hello?" Marilee's tone was urgent.

"I'm here." Jane shook her head, trying to banish the images crowding her thoughts. "What else, Marilee? What else did she say?"

"Nothing more. That's all. Rather, that's all that's fit to repeat. She is clearly an unstable individual. About the only rational thing she said was to tell you she had the shoe. What does it mean, Jane?"

"Do you have a number, Marilee? Did she leave a number?"

"No, no. In all the calls she has made, she never leaves a number."

"Caller I.D. Check your caller I.D. It should tell us something."

"No, we've done that. Her number comes up as 'No data sent.' "

Kyle motioned that he wanted the phone. Jane handed it over with a shaky hand.

"Marilee, when did this happen?" he asked.

"Just a few minutes ago. I didn't know the significance of the message, but there was just something about that woman, about the way she seemed so . . . so bent on reaching Jane. I'm concerned that she may try to find Jane at home. We would never reveal her address, but you know there are ways people can be found, Kyle."

"Listen, don't take any further calls on that line until I can call the police. And try to pinpoint the exact time of the call, will you do that? I'm no technical expert on this stuff, but there may be a way we can trace where that call came from."

"I'm talking on that line now," Merilee said in a worried tone. "Does that matter?"

"I don't know. Just unplug it from the jack in the wall if you have to. After I check with the people at the phone company and the police, I'll get back to you. I don't want to tie up your lines, but this may be our best shot at finding her." He paused before adding, "It was a woman. You're certain of that?"

"Yes, a very deranged woman."

"Okay, take care, Marilee. We'll be in touch."

"She has Max!" Jane cried the moment Kyle closed the phone. Her terrified eyes locked with his. "She's insane, and she has my baby, Kyle. She's the one! What can we do?"

"First thing is not to panic," Kyle said in a grim voice. "And we need to call Sam." He drummed his fingers on the steering wheel, thinking. "I can't understand, if she's the same person who's been calling you on your cell, why she would keep making calls to Child Search? She has your cell number. She could have given that message to you directly. Something is not making sense."

"It doesn't sound as if she's capable of making sense," Jane said bitterly.

"Make that call to Pitre," Kyle said, "and tell him what Marilee said, but call Melanie first. Warn her not to answer the door to anybody."

Jane's hands were shaking so that she had trouble opening her phone. Melanie's cell was on speed dial and she punched the number. After ringing five times, it went to voice mail.

"Melanie," she said in a voice that trembled, "it's Mom. Call me. It's urgent. If you're at home, lock the door and don't answer to anyone."

"Now, Pitre," Kyle said when she was done.

Sam's office number was programmed on her cell. Drumming her fingers on her knee, she waited while it rang several times with no answer. "It's past office hours," she said. "I bet he's gone." She chewed on her lip, thinking. "I'll call 911. Maybe they'll be able to connect me to his cell."

With panic clouding her ability to think, Jane took a deep breath, then punched in the number. It rang once and instantly someone answered calmly, "What is your emergency?"

Jane's words tumbled out. "I need to get a message to Detective Pitre. Sam Pitre. He's at N.O.P.D."

"I'm sorry, ma'am. This line is reserved for emergencies. You'll have to call the precinct where Detective Pitre is assigned."

"I know that! But I'm in a car and—" She made an anguished sound. "Hello! Hello!" She snapped the cell phone cover closed and turned to Kyle. "She disconnected me. She could have given me the number. That's her job!"

Kyle touched her arm. "Jane, we can get the number. Calm down."

Jane settled back on the seat and forced herself to take a few deep breaths. After a moment, she groped around on the floor of the car for her purse. "I just remembered," she said. "I have Sam's card in my purse. He wrote his cell on the back of it."

"Fear and panic," Kyle said quietly. "Makes people crazy."

She looked at him. He appeared shut down emotionally. Meanwhile, an overload of adrenaline and fear were roaring through her system like wildfire. But, looking closer, she saw that he had a death grip on the steering wheel. And a tiny tic moved near his mouth. Maybe he wasn't as calm as he seemed.

She finally found Sam's card and dialed his cell.

It was frustrating that they were on the Causeway, trapped for an interminable twenty-five miles to the end. Plus, the storm that was forecast for early evening appeared to be moving in. She hoped it would hold off until they exited. She'd been on the Causeway during violent weather before, and it was scary.

She realized, as Sam's phone rang in her ear, that Kyle was ignoring the speed limit, driving as if the devil himself were chasing them. Still, it wasn't fast enough for Jane. She felt a wild impulse to open the door and take off running, so intense was her desire to *do something*!

Sam answered, and she told him briefly—and breathlessly—about the phone call. "What should we do?"

"I don't see there's much of anything," Sam said in his laconic way. "I will try to trace the call to Child Search, but she could be halfway to Texas."

"And that's it?" Jane cried. "We do nothing but wait for her to do something else just because she likes to see us suffer?"

"You can try again to find a link to this person. It's there, Jane, somewhere in your professional or personal life. Or Kyle's. But that's about all I can suggest . . . on your part. I intend to work this case around the clock. You have my word on that."

Jane wanted to scream in frustration. Digging in her case files was just busywork, something Sam suggested because he didn't want her or Kyle hovering while he did whatever cops did in kidnapping cases.

"She'll call again," Sam said. "She's taunting you by telling you she has the shoe. She has the power right now, and she knows it. I don't know anything else to suggest."

Sam's calm demeanor took some of the steam out of her so that she was a fraction less agitated when she hung up. Panic and impatience were not useful. She needed to settle down to think clearly.

You need to pray.

The thought came to her as clearly as if someone spoke the words. But how could she pray when she was so frantic? She was almost sick with dread, imagining where her baby might be, who might be holding him. She was terrified that whoever took him was taking pleasure in tormenting her with hope when all along Max was—

No! She refused to think that. God had not brought her on this awful journey to let it end in tragedy. It came to her suddenly that she was once again on the threshold of a life-changing moment, just as she had been before Max was taken and Christine had almost persuaded her that she needed God in her life. With his disappearance, she'd turned her back on God. Now, at this moment, she was being tested. How she knew that, she did not question. She felt it. Knew it. She did not need Christine sitting beside her to guide her. She didn't need anyone to try to explain the inexplicable. She simply knew that God was near. She simply knew she had to put her fate—and Max—in His hands. She had to let go of her anger at God that Max was taken from her and trust Him now for the outcome. Could she do it?

Please . . . please, help me to bear whatever happens.

To her amazement, the pounding of her heart eased. The panic in her mind eased. She sat for a minute simply trying to take it in. How incredible.

She must have made a sound without realizing it. Or maybe Kyle spoke. She wasn't sure. She turned to find him looking at her curiously, at her hands, which, without her being aware of it, were clasped over her heart.

"God is going to help us through this, Kyle."

He was clearly intrigued. "How do you know that?"

"I don't know. But I believe it."

THAT SAME DAY, MELANIE stayed late at school doing research in the library for a special report in biology for which she'd get an extra grade. Since getting pregnant, she had become way more serious about her grades. She wasn't sure why that was. It just was. Now, looking nervously at the darkening clouds, she was glad Daniel's driving privileges had been restored after the Big Meeting so he could drive her home.

The Big Meeting. That's how she thought of the evening when she'd confessed how she'd come to be pregnant. Daniel told her his parents were really disappointed in him, and she felt bad about that. He said they talked about choices and stuff and that she hadn't put a gun to his head to make him have sex with her, but she knew she hadn't played fair. Although their friendship was on again, she worried they'd never be as close as they once were. Her fault, she took the blame for that.

The house was quiet when she unlocked the door and went inside. She headed straight for the kitchen, plugged her cell phone in the charger as the battery was gone, and went to find something to eat. She was always hungry now. And to prove it, she was putting on weight. She had a little bump in front, her little baby bump, she called it. And it needed to be fed. She opened the refrigerator and found blueberries and sliced cantaloupe in a bowl ready to eat. Her mom, she thought. Always thinking healthy.

She'd finished off the fruit and was looking for something else when the doorbell rang. Grabbing a bag of pretzels—telling herself they were a healthy snack—she headed to the foyer, checked the peephole, and saw a woman. A total stranger. No one would be looking for her mom or dad so early, she thought. Neither was ever home from work at this hour. She stood for a moment trying to decide whether to open the door. It was really hard to just ignore someone. Especially since it was an ordinary looking woman. Not like she was some kind of serial killer.

She opened the door.

17

"I'VE GOT IT, KYLE! It's been dangling out there in my head just out of reach and driving me crazy."

Kyle exited the Causeway and merged into traffic. "Got what?"

"I know who it is!" Jane was almost jubilant with discovery. "It's been nagging at me from day one. It's like a déjà vu thing, you know? All along I felt there was something I should have picked up on, but when I really concentrated, it slipped away. It's only now that she left that message about the shoe that it all fell into place."

Kyle stopped at a traffic light. "You know who kidnapped Max?"

"I think I do." She was shaking her head in wonderment. "I'm just flabbergasted that I didn't put it together before now."

"So . . ." Kyle said with an impatient edge in his voice. "Tell me."

"The day Max was kidnapped, everything was taken from his stroller—diapers, his bottle, his pacifier, everything."

"Yeah . . ."

"But when the cop brought the stroller back, there was only one thing in it, Max's shoe. At the time, nobody considered that significant. We figured that whoever took him . . ." Here her voice wobbled a bit, but she recovered. "Whoever took him would have been in a hurry to get away, naturally, so when he was lifted out of the stroller, we thought he probably just lost his little shoe in the shuffle. We never considered the possibility that it was left intentionally." She looked at Kyle. "You see?"

"Okay . . . she left it intentionally. But I don't see what that proves."

"Wait, I'm getting there." She was shaking her head again. "About two years ago, I represented a client, Mary Beth Rutherford. Her husband sued for custody of their infant boy, claiming his wife was mentally unstable. The judge agreed. Frankly, even to me, Mary Beth seemed eccentric to the point of weirdness. Anyway, the meeting was in my office the day the exchange was to be made."

Jane's expression softened, recalling the incident. "Mary Beth went ballistic. She was wild with grief and rage. I learned later from her husband's attorney that she was admitted to the state psychiatric hospital here in Mandeville."

"I remember this now," Kyle said. "You came home with several nasty scratches on your neck where she'd raked you with her claws."

"She was desperate at having her child taken from her," Jane said, remembering the look on the woman's face. "And, considering her mental state, we should have been prepared for her reaction."

"And why do you think she's the one?"

"Just this. And I'll never forget it. When Andrew left my office taking her baby, Mary Beth was sobbing hysterically and clutching his tiny shoe to her breast."

After Melanie opened the door, she wondered if she might have made a mistake. It wasn't the way the woman dressed or how she smiled. And she drove a nice car. No, it was something about her eyes . . . the way they darted this way and that, blinking too much. Sort of . . . weird.

"Hi, honey, do I have the right house? I'm looking for Jane Madison."

Melanie, still holding the pretzels, decided she'd talk to her outside, not in the house.

"I'm sorry, my mom's not here. Are you a client?"

"I am. I was in the neighborhood, and since I haven't seen her in a couple of years, I thought I'd drop in. She handled my divorce, and I thought she'd like to know how things turned out for me."

That sounded okay, so Melanie relaxed but not quite enough to invite her inside. Besides, she wanted to go upstairs and take a nap. "I'm sorry you missed her. Would you like to leave a message?"

"I believe I'll do that, yes, indeed." She smiled, but again, the thing with the eyes put Melanie off a little. She was reminded of a horror movie she'd seen a couple of months before where the bad guy smiled and showed a lot of teeth before doing awful things to people. Which was silly, she told herself. "Do you have a card or something?"

"Can you believe this? I'm all out. Oh, but wait." Melanie blinked when the woman suddenly snapped her fingers. "I've got a little notebook right here in my purse. I'll just write a message. I do need to put it in writing rather than having you give it to Jane verbally on the chance of it going all cockeyed. You've played that game, haven't you, honey?"

"Game?"

"You know—where you sit in a circle and whisper a secret to the person next to you and they tell it to the next person and by the time it gets around the circle it doesn't even resemble the original."

"Oh. Uh-huh." Melanie had played that game but not since she was about eight years old.

"I suspected Jane probably would not have left her office yet, so I came prepared." Chatting away, she rummaged in the depths of her purse, a huge, bulky thing big enough to hold a week's groceries.

"I could get you something to write on," Melanie offered. Anything to hurry her up so she could take that nap.

"No, no, not necessary. It's in here . . . somewhere. I'm prepared. I wanted to be sure Jane got my message."

Finally, out came a little notepad with a pen stuck in the spiral binding. As Melanie watched, the woman propped her foot on a big pot and scribbled her message. That done, she ripped it off and folded it. But when Melanie reached to take it from her, she backed away.

"No, honey, I think it's best that I just leave it here, maybe stuck in the door. That way, Jane is sure to find it."

"Don't worry; I'll give it to her."

"You would if you were here, I'm certain, but what if you're not?"

"I'm not going anywhere." Frowning now and getting an uneasy feeling, Melanie decided to go inside. If this creature wanted to stick a message in the door, have at it.

"I don't think I mentioned my name." She stuck out her hand. "I'm Mary Beth Rutherford, and you're Melanie, Jane's little girl."

Melanie couldn't think of a polite way to refuse her handshake. She reluctantly transferred the pretzels to her left hand, but kept contact as briefly as she could. "You know my name?"

"Oh, I know everyone in Jane's family. In fact, you might want to take a little ride with me and meet my family."

Melanie gave her a startled look. Could she be serious? "I don't think so," she said, reaching behind her for the doorknob. "I really have to go now, Ms. Rutherford. I'll tell Jane you dropped by, and I'll see she gets the note."

"But you won't be here, honey. You'll be going with me."

Melanie stepped back over the threshold alarmed. This woman was certifiable. She made to close the door but was caught off guard when Mary Beth grabbed her arm and almost yanked it off. Pretzels scattered all over the place. "Hey! Let me go!"

"No, honey, you're coming with me."

"No way!" Melanie struggled, but Mary Beth had her arm in a hard grip, and she couldn't budge. "What is with you?" Melanie demanded.

"You mean who is with me, don't you?"

"What? No! Let me go! I'm not going with you. Why would I?"

"Why? Well, honey, because I have Max. That's why."

Melanie froze in astonishment. "What?"

"I think you heard me. I have your little brother, and if you want to see him ever again, you'll come with me."

Melanie was shaking her head. "No, I don't believe you."

Mary Beth sighed, rolling her eyes. "I took him on Mardi Gras Day. You left him to flirt with those boys on the float." She shook a finger in Melanie's face. "You should be ashamed of yourself, honey. Look what happened."

"You could have read all that in a newspaper," Melanie said, but she was shaken. And scared. With her heart pounding, she looked beyond Mary Beth to her car. "Is he with you? Because I'm not going anywhere with you unless I see him."

Mary Beth reached into her voluminous bag and pulled out a snapshot. Handing it over, she said, "Is that proof enough?"

Melanie took one look. She made a distraught sound, then

sent a frantic look toward Daniel's house. She needed help. She could scream. Someone would hear and come running. Maybe.

"Don't do it," Mary Beth said in a harsh voice. "You yell and I leave. Goodbye Max."

"Where is he?" Melanie cried. "What have you done with him? You better not have hurt him."

"Only one way to find out." Mary Beth smiled. "But you'll have to come with me."

KYLE PULLED THE CAR into the garage and instead of getting out simply sat with his gaze fixed straight ahead. Looking at him, Jane's excitement in thinking she'd finally figured it out began to wane.

"Well," she said, "what do you think? Doesn't that make sense?"

"Yeah, it does," he finally said, but he still seemed distracted.

"But what?" she said. "I hear a 'but' in there."

"I'm just trying to figure out how Rutherford managed to be at the right time and place to take Max. How did she find you in that crowd? It was Mardi Gras Day. Thousands of people clogged the streets. And how would she have known you were going to watch the parades at all?"

"I don't have answers. To any of that." Jane's brow wrinkled as she considered how it might have happened. She had no answers, only a gut feeling that she was right. The crucial thing now was to find Max.

"All I know, she said, "is that I'm convinced we're on the right track. Mary Beth Rutherford took Max. And she left his shoe for me to see the day it happened because that was all she was left with when her baby was taken from her. I was her lawyer. She blames me."

She got out of the car and followed Kyle into the kitchen,

still talking. "It's the same thing, Kyle. It's crazy, but in an insane sort of way, it makes sense."

"Maybe."

She stopped and just looked at him for a long minute. She'd finally figured it out, and she so desperately wanted to be right. But could she be fooling herself? "Do you see it differently? Am I missing something?"

"I don't know, Jane. But we don't want to close other doors. I'll call Sam and run this by him. You should ask Melanie if Mary Beth may have called us here at home. Now that she's showing her hand, it's a possibility."

"We should go to my office and pull the Rutherford file," Jane added. "She won't be at the same address anymore but there should be other references, family, etcetera."

"Hopefully."

Jane paused at the counter, spotting Melanie's cell phone charging. "Melanie must be upstairs."

While Kyle dialed Sam's number, she headed to Melanie's room. A breakthrough at last! She knew it in the depths of her being. It was Mary Beth Rutherford. For nearly seven long months, she'd clung stubbornly to the belief that one day her baby would be found. Inside, she felt wild elation, but she was afraid too. She told herself she had to reject the possibility that what waited might be bad. She had to have faith that it would all work out for the best.

Please, please . . .

She found Melanie's bedroom door closed and almost walked away without knocking, recalling her own need for sleep when she was pregnant.

She tapped lightly on the door. "Mellie?" When there was no answer, she tried again, tapping a little harder. "Melanie, can I come in?"

Still no answer. Jane cracked the door quietly. The bed had not been disturbed. She stood looking uneasily around the room for evidence that Melanie had been upstairs at all after school. She backed out, thinking the bathroom was the only other place she could be. But she found it empty too.

As she stood at the top of the stairs, flickers of lightning signaled the storm outside was imminent. Melanie was freaky about storms. She would not be out in it. Worried now, Jane started down the stairs, thinking to call Daniel. Without her cell phone and a storm threatening, she wouldn't likely be anywhere else.

As she passed the foyer, she noticed a slip of paper stuck in the front door. So Melanie had left a note after all, Jane thought with relief. It was an odd place to leave it, but who could figure a teenager? She started across the floor to get the note and felt something crunching under her feet.

Pretzels. Scattered all over. Melanie wasn't the neatest person on the planet, but if she spilled anything right at the front door, she would have cleaned up. Truly anxious now, Jane took the note from the crack and headed to the kitchen to tell Kyle something was very wrong. She found him ending a call.

"Is she upstairs?" he asked.

"No." She waved the note. "I'm worried, Kyle. She left this stuck in the door and there're pretzels all over the floor." Jane began reading. "She hasn't been in her room and—" She stopped with a gasp.

"What is it?"

"Oh my God, Kyle. It's Max and Melanie." She threw the note on the counter as if stung. Kyle picked it up and read out loud.

"Jane,

I took Max. And now I have Melanie. What goes around comes around.

How does it feel?"

* * *

Melanie did not want to get in a car with Mary Beth Rutherford, but she had no choice. All it took was one look at the snapshot. No mistake. It was Max. If there was a chance to see Max again, a chance to bring him home, she was willing to do just about anything.

But thinking about what she was getting into made her feel sick. She winced when a fierce flash of lightning lit up the road. Between being kidnapped and being caught out in a thunderstorm, she had a right to feel icky. She put a hand over her tummy, over her baby bump, and closed her eyes.

Please, please, please, don't let this be a horrible trick. If this crazy woman really does have Max, please help me find a way to save him. And me.

"You're not feeling sick, are you, honey? You're looking a little peaked." Mary Beth was hunched up to the steering wheel, driving with both arms crossed over it. Melanie had never seen anybody drive in that position. Weird. But the more Melanie was around this woman, the weirder the woman seemed.

"No, I'm not feeling sick," Melanie said. "I'm okay." But she wasn't. She eyed the sky anxiously, not liking those dark clouds. And there was more and more lightning.

When they were several miles out of town, Mary Beth abruptly turned off the main highway onto a country road. Melanie didn't recognize where they were. And because of those mean clouds, it was getting dark fast. If this woman really did have Max, she'd need to know how to get out of here if she got a chance to escape with him. She would need a miracle to do that.

After several miles of nothing much besides farmland and a house now and then, she asked, "How much farther?"

"Not too far. I should warn you that the place is not real fancy, but you need to look beyond the obvious. It's actually just beautiful out here, tall trees, a river. There are deer and other wildlife too. It's truly nature's wonderland."

Melanie stared at her, chatting away in a conversational

tone as if they were friends. As if she wasn't a baby kidnapper. It made Melanie feel as if she'd been taken out of her real world and dropped into a place of crazies.

"Funny how you know things from your childhood and you forget," Mary Beth continued. "Because I was pretty desperate looking for a place. But one thing I'm good at is solving problems." She took her eyes off the road long enough to flash a grin at Melanie, who felt like cringing.

"Who's babysitting Max?"

Mary Beth sighed. "It's hard to find good help these days, isn't it?"

Melanie gave her a puzzled look. "But you found somebody, right?"

"Not really. But he was sleeping when I left, so he's okay. I wouldn't be surprised if he's awake now. He'll be glad to see us."

"You left him alone?"

"Only for a little while. I knew I wouldn't be gone too long."

"You shouldn't have left him at all, Ms. Rutherford," Melanie said in her best stern Jane-like voice. "He's only thirteen months old. What if he wakes up? He could fall out of his crib."

"He's not in a crib, honey. Where we're staying, there is no crib."

"Where does he sleep?"

"On my bed. And I've got to tell you, sleeping with a little kid is a pain. I'm totally sleep deprived. I'll be glad to turn him over to you. See how you like wrestling with him. He seems to grow six arms and legs when he sleeps. And he kicks and flops all night long."

Melanie winced at another streak of lightning while trying to process what she was hearing. Was this woman thinking she would be moving in with her to take care of Max?

"How long have you been living out here?" Melanie asked, frowning. With nothing but trees, trees, and more trees, where was a grocery store?

"Two days, but it seems like a month," Mary Beth said. "Plus babies are expensive. Diapers are not cheap, you know. But I will soon have that problem taken care of."

Taken care of? Melanie had a bad feeling. She had heard her parents talking about the possibility that Max could have been taken by a man who had been arrested for selling babies. Was this woman a part of that?

"By the way," Mary Beth said in the same chatty voice, "did you get my package?"

It took Melanie a minute before it dawned on her. "Do you mean the box with the bloody doll in it?"

"I needed to come up with something that would get Jane's attention."

"Pushing her down when she was jogging got her attention. That was you, wasn't it?"

"Yes, but the baby in the box was a better idea. I bet you thought it was a real baby at first, didn't you?"

"It was a cruel thing to do, Ms. Rutherford," Melanie said quietly.

Mary Beth took her eyes off the road to look at Melanie as if gauging her reaction. "Then she was upset?"

"Everyone in our family was upset. You used Max's clothes, and you poured red stuff all over to look like blood. It was horrible."

"Taking my baby away from me was horrible," Mary Beth said in a tone that was suddenly hard and harsh. The macabre normality was abruptly gone. "No matter what I came up with, it couldn't hurt as much as I've been hurt."

"But taking Max from us didn't make you feel better, did it?"

"Actually . . . it did, honey."

If Melanie had any doubt about the depth of this woman's evil intentions, that removed it. To say flat out that she wanted Jane to hurt was sick, sick, sick. It added to Melanie's worries about Max and what condition he might be in when they got to the place where this woman lived. Or worse yet was the fear that he wouldn't be there. That this was a cruel hoax. That something awful had already happened to Max and she had just put herself in the hands of a murderer, which would again bring more grief and pain to her parents. Was this her punishment for all the trouble she'd caused since Max was taken?

She was almost jolted off her seat when Mary Beth suddenly braked at a weathered sign advertising a mobile-home park. She turned onto a road—if it could be called a road—that had a crushed-shell surface but was now so washed out it was mostly potholes. Melanie looked around in dismay. She wasn't sure whether to be glad or sad. If Max was here, she might find help from some of the neighbors to get away. But she'd heard stories about people who lived in such places and worried that she might be in even more trouble.

But Mary Beth didn't stop. They bounced past a string of ramshackle double-wides crowding the road. Melanie saw junk everywhere, old cars, bikes, kids' toys. Trash lay in the unmowed ditches. Many of the mobile homes looked neglected, rusting away and needing paint. She didn't see any people. Or children. Maybe they were all hunkered down with the storm coming. Or was the place abandoned? The thought of Max being held here—even for a day—made her feel sick.

Mary Beth veered to the right at a fork in the road, leaving the mobile-home park behind. The forest seemed thicker here. Melanie cast nervous looks at huge, towering pines. She worried that lightning might strike one of those trees and somehow jump to the car. She hoped wherever they were headed would be a farmhouse and out in the open.

"I can't believe you found anything to rent way out here so far from civilization, Ms. Rutherford," she said.

"I don't believe I said anything about renting." She left it at that, and Melanie knew she wouldn't get more information even if she asked.

They weren't even on a road now, but some kind of overgrown trail. Mary Beth drove slowly about the length of a football field, and there tucked into a space smack in the middle of huge, tall pines was an old travel trailer. Out here in the middle of a forest? Pretty sad and dilapidated, Melanie thought. It must have been a campsite, like for hunting and fishing, but it looked as if it hadn't been used for a long time since the windows were all boarded up. But she didn't dwell on the reason why or the condition of the place. She was interested only in finding out if Max was inside.

Skeptical suddenly, she turned to Mary Beth. "Did you really leave Max out here alone?"

"He's safe," Mary Beth said, climbing out of the car. "The generator needed a little tinkering, but I managed to get the well and the AC up and running. And it's private." She flashed a grin. "Privacy is a must on my list."

Melanie was beyond speech as she got out of the car. Her heart was pounding and she had a knot in her stomach. As they got closer, she looked around to see if there was any sign of life in this desolate place. But, of course, there was no one. And now she saw that the door was padlocked! If Max was inside and there had been a fire, nobody would have known to rescue him. If he woke up alone and scared and crying, nobody would have heard him. She was so shocked at this woman leaving a little child out here alone with night coming on—and a storm!—that she didn't trust herself to speak.

Please, please, let him be here. Please let him be okay.

Holding her breath, Melanie took two steps up the metal steps and reached for the doorknob.

And that was when she heard a child crying.

18

JANE AND KYLE MET Sam Pitre at police headquarters in Mandeville. To his credit, he'd crossed the Causeway in record time after Jane called. It was out of Sam's jurisdiction, but M.P.D. welcomed him because of his familiarity with Max's case. Jane knew she'd sounded frantic on the phone, but she was absolutely convinced that Mary Beth Rutherford had both Melanie and Max. There was no time to waste. But it was up to the police to find her.

"You need to give us as much information about this woman as you can come up with," he said to Jane.

"I handled her divorce, but I haven't seen or heard from her in over two years."

"But you have a file," Sam said.

She handed him the folder. "I ran to my office and copied it while you were on your way," she said.

"Good," he said glancing at it as he laid it on the table. "We can check to see if she's had any run-ins with law enforcement, such as a traffic ticket. Maybe she's on our tax rolls or she's renewed her driver's license, that kind of thing. Also, we've called in the FBI. An agent will be here within the hour. They have resources we don't have locally."

"So, what do we do?" Jane said.

"Wait." Sam shrugged. "I'll keep you posted."

Kyle touched her arm. "Let's go." Jane let him walk her toward the door.

"One more thing," Sam said, moving to them. "I need that note so we can compare the prints on it with the prints on the package you received."

Thanks to Kyle, they'd had the foresight to seal the note in a plastic Baggie. Although the note was unsigned, Jane's certainty that it was Rutherford had convinced the police. She handed the note over. "She sent the doll, Sam. I know she did."

Sam nodded. "We'll just double-check to be sure."

"IT'S MARY BETH, I know it," she grumbled to Kyle on the way home.

"He wants to rule out Joseph Kaski," Kyle said. "It's his job to dot all i's and cross all t's."

"Has it occurred to you," Jane said, scanning the ominous look of the sky, "that Melanie is nervous when the weather turns nasty?"

Kyle's face was grim. "Yeah."

Looking at him, Jane realized he was as strung out as she felt, and he was beginning to show it. Her heart warmed. She reached over, stroking his arm in wordless comfort.

"Why don't we call Andrew Rutherford?" Kyle said. "He was married to her; he may know how to get in touch with her. Not that I can imagine he'd ever want to," he added dryly.

"Or he may know a relative. Even criminals have relatives."

ANDREW RUTHERFORD'S PHONE NUMBER had been changed to a private listing.

"Why am I not surprised?" Jane said glumly.

Kyle gave her a quick, sympathetic hug. "Hey, with an ex-wife who's a mental case, he would need to take extra precautions. We'll have to go to his house."

Jane savored the luxury of closeness with Kyle for a minute. "And how will we find his address? I know he moved. I remember his telling us that day he left with Andy. He knew Mary Beth would be trouble if he didn't keep her away from him."

"Cops will be able to access a database. Rutherford's car registration will show an address. I'll call Sam." Kyle let go of her and pulled out his cell. "While I'm doing that, why don't you go through Mary Beth's file one more time. There has to be something in there we can use."

Jane made a heroic effort to clear her mind and concentrate. Outside, the rumble of thunder told her the storm was advancing. Melanie would be petrified. But Jane put that out of her mind and focused on the original file she'd brought with her.

As she read, she was struck again by Mary Beth's personal history. She had an undergraduate degree in chemistry and a doctorate in biochemistry. But early on there was ample evidence of her unstable mental state. She'd been unable to hold a job for more than a year or so. Jane flipped pages, wondering why Andrew had not discovered her instability before they married.

She recalled her own hesitation about representing Mary Beth, but the woman had been a connection of Henri Robichaux's mother, and she'd had little choice when Henri asked. Maybe it was postpartum depression that had pushed Mary

Beth over the edge, Jane thought. She knew of several women who'd gone through very rocky periods after giving birth. Or if postpartum hadn't been the reason, perhaps Andrew's filing for divorce and winning custody of Andy had.

Jane stopped abruptly, looking up at Kyle, who was wrapping up his call to Sam. "I just remembered something, Kyle. Henri's mother knew her. There was some kind of connection there, but I don't know what. Maybe Henri can give us more information."

"Okay," Kyle said, pocketing his phone. He glanced outside as thunder boomed, shaking the windows. "We need to get moving."

Jane needed no reminder to leave. She was convinced both their children were in the hands of a woman who could be in a dangerous mental state. And hanging out there was incredible hope—and fear—for Max. If it was Mary Beth, what shape was he in after spending half his life with a crazy woman?

She called Henri and luckily reached him at his home. "I'm sorry to interrupt your evening, Henri, but this is an emergency. It's about Max."

"He's been found?"

"No, not yet. But we think we have a good lead on the person who took him. That's why I'm calling."

"What can I do to help?" he said instantly.

"Thank you, Henri. We need to find Mary Beth Rutherford."

He made a shocked sound. "You don't think Mary Beth is involved, do you?"

"Actually . . . yes. I know she's a connection of your mother's and—"

"I can't believe she'd do something so monstrous as kidnapping your baby. Are you certain you're on the right track?"

"Very certain." Jane closed her eyes and rubbed her forehead. "I hoped you'd be able to tell me where she's living."

"I'm so sorry, Jane. I've heard my mother mention that Mary Beth was brilliant growing up, but it was always obvious that she was . . . different. That scene in your office should have sent up a red flag for us. Why didn't it?"

It was a rhetorical question echoing Jane's own thoughts. Why had she missed Mary Beth's being a logical suspect when she'd scrutinized her files? Maybe *because* she was connected to Henri?

"I don't know, Henri," she said finally. "But we need to find her. And since she came to us through your mother, I thought maybe she could help us."

"My mother passed away last year, Jane," Henri said gently.

"Oh, I'm sorry, Henri. Of course." How could she have forgotten? She'd been out of town, so she'd missed the funeral. "Circumstances have me a bit unsettled tonight," she said, giving Kyle a dismayed look as another hope of getting some scrap of information faded.

"However," Henri said—Jane guessed from his tone that he was on his feet and walking somewhere—"I think I might be of some help to you. Mary Beth's aunt was my mother's friend. They played bridge together. It's reasonable to assume she keeps in touch with her niece. Let me see if I can dredge up the aunt's name. Hold on." He paused a moment while Jane held her breath, thinking she heard conversation. "Sophia is telling me something," he explained.

Sophia, his wife. Jane's nerves screamed with impatience while they talked.

He was suddenly back on the line. "Virginia Perkins," he said. "And before you thank me, it's Sophia who came up with the name. She has my mother's Christmas-card list with Virginia Perkins's name on it. Virginia lives in Madisonville. So you aren't very far from her, Jane."

"I need to talk to her, Henri."

"Yes, of course. And if I might offer some advice?"

"Please," Jane said.

"I'd go and see her in person rather than calling her. I think you'll get more information that way."

"Thank you so much, Henri."

"You're quite welcome."

Jane broke the connection after thanking him again and turned to Kyle smiling widely. "Yes!"

19

MELANIE PULLED THE DOOR of the trailer open and, to her astonishment, Max almost tumbled out. For a split second, she was so stunned she didn't move. He was bawling and obviously had been for a long time. His nose was running, he was dirty, and barefoot, and wearing only a T-shirt and a sagging, sopping-wet diaper, but he was Max! She gave a glad cry, her heart nearly bursting out of her chest with joy and relief. But when she reached for her little brother, he screamed with fright and dropped to the floor, crawling away from her as fast as he could go like a little crab.

He didn't know her!

Melanie felt the hurt like a sharp blade right to her heart. But he was just a baby, she reminded herself. After six months, she was a stranger. How could he know her?

"See? What did I tell you?" Mary Beth entered behind Melanie and stood looking at Max as if he were a puppy that wasn't potty trained. "He acts like he's an only child. They just can't entertain themselves. They need people around all the time."

"Stay away from him!" Melanie stepped between Max and Mary Beth. "Don't touch him again."

"Honey, I don't want to touch him," Mary Beth said, taking a seat on a rickety chair. "Why do you think I brought you here?"

Max still screamed bloody murder. How long he'd been crying, Melanie could only guess. Then, in the middle of his bellowing, his sobs suddenly caught as he was overtaken with a coughing spasm. Melanie ran to him and patted his back.

"Don't cry, Max," she said, her voice unsteady. Inside, she was shaking, furious and almost weak with a storm of emotion. Max was alive! "You don't have to be afraid, Maxi-Moo," she crooned. "It's Mellie. I'm going to take you home, little boy."

She gave Mary Beth a stern look. "I need tissues to wipe his nose. Where are they?"

"Are you serious? Tissues aren't on my grocery list." She left the chair and went to a tiny bathroom to get toilet paper. "Here, use this."

Max was still crying but not with the same abject fear as when Melanie first entered the trailer. She reached out and gently wiped his nose, then, unable to help herself, pulled him close and rocked him in her arms. "Oh, Max, I've missed you so much. I'm so glad to see you. I love you. Mom and Dad are going to be so happy we've found you."

Max was snuffling now, obviously confused, but calming down. Still teary and hiccupping, he looked up at Melanie's face, subjecting her to a curious and wary scrutiny. Her heart turned over.

"Where can I find a diaper?" she asked, frowning at Mary Beth. "How long has it been?"

Mary Beth shrugged. "He was okay when I put him down for his nap." But she got up and opened a cabinet, took out a disposable diaper and tossed it to Melanie. She didn't make a move to pick it up, but simply held Max in her lap and murmured soft words meant to reassure him. She hoped he would let her change him. "We're just gonna fix you all up nice and clean and dry, Maxie-Moo," she told him in a singsong voice. "You're gonna feel all better, you'll see."

To her relief, he lay back, still watching her warily as she quickly removed the soiled diaper. Wrinkling her nose, she sealed it up and dropped it on the floor beside her. She couldn't tell how long it had been since he'd been changed, but she was convinced that it had been longer than Mary Beth claimed.

"I need a baby wipe," she said.

"And I need a steak with lobster on the side," Mary Beth said.

Melanie turned and glared at her. "If you don't have baby wipes, could you please bring me a washcloth? Max has a diaper rash, and it'll only get worse if I don't clean him up really good."

With a huff of impatience, Mary Beth got a cloth from the cabinet, took it to the kitchen sink, and turned the water on. "You're not at the Hilton," she told Melanie, thrusting the cloth in her hand. "So, now that I've shown you where everything is, you won't need me. You can do it all for yourself."

"I won't need you, period," Melanie said. "I'm taking Max away from here as soon as I change him."

Mary Beth crossed her arms and smiled at her. "I don't think so, honey."

"You can't think I'm going to stay here. I'm calling my parents to come and get us."

Mary Beth stood, scooped up her bag, and walked to the door. Holding up her cell phone, she waggled it back and forth, grinning. "How are you going to call anyone? You don't have a phone."

Melanie felt a pang of unease. "Why can't I use yours?"

Mary Beth deliberately dropped the phone into that big, big bag of hers. "I'm taking it with me."

"Where are you going?" Melanie cried in alarm. "You're not leaving us out here, are you?"

"That's the plan, honey." Mary Beth opened the door. "And I'll soon know just how much Jane loves her two little kiddies and what she's willing to do to have you back."

"Wait!" Melanie jumped up from the couch, thinking to stop her at the door. She couldn't let Mary Beth close them up in here, padlocked in a desolate location with the windows all boarded up. Almost as scary was the fact that it was going to storm any minute. But their captor was already out the door, slamming it in Melanie's face. Panicked, Melanie grabbed the doorknob, giving a shocked cry when it came off in her hand.

"Mary Beth!" she shouted, banging on the door. "Stop! You hear me? Don't you dare lock us in here!"

Behind her, Max began to cry again. Melanie turned just in time to see his little bottom dangling off the couch, and she lunged over to prevent his falling to the floor. She sat down with him in her lap and began rocking and crooning to quiet him again, all the while her mind racing.

The ancient air conditioner had seen better days. What measly air it wheezed out wasn't cool, but at least it worked, sort of. Thankfully there was a generator, so they wouldn't be trapped in stifling heat. It was September, but it was still warm and humid.

And ready to storm any minute.

Outside, lightning flashed, sending a humongous boom that shook the trailer and sent ice-cold fear through Melanie. Max didn't seem to notice. He was snuggled in her arms and quiet again, so she couldn't give in to panic. Instead, she forced herself to calm down and think. Mary Beth obviously had some kind of plan, and it was sure to involve using Max and her to terrify Jane some more.

She kissed the top of her little brother's sweet head, knowing she had to stay calm for him. She stroked his back, feeling profoundly happy that Max was found and that he was alive. Inside, her heart was about to burst. She felt tears spring into her eyes, and her throat ached. But she couldn't cry. Not now. She had to figure out how to save them both.

"We're in a pickle, Maxie-Moo," she told him in a voice she might have used to tell him a story. "But we're gonna be all right, you'll see. I promise. Mellie's gonna take you home."

DUSK HAD FALLEN WHEN Jane and Kyle finally reached the neighborhood where Mary Beth's great-aunt Virginia Perkins lived. When Kyle stopped the car in front of a quaint Victorian cottage, Jane rolled down the window on her side to try to read the number. But with no porch light it was impossible.

"This has to be it," Jane said, studying the ornate wrought-iron fence. "It's too dark to tell, but it looks exactly as Henri described it."

Jane closed the car door and met Kyle on the sidewalk. "C'mon, I'm depending on you to charm her into letting us in."

He gave a short laugh and hugged her against his side. "And you'll talk her into giving up Mary Beth's personal information?"

"I am her lawyer, so that's the plan."

"Okay. Let's see if it works."

The wind was whipping up as they approached the gate, and when Kyle pushed it, it swung wildly, banging against the iron fence. Holding her hair with one hand, Jane bent her head against the wind and hurried up the walk to the porch steps. The aunt had lived in the cottage for over forty years, and, from the look of it, the confederate jasmine overtaking the porch hadn't been pruned in all that time.

"What's with this doorbell?" Kyle said, fumbling in the vines.

"It's one of those antique things. You twist it." She did so and instantly heard a bell rang somewhere inside.

Jane realized she was so nervous she felt sick. *Please, please . . . let this woman help us find Max and Melanie.*

Kyle slipped an arm around her. "You're praying again, aren't you?"

Jane nodded wordlessly. And just then, a light went on inside, revealing the silhouette of a woman through the lead-glass door.

Virginia opened it without hesitation, studied the two of them for a moment, and then said, "Sophia called. You may come in."

Jane reached out to take the old lady's hand. "I'm Jane Madison."

"And I am Virginia Perkins."

Scratch the old-lady part, Jane thought as she felt the woman's firm grip and got her first clear look at her. This was no elderly woman with one foot in the grave. Virginia Perkins was far younger than Jane expected and quite beautiful. Probably in her midsixties, she was trim and fit. Though her hair was snow-white, it was cut in a classic style. Her eyes were a clear blue, and her gaze direct.

Please let her be rational.

"This is my husband, Kyle," Jane said.

She extended her hand graciously to Kyle, then invited them into the house. "Come into the parlor, please."

The parlor. Jane wanted to smile. And what a parlor it was . . . chock full of antiques. Even as they entered, a grandfather clock was striking the hour, a sound that reminded Jane of visits to her grandmother in New Orleans. There'd be stories to go with these antiques, but for another day.

"You have questions about Mary Beth," Virginia stated after she'd seated Jane on an exquisite settee and Kyle on a chair so delicate looking that Jane winced. Would it hold a guy of his size?

Jane hesitated and then decided to be direct. "Mrs. Perkins, do you know where Mary Beth is at the moment? It is urgent that we find her."

"She lives with me," Virginia Perkins said. "Or rather, she did until a few days ago. Why are you asking about Mary Beth? Sophia said you and your husband are lawyers. Are you representing Andrew?"

"Andrew?" Jane was taken off guard. "No, no. Actually, I'm Mary Beth's lawyer . . . or I once was. To tell the truth, I lost touch with her, and something has come up that I really need to discuss with her. You say she's been living here with you?"

"Yes. And Ryan too, of course."

"Ryan?" Jane exchanged a startled look with Kyle. "I'm confused, Mrs. Perkins. Do you mean Andy? I was under the impression he lives with his father."

Virginia was shaking her head. "No, Andy is their first child. And it was an egregious miscarriage of justice that custody went to Andrew. Mary Beth was absolutely traumatized. I don't blame you for not knowing, of course. Andrew can appear such a gentleman. But once the bloom was off the rose in their marriage, as they say, it was simply unforgivable to take her child from her."

Their first child? Jane's head was spinning. "But they had only one child . . . didn't they?" she asked.

"No, Ryan is their second child. Mary Beth should never have remarried him, but she was always a headstrong girl. I knew nothing good would come of it, but I wasn't consulted. After remarrying, she ran off to Atlanta with him, and I didn't hear a word from her for the longest time. Not until she showed up here on my doorstep with Ryan. She didn't dare let Andrew know she was back in town."

"And when was that?" Kyle asked.

"Oh," she said, thinking. "Mid-February."

"Mardi Gras," Jane breathed.

"So you say Mary Beth and Andrew got married again?" Kyle went on.

"Yes, but it was just as troubled the second time as the first, according to Mary Beth. Andrew was always abusive, a violent man. Their marriage was a travesty, first and second. Mary Beth was forced to slip away in the middle of the night bringing little Ryan with her. I've been trying to persuade her to go to the authorities and rescue Andy. But she claims she's afraid he'll somehow manage to steal Ryan away from her too."

Jane studied her intently, realizing she believed what she was saying. It was amazing that Mary Beth could have lied so convincingly to her own family and gotten away with it. But Jane wasn't about to take a chance on antagonizing Virginia by setting the record straight. She might be the sole person on the planet who could lead them to Max.

"Mrs. Perkins," she began gently, "have you ever spoken directly to Andrew about this?"

"Oh, no. Just think. If I did that, he'd know right away how to find Mary Beth. No, it's best that she just put those two mistakes behind her and try to build a new life for herself and Ryan."

She paused to study their faces. "I can't understand why you seem so confused. As her lawyer, she must have been in touch with you from time to time."

"No," Jane said faintly. "I haven't heard from her in a long time."

"I admit it was somewhat of an adjustment getting used to a baby in the house, but he's such a darling." Virginia's gaze wandered to the top of an upright piano where Kyle had drifted over to look at a collection of framed photographs.

"And it was a bit of an adjustment for Mary Beth too," she went on, watching as Kyle studied a photo he held in his hand. "She is really quite brilliant, you know, but that doesn't necessarily mean that motherhood came as naturally to her as . . . well, chemistry, for instance."

"What do you mean?"

Virginia's gaze shifted back to Jane. "To tell the truth, I wound up shouldering more of Ryan's care than Mary Beth did. She meant well, but you know how demanding it is to have the responsibility of seeing to a child's needs. There's feeding and changing and keeping track of all the things babies need, adhering to a schedule, which I believe is quite good for young children. I must say, and I hope this doesn't sound disloyal, but sometimes I thought that her firstborn—Andy—was the child of her heart. She loved Ryan but not the way she loved that first child. She was almost obsessive in how she talked about Andy and how she missed him. It puzzled me that she was . . . well, honestly, she was a bit neglectful of Ryan."

Jane was dizzy trying to process these bizarre facts while a part of her was anguished at the thought of Max's being neglected. But how had Mary Beth managed to pull off such an elaborate hoax?

"Mrs. Perkins," Jane said gently, "Andy, Mary Beth's older child, lives with Andrew. Mary Beth and Andrew did not remarry, nor did they have a second child."

Virginia instantly bristled. "What an absolutely preposterous accusation. That child has been living right here in this house. I think I would know personal details of my niece better than you. You've just said you haven't been in contact with her for . . . how long did you say it was?"

"Two and a half years."

"Well then. I can't imagine where you came up with such an idea."

"I came up with the idea," Jane said, "because the baby you know as Ryan is really my son. And his name is Max. And seven months ago on Mardi Gras Day Mary Beth kidnapped him."

A look of total incredulity come over Virginia Perkins's face. "Mrs. Perkins," Jane said gently, "I can see I've shocked you. Please let me explain. And you can call Detective Sam Pitre of the New Orleans Police Department as soon as we're done here today to verify everything I've just told you. But first, just hear me out. The lives of Max and my daughter are at stake."

Virginia waved a hand and said weakly, "I don't believe you."

"I'm sorry, but it's true. Today, Mary Beth left a note at our house saying she had taken Max. And she somehow forced our sixteen-year-old daughter to go with her. Now she has both our children."

Virginia Perkins was pale with shock. She spread a shaking hand over her heart. "Mary Beth may have . . . problems, but she wouldn't do something like that. You have to be mistaken."

"Mrs. Perkins, can you honestly tell me you believe Mary Beth to be a stable person?"

"I . . . I think I need to sit down."

Jane regretted being the bearer of horrible news. But Max and Melanie were in jeopardy, and that had to be her priority now. She waited until the woman eased herself into one of her antique chairs. "I have a picture of my baby in my purse. Would you please look at it?"

Virginia hesitated but finally nodded. "I suppose I must."

Jane took it out and stood up to take it to her. At the same time, Kyle crossed the room, holding the framed picture he'd found on the piano.

"You may want to compare it to this photo," he said in a grim voice.

"Is it Max?" Jane asked him.

"Without a doubt."

Jane released a heartfelt sigh. Even though she was convinced they were finally on the right track, it was a relief to have it confirmed. Bracing herself, she looked at the photo. Pressing both hands to her mouth, she made a soft, distraught sound.

"It is Max, Kyle. It's my baby. We've found him!"

Looking shattered, Virginia said, "I am simply horrified. For Mary Beth to be a part of something like this is . . . is . . . What can I say? I'm shocked. I'm . . . speechless."

"Please tell us where she went, Mrs. Perkins," Kyle said.

"I really don't have the faintest idea," Virginia said. "I wish I did. For the past two or three weeks, she's been acting very strange. One moment making plans for a new life with . . . with the baby, and then the next, closing up in her bedroom and refusing to come out to take care of him."

"So she left with him?" Jane asked, trying to keep from showing how outraged she was. "Didn't you worry?"

"Naturally, I worried. But I've called her often, and she tells me she's found a place to stay and a job. She assures me the boy is fine."

"You called her?" Both Jane and Kyle spoke together.

"Yes, she has a cell phone."

Jane took a breath and asked softly, "Can we have that number, Mrs. Perkins?"

"Of course. It's new. She only got it a few weeks ago."

A throwaway and untraceable, Jane could have told her, but she kept that to herself as Virginia crossed the parlor to an old-fashioned secretary. But her hands were shaking as she lifted the slanted lid and took out an address book.

Kyle had his pen out and one of his business cards in his hand. He took the open address book from Virginia and copied Mary Beth's cell-phone number.

"Thank you," Jane said. "I don't suppose you know whether Mary Beth is financially able to stay in a motel?"

Virginia was shaking her head. "No. That is why I worried about where she would take her . . . the boy. I can't imagine where they could be staying. She has a little income from a trust her parents left, but . . ." She spread her hands helplessly.

Jane took the address book from Kyle along with another of his business cards. "Well, if you do think of some place she might be, I'm leaving my husband's cell number here for you so that you can call. Would you do that?"

"Yes, of course. But I don't know how else I might be able to help."

Kyle had his cell phone out. "I'll be calling the detective who has been on top of this case from the beginning, Mrs. Perkins. The FBI is involved too. They may want to put a trace on your phone in case Mary Beth calls again."

"Oh dear." Virginia put a hand to her cheek. "I'll cooperate, of course, but this is all so incredible."

Kyle urged Jane toward the door. "One more thing," he said. "Please don't call her. Let us try to reach her first."

Jane touched the woman's hand. "I know you must feel protective of Mary Beth, but Kyle's right. If she knows we're closing in, she may be tempted to do something desperate. We have to think of the children."

Virginia nodded, wringing her hands. "This is absolutely beyond my ability to comprehend. I'm so sorry." She looked at Jane with sad bewilderment. "I loved having them. There was a hole in my heart when my husband died in January, then right away they came. Ryan filled that hole. I love him, Jane."

Jane was touched in spite of herself. Max had been loved while away from her just as she'd prayed he would be. "Thank you for that."

After they left Virginia Perkins, Jane glanced over at Kyle and saw he was as stunned as she was. "Do you get the feeling that we've just left the Twilight Zone?"

He grunted, but whether yes or no, she couldn't tell. He

was busy dialing Sam Pitre. She waited while he filled Sam in.

"What'd he say?"

Kyle set his phone on the console. "They're putting a trace on Virginia's line as I thought they would. Whether they can locate her if she does call is dicey, but they're on top of it. I also gave them Mary Beth's cell number. If she uses it for anything, they'll know."

Jane gazed out the window. " "Do you think we should try calling Mary Beth?"

"I've been thinking about that. We don't know what her reaction might be if we call."

"Isn't that what Sam said? That it's difficult to anticipate the behavior of someone with a twisted mind?"

Kyle pulled into a service station. "I need to get gas. Why don't you go inside and get us two coffees. This may be a long night."

"Okay." But knowing Mary Beth's number and resisting her intense desire to call the woman made Jane as jumpy as a jackrabbit. She knew it was best to have a plan when they called, but nothing came to mind. Mary Beth might just hang up when she heard Jane's voice. Maybe if Kyle made the call, she'd be more willing to listen. Or at least to allow them to hear Max and Melanie's voices and prove they were unharmed.

As she paid for the coffee, she heard the signal for a severe weather bulletin coming from a television set mounted on the wall above the cashier's cage. With a sense of dread, she read, *Tornado watches issued for the following parishes: Tangipahoa, Livingston, Jefferson, Orleans, and St. Tammany from 7:00 p.m. until midnight. Be prepared to take cover in the event of a sighting.*

"What is it?" Kyle asked, as she approached the car.

"What else could go wrong this wretched night, Kyle? I just saw tornado watches issued for this parish."

Kyle simply shook his head. Jane was carefully placing the two coffees in the beverage holders when her cell phone rang.

Her heart gave a leap. She fumbled for the phone in her purse, praying it would be Melanie. Finally, she got it out and quickly scanned it only to read, "Unknown Caller."

Kyle looked at her over the roof of the car. "Is it Mellie?"

"I don't know. The number is blocked. It could be the crank caller."

"Answer it, Jane. Get in the car and put it on speaker." He opened the driver's side and got behind the wheel.

Jane's finger was shaking as she fumbled with the phone. The phone was on its final ring before going to voice mail when she clicked Talk. "Hello?"

"Hi, Jane. It's your old client, Mary Beth Rutherford."

Jane closed her eyes, fear and relief mingling. How to respond to a deranged kidnapper who held her children's lives in her hands? "Mary Beth. I got the note you left at my house."

"Oh, goody. Saves me the trouble of a long explanation."

"Do you really have Max?"

"I do."

"Is . . . is he okay?"

"He's just fine."

Jane swallowed hard, struggling to continue the bizarre conversation. She was vaguely aware of activity outside the car—people going about doing normal everyday stuff, getting gas, negotiating traffic, talking, laughing. "And Melanie?" she managed to say. "Do you have her too?"

"Yes, indeed. She's a little grouchy, but you know how teenagers are."

"But is she okay, Mary Beth?"

"She's fine. Same as Maxie-Moo."

Maxie-Moo. Melanie's pet name for her little brother. Jane felt like bursting into tears. Or screaming. She felt like climbing through the phone line and ripping this woman's face off. Instead she took in a calming breath and said in a normal voice, "We'd like to come and get them both, Mary Beth. Where are you?"

"Well, you see, that's not exactly what I would like." She paused and her voice turned hard. "What I would like, Jane, is to see you suffer as I have."

Jane met Kyle's eyes with dismay. "Mary Beth, think for a minute. You can't continue to hold two children. First of all, bad weather is forecast. There are tornado warnings. Please tell me where they are."

"No, Jane, and I want you to understand this, so please listen. For over two years, I have been living with a broken heart. And a broken life. It has been horrible. And all because I didn't have Andy. That's your fault."

"I'm sorry, Mary Beth. I'll try to make it up to you somehow. But won't you please let me come and get Max and Melanie tonight?"

"No, I won't. Not until you've had a taste of what I went through. Don't you get it? I have taken Max and Melanie because I want you to know how it feels." She gave a short cackle of a laugh. "So, Jane . . . how does it feel?"

20

SHE HUNG UP!" JANE threw the phone on the seat and grabbed the sides of her head in wild frustration. "She hung up! I'm going to kill her, so help me! When I see her, I'm going to shoot her! She's a lunatic and she's cruel and heartless. How do you deal with someone like that?"

Kyle reached across and hugged her. "Don't, sweetheart. That's what she wants, to make you crazy. To scare you, to torture you. Let's not give her that power. We have her number. We can call her. We just have to think about what we want to say when we make the call."

She allowed herself the comfort of his embrace for a minute. "Are you saying we should try calling her without first telling Sam that she phoned? Or asking his advice?"

"I'm trying to think what to do, period."

"I'm not sure we should call Sam," Jane said, frowning.

"You don't think she might be spooked if she knows the cops and the FBI are onto her?"

But Kyle was shaking his head. "We're at a crucial point here, Jane. I hear what you're saying, but I think we need professional help. They have procedures vastly superior to anything we come up with on our own. Think, we're two emotionally involved parents. If we screw up, we could lose our children." He looked directly into her eyes. "We have to call Sam and do what the FBI says."

Sam met them on the steps of the police station. "You did the right thing calling us. We're ready to record your conversation and try to pinpoint the cell tower. She could be out in the boonies somewhere, but we'll at least have a general fix on her."

"What if she won't talk to me?" Jane asked, hurrying to keep up with the two men. "Or what if, after I call, she stops using her cell phone? We'd lose any contact with her then."

"She won't discard it," Kyle said. "She needs it to torture you." He was looking at Jane.

"What's to prevent her using a pay phone?" Jane asked.

"She knows cops can instantly trace the location of a pay phone," Sam said, opening the door to the precinct and letting Jane enter first. "Your job is to keep her on the line as long as possible. She'll want to hang up before it can be nailed, count on it. She's smart."

Jane looked up at Kyle. "Are you okay with my making the call, Kyle? If I mess up . . ."

"You won't. And you're the one she wants."

"Any advice what to say?"

"I think you should wing it, Jane," Sam said. "Play her. Get her to give you as much information as she will."

Kyle slowed when they reached the room where the action

was. He waited until Sam went inside, stopping Jane. "When you get her on the phone, I know you'll make every minute count." Looking in her eyes, he reached over and stroked her cheek with the back of his hand. "You can do it, sweetheart."

Jane leaned into him for a moment. Through the window at the end of the hall, streaks of lightning danced across the night sky. Her baby was out there somewhere, and so was her pregnant daughter. She had to believe they were together. Max was with someone who loved him.

"I'm nervous, Kyle."

"Yeah, me too."

What to say if and when Mary Beth actually picked up the call? She knew what she wanted to say. Where is my baby? Where's Melanie? Tell me how to get there. All of which was bound to please Mary Beth because it revealed Jane's desperation and gave Mary Beth power. All Jane had was overwhelming mother-love and shaky faith.

She pulled away from Kyle and walked before him into the squad room that was a beehive of activity. She felt an instant lessening of anxiety. These were professionals. This wasn't a new and strange world for them as it was for her. Sam motioned her to a chair. And in ten minutes, after checking the technology, and the room hushed to silence, she was given a signal to go.

Using the number Virginia had given them, Jane dialed and waited while the phone rang, knowing her name would come up on the screen. But would Mary Beth pick up? She waited with her stomach rolling sickly.

"Hello, Jane."

"Hello, Mary Beth. I—"

"Stop."

Jane did as ordered, but sent a distressed look to Sam. He put his finger against his lips in a signal that she was to wait for Mary Beth. The kidnapper was calling the shots.

"You are not playing fair now," Mary Beth said. "I'm afraid that's going to cost you, Jane."

Not playing fair? This from the woman who had kidnapped her children? Jane breathed a prayer for patience. "Mary Beth, I was hoping we could talk for a minute."

"First, tell me how you got this number."

Jane gave up trying to be cagey and clever and thinking she could play games with this woman. "Virginia Perkins gave me the number. She's very worried about you and about Max."

"You mean Ryan, don't you?" Mary Beth chuckled gleefully. "But I guess the cat's out of the bag now, isn't it?"

"Are Max and Melanie with you now, Mary Beth? Or are they someplace else!"

She giggled again. "Wouldn't you like to know!"

Jane searched for a subject that might keep her on the phone long enough to get a location. "Can I ask you a question?"

"Depends."

"How did you manage to find us—Melanie, Max and me—in that Mardi Gras crowd, Mary Beth?"

"Oh, Jane, you're such a trusting soul. You didn't ever suspect that I was watching you?"

"Watching me?" Feeling chilled, Jane looked at Kyle.

"Every minute . . . well, almost every minute. I had to sleep sometimes, but it was easy. Your life is an open book, or it was then. And pretty boring, in my opinion. When I saw you pack up the car that day, I knew you were probably headed to Mardi Gras, so I just waited down the street, and out you came with your good buddy Christine. I followed you all the way to the Quarter and waited. Piece o' cake."

"But you—"

"Enough chitchat." Mary Beth's tone hardened. "Now that you've harassed my aunt, you've stepped over the line. You've no doubt turned her against me, just as you turned Andrew and his lawyer and the judge against me."

"Please listen, Mary Beth. I—"

"No, you listen, Jane. I might have been tempted to let you off the hook, but now I don't think so. I've been trying to come up with a suitable punishment. I ask myself, what kind of punishment would suit the crimes Jane has committed?"

Jane's heart went cold with fear at what Mary Beth implied. The ultimate punishment to Jane meant doing harm to her children. "Please tell me where Max and Melanie are, Mary Beth!" she begged, guessing that she had little time before the woman hung up. "Just tell me what you want and I'll do it!"

"And then you'll call the white coats to come and get me and lock me up again? Oh, you'd like that, wouldn't you, Jane?"

"No, I don't want to hurt you, Mary Beth. I just want my children." She heard the rise of desperation in her voice and knew Mary Beth heard it too. Loved it. In spite of trying not to, she was giving the woman what she wanted.

"Yes, I so understand, Jane. I've been there and done that. It's your turn now."

For a second, Jane froze, realizing she held a dead phone in her hand. And then she turned to Sam with an anguished cry. "She hung up! She's going to do something horrible. We've got to stop her!"

"Did you get a fix on her?" Kyle asked Sam.

"No. Sorry." Sam stood at a technician's shoulder. "The signal was too weak. We couldn't pinpoint it. Wherever she is, there's interference. Probably due to weather."

Jane turned her face into Kyle's chest and said brokenly, "What'll we do, Kyle? How can we find our babies?"

"We will find them!" His voice rang with fierceness as his arms went around her tightly. Over her head, he looked at Sam. "What's next? We don't just sit and wait for her to jerk us around, do we?"

Before Sam could reply, lightning suddenly flashed and thunder boomed. The threatening weather broke with a fury that made even the hardened cops in the room flinch. Wind howled and rain lashed the windows. Lightning was so constant, it appeared to be daylight outside.

Sam moved to the window. "We'll just have to wait—" He cringed as another spectacular boom literally shook the building. The lights went out.

"Not a problem!" One of the technicians called out in the darkness. "The backup generator'll kick in. It's not gonna give us full power, but it's better than nothing."

Barely were the words out of his mouth when the lights flickered on again. There was a sigh of relief throughout the squad room, but the failure of the team to zero in on the kidnapper was telling on the faces of the cops.

Jane looked at Sam. "The storm is going to cause technical difficulties all around, isn't it?"

"I'm afraid so, Jane." Same sent a dismayed look at the streaming windows. "We'll just have to wait it out."

Jane felt crushing despair. She stepped back from Kyle's embrace and, with a sigh, sat down on one of the hard chairs. She had been so confident earlier when she told Kyle they were going to find Max and Melanie. But now . . . her heart ached. Why was she being tested this way?

She was holding her cell phone in her hand, looking at it dejectedly, when it suddenly rang. "It's Virginia Perkins," she said, quickly gathering herself. "I'll click on speaker so everyone can hear. Hello?"

"Is this Jane Madison?"

"Yes, Mrs. Perkins. What—"

"I just thought of a place where Mary Beth might possibly have taken the boy."

"Oh, tell me . . . please."

"My husband bought some land above Covington that had a travel trailer on it. It was quite nice at the time, but that was a long time ago. He used it when he and his pals went hunting or fishing. Mary Beth knew about it because she spent a weekend there with her girlfriends when she was a teenager."

Jane's heart was beating fast. "Where is it, Mrs. Perkins?"

"To tell the truth, I haven't been in a long time, so I will only be able to give you general directions. Unfortunately, I don't think it will be easy to find in the dark, especially in this weather."

"Just tell me where you think it's located," Jane said.

Sam picked up a yellow pad. "Ask her if she has a deed to the property. If she'll give us legal description, we can look it up from records in the tax assessor's files. We can find it from that."

As Virginia told what she knew about the property, Jane repeated it to Sam.

"It's precious little," Kyle said when Jane hung up.

"She has the deed, but it's in the attic. She says she's going up there to get it and she'll call us when she locates it." Jane looked worriedly at the window now being lashed with rain. "Do you think it's safe for her to go climbing around in her attic with the weather acting up like this? She seemed determined to do it."

Kyle looked around at the activity going on in the squad room. "We'll drive over. I'll go up in her attic and get it myself."

"Hold on." Sam was watching a weather bulletin streaming from a TV set mounted on the wall. "The storm has already knocked down trees in some areas. There's flash flooding. The uniforms on the street have taken shelter. They won't venture out unless there's an emergency."

"This is an emergency!" Jane cried.

"We'll have to stay put until it passes, Jane," Sam told her.

"We can't just sit and wait, Sam," she said. "The storm could last for hours. We need to find that trailer."

"It's in a desolate area. It'll be a challenge to find it in daylight. In the dark, in a storm, with trees over the roads and flooding galore, it'll be next to impossible. I know you're anxious, I understand. But it'll be better if you let us handle it."

Jane watched Sam cross the room out of earshot. Dispirited, she leaned her head against Kyle's arm. "So remind me again why we needed the cops and the FBI?"

Wordlessly, Kyle dropped a kiss on the top of her head.

MAX WAS HUNGRY. MELANIE had made a quick search for food. She needed to rush because she didn't know how long it would be before Crazy Mary came back, and she was anxious to get away before she did. The cabinets were empty. The only food she found was in an ice chest. That, at least, kept out bugs. Melanie had seen plenty of those since arriving.

She scurried around like mad snatching milk and baby food out of the ice chest. She guessed that even though Max probably ate regular food, Mary Beth had no choice but to use jars of the baby stuff out here in the wilderness There were several gallon jugs of water too. She used that to wash out a sippy cup and filled it with milk.

He *was* hungry, she thought a minute later as she fed him. She felt outrage that anybody would neglect feeding a little kid. As she shoveled mixed veggies and chicken into his little bird mouth, he watched her with his eyes as big as blue marbles as if trying to figure out who she was. In spite of her urgency to get it done and get out, she chatted and teased him, but he didn't smile or make a sound. Still, he seemed okay being with her. She thought maybe somewhere back in his baby brain he remembered her as his big sister. It just melted her heart . . . plus it made her more determined to escape. Not only did she have Max to think about, but her own baby.

But how to get them out? The weather was really bad. Rain pounded on the trailer, and gusty wind rocked it so hard she worried it would topple over any minute. Anything that wasn't tied down rattled and rolled, including her and Max. But she told herself the trailer was ancient and if it hadn't toppled over yet, maybe it would hold together for one more storm.

Melanie hoped *she* would hold together.

It was pitch dark outside. Except for the weak overhead light and frequent lightning, it was difficult to see much of anything, but one thing she had found in the cabinet was a candle and matches in case the generator quit. She didn't know much about generators except that they ran on gasoline. When Hurricane Katrina hit, her dad had a portable generator that made it possible to have AC and lights. But when the gasoline was used up, the lights and the AC would go.

With that in mind, she had thoroughly scouted out the place while she could still see, trying to find a way out. She finally decided she would have to take the AC unit out of the window. It was the only way. The door was padlocked, and the windows boarded up. She'd need a screwdriver, but so far no tools anywhere. There were a few utensils in a drawer, including a couple of table knives that might work. If so, they could crawl out from there, but then what? They were miles and miles from civilization. Max was a baby. He couldn't walk very far and not at all in pitch blackness and a raging storm.

As scared as she was, Melanie vowed not to wimp out. If she did, Max would know. But she had to hurry. Mary Beth could come back any minute. She didn't know what the woman would do. Melanie had already decided she would protect Max with her life, if necessary, but it might not matter if Mary Beth showed up with a gun or something. She was just crazy enough to do that.

Finally, done with feeding Max, she wiped his face and hands and set him down on the floor. "Give me a sec, little buddy," she told him. "I've got to try and spring us from this place."

Max looked at her gravely, big blue eyes wary, and no smile, no nothing. But at least he wasn't crying. With wind whistling and howling, she went to work on the AC. Old and rusty, the screws didn't budge at first. Frustrated, Melanie gave it a hard smack with the knife handle, hoping to loosen it.

"Where's the WD-40 when you need it?" she muttered grimly.

Suddenly, she realized Max had sidled up to her. She looked down into his blue eyes, trusting eyes. She felt a rush of love and fear. He was relying on her to get him out of here.

But again, the big question . . . how?

KYLE STOOD WITH JANE, listening while Sam, two FBI agents, and half a dozen men from city and parish argued over what to do next. While they went back and forth, Kyle wrestled with more primitive emotions—anger, frustration, fear and deep father love. Above all, he burned to rescue Max and Melanie. He didn't believe it would happen here. There was too much push and pull for turf. Too much macho ego.

He touched Jane's arm. "Let's go. This isn't getting us anywhere."

"What? We're leaving?" Jane was forced to skip a little to keep up with his long strides. "Why?"

"We're going to Virginia Perkins's house."

With Jane at his side, Kyle left the building and waited beneath an overhang for a chance to dash through the rain and wind to his car. It was one of those Louisiana deluges, multiple inches of rain in a short span of time. With the chance of a tornado added, it made for a significant storm. But Kyle couldn't wait for it to run its course. With the lives of Max and Melanie at stake, it was time to act.

He popped their one umbrella open and snaked his arm around Jane's waist. "We'll get wet anyway, but this'll help. I hope you're okay with that."

"I am if you have a plan," she said. And with that, they stepped off the curb and sprinted across to his car.

Once inside, Kyle ignored his drenched clothes and buckled up. Beside him, Jane had found a few fast food napkins to blot her arms and face.

"So, what is our plan?" she asked.

"I'm going up in Virginia's attic," he said. "If that deed's up there, I'll find it. If the electricity's out, I'll use a flashlight. And once we pinpoint the location, we're taking off to find it. I'll call Sam and any others who choose to follow. But just to sit and wait for the storm to subside isn't an option. Every minute counts while Max and Melanie are at the mercy of a deranged woman."

"Melanie is so afraid of weather like this," Jane said, eyeing the fury of the storm with a worried frown. "I can only imagine how she's feeling wherever they are."

Kyle had struggled not to think what Melanie was feeling. If he let himself dwell on that, he wouldn't be able to act or think rationally. Time enough to vent when he had his children back safe and sound.

In a few minutes, they'd reached Virginia's neighborhood. Kyle turned onto her street and was forced to cruise slowly through rising water. "Another half hour and we wouldn't have been able to get to her house at all," he said.

"I hope you find the deed quickly," Jane said, sitting forward and looking anxiously at the street. "Everything is conspiring against us, Kyle. Absolutely the last thing we needed was this storm."

"I wonder what Christine would say about that," Kyle said thoughtfully.

"Why? Because the storm seems to be an evil obstacle to keep us from finding our children? That somehow God's hand is in this?" Jane went silent for a few moments. "I can't think like that anymore, Kyle."

"Why is that?" He glanced over, searching her face.

"Because I've felt God's hands in all of this despite the horrible things that have happened. I prayed that He would keep Max safe, and He did. He gave Max over to Virginia." She turned to him as he put the car into Park. "So, you see, I have to keep believing."

"Does that mean you're not afraid?"

"No, I'm still scared. But God's here."

He reached for her hand in that moment and gave it a squeeze. Then, gazing through the windshield at the torrent pummeling the car, he said, "Stay put. No sense in us both getting drenched again." He leaned over and kissed her on the mouth, then backed off with a crooked smile on his face. "You could use the time to pray I find that deed fast."

The umbrella was of little use when rain was coming down in sheets, Kyle decided. And there was no way to dodge puddles and keep his shoes dry. Water was up to his ankles. Grimacing, he slogged through it and finally reached Virginia's front porch. He was relieved to see the glow of candlelight through the lead-glass door since the power was out. But he had no time to ring the old-fashioned bell as the door suddenly opened and, despite nearly gale-force winds, Virginia grabbed his shirtsleeve and pulled him inside.

"I was just about to call you, Kyle." Obviously excited, she waved a legal sized envelope at him. "This is the deed. I found it in the attic. I don't know if Mary Beth is staying in that trailer, but I suddenly remembered her mentioning it, though it was a while ago."

Kyle decided he'd ponder later Jane's being in the car praying that the deed would be found quickly. "How did you get it out of the attic, Mrs. Perkins?"

"Why, I climbed the stairs and took it out of a box. How do you think I would get it?"

"In the dark? Using a candle?" Kyle was beginning to think

there was more spunk to Virginia Perkins than he'd originally thought.

"I used a flashlight, of course. It's the least I could do seeing as those children could be at risk with Mary Beth in a fragile state."

Kyle tucked the envelope inside his soaked shirt. Before turning to go, he leaned over and kissed Virginia's cheek. "Thank you, ma'am."

WHILE JANE USED A tiny flashlight from her purse to read the property description on the deed, Kyle wasted no time getting off the fast-flooding streets.

"You can check to make sure I'm right," Jane said to him, "but I think we need to get on the highway above Covington and head toward the Mississippi state line. The campsite looks to be somewhere in that area, and the highway won't be flooded."

"Lots of tall, thick timber around there," Kyle said. "I can see why Arthur bought in that area to hunt and fish, but it's the middle of nowhere."

"Which is why Mary Beth chose it," Jane said quietly. "If we're right in guessing where she is."

"Why don't you try calling her again," Kyle said. "If she's way out there, I bet cell reception isn't too good. If her signal is loud and clear, it might mean we're on the wrong track." But even as he said it, he knew his theory was iffy at best. With weather like this, cell signals could go haywire no matter where she was.

"We need to call Sam first, right?" Jane said.

"Yeah. Tell him we'll meet him at the service station where we filled up earlier. Tell him we aren't waiting for the storm to pass. If he wants to meet us, we'll wait fifteen minutes. No longer." He was done with waiting. He was done with seven months of going through proper channels while the search for his children moved like molasses in December.

Jane made the call to Sam, who, without arguing or trying to suggest something different, agreed to meet them. "He's coming with a couple of cops who aren't afraid of getting wet," Jane said after hanging up. "I guess we should be grateful for that."

"Try Mary Beth now," Kyle said.

Jane put the phone on speaker and dialed the number. It was picked up after only a single ring.

"You again, huh, Jane?"

"Hello, Mary Beth. I'm just calling to check that everyone is okay."

"Right as rain here, no pun intended. How's it going with you there?"

"There are tornado warnings up for this area. Were you aware of that?"

"If this is a sneaky way to find out where I am, you struck out, Jane. And before you start talking and trying to keep me on this phone so it can be traced, I've decided to tell you what I want before you can have your children back."

Jane shot Kyle a startled look. "What, Mary Beth? Tell me."

"I want Andy. Don't talk! Just listen. I want you to arrange a meeting with Andrew, and I want him to let me have my son. None of this supervised-visit stuff. I want to be with him without Andrew. And hear this, Jane. You won't get Max and Melanie back until it happens."

"You know that's not possible, Mary Beth. The weather alone prevents us doing anything like that. There is flooding in the streets, and, like I said, we're under a tornado warning."

"I can wait, Jane. You heard what I said, didn't you? I get Andy and you get your precious Max and Melanie. So, do your lawyer thing and get busy on the phone with Andrew. And don't try calling me again. I'm turning this phone off until tomorrow morning."

"Wait, Mary Beth!"

"One more thing," Mary Beth said. "If Andrew refuses, you will never see your kids again."

It was no surprise that after issuing her impossible ultimatum, Mary Beth hung up. Jane closed the phone and sat looking straight ahead for a minute. "Andrew wouldn't hand Andy over to her for even a supervised visit," she said quietly.

"But it's an opening, don't you see that?" Kyle said. "She's giving us a window of opportunity."

"But a very slim one," Jane said doubtfully.

Kyle turned the car onto a main thoroughfare. "I just want to find them at the campsite."

She looked out at the raging storm. "Me too."

21

While Melanie was busy trying to loosen the screws that held the AC in the window, she realized Max was literally stumbling with fatigue. She quickly made a makeshift bed from two chairs pushed together. Then, picking him up, she walked back and forth in the cramped trailer, rubbing his back and talking to him softly. It took only a couple of minutes until he was asleep.

All the while, she was wild with worry that any moment Mary Beth would come back. To keep her out, Melanie had barricaded the door. It had been a trick to figure out how until it dawned on her to use the mattress on the bed. It was now wedged against the door. Because the space was so cramped, it would take a lot to dislodge it.

The table knife had worked to remove the screws. Once she took the unit down, she didn't care if they were deep in a forest, she was taking Max and getting out of this horrible place. What worried her was the storm. It was really blowing and going now.

But it couldn't rain forever. Maybe she could find a sheltered place to hole up once they were outside. She did not look forward to that.

She was studying the AC unit to decide how to handle the weight of it when, through a small space in a boarded-up window, she saw a flash that was not lightning, but headlights. A car! Her heart gave a leap with the hope that it was someone to rescue them. No way to tell as she could hardly see anything outside. Thinking it was most probably Mary Beth, she hoped the mattress blocked the door.

In seconds, she heard a scrabbling and thumping at the padlock. She crossed the floor and stood ready to protect Max, if necessary. She had the table knife in the pocket of her jeans with her T-shirt pulled down to cover it. It was a puny weapon, but it was all she had.

Finally, the lock gave. It was Mary Beth. Even over the howling wind, Melanie could hear her cursing as she shoved and shoved against the door. The mattress hardly budged. Melanie felt a rush of relief. It was holding . . . for now.

"Open this door, you little twit! It's raining out here."

Ignoring her, Melanie scrambled over to the AC. She had to get it out and somehow push Max through the space, then follow him before that maniac managed to get past the mattress.

"When I get in there, I'm going to beat the living crap out of you and that kid! And don't think I won't. So you better get a move on and let me in."

The AC unit was stuck fast! Melanie jerked and heaved, trying to pull it out but couldn't. Had she missed a screw somewhere?

Suddenly there was a loud crash that shook the trailer. Mary Beth was using something to bash a hole in the side. Whatever it was, the trailer rocked with the ferocity of the blows. Panicked, Melanie looked around for something to protect her and Max if Mary Beth got inside.

But there was nothing. So she rushed back to the AC and frantically tried again to locate whatever was holding it tight in its frame. She was so caught up in the task that she didn't realize at first that the banging had stopped. She paused, listening, hoping. Maybe Mary Beth had given up.

Boom!

Melanie jumped and gave a strangled scream. She was back, and whatever she was using didn't sound like she was kicking and banging with her feet and fists, but with some kind of tool. And it was working. A hole appeared in the wall. Melanie could see now. It was a tire iron. She felt almost sick with terror. If Mary Beth managed to get inside and attacked them with that, she could kill them. Both of them.

Within a minute, Mary Beth had gouged out a hole big enough to climb through. As Melanie looked around desperately for something to defend herself and Max with, Mary Beth tossed her humongous handbag through the hole. Melanie snatched it up while Mary Beth worked her head and shoulders through, realizing it was heavy enough with whatever was in it to serve as a weapon. Melanie braced as the woman hoisted her rear end through, thinking to swing the handbag as hard as she could and hit her on the head. But she'd read somewhere that it took a really hard blow to knock someone out. She didn't think it could be done with a handbag.

Dropping the handbag, she moved close to Max as Mary Beth got to her feet sort of like a beached whale. She watched warily as the woman gave a disgusted look at the mattress blocking the door.

"Think you're a smart one, don't you?" she said with a sneer.

"I was only trying to protect Max," she said, making her

voice meek and mild. She didn't want to say or act in a way to set this crazy woman off.

"Then since you were so smart as to move it over there, you can just move it right back."

"Okay." Melanie noticed with relief that she hadn't brought the tire iron inside. She was way bigger, but Melanie at least stood a chance fighting her off if it came to that. But only if she didn't have a gun in that big purse.

Mary Beth raked a hand over her wet head, spraying water everywhere. "You're going to pay for blocking that door, missy."

Melanie's heart went to her throat. She moved over to the chairs where Max slept. "You better not hurt Max."

"Who said anything about Max? It wasn't Max who moved that mattress." She jerked a dingy towel off the couch and made a few swipes at her hair. As Melanie watched, Mary Beth seemed to be talking more to herself than to Melanie. "You're too much like Jane. Bet she's in a stew right now, wondering about her kids. I'd give both of you back except I want her to suffer."

"What has she ever done to you?" Melanie cried.

"She took my baby!" But as quickly as her temper rose, it died. She glanced over at Max. "Glad to see he's sleeping. I'm fed up with his whining."

"He was tired and hungry," Melanie said in a carefully neutral tone. Trying to gauge this crazy person's mood was like walking a tightrope. "I fed him and made him a safe bed."

"I don't know how safe it'll be," Mary Beth said dryly. "Tornado warnings are up for this parish."

"Are you serious?" Melanie felt her tummy take a sickly dip.

"As a heart attack." She began drying herself with the towel. "The roads are already flooded, especially out here." She gave Melanie her best crocodile smile. "So if you're thinking to be rescued by Jane, think again."

"If that's true, shouldn't we get out of these woods?" Melanie asked, her heart racing. "This trailer is old, and if a tornado strikes, it could smash it. Or if a tree fell, we'd all be crushed. I can carry Max to the car."

"We aren't leaving." Mary Beth kicked off her soaked shoes. "Get over it."

"You've knocked a hole in the trailer!" Melanie said, hoping to try to reason with her. "It's even less safe than before."

"And whose fault is that? It was your bright idea to block the door."

"But rain's blowing in. In a minute we'll be as wet as if we were outside. It's dry in your car."

"Shut up!" Mary Beth threw her soggy socks at Melanie, who ducked and grimaced. "If I wanted advice from a teenager, it wouldn't be one of Jane's brats. Now get your butt in gear and move that mattress."

"What do you plan to do if there's a tornado?" Melanie persisted. "Hide under your mattress while the trailer is sailing through the air?"

"It's not happening." She balled up the towel and stuffed it in the hole in the wall. "Just think, how many times have you even seen a tornado?"

"One time," Melanie said promptly. "And I don't want to see another one." She'd been on a Girl Scout camping trip when she was eight years old and a tornado had touched down. She would never forget seeing trees snapped in half and a chaperone's car picked up and tossed like a toy. Miraculously, nobody was hurt, but total destruction was all around.

"Tough toes. We'll just have to take our chances." Then, with no pretense at modesty—and no warning—Mary Beth suddenly stripped out of her soaked shirt and pants down to her underwear. Startled, Melanie turned away in disgust.

"Jane really ticked me off tonight," Mary Beth said.

"Jane?" Melanie said, shocked. "You talked to Jane?"

Melanie's mind raced as MB rummaged around in plastic

bags. She did not want to see the woman stark naked. On the other hand, she thought suddenly, if she was naked, now might be a good time to try to take Max and get out of the trailer. Mary Beth would have to take time to throw on clothes to follow. Oh, but that wouldn't work since she hadn't moved the mattress yet and she wouldn't be able to squeeze herself and Max through the hole in the wall before she grabbed them both, and then what would the consequences be?

Melanie felt like tearing her hair! Grrr! "So," she said, "what did Jane do?"

"I was going to be reasonable and send you two little darlings back to her after I felt she'd suffered enough, but she threw a kink in my plans by going behind my back and talking to my aunt. I gave it some thought and finally decided what her punishment should be. You can look now."

Melanie turned to find Mary Beth wearing a gown with the words MY PSYCHIATRIST WENT TO CANCUN AND ALL I GOT WAS THIS STUPID SHIRT printed on it. It wasn't the shirt that was stupid, Melanie thought darkly. "My mom talked to your aunt? Who is she? How did she find her?"

"I don't know. But she shouldn't have done that." She stopped with a frown. "I told you to move the mattress. Get going!"

"I'm sure my mom was just trying to find Max and me, Ms. Rutherford." Melanie began dragging the mattress away from the door, grunting with the effort, then sliding it on its side to the bed frame. "She's probably so worried."

"Good, that's what I want." Mary Beth watched without lending a hand while Melanie settled the mattress in place. "I want her to be sick with worry."

"I know you don't care about a mother worrying about her child," Melanie said, looking her straight in the eye. "But you can put yourself in Jane's place when you think about Max. He's an innocent baby. You can't feel good about hurting him."

"I haven't hurt him. Jane is the one I want to hurt." She flopped down on the bed, no sheets, no pillow. "If you're thinking about stealing my car and leaving with the kid, forget it. You'll never find the keys. And no matter how much you'd like to leave, you can't in this weather."

Melanie stood looking at her, frustrated and seething, so much so that she was almost able to forget the storm raging outside. She had a bigger storm raging inside her. She had to get them away from this woman . . . somehow.

"THIS PLACE DOESN'T LOOK very prosperous," Jane said nervously as Kyle drove through a run-down mobile home park. "In fact, it looks pretty much deserted."

"Would you be outside in this weather?"

"Good point." She sat forward in her seat, trying to make out any landmarks. "Are you sure we're going the right way?"

"According to the map, it's up ahead, past a fork in the road," Kyle said.

"Maybe we should have waited a little longer for Sam."

Kyle's glance was ironic. "Weren't you the one who said let's go after we waited exactly fifteen minutes?"

"Maybe you should have talked me out of it."

Kyle's expression told her he wasn't touching that one. She flinched at a boom of thunder. Between the wind gusting and the water rising, the threat of a tornado, and her children in jeopardy, Jane felt she was in a horror movie. Flashes of lightning illuminated the road that was now a faint track in the woods. All they needed to make the surreal night complete was to encounter Bigfoot coming out of the woods.

"I'm thinking that having one of the police SUVs ahead of us would have been a good idea," Jane said as Kyle slowed at a low point to plow through foot-deep water. She'd once driven in one of Mandeville's flash floods, when her car stalled and began floating off. A police unit rescued her. It was an experience she didn't want to repeat.

"Too late now. If we need Sam and the cops, they'll be here."

But would it be too late? Jane wondered.

Kyle suddenly sat forward, straining to see as his wiper blades swished wildly. "Look, I think we're at the fork in the road. It shouldn't be much farther."

"If we've taken the right turn," Jane added. She checked the map one more time. A couple of the parish deputies had pinpointed the property described in the deed and marked it with yellow highlighter. If they were on the right track, they should spot the trailer any minute. Jane was getting more concerned about the storm. Trees were bent over by the force of the wind, and rain was coming down in sheets. But fortunately nothing blocked the road. So far.

Worried, she said, "This is a full-fledged tropical storm, Kyle."

After Katrina, she knew flooding could be as dangerous as high winds. She couldn't help being spooked, knowing today's date was within a week of the anniversary of the famous hurricane.

She settled back, hanging on to her conviction that she was on the verge of finding Max and Melanie. But doubt and fear were eating at her. How would she bear it if—

No, I can't let myself think that way now. Please, God . . .

Suddenly, on a flash of lightning, a bridge materialized just ahead. But Jane's heart sank. It was submerged in rushing water and debris. Too late, Kyle stood on his brakes, but the road was muddy and slick, and the car kept going. His brakes didn't hold. With a shout, he wrenched at the wheel a split second before the car would have plunged into the creek. As Jane braced herself, eyes wide with fright, the car fishtailed and went sliding sideways, its momentum taking it across a flooded ditch and crashing into a tree.

Both sat shaken for a moment. Kyle turned to Jane. "Are you okay?"

"I think so." She fumbled for her seat belt. When it gave, she peered out the window on her side of the car, but all she saw was darkness and rain and the hulking outline of dense forest. The car's motor, she realized, was still running. "Can we get back on the road?"

"We'll soon know," Kyle said grimly. Putting the gear in reverse, he accelerated cautiously. The wheels spun, and the car stayed put. Muttering, he tried again, this time giving it more gas. The rear of the car shifted sideways, but he could not get traction to move forward.

Jane felt like screaming in frustration. The car was stuck. And Max and Melanie were somewhere out there in this wretched place. In mortal danger.

Where was God when you needed Him?

SLEEPY AND BATTLING EXHAUSTION, Melanie settled down beside Max to wait out the storm. There was nothing else to do. After being certain Mary Beth was asleep, she'd searched for the car keys. No luck.

"They're probably in the pocket of that stupid nightgown," she muttered as she stroked Max's back. Meanwhile, the storm didn't appear to be letting up. If anything, it was worse. She had already decided that if and when it stopped raining, she was taking Max and leaving . . . on foot. With the handle off, the door could only be locked from the outside, so there was nothing stopping her . . . except the storm. Leaving was risky, since she knew Mary Beth would come after them the minute she discovered they were gone.

After a few minutes, in spite of trying to stay awake, she dozed off. But something—she didn't know what—brought her awake. Rain rocked the trailer, and the wind whistled around it. But something else was happening. She eased herself away from Max and went to the door. It appeared to be stuck. Had that stupid woman locked it from the outside? But with another mighty jerk, it came loose. Probably the force of wind had been holding it, she decided.

Bracing to keep it from swinging wide, she peered through a small crack. Suddenly, her heart stopped. She realized why she'd come awake. She knew that sound, that roar. And it wasn't thunder. Or raging wind. Terrified, she slammed the door. It was a tornado!

JANE PROVED TO BE of no help at the wheel when Kyle went outside and attempted to push their car back from the tree so he could drive it back onto the road. After ten futile minutes, he was on the point of giving up when two parish deputies in a police SUV appeared.

"Are you sure the car can be driven after this?" Jane asked from the passenger seat.

"We'll soon find out." Kyle, dripping wet from helping hook a chain to the back of his car, raked a hand over his face and wiped it on a paper napkin Jane had found in the bottom of the console. He glanced in the side mirror at a deputy with a flashlight signaling a thumbs-up. Lifting his hand in acknowledgment, Kyle put the car in gear. "Here goes."

Holding her breath, Jane was turned so she could watch as the squad car backed slowly with Kyle's car in tow. Fortunately, the SUV was equipped with tires made for traction.

"How did we take the wrong turn, Kyle? We were carefully following the map."

"Simple. The map was wrong." Kyle kept his eye on the deputy's reflection in the side mirror as he steered.

"Whose fault was that?"

"Nobody's fault, Jane. Maybe in the years since the deed was filed, the road has been rerouted. Who knows?"

Now with his car back on the road, he shoved the door open, ready to get out and help the deputy unhook the chain. But he was waved back into his car before getting drenched again. While they worked, two more police SUVs arrived. Jane suspected Sam was in one of them, but with the rain coming in torrents, it was impossible to tell. The two parish deputies, Jane noted enviously, wore full rain gear.

Now that it was determined they'd taken the wrong fork—thanks to the inaccurate map—Kyle fell in behind the three squad cars backing in tandem in search of a place to turn around and head in the opposite direction.

Jane settled back in her seat. "You aren't quitting, are you?"

Kyle looked at her. "Is that a serious question?"

She picked up the map and, ignoring the yellow highlighted route, began studying the road they should have taken at the fork. "Just asking."

It took about half a mile, moving in reverse while being whipped with gale-force winds and relentless rain before they found a place to turn around. And once they were on their way again—Kyle decided to be moved to the second-car spot in the lineup this time—they didn't see anything resembling the vague landmarks Virginia Perkins had mentioned.

Jane was beginning to think they were again on a wrong course when she suddenly sat forward. "Look, Kyle, Sam's on his brakes. Maybe he sees something."

"I'm paying attention, Jane," Kyle said dryly. Slowed to a crawl on the muddy road, he appeared to be taking no chance of another crash. Like Jane, he sat forward trying to make out the reason Sam stopped. "It's a turnoff, I think."

"I'm rolling down my window so I can see better," Jane said. In spite of heavy rain, she managed to make out a crude trail.

"That's his signal," Kyle said, as the blinker on the squad car began to flash. "I think this is it, Jane. I'm turning."

Jane sat frozen with hope and fear as Kyle cautiously turned onto the overgrown trail that, hopefully, led to the Perkins' camp. She saw Kyle's hands tight on the wheel, telling her he was as tense and anxious as she was.

They headed deeper into the woods. And the farther they went, the worse it got. Kyle dodged ruts washed out by the storm and crevasses worsened by the years. Once or twice, they almost wound up in the ditch. Jane didn't know how he managed to keep the car on a straight course. Plus, it was hard to see anything. And then, after about a quarter mile, the road took a slight bend.

Suddenly she saw it. The trailer.

"Kyle! We've found them! Oh, thank God, we've found them."

She would have jerked the door open in that instant, but Kyle reached out and caught her arm. "Wait, Jane."

"What? What?" She shrugged away from him impatiently, thinking only to leave the car and get to her baby.

"We don't know if Mary Beth has a gun. We can't just charge in there." He paused. "Wait a minute."

"What?"

"Do you hear that?"

Jane managed to calm herself. What she heard was rain drumming on the roof of the car. Wind whistling through the trees. But over it all another sound. A deeper, darker, more ominous sound. She looked at Kyle with terror in her eyes. "Is it—?"

"A tornado. Hold on!"

* * *

GALVANIZED BY FEAR AND a basic instinct for survival, Melanie rushed to Max. She had to find a place of safety for her and her little brother.

"What's happening?" Mary Beth sat up in bed, groggy and sleepy, her hair all crazy and her nightgown twisted. "What are you doing?"

"It's a tornado!" As Melanie scooped Max up, the sound increased. It was a sound like no other, a roar, a growing, growling, horrifying sound that seemed to come from the depths of hell. She settled a sleeping Max on her shoulder and headed to the door. "We've got to get out of this trailer!"

Mary Beth stared at her. "Are you crazy? And go where?"

Yes, go where? Melanie hesitated, but as the monster roar grew louder, she knew staying inside was not good. Outside was worse, but maybe the car . . .

"You can stay in here if you want to, but I'm taking Max and getting out of this trailer. It's the worst place to be." She fumbled at the door, but again it wouldn't give. It was stuck! Something—the force of the wind?—must be sealing it shut. She made a desperate sound as she fumbled with her free hand to jimmy the door open, but it was difficult with Max on her shoulder. The deafening sound grew louder with every passing second.

Panicked, she turned back to Mary Beth. "Help me get the door open, please!"

As reality dawned, Mary Beth's face paled with fright. Ignoring Melanie, she rushed back to the tiny bedroom and threw herself down on the floor in the narrow space between the bed and the wall.

There was no room for her and Max there. If they were going to be hit by the tornado and she couldn't get out of the trailer, she had only seconds to find a place to wait it out. She looked around frantically as the terrifying twister bore down on them. Still holding Max, who was awake now and beginning to whimper, she grabbed a blanket from Mary Beth's bed and went to the opposite end of the trailer. She put Max down on his feet, scooted under a tiny dining table that was fastened to the wall and pulled her little brother into her arms and covered them both with the blanket.

The trailer rattled and shook on its wheels from the force of cyclonic winds closing in. To Melanie it sounded like a thousand shrieking animals. Hunkered down, she wrapped her arms tightly around Max.

Please, God, please . . .

22

HOLD ON!"

Jane braced herself as Kyle floored the accelerator. The car shot forward, hydroplaning on mud and water, and somehow miraculously missed every tree. The car skidded to a stop a few feet from the trailer just as the tornado ripped through a stand of timber right in front of their eyes.

Transfixed with fear and horror, they could see in the gleam of the headlights countless trees being snapped in half, branches shorn off like toothpicks and all kinds of debris swirling through space. As they stared in shocked awe, a car parked nearby was lifted up like a toy and hurled into the sky. The sound was deafening.

"Look out!" Kyle yelled as the roots of a gigantic tree nearby were suddenly ripped from the ground. "It's going to fall, Jane. Get down."

But she didn't. She couldn't. She was frozen, knowing her

children were in peril and she could do nothing. She watched in horror as the tree, mortally damaged, began to list . . . and tilt . . . and lean . . . inch by inch as if in slow motion.

Kyle's arm went around her, pulling her down to the floor of the car. As both huddled in the cramped space, the tree finally fell in a colossal crash so deafening that, even over the shrieking wind, it made an awesome sound.

Jane didn't move. Then she realized with a shudder of relief that the tree had missed their car. She raised up with a frantic look around and felt a fresh rush of terror. The tree had missed them, but it had fallen on the trailer.

Jane screamed. Tearing free of Kyle's arms, she fumbled at the car door with only one desperate aim—to get to her children. She realized the wind no longer howled. The tornado had moved on. Still, rain stung her face as she fought her way through debris and mud and water to the fallen tree now covering the pile of rusty metal that was once the travel trailer. But she could see nothing—tell nothing. The camper was smothered in thick branches, and there was no way she could get to it.

"Jane . . ." Kyle caught her arm and pulled her close to his side. With rain lashing them, he spoke in her ear, forced to shout so she hear. "There's no way we can clear a tree that size away . . ." He stopped, drew in a shuddering breath. "The cops can do it."

She was vaguely aware of the three squad cars now stopped, their headlights fixed on the site of the destruction. And at the same time—oddly—the rain had lessened dramatically along with the dying wind. Nature's tantrum was over.

But Jane couldn't leave it to strangers to find her children. She moved out of Kyle's embrace, gripping her arms in fear and trepidation, and walked over to try to find some sign of life in what was left of the trailer. The tree was massive. She saw now that the trunk seemed to have missed a direct hit on the trailer, but the thick branches were more than heavy enough to do horrible damage to such a puny metal thing. Even obscured by limbs and leaves, she could see enough to tell it was basically demolished.

And then she heard a child crying.

She gave a glad sound and would have leaped into the green thickness, but Kyle caught her arm. “Wait, Jane. I hear him, too. But let’s go carefully. If he’s hurt, we don’t want to make it worse.”

Jane clasped her hands at her breasts, holding back joyful tears as Max’s howls grew louder. “It’s my baby, Kyle. I can’t believe it, we’ve found him.”

“Mom, is that you?”

Jane cried out again in glad surprise. “Melanie?”

“I’m back here, Mom. With Max.”

She held her breath. “Are you hurt?”

“No. I don’t think so. Max’s scared. But we’re stuck under a lot of tree stuff.”

“Hold on, Mellie,” Kyle said. “We’ve got help coming. We’ll get you out of there real soon.”

“Dad, you should check on Ms. Rutherford. She’s somewhere in all this.”

But it was two parish deputies, not Kyle, who headed around the opposite side with flashlights to search for the woman who’d held Max and Melanie hostage. The trailer was now just a pile of rusty metal. Its once shiny white siding was twisted and crumpled as if it had been no more substantial than a Coke can. As a dwelling of any kind, it was unrecognizable.

Sam appeared with two more deputies, both carrying chain saws.

“Where did the saws come from?” Kyle asked.

“Deputy Martinez had the foresight to grab them from the equipment room as we were leaving.”

“God bless him,” Kyle said, watching gratefully as the two

men tore into the part of the tree where Max and Melanie were trapped.

There was nothing louder than a chain saw, Jane thought, but between bursts of motorized sound, she realized that Max had stopped crying. From time to time, she could hear Mellie talking to him, soothing him. It was hard for Jane to stand and wait when she wanted with all her heart to be the one to croon and soothe her baby now.

The two deputies suddenly appeared out of the shadows, one scratching his head and frowning. "No sign of her back here," he said. "We found what was left of the bed, but it's smashed flat. She'd have to be somewhere near where the kids were in the trailer to survive. The rest of it is pretty much toast."

"If there's any justice, she's mashed flat under the trunk of this tree," Sam said in a low tone meant only for Kyle. "It'll be daylight before we can get to her."

Jane heard him. "And if she's not under that tree?"

"She can't get away in her car," Kyle said. "We saw it flying through the air."

"If she isn't under the trunk of this tree," Sam said laconically, "which is where I think she is, the sheriff will be out here with a full contingent at daylight to flush her out. She can't go far in these woods under these conditions, Jane. Trust me."

Jane told herself she would feel something later, maybe regret for a wasted life or sadness for a tortured soul, but right now, waiting for the first glimpse of her baby after almost seven months as a captive of this woman, she felt nothing for Mary Beth Rutherford. The woman was a demented criminal.

"We're almost there, Mellie," Kyle said, pitching in to help the two deputies as they stripped away the limbs trapping the two kids. "Is Max okay?"

"He's fine," Melanie called from beneath the tree rubble. "He's gonna be so glad to see his mommy and daddy, aren't you, Maxie-Moo?"

Jane paced anxiously. They would need larger equipment for the tree trunk. It was gigantic, at least two and a half feet in diameter. How it had missed crushing Max and Melanie was a mystery. And a miracle.

"Okay, we're clear," a deputy shouted, shutting down the chain saw.

Jane held her breath as Kyle tossed a last branch of the tree aside and peeled away a surprisingly intact piece of the trailer wall. Underneath, both children were huddled in a nest of blankets.

Melanie was crying. She stood up and instantly handed Max over to Jane.

"Here, take him, Mom. He wants his mommy," she said.

Jane reached for her baby with tears rolling down her cheeks. Her instinct was to take him in her arms and hold him tight, to kiss him all over, to never let him go again. But his blue eyes were wide and wary as he gazed at her, his sweet bottom lip trembling, working up to cry.

Jane calmed herself, and like Melanie, began to talk to him softly, lovingly. And in a minute or two, when she cautiously gathered him close, he allowed her to tuck his precious head into the curve of her shoulder. In that minute, when she felt him relax in her arms, she closed her eyes in a heartfelt sigh.

Thank you, thank you . . .

"Jane!" Kyle shouted. "Look out!"

Confused, she turned to see, but was blinded by the bright headlights of a squad car barreling toward her, its powerful engine revved to top speed. In one part of her brain, she realized she—and Max!—were about to be broadsided by a runaway vehicle. In another, she thought this could not be happening. Frozen in shock, she was riveted to the spot where she stood.

Kyle rushed at her from a dead standstill six feet away. The force of his tackle knocked the breath out of her and sent her and Max flying. They landed like stones on the bed of tree debris, covered by Kyle's body as the car zoomed past, missing them by a whisker before it crashed into the trunk of the massive tree.

For a beat or two, people were too stunned to move. Sam, recovering first, shouted an order. "Secure that vehicle!"

While deputies swarmed over the squad car, weapons drawn, Sam went to Kyle who was shifting his weight off Jane and his son. He lifted his bawling baby and handed him over to Sam.

"Jane," he said urgently. "Jane, talk to me."

Jane heard him as if from a long distance. Her head rang and she was dizzy. She heard Melanie's voice beside her, but she couldn't seem to open her eyes.

"Mom, Mom, don't die!"

"She's not going to die," Kyle said sternly, but he was pale and breathing hard. He took Jane's hand and rubbed it briskly. "Jane, wake up."

"I'm okay," Jane said groggily. "Just . . . catch my breath." She made a move to sit up. "Max. Is he okay?"

"He's right here. He's okay. Bawling his head off."

Sam handed Max over to Melanie and with a grim look strode to the squad car. Mary Beth Rutherford was slumped over the steering wheel. But the deputies were not able to get the damaged door open.

Kyle took Jane's hand and helped her to her feet. "You need to take a minute, Jane," he said. "You were almost—"

"I'm not sure what happened," she said, still dazed. "That car, what—?"

Kyle looked over at the wrecked squad car. The door was pried open with a mighty yank from one of the deputies. The process of removing the unconscious woman from the driver's seat began. "I don't know how she survived the tornado, but she did. And somehow she managed to sneak into that car."

"She wanted to hurt you, Mom," Melanie said in a shaky voice. "She hates you."

Jane spared hardly a glance at her nemesis. She turned to Melanie and held out her arms to take Max, a bewildered, frightened little boy. She gathered him close and looked at Kyle.

"Let's go home."

MIDNIGHT. AND JANE STOOD at the door of Max's room, content just to watch her son sleeping peacefully—to her amazement—in his bed. She had a full and grateful heart, although she was still shaky and a little dazed by the events of the day. Her children had escaped the clutches of a deranged kidnapper, her family had survived a tornado unscathed, and she and Max had been plucked in the nick of time from the path of a runaway police car. And all within the space of a few hours. How many close calls did a person get in this life? It left her feeling humbled and truly convinced of what Christine had been telling her for so long—that God loved her and that He'd never forgotten Max. He'd heard her prayers, and He'd sent Virginia Perkins to care for him and had even used Melanie's abduction to protect her boy in the storm.

"Here you are." Kyle came up behind her and slipped his arms around her waist. "I should have known where you'd be."

"Pinching myself to be sure it's true. Max is back."

"And all's right in your world."

"Close enough." She covered his hands with hers. "What about you?"

He hesitated, then turned her so that he could see in her eyes. "I'm wondering if some of the angel dust that has been sprinkled around today has landed on me too."

"You have your son back, your daughter is safe. We're a family again. What more do you need?"

"I need to know that you've forgiven me, Jane." He gave her a look of genuine entreaty. "Have you had enough time and space? I need to know how to make you love me again."

"You can't make me love you again, Kyle," she said softly. Then when he looked so hurt, she touched his cheek. "You don't make a person love you. They do or they don't." She raised her arms and settled them around his neck, gazing into his handsome face. "I love you," she said. "I never stopped loving you."

He made a sound as if a strong emotion was wrenched from deep inside. He pulled her close, locking his arms around her in a fierce embrace. "Jane, Jane, I've missed you so much."

She closed her eyes, feeling a rush of joy. "I've missed you too," she whispered.

"I never knew nights could be so long," he said gruffly. "It only took one night without you for me to learn that." She rested her hands over his heart. She could feel it beating, strong and even, and knew it belonged to her.

"Don't ever pull away from me like that again."

"Never." With his thumb, he tipped up her chin and slowly kissed her. It was a gentle kiss, a sweet, soft touch of his lips to hers. A tentative kiss, not the kind they'd shared a thousand times as husband and wife. It was—she searched to define it—a new beginning.

For moments they remained that way, swaying a bit, touching, not speaking, familiar as seasoned lovers, contented that differences had been smoothed and obstacles overcome.

"I missed this," he said, holding her close.

"Me too."

He hesitated, then caught her face in his hands so that he could see right into her eyes. "Now can I move my things back to our bedroom?"

She leaned back, flush against his hips, letting him see

laughter sparkling. “I thought you were going to be satisfied with just my forgiveness.”

“I lied.”

She threw her arms around his neck and laughed out loud. “Bring yourself back to our room tonight, Kyle. Move your things tomorrow.”

23

THREE MONTHS LATER

JANE GENTLY PUSHED MAX a safe distance away from the stove and opened the oven to look at the turkey she had put on to roast that morning. "Hmm, it's looking good," she said, inhaling the delectable aroma. "That little plastic thing has popped, so I believe it's ready. What do you think, Christine?"

Christine, who was busy mashing potatoes, craned around Jane to see. "Oh, I think you're right. And browned to perfection."

"Can we eat soon?" Melanie asked. "Why do we have to wait until two o'clock? I'm starved."

"You're always starved," Jane said, giving a loving pat to Melanie's baby bump. At six months, her pregnancy was obvious. "But first, go into the den and get one of the guys to come in here and take the turkey out of the oven. It's heavy."

"Turk . . . eeee," said Max, flapping his arms and pumping

his short legs in a dance. It was a trick he'd learned from a book Jane had been reading to him about Thanksgiving.

Jane bent down and kissed his nose. "You're Mommy's little turkey, aren't you?"

"Who's a turkey?" Kyle came in from the garage carrying several sticks of firewood in a canvas caddy.

"Ben," Christine replied promptly, "unless he gets up off that couch and comes in here and takes the bird out of the oven for Jane. Go tell him I said that, Kyle. We've been slaving in the kitchen since daybreak, and all he's done is watch football and wait for dinner to be served."

"Daddy," Max said, toddling over to Kyle and offering a toy train.

"I can't play right now, son. Daddy's got to stoke up the fire."

"Hot!" said Max, shaking his little head in a no-no.

"Jane, I'll be back to lift the turkey out after I take the firewood to the den," Kyle said.

"No," Christine said. "I'm serious. Tell Ben to come in here and make himself useful. You'd think the game would grind to a halt if he took his eyes off the TV."

"Okay, ladies, smile." Daniel stood in the doorway holding the camcorder, panning the kitchen. But instead of filming the cooks, he moved in for a close-up of a coconut cake. "Yummy, can I have a piece of that?"

"Before dinner?" His mother gave him a you-can't-be-serious look. "I don't think so."

Daniel shrugged, grinning. "It was worth a try." He turned the camera on Melanie. "Let's have a profile, Mel. Show the baby bump."

Jane smiled, listening. It had been gradual and not always a smooth road, but Daniel appeared to have a sense of acceptance about the baby. And even joy.

Melanie, holding two large salad servers, turned, exaggerating her rounded tummy. "How's this?"

"Cool," Daniel said. But Jane noticed that the camera moved up and lingered, not on Melanie's baby bump, but on her face.

"After you're done clowning around," Christine said, "tell your father the turkey awaits. Oh, and tell Rachel and Ruthie it's almost time to eat. Where are they anyway?"

"In Melanie's room upstairs playing video games."

Christine looked at Melanie. "Is that okay, Mellie?"

"Sure. There's nothing they can get into in my room."

"Except your makeup and your clothes," Daniel said.

"They're okay in my room, Daniel," Melanie said quietly. "They're just curious."

"And, Daniel, please take Max with you to the den," Jane asked as she rooted around in a cabinet looking for a dish suitable for her special cranberry sauce. "If he stays in here, he's liable to get stumbled on."

"Not a problem." Daniel shifted the camcorder to his left hand and scooped Max up. "Here we go, big guy. They've got a girly thing going in here. We men are supposed to be in the den watching football."

For the next few minutes, Jane, Christine and Melanie worked in classic harmony putting the final touches to the Thanksgiving meal. Jane had done much of the preparation the day before with Melanie's help. They'd mixed the cornbread dressing, made a cranberry-orange relish, baked the coconut cake, bought French bread and fresh green beans, and chopped the veggie appetizers that were now on a platter in the den. All of it had been a labor of love for Jane. And having Christine's family to celebrate the holiday made it all the more wonderful.

Thanksgiving had always been special to Jane, but this year just calling it special did not begin to describe what she felt. From now on, Thanksgiving would not be just a lovely holiday, not just an occasion when she counted her blessings. Thanksgiving now would always mean celebrating faith and family and friendship, yes, but it would mean so much more. It would be a day set aside to honor God and to thank Him for healing her broken spirit, for returning her children, and for rejuvenating her marriage.

She'd pondered all this when she got up early to put the turkey in the oven. Standing at the French doors looking out at the woods, she'd watched a flock of white egrets flying low and then, as if of one mind, suddenly swooping down, settling in the branches of the cypress trees. The sun was barely up, the sky a beautiful lavender and orange spectacle. It promised to be crisp and cool, a perfect Thanksgiving Day. A line from Robert Browning suddenly came to her.

God's in His Heaven, all's right in the world.

Well, maybe not quite. There had definitely been a few hiccups along the way since Max returned, but thanks to the resilience of babyhood—and Virginia Perkins—he seemed fine, for the most part. She'd worried about psychological damage to Max as a result of living for more than six months with Mary Beth Rutherford. Jane had taken him to visit Virginia several times, thinking to ease his transition from one home to another. Virginia had teared up when, on seeing her, Max had smiled and dove into her arms.

Marilee left Child Search when her husband was transferred to Washington. So after giving notice to Henri Robichaux, Jane jumped right in where Marilee left off. She took Max with her every day where he was spoiled shamefully by the volunteers and staff. When he reached age three or four, Jane told herself, maybe she'd be willing to put him in a pre-K program for a couple of hours a day, but not now. Now she had to be with Max daily. He'd been given back to her, and she treasured him as the precious gift he was.

As for Melanie . . . she wasn't the carefree girl she'd been before Max was taken, and she never would be again. Pregnancy changed her life. All her friends—all the world—knew, and because of that, she was once again in therapy. But she was surprisingly optimistic. Jane and Kyle would definitely adopt the baby. A sonogram revealed it was a boy. Jane looked forward to having a little brother for Max so close in age. Melanie would complete high school, go on to college, and build a life that might well take her far away from the child who would know her only as his big sister, not as his mother. Whether Daniel would be a part of it remained to be seen.

Mary Beth Rutherford would always be a shadowy specter. She was hospitalized in an institution for the criminally insane, which was where she belonged . . . at least for now. She had sustained a serious concussion, several broken ribs, and a punctured lung when she crashed the squad car, trying to kill Jane.

Sometimes Jane was struck by the way things turned out so that she wouldn't have to contend with the prospect of Mary Beth and her twisted mind. She sometimes thought of Mary Beth when she watched Max sleeping and playing and blossoming with health and happiness, and she wondered at her great good fortune as a mother, knowing Mary Beth would forever be denied that joy.

But other times when she dreamed that Max was still gone, she would wake in the middle of the night to find herself shaking, her heart pounding, tears streaming, and it would all come rushing back, a ghastly nightmare. At those times, she'd have to get up, go into Max's room, touch him, and sit in her rocking chair and watch him until the terror passed. At those times, no, she didn't feel much sympathy for Mary Beth.

But today was Thanksgiving Day, and she had Max and Melanie and Kyle and Daniel and Christine and Ben and the girls to celebrate with. The turkey was ready, the cooking done, family and friends famished and waiting. She stood looking at the table laden with the bounty of the season and knew she was truly blessed.

One last thing, she thought. Striking a match, she lit two tall tapers and, for a moment, in the gentle glow of candlelight, let herself enjoy what was to come.

"Now can we eat?"

It was Melanie, hungry as usual.

"We can." Jane gave her a quick hug and went to call everyone to dinner.

ACKNOWLEDGMENTS

THIS WAS A DIFFICULT story to write. I'm indebted to many for help and encouragement. To start: Thanks to my incredible brainstorming group—Jasmine Cresswell, Diane Mott Davidson, Connie Laux and Emilie Richards—whose insight and talent shine when we meet to talk about our current work-in-progress. To Debbie Macomber—your generosity knows no bounds. To Deborah Raney and DiAnn Mills—thank you both for your willingness in answering my questions and showing me the way in the CBA. To Alison Simmons for phenomenal publicity and marketing ideas. To Dave Lambert for excellence in editing. To Traci DePree for beautiful line-editing. And finally, to my agent, Wendy Lawton, who believed in this book upon her first reading of the proposal. Thank you, Wendy.

DISCUSSION QUESTIONS FOR *MISSING MAX*

1. Jane and Kyle faced parents' ultimate fear—a kidnapped child. Do you think a strong faith is essential to coping with tragedy? What about people who aren't believers?

2. Christine tried to persuade Jane that faith would help her through this nightmare, but Jane hardened her heart. Have you known a friend going through a terrible tragedy? How did you help?

3. To cope, Jane volunteered at Child Search, a group who helped other people who'd lost a child. Kyle felt rejected and withdrew into his job. Melanie acted out with rebellion and anger. Each coped in different ways. Was there a better way to deal with tragedy? Or was the situation simply too horrible? How would you cope in a similar situation?

4. Jane's career suffered when she neglected her job by throwing herself into volunteering at Child Search. Have you experienced a situation that affected your job performance? How were you able to get beyond that?

5. Max was taken when Melanie turned her back briefly. As a parent, have you done the same thing? Looking back, do you recall a careless moment when the unthinkable could have happened, but thankfully didn't?

6. Was it believable that Melanie got pregnant to "replace Max"?

7. Were Jane and Kyle's reaction to Melanie's pregnancy typical of most parents?

8. What theme came through to you when reading *Missing Max*?

9. What is your belief when dealing with the age-old question: Why do bad things happen to good people?